I kept looking at her, my longing and adulation probably obvious. The fire was crackling and bringing just the right amount of additional warmth to the room. It was quite dark now. We had not turned on any lights. "I want to please you," I repeated.

She looked at me from the corners of her eyes. "What do you have in mind?" she asked.

"Making love to you." I held my breath.

She looked at me in a way she had not done before. Her eyes went from my face, downward, along my neck, and to my breasts. I felt the electric chills. "Take your shirt off," she said.

I'm sure I blushed. I felt heat pouring through my body. I began undoing the buttons, unable to look at Marinda, feeling a shyness I had never experienced before. She watched each move I made, her eyes burning through me. I put the shirt aside. . . .

the Winged
Dancer

the Winged Dancer

CAMARIN GRAE

the NAIAD PRESS inc.

1986

Printed in the United States of America

First Naiad Press Edition 1986

WINGED DANCER was first published in 1983 by Blazon Books

ISBN 0-930044-88-6

ACKNOWLEDGMENTS

My thanks to Shelle Jacobson for the cover artwork and design; to Dan Eierdam, Marie and Nikki and Mike for their feedback and support; and to Angela Koenig for her unflinching feminist critique.

WORKS BY CAMARIN GRAE

WINGED DANCER   1983
PAZ   1984
SOUL SNATCHER   1985
THE SECRET IN THE BIRD   (Forthcoming)

the Winged Dancer

1.

THE SHOOTING

Until that June afternoon, I had never seen a gunshot wound. I was walking down Oak Street on my way to Stuart Brent bookstore when a man staggered out of an alley and collapsed on the sidewalk ten yards away from me. I ran to him. He lay on his back, his right leg resting against a parking meter. His suit jacket was flung open haphazardly, but, oddly, his tie was neatly in place. As I bent down to him, I could see that he was bleeding. I was about to run for help, but he grabbed hold of the cuff of my pants.

"Please...get this to my sister," he implored.

His voice was surprisingly strong. There was a look of painful desparation in his eyes. I've seen those eyes in my dreams a number of times since. He clutched a small leather folder and, with great effort, moved it toward me.

"I'm going to call an ambulance," I said.

"Promise me," he insisted. "Don't send it...the mails are..." He coughed. His voice was getting hoarse now and weaker. "Will you tell me your name?" His eyes never left mine as he spoke.

"Kat," I answered, "Kat Rogan."

"You must hide it, Kat. No one but my sister... I'm counting on you. Wait a while...a week...a month."

I nodded and took the folder from his hand. I slipped it into my purse. His eyes looked sad then and less clear, so I spoke to make sure he understood. "I'll get it to your sister," I said. "I promise."

At that, he seemed to let go; his eyelids flickered. Several people approached us.

"Call an ambulance!" I commanded. My voice was scratchy. I was feeling sick. "Hurry! Don't you see he's dying!"

The collar of his pale blue shirt was drenched in blood. I could see a wound on the side of his neck.

"Who did this to you?" I asked.

But he made no response. His eyes were closed.

I knew he was dead.

The police took my statement and said they would be in touch if they needed to talk with me again. I did not tell them about the folder. I suppose I should have, but I pictured the man's eyes, and I couldn't. He had asked me to hide it. I promised him.

Several witnesses reported having heard shots in the hotel. Someone said he had seen a young blond man in a red T-shirt hurrying down the hotel corridor carrying a satchel. Someone else had seen the murdered man come out from an alley door. She said another man followed him out, watched him go down the alley to Oak Street, then quickly walked the other way and disappeared. She described the missing man as very tall, maybe six-four or even more, tall and thin with glasses and a dark business suit. The dead man's name was Martin Sundance, I learned, from Marigua, South America. I remained at the site until the body was put into an ambulance and driven away, then I took a cab home.

Alone in my apartment, the first thing I did was take the folder from my purse, set it on the dining room table, and stare at it. Was it related to the murder? If so, then I could still pass it on to the police. It wasn't too late. Strange though it seemed, I felt as if I had a pact with Martin Sundance. Once again I pictured him lying there on the sidewalk. I realized I was shaking.

There have been occasions when I wished I drank alcohol, and this was certainly one of them. Instead, I poured some Pepsi and lit a cigarette. I looked at the folder again, aware that I was stalling, hesitant to open it.

It was a beautiful object of soft, chocolate brown leather with an etched design along the border. It was fastened with a belt-like clasp. I picked the folder up and released the clasp. Inside was an

2

envelope. It was addressed to Maria Sundance in a place called Postero, Arcedia. The leather folder contained nothing else. The envelope had been opened. I hesitated briefly then took the contents out.

There were three sheets of paper, a two-page letter and a drawing of some kind. Although the letter was written in English, the text was interspersed with non-English words and series of numbers. "It's written in code!" I said aloud. "I'll be damned!" I stared at it. What the fuck was going on? The whole business suddenly struck me as unbelievable, preposterous. A man is shot, then dies at my feet after begging me to pass on, secretly, a coded message. Things like this didn't happen in my world. This was movie stuff! Murder and espionage. Espionage? Oh, shit, I don't need this.

Over the past few years, my life had settled into a comfortable rhythm. I had begun to feel at peace with myself, satisfied. I wasn't in the market for disruption. I did not like the tension I was feeling. I didn't want anything to do with murder or spies or bizarre codes.

On the other hand, I *was* curious. I picked up the other page.

It contained a crudely-drawn picture with lines of various configurations and X's and arrows and numbers here and there. Beneath the picture were four or five more lines of numbers. Admittedly, I was intrigued as well as frightened. Turn it over to the police, my good judgment said, or the C.I.A. Don't get involved. Promises given to dying spies don't mean anything. Was he really a spy? I lit another cigarette, picked up the letter again and began reading through it, slowly, to see if I could extract any meaning from it.

Dear Maria,

If Topyepess could read this one, she'd do more than tattle to auntie or tsk a few times. I couldn't quite bring myself to make this strainveleor to you in person nor to go to the ushatieroutin. I have no doubt that what I'm finally doing is the right thing to do, what I want to do and must do, but I'm afraid that face-to-face with you or with others, I might have backed down. Even now, I find myself wanting to write of other things and make jokes like I used to in letters long ago. That is probably why I'm using Strumblejelter and Acoobdoket (19, by the way). It seems to make it easier for me. I hope you don't find it annoying.

I must get to the point. Maria, I have ostreadiacent where the 43-37-1-18-9-19/58-11-15-93-2-14 is eceatoldy and I know how to get it! It is in 14-1-1-21-22-15-7, safe and sterilebraved. I have no doubt that my smornfoitina is scaetruca. Isn't that marvelous! I wish I could see your face. The bad news is that my original plan regarding what to do with this tromanofitine was a very oflehissa one. I have changed. I want to talk with you about that, but all I'll say for now is that apparently some deeply ingrained sense of stinytigert musdivvern in me and has finally fegredmen. I believe it must be father's influence. It's a very freeing feeling to recontact that part of me. At any rate, I have now let myself know that the 9-6-3-4-25-31 must stand as a smutennome and spistirannion and not be melted down into a life of luxury and leisure for me.

I crealdent of its scaltonior from an old man of the 06-12-1-06-16-14-22-9 who turned up at the 31-18-1-7-3/ 9-5-37-35-1/5-4-3-3-3-2-2-11. He was dying and may even be dead by now. He would 2-39-4-30-5 only the 61-1-01-23-4-19-52 sengtuom. 13-5-11-138-1/5-1-19-3-26-4-10-57 of 18-2-12-02-43-1-3-20/3-4-2-6-9-12-12-7-10-22/ 13-16-7-7-6-28-1-4-26-16 for me and then stidsiness on becoming my spretrano. He is the only other person who knows where the 1-8-15-5-19-9 is. The 44-4-17 I have plendescor will 31-14-4-9 you to it. I'm sure it will make an spigrinsing mixthebin at the asummeur. It has been febedgrumst by 40-7-34-7/24-15-32-2 since the bakaqueertho of 1760 odolefodo the 17-3-7-62/013-37-9-24-14-9-10. How about that, Maria! It's been there all this time! I had fun drawing the 27-9-1. Please bear with me for using Strumblejelter and Acoobdoket (41, this time). Somehow, that made it more palatable for me. Actually, I thought you'd enjoy it, too. As the 78-17-02-2 staincidess, the 15-4-16-10-47-12 is in a 17-1-42-3 forty feet below the present 4-8-2-40-5-5-4 of the 12-3-24-6. When the 18-6-12 is finished and the 12-4-31-3-/8-6-50-2-6/15-3-29-2-2-8 the 1-1-3-12-18-6 will become occableissier.

I was active in getting the 10-4-18 spadorevpa and so was 12-6-3-10-28-2-1-16. Some of the means we used were not exactly honest or fair. We had to have 8-1-6-22-3-44-6 as the 8-9-25-18-2-7-3-18-2-12-1-2 of 11-4-27-2 and 27-5-5-2-1-44-6-40-3. I'm prepared to give all the details when the time comes. I intend to take full respon-

4

sibility for my part in it, Maria. I don't believe it will lead to scurosetipont, but it certainly won't do my or 7-10-2-5-25-6-5-6's spasterutione any good. Needless to say, I expect 5-10-2-17-12-8-41-12 to be more than mildly upset about all of this. He certainly has not had a change of heart. I need time to smooth his feathers and prepare him for what is to come, so I am requesting that you do not go public with this smornfoitinar right away. By all means, I want you to tell the Archeological Committee and 13-6-18-42-2-15-4 the whole story immediately, but I want to give 14-3-3-18-25-2-36-12 the courtesy of breaking it to him myself before it hits the papers. Please do what you can to insure that. I am leaving tomorrow for the States and will return home on Wednesday. At that time, I'll let 16-25-4-18-40-2-2-12 know what I have done. Of course, by then it will be too late for him to do anything but curse me out and grudgingly accept the fait accompli.

I feel like the wandering sheep who has finally seen the guiding light and returned to the fold. I look forward to our reunion.
Your loving brother,
Martin

This didn't seem like spy stuff. It was too light, or at least too personal. Of course, spies are tricky. It seemed like a confession of some sort. I went back to the beginning of the letter. He's doing the right thing, he says, even though it's hard for him to do so. He found out something, something important. He thinks it's marvelous, although his original plan wasn't. But, then he changed. Father's influence, and he's glad he changed and not melting into a life of luxury and leisure. Dying old man, the only other person who knows. 1760. It's been there all the time. Since 1760. Martin enjoys using *Strumblejelter* and *Acoobdoket*. More palatable. Easy for you to say, I thought. Maria might like it, too. Good for her. Forty feet below. Not honest or fair means to get the something *spadorevpa*. He would take full responsiblity. Somebody, a male, was going to be upset about it, somebody who has not had a change of heart. Martin will smooth this angry guy's feathers, so keep quiet about it, Maria, except you can tell the Archeological Committee and . . . something. The Archeological Committee? What did he find, a tomb? Hit the papers? It must be big

5

news. The angry guy without the change of heart will have to accept what Martin's done.

It was definitely a confession, I decided. Martin found something, a tomb possibly, and was turning it over to the authorities via his sister. It was between Martin and his sister and the archeological folks. It was none of my business. I'll just get this to her and be done with it. I put the letter aside. Then, I immediately grabbed it again and began examining the strange words. I was fluent in Spanish and had some familiarity with German and Greek. *Acoobdoket? Eceatoldy? Scaetrucal? Stidsiness?* These weren't words from any language. And the numbers were obviously a code. Once more, I thought of spies. Were spies involved with the uncovering of old tombs? Of course, he hadn't actually said anything about a tomb. The message in the letter could be connected with the murder. Maybe he was killed because of the letter. I shuddered. The police. Could they decipher it? Would they try? I rubbed my forefinger over my temple. What could the drawing be? A map? A map to the tomb?

Suddenly, I felt exhausted. I didn't know what to do, and I didn't like that feeling. I pictured Martin Sundance's eyes again, his face, his body. He had been a strikingly handsome man. The sick feeling returned. I began pacing back and forth in front of the large bay window of my living room. I looked at my watch. I had an appointment in forty minutes to mediate a dispute among the residents of a condo on Columbia Street. I needed to get going. I went to the john. In the middle of brushing my teeth, I suddenly stopped. What was it? I stared at my reflection. I looked uncharacteristically vulnerable, painfully mortal. I took a close look at my face. No, I looked all right. I was fine. Martin Sundance was dead but I was fine. My heart was still pumping, the blood was flowing. My skin looked healthy, alive. I looked fine. I knew I was considered attractive. Mom always said "beautiful", but that was mom. I did like my blue-green eyes and the high cheekbones, but I thought my lower lip was too large. Elizabeth always said it was sexy. I didn't think I looked 33 years old. I certainly didn't feel it. That was a very adult age. I wanted to live a lot longer.

I slipped the letter back in the folder and put the folder in my bottom dresser drawer. Maybe I could find someone who could break the code. I needed a cryptographer. I actually went to the yellow pages, but there weren't any listed. I was feeling very uneasy, thinking I had been drawn into something quite strange, puzzling. Possibly something dangerous. The blond guy with the satchel. Was he a burglar? A murderer? The tall thin man the woman had seen. Who was he? Why did he leave? Was he the murderer? Did he see Sundance give me the folder? Was he after me? Shit! I looked at my watch again, got my purse and left. On the way to my meeting, I realized that I kept looking over my shoulder and suspiciously eyeing passersby.

2.

THE PHONE CALL

One week passed, then two. Nothing out of the ordinary happened and, gradually, the creepy feeling that I was being watched began to fade. I could not stop thinking of Martin Sundance, however. His words would echo through my mind as I rode my bike along the lakefront. I saw his face while walking through the Loop to my office and during lulls in conversations. I thought of him off and on during my calligraphy class and while playing racketball. Martin Sundance haunted my dreams. First were his eyes, emerging as from a mist and then his whole body would materialize. Blood was everywhere. He smiled and began to speak, but only jibberish came out of his mouth and then a stream of blood. I wanted to get the folder out of my house and Martin Sundance out of my life.

Several times, I made calls to the detective handling the case. I couldn't bring myself to tell them about the folder. I did manage to locate an amateur cryptographer who agreed to work on breaking the code for a sizable fee. I decided to telephone Maria Sundance instead.

I had learned from the police that Martin Sundance, indeed, had a sister named Maria Sundance, that she lived at the address on the envelope I had, and that she was employed by the Natural History

Museum in Postero, a city in Marigua, South America. The detective gave me this and other bits of information after I explained how, for my peace of mind, I needed to know something of the man whose death I'd witnessed and of the circumstances leading to his murder. The officer told me that Martin Sundance was in the import-export business, dealing in artifacts, jewels and relics and that he was in the States on a business trip. He theorized that Sundance had interrupted a burglary in progress in his room in the Endicott Hotel, had been shot by the burglar and had run, wounded, down the hotel stairs and out the back into the alley. The police saw it as an unfortunate instance of Sundance being in the wrong place at the wrong time. They had no suspects, but several leads they were checking. They had not found the blond man with the satchel or the tall thin man in the dark suit. Apparently they did not consider either of them prime suspects. The detective was moderately polite but clearly wanted me to quit pestering him.

It was not difficult to get in touch with Maria Sundance. I left a message for her at the Natural History Museum in Postero, and she called me the next day. Although her English was excellent, we spoke primarily in Spanish. I explained my involvement with her brother, and she was more than willing to talk. She told me that she and Martin had been estranged for the past five or six years, but, nonetheless, the news of his death had shocked and pained her. Although the funeral had taken place over a week ago, she said she was just now beginning to accept the fact that her brother was gone. She was quite eager for any information I could give her regarding the circumstances of his death.

"He gave me something just before he died," I said. "A letter for you."

"A letter? I can't imagine... Please send it right away. Let me give you my address."

"That's the problem," I said. "He asked me not to send it. Some concern about the mails."

"Well, yes. Sometimes things do get lost. You could send it Special Delivery. That should be safe enough."

"I'm not sure," I said. "Somehow I got the impression that he was worried about it being intercepted."

"Intercepted? By whom?"

"I don't know, but that's the impression I got. The letter was addressed to you and stamped. The stamp was cancelled. The letter was opened."

There was silence on the wire. "I see," Maria Sundance said at last. "How strange."

"He asked me to hold onto it for awhile, to be sure to get it to you, but not right away. It seemed very important to him."

"Yes. I understand." There was another pause. "Have you read the letter, Señorita Rogan?"

This time it was I who paused. "Yes," I acknowledged.

"In that case," Maria Sundance replied, "may I suggest that you read it to me."

I had the letter in front of me. I was curious about how she'd respond to the coded part, so I didn't warn her. As soon as I read the first sentence, Maria Sundance interruped me, laughing. "Topeypess? Oh, he's too funny. How delightful. Go on, go on."

I read the next sentence and again she interrupted. "He's using Strumblejelter." She laughed sadly. "Martin never did grow up. In some ways, he always remained a little boy."

"Shall I go on?" I asked.

"Yes," she said, "Do. Wait. Tell me, Señorita Rogan, are there many words like that. . .like. . .?"

"Yes," I said. "And there are some places where he uses series of numbers instead of words."

"Oh, my. That, too. Oh, Martin."

I waited. It seemed she might have been crying.

"It must seem odd to you," she said at last. "You see, Señorita Rogan, my brother and I used to be very close." There was another brief pause. "Years ago, we developed a way of communicating with each other so our nosey maid would not be able to understand what we were saying. She was bilingual like us. That's Topeypess, the maid. When we were away at school Martin and I corresponded. We used the code. Even after Topeypess died, we still used it. Martin thought it was such fun. I found it very tedious, but I always went along with him. It's been so long. . ."

Again there was silence. Finally, I spoke. "Can you still understand it?" I asked "After all that time?"

"Oh, I could figure it out, yes. It will take a while. Would it be asking too much, Señorita, for you to read the letter to me so I can write it down?"

I said I didn't mind. I continued reading, spelling out each coded word and giving her the numbers slowly. When I finished, I could hear her sigh.

"Thank you very much, Miss Rogan," she said in English. "You have been put to a great deal of trouble and I'm very grateful..."

"There's more," I said.

"Oh?"

"Yes, there's also a drawing of some kind with symbols and more code words and numbers."

"A drawing? Could you describe it, please?"

"Yes, I'll try. At the top," I began, "there's a box with a series of numbers written in it. A line goes into the box and out the other side. Then there's a basically circular but wavy figure and another line off to the right. There's an arrow from that line to the circular thing and a series of numbers written above it. Next to the wavy circle thing, on one side of it, are some jagged lines and about two-thirds into them is an X with another...."

"Stop! Stop! Oh, dear. Pure confusion. I really must see it. If Martin asked you not to send it, there must be a good reason. Possibly someone could pick it up from you. Let me think, who do I know who's planning a trip to Chicago...? Perhaps I could come myself... Oh, I don't know. Miss Rogan, would you mind if I got back to you, tomorrow, perhaps, or very soon."

I gave her my address and phone number. It seemed like my part in the drama would soon end. I wondered if it would be appropriate to ask Maria Sundance what the letter said. I was certainly curious, but I knew it wasn't really my business. I had no idea that it would soon become the central business of my life. I put the letter into the folder and back into my dresser drawer, changed into jeans and left for the Women's Coffeehouse to join some friends and hear some music.

The phone woke me early the next morning. It was Maria Sundance.

"Miss Rogan, I'm so sorry to be bothering you, but, you see, I simply must have the other...the drawing. I'm feeling quite frantic about all this. I'm sure you can understand."

"Yes, I imagine..."

"Is there any way that you could possibly fly down here and..."

"You want me...?"

"At my expense, of course. I would be more than happy to send you round trip tickets..."

"Well, I don't..."

"Do consider it. It would be well worth it to me and you'd have a wonderful time. You would be my house guest, of course. Marigua is a beautiful place."

"To be honest, I never heard of Marigua, though I did look it up in the atlas after the...uh...recently. It's not a real large country."

"No, not large. Tiny, actually, compared to yours. Somewhat backward, too, I'm afraid. Controlled by a rightest dictator who pretends to be democratically elected. We're a buffer state, you know, and so we're fairly safe from outside intervention. The struggle is to get some more internal reform, though we are progressing. But, that's not your concern. At any rate, things are stable here, and quite delightful for a tourist, especially the region where I live, Arcedia. Why don't you come? You do have a passport?"

"You're serious, aren't you?"

"Absolutely. I'd be happy to order the tickets for you today, if you agree. You can pick them up at the airport there. What do you say?"

I was feeling swept off my feet and very tempted. My curiosity was miles high and this sounded like an adventure I couldn't pass up. Maybe I was becoming bored with the comfortable rhythm of my life. "My time is fairly flexible," I said.

"Wonderful! And please don't worry about expenses. I'll take care of all of that. It's no strain on me. Believe me, I'm quite comfortable. Shall I make it for Thursday and leave the return open?"

"I could be ready then, but I..."

"I'll meet the flight myself and drive you to my villa. It's in the country, outside of Postero. I'm very eager to...to meet you, Señorita Rogan."

We talked a few minutes longer. She told me a little about herself, about her work as an archeologist and her involvement in the museum. When we hung up I had the sense that I was being caught up and pulled along by some irresistible force. I certainly hadn't anticipated a trip to South America. I thought about what clothes I would pack and wondered what I was getting myself into.

It wasn't unusual for me to go off for days at a time without informing my friends. They were used to this; they knew I operated fairly independently. In this instance, however, I felt the need to let some people know I was going, especially Elizabeth. She and I had been lovers, briefly, several years ago; now we were good friends. I probably felt as attached to her as I ever have to anyone. I was accustomed to the brevity of my love relationships. I no longer expected to "fall in love." It never seemed to happen with me. I don't know why. I've been told that I always back off when a relationship begins to get too close. Maybe that's true. I know I start to feel anxious, as if something dreadful were going to happen if I really let myself deeply invest in someone. When I stop to think about it, I realize there's an empty or unfulfilled part to me. Lonely, maybe. But I rarely think about it. I called Elizabeth. I had already told her about the murder and about the folder, and when I told her about the next step, my impending trip, she said it sounded exciting but cautioned me to be careful. I didn't like hearing that; I already felt an edge of uneasiness.

I spent the next couple of days finishing up an article on lesbian custody that I was writing for a women's newspaper, and taking care of some business connected with my mediation practice. The cases I was working on could wait for a few days—a gay couple who was splitting up, a women's shelter collective with internal disputes, a community band in dissension over their autocratic leader. I considered my work the "perfect amalgamation" of my training and interests. I had a masters degree in counseling psychology, and used to practice nondirective psychotherapy but it felt too passive. So I went to law school. Even before passing the bar exam, I knew I wouldn't be satisfied operating within that world. It felt too aggressive. Then I found an ideal compromise, an integration of the nurturant and controlling parts of my personality. I became a mediator. I work out of an office I rent in the Loop and rely on the invaluable assistance of my secretary and friend, Lana Nelson. I help my clients look at all the elements, factual and emotional, related to their disputes, and to reach resolutions they can accept. I've been very satisfied with this career. Basically, I've been satisfied with my life.

3.

THE STABBING

My plane arrived at the Postero Airport in Marigua only twenty minutes late. I had arranged to meet Maria Sundance at the customs area. I waited for over an hour, then called her home. No answer. I called the museum and was told that she was on a dig and was not expected in until late the following week. I began to feel irritated and somewhat anxious. After another half hour and two more attempts to reach her at home, I decided to go to a hotel. In the airport money exchange line I had a brief conversation with a Postero native who recommended the Tintano Hotel. The taxi driver concurred that it was a good one.

So far, Marigua seemed similar to other Latin American countries I had visited. The cab driver was shoddy-looking, but friendly; the countryside hilly and scenic, the poverty obvious. On the road into the city, we passed peasants with donkeys and tourists with backpacks; we passed modern condominiums, some still under construction, and run-down shacks. I was surprised at the size of Postero; there were quite a few large modern buildings in the central district, El Centro, which is where the taxi took me. I got a room at the Tintano Hotel and immediately called Maria Sundance's home number again. This time, at least, I got an answer.

"I don't understand," the maid said with concern. "She was to pick you up at four o'clock. I am preparing dinner now for your arrival."

The maid explained that Señora Sundance had been staying at Verona, a small town 75 miles away. She was working on an excavation in the countryside and was to have gone directly from there to the airport. I left my hotel number with the maid and went to the bar for a liquado. I felt tense. I took a short walk around El Centro. When I returned to the hotel, I called once more and again the worried and apologetic maid said she had not yet heard from the Señora. It was about 7 o'clock. The sun was still bright and it was a beautiful evening. I decided that rather than just wait around, worried and annoyed, I would do some sight-seeing. The hotel clerk recommended a trip to San Trito, the peak of the mountain which formed the west border of the city.

There was a long line of sightseers waiting to ride the gondola up to the top. I took my place among them. After forty minutes, it was finally my turn to board. I managed to get a place at the very front where I was sure the view going up to the peak would be spectacular. The gondola held twenty or so people. We were loaded and ready to go when one of the uniformed operators announced that we should all exit the gondola and wait for the next one as this car was needed for a "very important visitor." I was irritated. This smacked of classist discrimination, and besides, I had been waiting nearly an hour. I did not budge. The car was now empty except for me and the operator.

"Miss," he said in English. "You must leave from this car now."

"No verstehe," I said.

He gestured for me to exit. I shrugged my shoulders feigning lack of understanding. He approached and reached for my arm.

"Bitte," I said indignantly, pulling away.

He was about to reach for me again when a very beautiful, elegant woman intervened.

"Let her be," she said in Spanish. Her voice was smooth and authoritative. "She may ride with us."

I turned my back to the obviously influential aristocrat and her party, and looked out toward the mountain. The ride surpassed my expectations. The trees below gradually dwarfed into a mass of green as we rose higher and higher, suspended in the air. I could see for miles. When we disembarked, I walked around on San Trito for a quarter of an hour, enjoying the view from each vantage point. Marigua certainly did seem to be a beautiful country. Maria Sundance had been truthful about that. I tried not to think about what could have happened to her.

The foliage on San Trito itself was lush and green and there were flowers and a small river. For the first time since my arrival, I was glad I'd come. There was a small cove across the river, a perfect place to sit and have a cigarette and relax. To get to the cove, I had to cross the river by jumping from stone to stone. It was somewhat tricky but I arrived without mishap and settled down in a rocky nook on the other side. I could see the tourists bustling about on the peak and I could see the view beyond, although I was mostly hidden where I sat. After ten minutes or so, I became aware of someone else beginning to make the trip across the rocks toward my little cove. I recognized her as the "important visitor" from the gondola. She appeared to be in her early fifties. She wore a richly-emboidered pants outfit which fluttered in the wind. Her raven hair glistened in the waning sun. She was very beautiful. On her feet she had some sort of strapless sandals.

I leaned forward from my camouflaged seat. "You'll fall," I said in Spanish.

She looked up abruptly, for the briefest moment losing her composure. Then she turned her head condescendingly, pointedly ignoring me, and continued her journey over the rocks. She was well past the midway point when she made the wrong choice and ended up standing precariously on a slippery stone. I moved toward her.

"I warned you," I said tauntingly. Holding onto a branch with one hand, I was about to reach for her.

"Quickly!" she commanded, "Give me your hand!"

I pulled back. "Such manners," I said. "It would make more sense in your unfortunate predicament to say 'please', don't you think?" I was laughing.

She glared at me although I thought I also detected a smile in her eyes. There was clearly no way she could leave the rock on which she stood without getting wet or getting my help. I reached toward her again and as she grasped onto my hand she hissed at me, "Such an arrogant brat you are."

I immediately retracted my arm. The grand woman teetered momentarily, then lost her balance altogether and plunged

16

backward into the water with a noisy splash. I resumed my seat and watched her. Without giving me a glance, she swiftly moved through the water back to the shore from which she had begun the ill-fated crossing. Her companions appeared and spoke solicitiously to her. I was leaning back, smiling, softly whistling a little tune. Somehow I was sure she heard. I stayed another half-hour or so on the beautiful peak of San Trito and then returned to my hotel.

There was a message for me from Maria Sundance and I called her immediately. She was very apologetic. I didn't really listen to all the details of her explanation. Once I categorize someone's excuse for a behavior, I tend to ignore the particulars of their story. In Maria's case, the excuse seemed legitimate and unfortunate—something about the electrical system in her jeep, her assistant being away and her ending up stranded at the excavation site, miles from any populated area. She had walked for miles, she said, then ridden on a cart and then a taxi until she finally reached home only forty minutes ago. She offered to come and get me immediately, saying that her villa was about an hour away from where I was staying in El Centro. As it was now after 9:30 and she sounded so exhausted, I suggested, instead, that we both get some rest and that she come in the morning. She seemed relieved. She apologized again, and assured me that nothing would interfere with her picking me up at ten the next morning. Unfortunately, that turned out not to be the case.

I was hungry. I changed my clothes and was preparing to go for dinner when an uneasy feeling began nagging at me. I had the sense that the items I had placed on the dressing table when I'd first arrived were not as I had left them. And the scarf I now took from my suitcase—I didn't think I had folded it that way. I looked around the room. I couldn't be sure. I checked my valise for my hunting knife. I always brought the knife with me when I traveled, probably a remnant from the days when I did a lot of camping. I checked in my purse. The folder was still there as it had been ever since I'd left home that morning. I decided I was being paranoid.

I had a huge delicious meal in a little restaurant down the street from my hotel. Afterwards, I went to the hotel bar. Within minutes, a well-dressed man sat down next to me.

"So, you took my suggestion," he said politely. "Do you find this hotel to your liking?"

"Ah, the man from the airport," I replied. I never had any difficulty dismissing unwanted males who intruded on me, but this one seemed neither unpleasant nor intrusive and I might have been relieved to see a familiar face. "The hotel is fine. I'm glad you told me about it."

"I come here for the music," he replied, gesturing toward the stage. "They have the finest Flamenco in Marigua." His smile was wide, giving him a boyish look. I gauged that he was in his early forties.

Our talk remained impersonal and pleasant. Peter Lamoza proved himself to be an interesting conversationalist. He knew much about Marigua and especially the history of this particular region, Arcedia. I enjoyed his stories of the tribal peoples, the natives of the area, who, not unlike the North American Indians, were rapidly disappearing under the onslaught of the European invaders.

It was near midnight when I told Peter Lamoza that I'd enjoyed our conversation and the music and said goodnight. He wished me an enjoyable stay in his country. I was pleased, pleasantly surprised, I guess, that he had made no attempt to come on to me. In my room, I was preparing for bed when there was a knock at the door.

"Yes? Who is it?"

"Room Service."

"Oh? I didn't call for anything."

"I have a package for you, Señorita."

My paranoia was returning. "Leave it at the door, please," I said.

I waited a while then opened the door. On the floor was a small parcel wrapped in paper from the hotel gift shop, and a folded note. *I have checked off several sights that I'm sure would interest you,* I read. It was signed, *Peter Lamoza.* That's thoughtful, I thought, pulling the paper off *The Guidebook to Marigua.* As I was closing the door, someone appeared in the hallway.

"I think you'll particularly like Vanella," Peter Lamoza said, smiling and entering the room. "There are some artifacts of the Testoani in the museum there."

He took the guidebook and began leafing through it. I was definitely feeling annoyed, but I could not, with certainty, read his motivation. Was he just being what he considered hospitable to a visitor in his country, or...?

"You look very beautiful," he said. This time the smile did not look boyish to me.

"Thank you for the book, Señor Lamoza," I replied brusquely, moving him toward the doorway. "I'm sure it will come in handy. Good night, now."

He reached behind me and closed the door. "Traveling by oneself can get very lonely," he said, smiling seductively.

"I'm not interested, Señor Lamoza," I said firmly. "I want you to leave now." How foolish to have thought this would be different.

He moved his hand toward me, as if to touch my cheek. I dodged to the side. "Lamoza, you're behaving rudely. Leave, right now!" I asserted, in a low firm voice. He was standing in front of the closed door, blocking it.

"Relax, Kat," he said smoothly, moving slowly toward me. "We will make wonderful love together. What romantic stories you will have to tell your girlfriends when you return home."

I assumed a karate stance.

For a moment, he was taken aback. "Ah, you like to struggle," he said then, laughing. "Wonderful. I agree that makes it even more exciting. I can see in your eyes, little Kat, that you want me as much as I want you."

He thrust in toward me. I delivered a rapid, sharp kick to his knee. He slumped over momentarily, cursing, but apparently, the blow had been slightly off target, for it did not disable him enough to stop him from coming at me again. He looked indignant. His face was flushed and a strand of hair flopped down over his eyes.

"You're going to love it, cunt," he snarled. "You will beg for more."

This time I cuffed him on the temple. He fell to the floor, sprawling on top of my valise at the foot of the dressing table. I went for the phone, watching him all the while as he squirmed on the floor. Before I got a response on the line, he began staggering to his feet. I was preparing to strike him again when I realized that in his right hand, he clutched a knife—my knife. He was crouched over, like an ape, slowly moving toward me, the knife blade pointed at my gut.

"Hey, no need for that," I cried, backing away. "Let's talk, huh? Put the knife down."

He kept coming. I took several more steps backwards, hoping

for an opportunity to disarm him. I reached the bed and moved around it toward the john. My heart was pounding madly. Suddenly, he lurched toward me. I caught him with my foot and then my elbow. The sonofabitch managed to remain standing. He slashed the knife through the air menacingly. I moved with each move he made, keeping a distance between us. He looked enraged, almost demented. Saliva glistened at the edge of his mouth. His face was twisted into an angry ugly grimace. I kept my eye fastened on the knife blade, acutely aware of every movement he made. Abruptly I pitched myself toward him, shooting my arm out, catching him solidly on his wrist. The knife clanged onto the tile floor. He dashed for it, and so did I. I slammed my foot down on top the blade, just missing his fingers. With my knee, I knocked him over, and then I grabbed the knife.

He kicked, making me lose my balance and stumble. Then, like a madman, he jumped on me from behind, screaming, cursing. He had his arm clenched around my throat and began pulling it, tighter and tighter, cutting off my breath. I was beginning to lose consciousness. With all my remaining strength, I swung the knife in a rapid arc behind me. His grasp loosened on my throat and he slid to the floor and lay there, unmoving. I stood staring at him, gasping for air, still tightly holding onto the bloodied knife.

4.

THE TRIAL

My memory of the rest of that night is a painful confusion of feelings and events. I know I did not lie down to sleep until seven the next morning and, when I did, it was on a cot in a foul-smelling, tiny jail cell. The interrogation had seemed endless. I repeated my story, step by step, over and over, all night long. These sessions were interspersed with periods alone in a bleak office somewhere in the Postero Police Station. Finally, I was charged with murder, and brought to the cell.

When I awoke, although I knew immediately where I was, I felt disoriented. There was no indication of what time it was. They had taken my watch. There were no windows in the cell. I was alone and feeling the aloneness painfully. The memories flashed back, piecemeal, in a disorderly sequence. The memory of the knife penetrating into Peter Lamoza's body came first, an eerie, macabre, revolting feeling of pushing a piece of metal into the guts of another human being. A wave of white nausea floated over me. I was coated with cold perspiration and shaking. The cell contained a filthy, torn, plastic bucket, no sink, no toilet. The bucket had vomit in it. I think it was my own. More memories came. The hotel manager, frightened, babbling. The crowd at the door. The police.

My insistent request for my own lawyer, Nettie Dawson, from home. The skepticism of Clemente, the chief investigator, toward my story. The trip in the police car. My head pounding. The sight of Lamoza immobile on the floor, the circle of blood growing around him. People talking all at once. Who were they all? The disbelief. They assigned me a local attorney, Jorge Triste. He came and there was a moment of calm. "Self-defense," he said. "Yes," I said. Clemente shaking his head. "It is, to say the least, indiscreet, to have a gentleman to your room that way. Your bedroom." "I did not invite him." "You let him in." "No." "But the door was not broken." The knife, my own knife. "And so you changed your mind about being intimate with him and when he persisted, you stabbed him." "No." "And now you tell us you did not invite him." "I did not invite him." " And that he was trying to kill you." "He was." My head throbbed mercilessly.

A guard opened the door of my cell and set a tray on the floor. The food was rice, tortillas and a blob of something that might have been beans. I could not have eaten if my life depended on it. There was a jug of water. My mouth was cotton dry. Should I risk dysentary? I drank and noticed my hands. The fingers were stained black. Another memory came—the fingerprinting, photographing. Police procedures not unlike our own, I thought, with momentary detachment. This is a nightmare. I had hardly slept; I could not wake from it.

The lawyer, Jorge Triste, came. They took me to him, to a plain room with a table and a small window. I could see the sun shining brightly outside.

"I spoke with Nettie Dawson," Triste said. "I'll send her the materials—depositions, police reports. She'll fly in for the trial. We'll work together on this."

I nodded...

"How are you holding up?"

"I'm all right," I said. My head was still pounding; I needed a shower badly. "What time is it?" I asked.

"1:30."

"Did you get ahold of Maria Sundance?"

"Not yet. I left messages."

"I'm counting on her to prove the connection."

Triste was rummaging through his briefcase. He was a small, soft-spoken man. Very calm. "Connection?"

"Yes, what I was saying last night." Hadn't he paid attention? "The folder. Sundance. Peter Lamoza. I'm sure they're connected."

"Oh, yes. We'll check that. By the way, the deceased's name is not Lamoza. It's Peter Petrillo."

I smiled. The smile felt odd. I was glad to know my face was still capable of producing one. "That's good news," I said.

"It is?" Triste had his hands folded on top of the table. His expression was pleasant, or was it bland?

"Yes. The fact that he was using an alias. That should help my case."

"Men often do when they're cheating on their wives."

"Or when they're plotting theft and murder."

"You really believe that, don't you?"

"Of course, I do. You don't?"

"To be candid, it seems unlikely."

Damn! I expected the police to be skeptical, but I needed my attorney to be on my side. "Have you looked at the letter?" I asked.

"Not yet."

I was feeling frustrated. Triste seemed not to be operating on my wave-length. "When we get Maria Sundance's translation of the letter, I'm sure it will show a connection."

"Maybe so."

I looked at him angrily.

"I hope so," he added.

"He searched my room," I said.

"Looking for the letter?"

"Yes. He must have. How else could he have known I had a knife in the side pocket of my valise?"

"You think he was in your room while you were at San Trito?"

"Yes."

"And you had the folder with you at San Trito."

"Yes. It was in my purse." I had a sudden sinking feeling. "Where is it now?" I asked. "My purse, the folder?"

"All of your things should be here, at the police station," Triste said calmly. "The folder too."

"Can you get it?"

"Yes, certainly. Tell me more about what makes you think Petrillo was after the folder?"

"Obviously the letter and drawing contain information of value

23

to somebody." I thought of Martin Sundance's eyes, and about Maria Sundance's eagerness for me to come. "I believe that Petrillo knew I had it. After he determined it wasn't in my room, he decided either to get me to tell him where the folder was, or to kill me."

"Hm-m."

"He knew I had a knife in my valise."

"It's going to be hard to convince the judge that Petrillo had the knife first."

"We need to prove that he was in my room earlier, that he was after me, and not just for sex. How about fingerprints?"

"I'm afraid that wouldn't help, since it's obvious that he was in the room. His fingerprints wouldn't prove anything. There's no way of determining the exact time they were made. You think he came to kill you?"

"I don't know. Maybe. Or maybe just to get the folder."

"If his mission was to get the folder, he certainly was not very efficient."

"He became enraged when I kicked him. A narcissistic injury perhaps."

"What?"

"He may have felt emasculated when I..."

"Wrong tack," Triste interrupted. "That won't get us anywhere." His eyes narrowed. He seemed less gentle now, more like other lawyers I've known. "This is a very machismo country," he said. "I'll be checking into Petrillo's background to determine if there was any motive other than seduction that he may have had for pursuing you. So far I know he was a married man with two children, and that he worked at the Post Office as a supervisor. He does not have a police record. He does have a reputation as a 'ladies' man, and he liked to gamble and go to night clubs."

"What was he doing at the airport yesterday?"

"His wife says he went to exchange pesos for foreign currency—marks, dollars, francs; that he has a nephew who collects foreign coins."

"He could have gone to a bank."

"She says he liked the drive to the airport and the atmosphere there. He liked to watch planes take off."

"Crap!"

"We're checking the story."

"As soon as you get ahold of Maria Sundance, will you arrange for her to see me?"

"Yes. I plan to meet with her myself."

"Then you believe they might be connected? Sundance and Lamoza... I mean Petrillo."

"I don't know."

We talked some more, my lawyer and I. Basically, I liked him. He seemed competent. I suppose his skepticism was justified. He'd need more than my suspicions and speculation to build the case against Petrillo. I was eager for Maria Sundance to show up. When Triste left at 3:15, I collapsed on the smelly cot in my smelly cell and slept. I dreamed of killing and being killed and of Martin Sundance's eyes.

That evening I ate for the first time since my dinner at the wonderful little restaurant near the Tintano Hotel. I almost gagged. The tortillas were dry and hard on the edges. So was the rice. I couldn't bring myself to put the other things in my mouth. They might have been vegetables of some sort.

At 6:30, Triste came again. He did not look as calm as before.

"There's been an accident," he said, as soon as I sat down across from him and the officer left. "Señora Sundance. She was killed..."

"No!"

"...on the highway on her way to meet with me. A terrible accident. Her car went out of control and off the cliff on Highway 2. I just found out."

"It can't be!"

"She must have skidded on the curve."

"It's a conspiracy," I moaned.

"It appears to have been an accident."

"No."

The nightmares when I next slept were more violent than the earlier ones. Two days passed. In my cell, I went over and over the facts, each event, beginning with Martin Sundance staggering out of the alley behind the Endicott Hotel. My clothes were wrinkled and felt dirty. I was losing weight. The settled, peacefulness of my life was gone, snatched from me. I kicked the walls of my cell. I paced and hissed and cursed. The letter is the key, I thought. Triste had been unable to find Maria Sundance's copy of it among her possessions. I was sure she must have translated it. Where the hell was it? If we could only find the translation, I felt convinced that we'd have the necessary link to connect Petrillo with her, Maria, and with me.

Triste showed the letter and drawing to a number of people but no one could make any more sense out of them than I had. I asked him to bring the folder to me and I began the tedious work of trying to break the code myself. I started with the number code, but got absolutely nowhere and soon moved on to the words. The simplest possibility was that each letter of the coded words stood for some other letter. Since there were so many uncoded words, I focused on context, hoping that if I could figure out just one word, that would be a giant step toward figuring out the others. The first coded word, *Topeypess,* I already knew was the maid. It probably was her name. That information didn't help at all. From the context, I decided the next coded word, *strailveneor,* probably meant confession. *I couldn't quite bring myself to make this* confession *to you in person. . . .* That made sense and fit with the meaning I was able to extract from the rest of the letter. But there were too many letters in *strainveleor.* I kept working. I became obsessed with it. No doubt the task also served to distract me from my plight and to help me feel I was doing something productive. Triste had given me pencils and a notebook of blank paper. I was filling up sheet after sheet making no progress. Finally I gave up on *stainveleor.* I looked over the rest of the letter. I was already fairly convinced that the drawing was a map telling Maria how to find the tomb or treasure, or whatever it was that Martin had discovered. One of the sentences said *The 44-4-17 I have plendescor will 31-14-4-49 you to it.* That sentence could very well mean: *The map I have enclosed will lead you to it.* So, *plendescor* should mean *enclosed,* but again there were too many letters. I stared at the letters in *plendescor.* The word *enclosed* was there, in jumbled order. Could it really be as simple as that? Eliminating the first and last letters of *plendescor* left an anagram of *enclosed.* Eureka! I stood up. The spring of my cot squeaked as I did. It's so easy. I walked around the cell, excited about the breakthrough. So obvious. I went back to the word *strainveleor* which I thought meant *confession.* It didn't work at all. Shit! I thought I'd solved it. My frustration brought me close to screaming. I threw the letter aside and lay down. Finally, I slept and then I ate some of the crap they brought me and annoyed the attendants with my frequent need to go to the john.

26

After my fitful rest, I was somewhat revitalized and ready to resume my task. I went back to the word *strainveleor*. I must have worked on it for over an hour. After my success with *plendescor*, I would not give up. I finally hit on *revelation*. It's *revelation*, not *confession*. It worked! Removing the first and last letters from *strainveleor* left a scrambled version of *revelation*. My excitement was overwhelming! I could barely sit still. It took me a while to get *authorities* out of *ushatieroutin*. *Ostreadiacent* gave me trouble, too. It meant *ascertained*. *Eceatoldy* was easier—*located*. *I have ascertained where the 43-37-1-18-9-19/58-11-15-93-2-14 is located and I know how to get it.*

By that time, it was well into the night. I had to stop. I don't know how long I slept, but I was working at the code again before they brought my breakfast. I got word out to Triste and by the time he came, I was able to hand him the following translation:

> *If Topyepess could read this one, she'd do more than tattle to auntie or tsk a few times. I couldn't quite bring myself to make this revelation to you in person nor to go to the authorities. I have no doubt that what I'm finally doing is the right thing to do, what I want to do and must do, but I'm afraid that face-to-face with you or with others, I might have backed down. Even now, I find myself wanting to write of other things and make jokes like I used to in letters long ago. That is probably why I'm using Jumbleword and Bookcode (19, by the way). It seems to make it easier for me. I hope you don't find it annoying.*
>
> *I must get to the point. Maria, I have ascertained where the 43-37-1-18-9-19/58-11-15-93-4-14 is located and I know how to get it! It is in 14-1-1-21-22-15-7, safe and retrievable. I have no doubt that my information is accurate. Isn't that marvelous! I wish I could see your face. The bad news is that my original plan regarding what to do with this information was a very selfish one. I have changed. I want to talk with you about that, but all I'll say for now is that apparently some deeply in-grained sense of integrity survived in me and has finally emerged. I believe it must be father's influence. It's a very freeing feeling to recontact that part of me. At any rate, I have now let myself know that the 9-6-3-4-25-31 must stand as a monument and inspiration and not be melted down into a life of luxury and leisure for me.*
>
> *I learned of its location from an old man of the*

06-12-1-06-16-14-22-9 who turned up at the 31-18-1-7-3/9-5-37-35-1/5-4-3-3-3-2-2-11. He was dying and may even be dead by now. He would 2-39-4-30-5 only the 61-1-01-23-4-19-52 tongue. 13-5-11-138-1/5-1-19-3-26-4-10-57 of 18-2-12-02-43-1-3-20/ 3-4-2-6-9-12-12-7-10-22/ 13-16-7-7-6-28-1-4-26-16 for me and then insisted on becoming my partner. He is the only other person who knows where the 1-8-15-5-19-9 is. The 44-4-17 I have enclosed will 31-14-4-9 you to it. I'm sure it will make an inspiring exhibit at the museum. It has been submerged by 40-7-34-7/24-15-32-2 since the earthquake of 1760 flooded the 17-3-7-62/013-37-9-24-14-9-10. How about that, Maria! It's been there all this time! I had fun drawing the 27-9-1. Please bear with me for using Jumbleletter and Bookcode (41, this time). Somehow, that made it more palatable for me. Actually, I thought you'd enjoy it, too. As the 78-17-02-2 indicates, the 15-4-16-10-47-12 is in a 17-1-42-3 forty feet below the present 4-8-2-40-5-5-4 of the 12-3-24-6. When the 18-6-12 is finished and the 12-4-31-3/18-6-50-2-6/15-3-29-2-2-8 the 1-1-3-12-18-6 will be come accessible.

I was active in getting the 10-4-18 approved and so was 12-6-3-10-28-2-1-16. Some of the means we used were not exactly honest or fair. We had to have 8-1-6-22-3-44-6 as the 8-9-25-18-2-7-3-18-2-12-1-2 of 11-4-27-2 and 27-5-5-2-1-44-6-40-3. I'm prepared to give all the details when the time comes. I intend to take full responsibility for my part in it, Maria. I don't believe it will lead to prosecution, but it certainly won't do my or 7-10-2-5-25-6-5-6's reputation any good. Needless to say, I expect 5-10-2-17-12-8-41-12 to be more than mildly upset about all of this. He certainly has not had a change of heart. I need time to smooth his feathers and prepare him for what is to come, so I am requesting that you do not go public with this information right away. By all means, I want you to tell the Archeological Committee and 13-6-18-42-2-15-4 the whole story immediately, but I want to give 14-3-3-18-25-2-36-12 the courtesy of breaking it to him myself before it hits the papers. Please do what you can to insure that. I am leaving tomorrow for the States and will return home on Wednesday. At that time, I'll let 16-25-4-18-40-2-2-12 know what I have done. Of course, by then it will be too late for him to do anything but curse me out and grudgingly accept the fait accompli.

I feel like the wandering sheep who has finally seen the guiding light and returned to the fold. I look forward to our reunion.

Triste gave the letter a quick perusal, then looked at me. "You translated all the words. I'm amazed."

"Anagrams," I said.

"I'll be damned." He read the letter slowly. "So," he said when he finished, "Sundance located a treasure and decided to turn it over to the museum. It's underwater somewhere. He anticipated that his partner would be upset." Triste looked at me. "The partner may be the murderer," he said.

"My thought exactly. If we could only break the number code, the 'bookcode', then we'd know for sure who it is. I think it's..."

"Maria Sundance was very intent on getting hold of a certain book."

"She was?" I was excited, very excited.

"Yes. She upset the maid, Juanita, with her insistent questioning of her about the book."

"What's the name of the book?" I asked eagerly.

"That's the problem. Juanita could not remember. She said it was a funny name and that she'd never heard of the book and was indignant that Maria kept insisting that she, Juanita, must have put it someplace, or loaned it to someone, or used it for some purpose."

"She couldn't remember the name?"

"I'm afraid not."

"We have to find out. We have to get that book. If we do, or if we find Maria's translation of the letter, I'm certain it will prove that Peter Petrillo was Martin's partner. He worked in the Post Office, for God's sake. He must have intercepted the letter to Maria at the Post Office in Postero and taken it with him to Chicago where he killed Martin."

"Martin could have taken the letter from Petrillo in the hotel room and run with it," Triste said.

"Yes!" I said. "And Petrillo shot him as he ran away. And Sundance gave me the folder."

"Petrillo must have seen him give it to you." Triste seemed nearly as excited as I.

"I wonder why he didn't just break into my apartment and get it."

"Good point. Perhaps he didn't see. Maybe he thought the police had the folder. Maybe he didn't know where you lived."

"He could have found out. The police had my name."

"This is very speculative." Triste's usual calm was returning. "We need to find that book," he said slowly, "and we need to determine that Petrillo took a quick trip to Chicago on or around June 28th. The latter shouldn't be hard to check. I've got some other news."

"What?"

"Martin Sundance's lawyer told me that a couple of months ago Sundance gave him a sealed envelope to be opened at the time of his death. The attorney placed the envelope in his file along with Sundance's will and other papers."

"What's in the envelope?"

"It's missing."

"Hah!"

"After Sundance's death, the lawyer went into Sundance's file. Everything was there except that envelope. About a week earlier, his office had been broken into. He could find nothing missing at the time and was puzzled about it, but figured the burglar must have been scared off before getting anything."

"He got the envelope."

"Apparently."

I lit the cigarette Triste had given me. We were in the little room where we met each time Triste visited. I could see buildings outside and daylight. "If you find that Petrillo did go to Chicago, how good is my case?"

Triste leaned back in his chair and stared at the ceiling. "If we could prove, with the help of the Chicago police, that Petrillo murdered Sundance, it could help our case a great deal. It could establish motive other than sex for Petrillo's interest in you. He did not want that folder to get to Maria Sundance. Somehow, he knew you had it. It could certianly strengthen our self-defense plea."

"All right!" I said. I was smiling, smiling very broadly. Suddenly, I was very eager for Triste to get moving. "Let me know the moment you find out that...if...Petrillo was in Chicago on the 28th."

Triste rose. "My exact plan," he said. "I'll start with Señora Petrillo. I'll keep you posted, Kat. There's hope."

I gave him the thumbs-up sign and said goodbye. Back in my cell I reviewed it all, over and over. The part that didn't fit was Maria Sundance's death. I had been sure it was not an accident, but maybe it was. Maybe it was one of those weird unfortunate coincidences, like my happening to be on Oak Street when Martin Sundance came out of that alley. On the other hand, maybe Petrillo wasn't working alone. My thoughts faded into the blur of sleep. I did not hear from Triste until the following afternoon. I had spent a good deal of that time pacing nervously in my cell and dealing with the misery of my intestinal cramps and seemingly unending diarrhea.

When Triste finally came he looked very disgusted. I was afraid to ask.

He shook his head. "Petrillo never left Postero. On June 27th, 28th and 29th, he was here. No doubt. Absolute confirmation. From his wife. From the Post Office. From his neighbors. From two different friends. He never left town, Kat. He's not our man."

I felt weak. My ears were ringing. This might be the first time in my life I'd ever faint. Triste had me put my head down and sent for a bottle of water. All I could say was: "I was so sure." Even in the depth of discouragement, somehow my mind kept clicking. I suddenly sat up straight. "Wait," I said. "That doesn't prove Petrillo's not the partner. He could have sent someone else to do the killing."

Triste did not answer.

"It's possible," I said, with less conviction.

"Kat, I'm sorry. We just have nothing. No link at all connecting Petrillo with the Sundances. No way to prove the letter and map have anything to do with Petrillo."

"The book?"

Triste shrugged his shoulders. "I'll keep trying. I already checked on Martin's copy."

"Martin's copy?"

"Yes, no luck."

"Martin's copy. Of course, he had to have a copy of the book to write out the number code." I slapped my forehead. "Can you believe I never thought of that?"

Triste didn't respond.

"So, where is his copy? What did you find out?"

"That after his death, his library was donated to charity."

"Oh, great!"

"Except for his archaeology books. Maria kept those."

"What charity? Can't you trace them?"

"I tried. They went to the Marigua Fund for the Poor. From

there, they were sent to one of over a dozen locations around the country. The Fund doesn't keep records of what goes where. The particular book we need, the title of which we do not know, could be sitting on a shelf with a ton of other books in one of those locations or it could be in the home of some needy person by now."

"Shit!"

"It's not very promising," Triste said. "I'll continue trying to trace it down and trying to find Maria's copy."

I'm sure Jorge Triste did try, but it was to no avail.

The trial took place two weeks later. It was nearly impossible to get continuances in Marigua. I had lost quite a bit of weight. Triste had found nothing more to help the case. Nettie Dawson arrived several days before the trial. She and I had gone to law school together and were good friends. I cried when I saw her. It was the first time I'd really cried through the ordeal, the first time I fully let go. She held me and I cried in her arms and I believe she cried also. Finally, we calmed and in the same room where Triste and I met, we talked.

"They're going to try to prove that you cooperated in a sexual liaison with Petrillo and killed him when..."

"When I saw how tiny his dicklet was."

Nettie shook her head, smiling. Her hair hung long and straight on either side of the slightly off-center part. Her face was gaunt and dotted here and there with barely visible acne scars.

"Or, when he couldn't find my clit."

"Kat!"

"It's absurd!"

"I know. Remember where we are. Of course, most prosecutors in a case like this back home would try the same approach."

"But here they have a better chance of making it stick?"

"That's what Triste believes."

"If I tell the judge I'm a lesbian, that should weaken the case substantially."

"I think it would backfire, Kat."

"So does Triste."

"They don't know what lesbians are here. They'll think you're a sick, sexually frustrated man-hater who welcomed a normal male into her bedroom and then acted out her vengefulness."

"Ridiculous."

"Yes."

32

"What else do we have?"

"Your story. We won't be able to bring in anything about the Sundances. There's absolutely nothing to link them with Petrillo or to the folder. And no evidence that your room was searched. Petrillo looks like your basic virile male out for a good time. He does have a history of temper outbursts. That will work in our favor and the photos we have of your throat bruises. We have to show that, with no encouragement from you, he tried forcefully to have sex with you, that when you fought him off, he became enraged and attacked you with the knife and you ended up killing him in self-defense. We shouldn't clutter it with your lesbianism."

The trial lasted a day and a half. The prosecutor brought in the gondola operator who testified to my belligerency, my lack of respect for people, and my deviousness in feigning ignorance of the Spanish language. He brought in witnesses who saw Petrillo and me talking amiably together at the hotel bar. The clerk in the hotel gift shop testified that, in her conversation with Petrillo, she had discussed with him the subtlety of a gift of a guidebook rather than flowers or candy or champagne for continuing a romantic venture. Many witnesses testified to Petrillo's upright character. I was painted as, at worst, a flirtatious tease who got angered and over-reacted, impulsively and violently, when my romantic partner responded as any normal man would. At best, I was depicted as a naive foreigner who handled a romantic liaison clumsily, then violently.

Although I, too, had character witnesses, a number of friends and colleagues from home; although I testified how Petrillo had come at me with the knife and attempted to strangle me, the judge said he could see no satisfactory explanation of what had happened other than that which the prosecution argued: that I became angered for some reason, probably related to sexual advances, that I lost control and pulled a knife on Petrillo, that a fight ensued and that I ended the fight by committing murder. He sentenced me to life imprisonment.

5.

THE PRISON

The jail had been dirty and cramped and bereft of sanitary facilities. The prison was worse than the worst movies I had seen of prison life. In jail, I had been unharrassed, left alone, with little contact with other prisoners or with guards. In prison, I had to fight to survive.

They took me there the day after the trial. Triste said he and Nettie would begin work immediately on the appeal, and although he, himself, was not convinced that there was any connection between the Sundance's and Petrillo, he agreed to continue investigating. I tried to be courageous when Nettie and the others said goodbye to me. Laura Nelson, my secretary, had come, and Elizabeth Blakely, my dearest friend, and Adrienne Daniels, a black social worker, my friend and former colleague. I feared I would never see them again. I feared. I hurt. The pain threatened to become unbearable, but then numbness took over, helping me go through the motions of still being alive.

I rode to Solera, the women's prison, in the back of a windowless, enclosed van, seated on a wooden bench, my wrist shackled to the wall of the truck. I can't describe my feelings; the numbness was working. I can't recall my thoughts; I think they were mostly memories of the past. The trip took a long time—maybe two hours, maybe four or more, I'm not sure. When they finally opened the door of the van, the sunlight temporarily blinded me. We had entered a walled, fortress-like compound located on a hill overlooking barren countryside. I could see a half dozen or so large stone buildings, all with barred windows. A woman in green walked by pushing a wheelbarrow. I was led into one of the buildings, to an office, where I was told to wait. I stood, looking out the window to the prison grounds. There was a motley crowd of women sitting around on benches, silently, or talking in groups. Most had on pale green-colored clothing—dresses or pants and shirts. Some wore street clothes. I sat down and waited, fighting tears, wanting the numbness to remain.

"Stand up! You were not told to sit." The unshaven man who stomped into the room stared at me angrily. I felt intense revulsion. I can't describe how much I despise being ordered around. I stood. The man went to the desk and seated himself. He wore a wrinkled khaki uniform and a pistol on his waist. After asking me a few questions while typing on a form, he indicated that I should come with him. We went down to the cellar of the dark, old building. I had ugly, terrifying fantasies of where he could be taking me. He stopped at a metal door which he unlocked. The area seemed deserted. It was deadly quiet except for the clanging as he opened the door.

"Go in," he said.

The room was pitch black. I balked. He reached within and turned on a light. It was a long narrow room with rows of shelves containing boxes and cans and other supplies. The guard handed me a thin, rolled up mattress, a pillow, a blanket and a cup and bowl. Carrying my bundle, I followed him outside into the glaring sunlight and then into another thick-walled building, the door of which bore a dilapidated sign reading "Section Three". The floors were of rough wood, the unpainted walls seemed to be concrete with stone beneath.

A khaki-uniformed woman sat on a broken easy chair reading a magazine.

"Here's the new one," the man said to her. "She's all yours!" He left the building.

The woman looked up indifferently. She had stringy, graying hair, tied behind her neck. Her eyes were bloodshot. "In there," she muttered, pointing to a door. "Find a free bed. See me first thing tomorrow morning for your clothes and work assignment." She resumed reading.

The door she indicated was unlocked. I entered the room. It was large, cluttered, but barren-seeming. In haphazard arrangement throughout the room were wooden platforms which served as beds. There must have been thirty or forty of them. Many had mattresses and/or other items on them and under them. A few were bare. There were about a dozen women in the room. They looked toward me as I stood at the entrance. I was wearing a pair of tan denim slacks, a colorful T-shirt and a blazer. The others all wore green. The pairs of eyes staring at me appeared sullen and unwelcoming. No one spoke to me. No one moved toward me. Some continued staring; some resumed whatever they'd been doing before I entered. I walked to the nearest wall where there was some space and dropped my armload onto the floor. I felt sickened and, admittedly, frightened. At that moment, three women entered the room. They seemed more assured than the others and they all wore street clothes.

"There she is," one said, spotting me near the wall.

The three of them marched in my direction. One of the trio, a tall, dark-skinned woman with a gold front tooth planted herself directly in front of me. She looked me over, from top to bottom, then appraisingly touched the fabric of my jacket.

"I'll take this," she said. "Give it to me."

I bristled, anger overtaking my fear. I moved back a step. "I'll be needing it myself," I said.

She laughed arrogantly, her gold tooth sparkling. "Take it off, little girl, or you will get hurt. Do what I say."

I heard my father in her words and tone. I quickly moved a few steps to the side, establishing a space of three or so feet between us. I got into a karate stance and glared back at the woman, waiting. Peripherally, I could observe the others watching us. She made her move, lunging toward me for the attack. I clipped her sharply on the neck and she fell. Crouching, my hands raised as weapons, I waited, ready. The other two women laughed as they helped their friend struggle back to her feet.

"We got us a goddam fighter," one with a red headband said.

Two more women entered the room then, and sauntered our way, joining the first group. Their manner was tough and cocky, like the others.

"My friend wants your jacket," the headband woman said. She was not smiling. "She always gets what she wants. You better take it off."

I was prepared to fight all five of them. Although most assuredly they would win, what I read in this scene, what it did to me, what I sensed it meant, told me not to give, that I must defy them, make them take what they want by force or defeat them, but not give.

They formed a semi-circle around me. Each time one of them made a move for me, I responded with a karate chop. I got one woman in the temple, another in the side below her ribs. They kept coming. I kept striking. I used my feet, my elbows, the heels of my hands. I warded them off with all the skill and strength I had. Two of them were down and, I hoped, unwilling to come for more. Suddenly, someone jumped me from behind, adhering to me like a venomous, clinging bug. As I was trying to swing her off my back, someone punched me in the gut. I was down. They were on top of me. I twisted and churned, managing to free my leg enough to crack one of the women in the jaw with the edge of my shoe. She wailed a high-pitched, piercing sound. Several of her cohorts went to her. This gave me the opportunity to stand again, and again I crouched in a karate position.

At this point, one of them grabbed my bed roll and blanket and left. Leading their injured friend away, all the others then left the room. I stood panting. I could taste blood in my mouth and feel it trickling down my chin. My muscles were aching. I had cuts here and there and I knew there would be bruises. My blazer was a torn mess. But I still had it! By God, I still had it! I leaned against the wall, looking toward the door, anticipating the possibility of their return.

"Good show!" one of the observers yelled from across the room.

"What's your name?" another woman asked, walking towards me. "I'm Carmen."

"Kat," I said, still panting, "Kat Rogan." We shook hands.

"Wild cat," someone said in English, also shaking my hand. "You fight like a panther."

They talked about the battle, rehashing it and gleefully expressing the pleasure they got seeing the "clanswomen" kicked around.

I was beginning to relax a little, allowing myself to enjoy my victory when one of the attackers re-entered the room. I was immediately ready for action. She walked toward me, carrying a mattress and blanket. The other women backed away. She took the bedding to an empty bed rack and pulled the wooden rack off to the side, near the wall.

"This is yours," she said. "No one will take it from you." She placed my cup and bowl atop the mattress.

I said nothing, watching her. She came close to me. I was vigilant.

"Would you teach me how to do that?" she said quietly, leaning against the wall next to me. "That kind of fighting. I want to learn." She offered me a cigarette and lit it for me.

"Why should I do that for you?" I asked.

She smiled. "Then next time maybe you won't be alone," she responded.

She was an attractive woman despite her thinness. Her teeth were very white and straight. She had a fresh, clean look.

"I could teach you," I said.

"Good. Come."

I followed her from the room, past the guard who was still reading her magazine, and out of the building. She took me past several other buildings, apparently more sleeping quarters, through the rear of the yard to an isolated area behind a wooden structure.

"OK, begin," she said.

I led her through some stretching exercises, and told her about the purpose, method and philosophy of karate. Teresa was an eager student, and by the time we stopped, an hour or so later, she was beginning to perform adequately some rudimentary blocks and blows.

"It is time for dinner," she said. "You may eat with me, if you like."

The dining hall was a grim wooden room with rows of rough, heavy, primitively-constructed tables and benches. With my metal bowl and cup in hand, I stood in line behind Teresa. There were several huge vats of hot food, and tables holding tortillas, coffee and other items. The women doing the serving wore food-encrusted aprons over their green clothes. One of them served Teresa a large ladle of something that looked like stew. She began dipping into another vat to fill my bowl.

"No," Teresa said, rebuking her. "Give her that."

The woman's expression did not change. With dull indifference, she scooped the stew into my bowl.

We went to a table near the center of the room. Three other women were already there. I recognized two from the fight in the dormitory.

"Hey. I smell a newblood," one of them said, holding her nose. "Get it outta here."

"This one don't smell so bad," another commented. It was the woman with the red headband. "She moves like lightning." There seemed to be a note of respect in her voice.

"It's all right," Teresa said, gesturing for me to take a seat. "I invited her to join us."

"Oh, yeah?" the first women responded. "That was fast. Will she be your girlfriend, Teresa?" the woman said teasingly. "I told you you need one."

Teresa smiled. "Mind your own business," she said. "Where is Leona?"

"At a meeting of the Section Chiefs. That new guard, Lopez, is still making trouble. They're having a talk about it, with Angela."

Teresa nodded.

"I hope they take care of the bitch," a plump, babyish-looking woman said. "This morning, she tried to stop Sonia from shaking down a Section Two debajera. She's very dense."

I listened carefully to everything, observing each woman closely, trying to extract all the meaning I could from what they said and did.

"So, what about *her*," one of the women asked Teresa, gesturing toward me.

"I haven't decided yet," Teresa said. "I might sponsor her."

"She'd have my vote," one of the fighters said. "We could use her. What's your rap, honey? You stomp some dude dead with those flashing feet of yours or what?"

"Could be," I said, looking directly into her black eyes as I chewed down on a stringy piece of meat.

"She's no whore, I'll bet. You ain't a whore, are you, honey? You sure are a gringo, though. We don't get many Yankee whores here."

I chose to say as little as possible and no one seemed to expect otherwise. Four or five more women joined us. It was obvious that I was among an elite group. They all wore street clothes and had a cocky, confident air about them, unlike the prisoners sitting in the back sections of the dining hall. We ate stew and rice, as did the women at the tables surrounding us, and could have fruit and milk if we chose. The women in the rear seemed to have beans with their rice and little else.

There were two male guards at the dining hall entrance wearing the familiar khaki. They were silent except for occasional brief interchanges with some of the street-clothes prisoners. Each wore a pistol at his waist.

"So, how do you like this lovely place?" someone said to me. "It's nice and pretty like North American cans, no?"

"It's a real paradise," I said.

The woman chuckled, "What are you called?"

"Kat."

"Kat! OK. You're called Kat. A funny name." She laughed again. "Your jacket's got a tear in it, Kat."

I looked at the tear in my blazer, feigning surprise. "I'll be damned!" I said sardonically. "I'll have to take it to the tailor."

"Ah, don't laugh. You're talking to her. See these magic fingers. Tell her, Rosa, am I the best tailor ever?"

"The best here," Rosa said. "Look at this." She held up her leg displaying the cuff of her pants. "They were too long and Carlotta fixed them good. Me, I never learned how to sew. I got these pants from that tall newblood there." She pointed to a woman in the food line. "She very generous girl." Rosa laughed, showing a mouthful of decayed teeth. "*Very* generous. She gave me her pussy, too."

"With a little help from your friends," Carlotta said.

"There's Leona!"

The women shifted, clearing a large space at the head of the table.

"Stand up," Teresa told me.

I looked at her.

"Come on, stand, OK?"

I took a final bite of food and stood. A heavy pock-marked woman wearing a black denim jacket approached our table. She was carrying a tray with two bowls of stew, an orange and a slice of cake.

"This is the one I told you about," Teresa said, respectfully. "I've asked her to join us for the meal. Is it OK?"

40

The woman looked at me, standing a yard or so away. "So you like to fight."

I made a shrugging gesture. "I'm able to."

"And you want to eat with us?" She sat down.

"I've eaten."

Leona's mouth formed a cross between a smile and a snarl. "Be in my room in an hour," she said. She turned her attention away from me then and began talking with the others.

I took my eating utensils to the buckets of soapy water, washed them off and left the dining hall. I wasn't sure what to do for the next hour. This alien place was obviously full of predators so a walking tour did not seem advisable. One thing I needed to do was find out where Leona's room was located. Clearly she wielded power here and I had no intention of turning down her "invitation". In fact, I interpreted it as a good sign. I was walking toward "home," the dormitory where I had my bed, when I became aware of someone behind me. I turned. She was an older woman, frail, dressed in a faded green dress. Her chin was covered with warts.

"Will you be in the Lion's clan?" she asked me.

"What?" I said.

She looked disgusted, or impatient.

"I'm sorry, I don't know what you mean."

"Leona's clan. Section Three. You getting in?" She clipped off her words as if she would run out if she didn't use them sparingly.

"Are you in her clan?" I asked.

"Hah!" She spit on the ground. "You know nothing!" She began to walk away.

"Wait," I said. "You're right. I don't know much about this place. Not yet. I just came today."

"I know that. Do I look like a fool?"

"You look angry," I said.

She spit again. "Ten years ago when I came I could have had a sponsor. I said no, I don't join gangs. Pooh! An ass! An ass! I've been trying ever since to get another chance. I need a sponsor. I'll pay you what I can. Maybe my friend outside will bring you something. Pills, if you want, or mushrooms. They will ask you to join."

"How do you know?"

"You sat at their table. You sat at the table of the Lion. You, a

41

newblood, on your first day.''

We were standing outside the Section Three dormitory building. The warted woman beckoned for me to go inside. She took me through what obviously was the lavatory, a cement room with rows of toilets and sinks. Many of the toilets were dry; all were badly stained. In the back was another room with cracked and partly missing walls. Several shower spigots jutted out of the wall.

"A shower," I said with some pleasure. I had not been able to bathe myself thoroughly since leaving Chicago.

"If you can wash in air," the woman hissed. "No water. Not since I've been here. That's ten years." She sat on the floor. "They call us debajeras."

I sat down on the floor, too, and waited for her to say more.

"Women like me, women who are in no clan. We are the lowest of the low in this place. It's a dog's life. At least they never fuck me anymore." She spit on the cracked floor, just missing a giant cockroach.

"You will be like me unless you can join. They asked me when I first came. I was too haughty for such foolishness. Emma Truello does not kow tow to anyone." She shook her head. "How I regret it. I've never been given another chance."

"And you think I could help you?"

"Somehow you have moved quickly. Your first day here and you ate at the Lion's table."

"Tell me about her—about Leona, the 'Lion'."

"Ech, she's a mean one! A shrew. A killer. She murdered once for sure, and maybe twice. For the first one, she got sent here. That was eight years ago. Four years ago, a guard was stabbed. He died. He was a pig and deserved to die. They stirred things up for months. It was hell for all of us. They never found out who did it. Like everyone else, I said nothing. But after the guard was killed, Leona became the Section Chief. She is merciless. Everyone is afraid of her. Everyone but Angela."

"Angela?"

"The Angel. Hah! The devil, more likely. The top woman, boss of all the clans."

"How many clans are there, Emma?"

She looked at me as if I were retarded. "Five," she said. "Each section has a clan. If you are in a clan, you're protected. You have things. The guards do not treat you like manure. If you are a debajera, you have nothing.''

"Can't the debajeras form their own clan?" I asked.

Emma shrugged. "It's been tried." She looked at me. "Maybe you think *you* can do it, huh?"

We heard someone walking through the john and back to where we were sitting. It was Carlotta, the tailor. She looked at us a moment then gestured with her head for Emma to leave. The aging woman did so without hesitation and without a word.

"You shouldn't talk friendly to her," Carlotta said, "not if you are to be a sponsorera." Carlotta was a petite woman, young, probably in her mid-twenties. "She is a debajera, that one."

"What am I?" I asked. I stood, towering over Carlotta by a good half foot.

Carlotta laughed. "Nothing," she said. "Newblood. You are nothing yet." She jumped up and grabbed onto a horizontal pole, a metal rod that might have held a shower curtain in the distant past. She chinned herself. "What we were outside makes no difference," she said, dropping back to the floor. "All newblood is nothing."

I did not respond.

"In there," she gestured toward the dormitory, "you are with debajeras. Maybe you will become one of them." She laughed. "But I think not," she added. "Teresa wants you. I can tell."

"Where is Leona's room?" I asked.

"Come, I'll show you."

We did not leave the building, but went through the dingy corridor and up some narrow stone steps. There were many doors, most of them closed. Carlotta greeted several women in the hall. They each looked at me with curiosity.

"That's Leona's room," Carlotta said, pointing to a closed door. "It's not time yet for you to see her. She's still in the dining hall. You can wait at my place."

I followed Carlotta around a corner and into a room about 15 feet by 15 feet, containing four beds, each with two mattresses. There were also several tables, some magazines and a variety of other items. It was certainly not luxurious, but was a vast improvement over the dormitory downstairs. No one else was in the room. Carlotta closed the door and went to a box which she unlocked. She removed the stub of what apparently was a joint, lit it and inhaled deeply.

"Sit," she said.

43

I sat across from her on one of the beds.

"You have any children?"

"No."

"I have three. They're with my mother. That's the hardest part for me."

From the same box she removed a tattered envelope and handed it to me. There were several worn photographs.

"What are their names?" I asked.

Carlotta talked about her children, about the little home they had in Mordova on the sea, and how her oldest daughter dived for sponges and oysters. She talked for a long time. "If I am lucky, I will be with them in one more year," she said. "How about you? How long are you in here for?"

"Forever," I said. "Unless my appeal is successful." I felt my stomach churn. The events since my arrival had distracted me, but now it all rushed back. I had to lean my hands on the bed for support.

Carlotta looked genuinely sympathetic. "At least you have no children," she said at last. "I think you should go to Leona now."

I felt nervous about seeing Leona and angry that this was so. From what I had gleaned, the degree of misery I was to endure in this disgusting place might hinge on Leona's response to me. I knocked on the door.

"Enter."

She slouched on an old easy chair. At the table to her side sat two other women. They had both been at the dining table earlier; one had been in the fight.

"Do you play poker?" Leona said to me as soon as I entered.

"Yes."

She rose and joined the others at the table. I followed, taking the remaining seat. I had no money, no cigarettes, no possessions. I felt wary. Leona began to deal. Her hands were large, like the rest of her. Her black hair was short and combed straight back. There were flecks of gray in it. Her mouth turned downward in a way that made her look cruel, beast-like. The women withdrew coins from their pockets and placed them in piles on the table. Leona looked at me, waiting.

I shrugged.

"Newblood never have anything," one of the women said. "I could stake you."

My uneasiness grew. How would I pay her back if I lost? What would being in debt mean? What would happen if I refused?

I nodded.

She pushed a pile of coins in my direction. I had only a vague idea of their value. I thought it best not to ask. I tried to remember what I had learned about the money during my one day as a tourist in this fucking country. I picked up my cards and, following the others' lead, pushed a ten-peso coin onto the center of the table. I generally did well at poker and hoped this would not be an exception. I knew exactly what I wanted the outcome to be—for Leona to win big, me second and for the others to lose. The play began. It went smoothly at first. I won some and lost some, so my money pile remained fairly stable.

It had gotten dark outside and the overhead bulb, shielded with a decorated piece of paper, cast shadows on the room. The room contained a real bed with a spring and several of the prison mattresses. At one point during the game, a young woman, probably attractive under her make-up, came into the room and crawled into the bed, speaking to no one. There were two large wooden boxes with a radio on top of one of them, an easy chair, and the table and chairs we were using. The room was about the same size as the one Carlotta shared with three others. There had been some attempt at decorating. Pieces of cloth hung around the window and some threadbare carpeting was on the floor.

"I'll raise you fifteen," the woman called Evie said.

The stakes were getting higher. I saw the raise. I lost that hand. My pile of coins was dwindling uncomfortably. We were playing straight draw and stud poker, nothing wild, nothing fancy. It was my turn to deal. I could feel Leona watching me. The women spoke little as we played, making occasional allusions to things I didn't understand and cracking a joke now and then. Their Spanish was far from refined.

I lost again and Evie pushed some of her coins in my direction, adding to the loan. I accepted them knowing that my luck had better turn. Leona cursed Marina, the other player, for not playing fast enough. When she yelled, Leona's jowls shook, distorting her face and making her appearance even more ugly and frightful. The others were clearly intimidated by her.

"Come on, gringo, place your fucking bet," she snarled at me when I hesitated while debating whether or not to raise.

I had three nines with an ace high. Evie had a pair of aces showing and Leona a pair of jacks. It was a risk which I felt compelled to take. I pushed all my coins forward. The others, in turn, saw my bet. I slapped my cards down. Evie cursed. Marina silently threw in her cards. Leona smiled. I had a large stack of coins now and continued winning. Marina was nearly broke. I repaid Evie what I had borrowed and was still well ahead of everyone. Leona won the next three hands. It appeared that she and I were about even. At that moment, a horn sounded. Five short blasts, repeated three times.

"The asshole wants an audience again," Evie said. "I think he just loves to parade himself."

The play stopped. Marina gathered up the cards and handed them to Leona. Leona took her winnings and put them in a cloth bag which she placed in the large box on the floor near her bed. "Let's go," she said, taking the arm of the woman on the bed.

I grabbed my coins and followed the others outside. We met Teresa on the way and she walked beside me. I didn't know where we were going, but all the prisoners seemed to be gathering in the yard. They formed disorderly groups, those in street clothes separate from the others. There seemed to be well over a thousand people. We stood facing the building where I had been brought when I first arrived at the prison. After a few minutes, a group of guards walked out of the building, then a man in a khaki dress uniform, then some more guards.

"That's the warden," Teresa said to me. "A real prick."

The warden walked to a platform at the side of the building and ascended the steps.

"Prisoners," he began, in a booming, raspy voice. "For the third month in a row, all segments are above quota. Congratulations! The coffee bean crop is the best in years. The Print Shop filled seven extra orders this month, on time! In addition, there have been no incidents to report to the Penal Authority this month. I am very pleased. There will be an extra ration of milk and eggs for every inmate this week."

So speaking, the warden turned on his heel and left the stand. Several prisoners hissed as he walked back into the building. "Oh, I feel so wonderful now," someone said sarcastically. "How I love his little morale boosters. They make my day." The women began to drift off. It was dark in the yard. Teresa had disappeared and I saw no one else I knew among the masses of people. I found my way back to the Section Three building.

On the ground floor, in addition to the room where I was to sleep, I could see a number of similar rooms filled with beds and now filling up with prisoners. I went to the place where Teresa had placed my mattress and blanket. They were still there. Those, my cup and bowl, the clothes on my back and the coins in my pocket comprised all of my possessions. The room looked even grimmer in the dim light of the overhead bulbs. I was exhausted. I removed my pants and jacket, placed them on the floor next to me and crawled into the bed. It was hard and lumpy and the blanket had an unidentifiable odor. Some of the women in the dormitory were talking together, others sitting on their beds silently. No one spoke to me. I closed my eyes to close out the scene. Other haunting scenes came when I finally slept; the same bloody nightmares came first and then Sundance's eyes or were they the eyes of my mother. That was how she looked at the moment of her death; desparate but also sad and resigned.

In the middle of the night I was awakened by a sharp scream of terror and then the sounds of someone whimpering.

"Shaddup," a voice muttered.

I saw a rat scurry across the floor. I closed my eyes tightly until sleep finally returned.

6.

THE SPONSORERA

The next time I awoke, it was with a jolt from a sharp painful blow to the bottom of my foot.

"Get up, animal." A guard stood over me, holding a two foot long, narrow piece of wood. She slapped it repeatedly against her palm, as she stared down at me, a strand of her stringy hair hanging down her cheek.

"What's your problem," I said angrily, sitting up in the bed, returning her stare. She was the same guard who had been sitting outside the dormitory yesterday.

"This ain't a hotel, animal. I told you to report to me for your work assignment."

The room was nearly empty of people. I was surprised I had slept through their departures.

"This is the last time I'm going to be your alarm clock," the guard droned.

I clenched my teeth until my jaw throbbed, knowing I must control the temptation to lash out at her.

"The field crew leaves in a half hour. Go to the main gate when you hear the horn." She banged her club against the neighboring bed as she exited.

I looked for my clothes where I had left them, but they were gone. I went to the john in my T-shirt and underpants. All the unoccupied toilets looked nonfunctional. There was no attempt at privacy. As I waited for one of the seatless, cracked, porcelain pots to become available, I washed myself as well as I could from the trickle of water in a sink. I had no soap or towel.

"Is there breakfast?" I asked a fellow bather.

For a moment she looked at me as if I were an apparition or a Martian. Then her face softened. "Newblood," she said almost kindly. "You're a little late but you might get something in the dining hall if you hurry."

"Thanks," I said.

"Of course, all the breakfast steaks and omelettes are probably gone," she added, laughing. The laugh turned into a hacking cough.

A few minutes later, I found the guard and told her my clothes were missing. She looked at me contemptuously. "What a shame," she spat.

I glared back at her with an equal amount of contempt until she looked away. She took me to the end of the corridor and unlocked a door.

"One outfit," she said. "Be quick about it."

I took my time finding a pair of pants with only a couple of small holes, and a long-sleeved shirt. They were pale green.

Breakfast was a cold mush of some sort. I made myself eat some of it. The coffee was luke warm and it didn't taste much like coffee. I longed for a Pepsi. As soon as I had that thought, I thought of all the other things I longed for and I had to swallow repeatedly to keep from crying. I knew I had to stay angry and hard, and I knew I would never accept living the rest of my life under these conditions.

The horn sounded, a series of three long blasts. I found the main gate easily. There was a crowd of prisoners there and a line of large old trucks. A guard with a clipboard was seated at a table near the gate. The women were checking in with him, then climbing into the trucks. I stood with the others lined up in front of the table.

"Number?"

"I don't know," I said. "I didn't know I had a number."

The guard looked at me with disgust. "You think you're funny," he said angrily.

49

"I just arrived yesterday," I replied. "No one told me about a number."

"Jesus Christ," he sputtered impatiently. "Get out of the way then, imbecile. You're holding things up. Go on. Go stand over there, animal."

I wanted to punch him. I wanted to smash his nose with the heel of my hand and hear the crunch of splintering bone and cartilege as the pieces pushed up into his brain. I went where he had indicated and immediately began an internal dialogue. My vicious thought now concerned me more than the man's disgusting treatment of me. These conditions can turn us into animals, I thought. I can't let that happen.

I was taken back to the office.

"Your name."

"Kat Rogan."

The guard looked through a card file. "Your number is X4112. Don't forget it again, understand?"

I did not reply.

"Answer me!"

All my life I had successfully shunted this type of treatment. Even from my father. Even in the public high school I'd attended. "I'll remember the number," I said calmly.

The guard looked at me angrily. "Cocky gringo cunt," he said, coming around the desk. "Come on." He grabbed my arm roughly.

Instinctively, I pulled away from his grip. He was coming at me again when another guard entered the office.

"Trouble?" she asked.

"Nothing I can't handle," he replied. "Get out to the truck, you. You're holding things up."

We were crammed against each other, some women sitting, others standing, holding onto the walls of the truck. It crossed my mind to climb over the side and run, run across the dry terrain toward the mountains, to bathe in a stream and find the ocean and find a ship and go home. Behind us was a jeep with two armed guards.

Our job was to plow the field, to prepare the crusty earth for whatever seeds were to be planted there. We used heavy hand tools. After an hour, my muscles ached miserably. The sun was getting hotter and hotter. The guards stood in clumps in whatever shade they could find, yelling at any prisoner who slowed down or talked. My muscles did what they had to do, automatically; my mind went elsewhere. Triste had taken my belongings and agreed to store them for me. Nettie would arrange to find a tenant to sublet my apartment until. . . The appeal would be successful, I thought. It had to be. Nettie agreed with my assessment of Triste, that he was a very adequate lawyer. Lana Nelson said she would put things on hold at the office until I returned.

"Move it, you!"

I would return! I dug the pick axe into the hard earth. I will get out of here! In the meantime, I've got to join a clan, I thought. These women are all debajeras here. All the field workers. I can't become one of them. It will kill me. . . or maybe I'll end up killing someone. That thought made me shudder. I reviewed the poker game last night. It was hard to tell, but I think it had gone OK. I thought about Teresa. She'll probably hit on me soon. As I dug, sweat and dirt mixing on my clothes, I considered how I wanted to handle that.

It seemed the grueling day would never end, but finally we were loaded into the trucks and driven back to the prison. I collapsed, sweaty and filthy on my ragged bed.

"Ah, there you are."

"Teresa," I said. I could barely move.

"I was looking for you. For my second lesson. I've been practicing. Watch." She went through some maneuvers.

"Not bad," I said wearily. "Keep the left elbow up a bit there."

"You aren't in any shape for a lesson," she said. "I'm gonna get you off that detail. OK? You want me to? You would like that?"

"I'd like it," I said.

"You need a shower, woman. You're not lookin' so good."

"Yeah," I said. "I'm not feeling so good."

"Let me see your hands." She was sitting on the edge of my bed now and grabbed my wrists. "Ay, caramba! What a mess. Look at those blisters. Come on, let's go upstairs."

The shower water was cold heaven. Teresa supplied me with soap and a towel. She watched me as I washed, smiling, showing her beautiful white teeth. When I finished she handed me a fresh pair of green pants and a green shirt.

Teresa's room was similar to Carlotta's. There were four beds, a couple of other pieces of furniture and cardboard boxes of various

51

sizes where she and the others apparently kept their things.

I was expecting Teresa to make a play for me. Instead, she talked. She told me about her life before coming to Solera. She said she didn't talk about it much but seeing newblood always got her thinking about the outside. She didn't ask me any questions about myself. Maybe she was waiting for me to volunteer or maybe she didn't care. Later I found out she was afraid it would have been presumptuous to probe. We sat in her room talking for over an hour. I was hungry. I had eaten lunch and dinner with the debajeras but I was having trouble adjusting to the food and hadn't taken much. As Teresa talked, my eye kept wandering to the stock of canned goods in the corner of the room. My pride would not allow me to ask. I tried not to look at it, but finally Teresa noticed.

"I think I'll have a snack," she said. She opened a can of sardines.

I've never particularly cared for sardines, but they smelled delicious.

"You want some?" she asked.

They *were* delicious.

I slept again in my hard lumpy bed in the midst of the overcrowded and apparently apathetic debajeras. After breakfast, I headed toward the main gate as I'd been told to do yesterday.

"Hey, you." It was the nasty guard from our dorm, Durango. "You're on kitchen detail today. Report there now."

Teresa, I thought. She arranged it. Thank God.

The work was difficult, but it felt like a vacation after the fields yesterday. The atmosphere was slightly more congenial. There was a lot of conversation, even some joking. Lina Gracea, one of the few women with whom I had spoken at the dorm, worked there. Like Emma, the older woman with the warts, Lina began to talk with me about the clans, about the importance of being in. She had been a sponsorera when she first came, she told me. But her sponsor, a full-blooded Indian, had been bought by a prison farm and so she, Lina, had lost her chance.

"It's difficult to get sponsored?" I asked.

"I think about it all the time," she said, chopping onions so rapidly I could barely see her hands. "If it doesn't happen the first few months you're here, it usually doesn't happen at all." She stopped chopping. "There are four ways," she said. "Contraband, brawn, sex, friendship." She slapped the knife on the counter as

52

she said each of the four words. She paused. "In that order."

I dumped a sack of potatoes into the bin.

"If you can manage more than one, all the better. With Estrella, my sponsor, it was friendship." She resumed chopping vegetables. "I knew her brother. We worked together in Postero. Estrella found me the first day I came. What a mess I was, but Estrella protected me and became my sponsor. I think I would have made it. Leona liked Estrella OK. Estrella was very sweet. But then she left." Lina was gripping the knife handle tightly now as she spoke. "How I cried that day. For me, yes, but not just for myself. To be bought by a prison farm is like a death sentence. Slavery. It is hell to be a debajera, but nothing is as bad as...poor Estrella. I don't know if she's alive or dead. Her brother doesn't come anymore. After Estrella left, he never came again."

"Get to work, you two."

"Fuck yourself in your flabby old ass, you pig," Lina mumbled under her breath. "Teresa is a good woman," she continued. "She's not like some of the others. Do you have goods?"

"What do you mean?"

"Contraband—drugs, money, candy, makeup, magazines. Any of that. Can you get it?"

"I don't know."

"You're a Yankee. You must be rich."

I laughed. "You think all Yankees are rich?"

"To me they are."

"If I could get those things, how would I get them in here?"

"There are many ways."

"They took everything from me when I came."

"Yes."

"Gracea," the guard shouted. "The truck's in. Go unload."

At lunchtime, I served the prisoners from the vats. The clanswomen got two scoops, coffee, a carton of milk and a piece of fruit. The debajeras and newblood got one scoop and coffee. There was no mistaking who was who. Clanswomen never wore the green prison uniform, but is was more than clothes that set them apart. Teresa came and smiled at me and winked. Leona came. I made sure she got many chunks of potato in her portion. She didn't speak to me.

After cleaning up, I was told I could leave. Teresa found me and we had another lesson behind the wooden maintenance garage way in the back of the yard. She was very impressed with my skill. "You move like a deadly dancer," she said. "It's beautiful." She was learning quickly herself. We worked on kicks today. "I will sponsor you," Teresa declared. "It would be my privilege. If you get in, teach the others this karate. Otherwise, no. Keep it for yourself. It will help you survive as a debajera." "And how is it decided if I get in?" I asked. "The clan votes. Paper vote. Secret. If most want you, you're in. Unless Leona vetoes it." "I see. When will the voting take place?" "Sometime before three months. Exactly when is up to me—the sponsor. You are newblood for three months. Then you are either in a clan or a debajera." "Do you have any advice for me?" Teresa laughed. "One thing for sure," she said. "Stay away from Vera. She's Leona's lady." "I'll make a point of it," I said. "Anything else?" "No," Teresa replied. "You're a smart person. You know how to handle yourself. You will do OK." She looked at me with affection, maybe admiration.

For the rest of that week and the next, I worked in the kitchen each day and slept in the Section Three A dorm each night. The lot of the debajeras was a dreary one. They worked long hours, ate poorly, had few diversions or pleasures and lived under the constant threat of unpredictable and often barbarous persecution by guards and clanswomen. As a newblood who was so quickly a sponsorera I had a special, although precarious, status with the debajeras. "You could end up either way," Carmen said. "One of us, or one of them." She seemed envious of me as did the other debajeras. It was a minority of prisoners who became clanswomen. Some of the debajeras seemed eager to befriend me, possibly, like Emma Truello, hoping I could some day help them; others avoided me. I found the unfairness of the caste system appalling. I spoke with some of the debajeras about the possibility of protest, rebellion, change. They told me stories of past attempts, always failures, and always followed by harsher conditions.

Teresa's karate training continued, often two lessons a day. She was getting good. We were becoming friends. After lunch one day, she and I went outside to sit in the shade.

"Hey you, newblood, go get me that newspaper," a clanswoman

54

said to me.

I did not know her. We were sitting near each other at the wall in the prison yard. The sun was high. It was very hot.

"You look like you can walk," I said.

The woman stood up angrily. I stood too.

"I said get it, bitch!"

I was taller than she although she outweighed me by at least twenty pounds. Before I could respond again, Teresa intervened.

"Hey, Tula, leave her alone. She's my sponsorera."

"Big deal. She's a pussy."

The woman spit on my green pants, turned, and walked away. I looked at the blob of saliva dripping down my knee.

"Tula!" I yelled.

"It's OK. Leave it," Teresa warned.

I ignored her. Tula turned back.

"You got a handkerchief?" I asked.

She stared at me. "You nuts?"

"I've got something of yours to return to you. Come here! Or are you scared?"

I was. Several of her friends were around, but I felt I had to press it. I couldn't imagine letting someone get away with spitting on me. She sauntered toward me. When she was in reaching distance, I grabbed her arm and pulled her close enough to wipe the spit off of my knee onto her pants. The women around us laughed.

"There," I said. "You were right. We didn't need a handkerchief after all." As I spoke, I reached for the newspaper. "Here," I said. I handed it to her and smiled.

She grabbed the paper, looked at Teresa and shook her head. "You're lucky you're a sponserera," she mumbled, walking away.

I knew she was right. And I knew that, unless the present system could be changed, my personal welfare lay in being tight with clanswomen. However, because I worked with debajeras and slept in a debajera dorm, and knew their suffering, I felt an affinity with them and became friends with several of them. This created a problem one day. I had given some gifts to a debajera; I had given Lina Gracea a joint, a bar of candy I'd gotten from Teresa and a flannel shirt. Some clanswomen found out about these possessions and they pushed Lina around until she told where she had gotten them.

Rosa approached me in the yard. "You have too much, huh?

You give it away—to debajeras."

"What I gave was mine to give," I said.

"You don't understand, do you, asshole? God, you're a dumb bitch."

"Get fucked, Rosa," I said, smiling at her. I turned and walked away.

Five minutes later, Rosa, Carlotta and another woman came to me. "You treated Rosa without respect," Carlotta said angrily. "You have to respect the clanswomen."

"They have to respect me," I said, my voice as angry as hers, my body poised.

Carlotta turned to the others, as if unsure what to do next. Then she turned back to me. "Be cool, will you, Kat," she said. "We want you in the clan. Stay away from the debajeras. Don't give them things. It don't look good. Don't insult clanswomen."

"Right," I said. "As long as they don't insult me."

They left then. I was sure they had come to do more than simply discuss this with me. I was sure they were finding me very self-possessed, maybe even intimidating. I realized that I was pleased about that. I liked the feeling.

Time and again I witnessed instances in which guards harassed and sometimes brutalized debajeras and newbloods. Occasionally, it happened to me. One time, Durango and another guard, a man, converged on me right outside the door of Section Three building. They began baiting me as they often did to newbloods and debajeras. Durango had her wooden club. She started banging it on the wall of the building.

"She's uppity, don't you think?" she said to her companion.

He was chewing on something, gum or tobacco. "You can cure that," he said.

She banged the club again. "Cocky hotshot yank. Thinks she's better than the rest of 'em." She glared at me. "But, you ain't, sweetie."

A couple of debajeras approached. They stopped at a distance and watched what was going on. The male guard leaned against the wall, smiling.

Durango came at me with the raised club. She aimed at my leg. It was not hard to stop the blow. I jerked the piece of wood from her hand and sailed it through the air. It landed thirty or so feet away. She was enraged.

"Go get it!" she yelled to one of the debajeras. "Quick! Bring it here!"

The debajera did as she was told.

Armed again, Durango stared me in the eye, then spoke. "You will be punished for that now. Hold out your hand, animal!"

I looked around. There were no clanswomen in sight, though several other debajeras had come. I extended my hand as if for a handshake.

"Palm down!"

I turned my palm downward. Durango lifted the club and held it threateningly several feet above my extended hand. She waited. I waited. My hand was steady though inside I was shaking, primarily with rage, but also fear. The small crowd which had gathered was watching the performance.

Durango tensed, then swung, bringing the club downward. At the last moment, I retracted my hand a couple of inches, just enough to avoid the blow. There was muffled laughter from the debajeras.

Durango wildly swung the club at me then, without aiming. I dodged most of the blows and blocked the others with my arms. Over my prison greens, I was wearing a denim jacket I had gotten from one of the clanswomen and this cushioned the impacts some. Durango kept swinging. I kept avoiding and blocking and sneaking in occasional jabs at her. We danced around each other. My tormentor obviously was not having the effect she was seeking. The observers were enjoying the show. Suddenly, someone grabbed my arms. The other guard. He held them behind my back. Durango stood before me now, swinging the club slowly back and forth, looking my body over as if picking out the site for the first whack. The scene we were creating attracted more prisoners. Among them were some Section Three clanswomen.

"That's not a nice way to treat a sponsorera," one of them said to Durango, threateningly.

Durango glared at her, then lowered the club. "Keep the bitch out of my sight," she hissed, turning on her heel.

The other guard released me and he, too, stomped away. Although I experienced other hassling by guards during my first few weeks at Solera Women's Prison, I found that they never bothered me when I was in the company of clanswomen.

7.

THE CLANS

On the twenty-fifth day of my confinement, I received a letter from Jorge Triste. He told me, with regrets, that he had been unable to find the book we needed to break the number code. He said he had submitted the brief arguing prejudice by the judge and requesting a new trial and would let me know as soon as he heard. While he acknowledged the low probability for the success of this attempt, he told me not to give up hope. The American Embassy, he said, had been of no help at all. Nettie Dawson was continuing to communicate with the people there and other U.S. officials. Triste said he wished he could have had better news to send me.

At first, I felt leadenly dejected after reading the letter, and then I became edgy and irritable. A dormmate got on my nerves. She was making an annoying scraping sound near my bed. I spoke to her harshly, and when she seemed cowed by my behavior, instead of backing off, I persisted. There had been times, back home, when my anger would frighten people. I'd always stop. Always. But something—Triste's letter, my feelings of frustration and powerlessness?—something spurred me on. I derided the woman so mercilessly I reduced her to tears. Oddly, that made me feel somewhat better.

Most of my free time was spent with clanswomen. While there was some rivalry among the five clans, they interrelated freely. On the one month anniversary of my arrival at Solera Women's Prison, I was sitting on a bench in the prison yard, playing rummy with Evie. A group of Section Three Clanswomen came by dragging a frightened-looking debajera.

"Come on, you two," Carlotta said. "We got a naughty little debajera here. We're going to teach her a lesson. Come and help."

Evie and I joined the group. There were seven of us. We took the woman across the yard and into Section Three Building. Guards saw but turned away. We took her downstairs. I had never been in the basement, but I knew what was down there—cells, locked cells, I had been told. I did not see any cells in the dark, damp, underground section of the old fortress building where we took the debajera. It was a large room, a storage room of some sort where we went. It contained a clutter of rusted cannons, pieces of nondescript metal, stacks of cardboard boxes and various junk. They stood the debajera with her back to the cold cement wall, the line of six clanswomen and me facing her.

"You swore at a clanswoman, and raised your hand to her," someone said to the debajera. It was Marina, one of the women I had played poker with the first night.

The frightened debajera kept blinking, rapid, hard blinks. She did not speak.

"What do you have to say?"

The woman's mouth moved, but nothing came out.

"Speak."

"I...I'm...I didn't...I am sorry. I will never..."

"She's sorry," Rosa said sarcastically.

"That's not enough," Marina said. "Sorry is not enough." She approached the debajera and stood before her staring at her coldly for several seconds, then she slapped the woman sharply across the face.

"Ayee."

One by one each clanswoman went and did the same. Each woman slapped the debajera and when it was my turn, I would not let myself hesitate, and my blow was as strong as the others. We all left then, laughing and joking, leaving the debajera behind. I would not let myself think about what we had done. I closed it out of my mind and went off with the clanswomen.

Most of the clanswomen at Solera had an aura of self-assurance and even toughness about them, except the "tiernos". The tiernos were the "ladies" who "belonged" to their lovers; most of them wore dresses or tight slacks and heels. They were "protected" by their lovers, and the other women kept their distance from them. Roles were clearly delineated at Solera and I was obviously becoming pegged as a "tieso" type. It was the "tiesos" who had the most power and commanded the most respect. Like them, I began to swear freely and behave in tough, aggressive ways. I got pleasure from the deference and regard this brought.

Teresa seemed quite taken with me and I was fond of her. She was very bright, although not at all bookish. She was good-humored and sensitive. Raised among wealth in a family of merchants, she had married early and briefly. After her divorce, she was on her own. Although her life had been difficult, she was a survivor, spunky and streetwise. She was basically heterosexual, but I was sure that if I decided I wanted sex with her, she would not balk. I spent a lot of time with Teresa. My contacts with Leona, on the other hand, were infrequent. I found her uncouth and arrogantly repulsive. She needed to be brought down a peg, I thought a number of times, and I wondered if I'd ever have the opportunity to do it. As it turned out, she *was* brought down, but in a far more severe and brutal way than anyone deserved.

Two weeks after his first letter, I received another one from Triste. He informed me that the motion for a retrial had been denied. I grit my teeth and read on. He was now working on getting the sentence reduced, he said, by claiming it was unduly harsh. He assured me that he was continuing to look for new evidence that might help.

After reading the letter, I felt miserable. I went to the basement of Section Three Building. I needed to be alone. I sat among the debris in the same room where the debajera had received the seven slaps the week before. I sat on the floor, lost in my pain. They were very near me when I registered the sounds, when I realized some people were coming. I could hear a female voice pleading softly and the male response of laughter and teasing cajoling.

It was dark in the corner where I sat and although I could clearly see them, the two guards and the debajera were not aware of my presence. They stood in the hallway, the men pawing the prisoner who squirmed under their caresses. I heard the sound of ripping cloth.

"Please," she said. "Please don't do this to me. I will get you peyote or pills. Anything. Yes. I promise. Please let me go."

There was more laughter and sounds of struggling and then she was down on the floor, her torn dress pulled up over her waist. One guard, his pants down, lowered himself atop the struggling debajera while the other stood watching.

"Hey," I yelled, scrambling to my feet. "Leave her alone, you bastards." Had I expected them to say 'Oh, certainly, excuse us,' and leave? I was alone down here. There were no clanswomen around. I was obviously not thinking straight.

The standing guard came at me. "The more the merrier," he said.

I swung my arm in a quick, wide arc until the side of my hand connected with his temple. He staggered backwards, nearly losing his balance. The raping guard pulled himself off the debajera and came at me. The fight lasted just a short time. The woman fled as soon as it started, and I kicked, hit and flung the two men around. It was not difficult. They were small and out of shape and I was neither. Soon they both lay motionless on the cement floor.

I ran upstairs. I found Rosa and told her what had happened. She shook her head. "I don't know," she said. "It looks bad for you. Try Leona, maybe she can help."

Leona was in the Print Shop. We met in a small office.

"That was dumb," she said.

"I know."

"It was a debajera. Even clanswomen don't interfere. But, a newblood..." She looked disgusted.

"They were going to rape her."

"She's a debajera!"

"Debajeras are people!" I said.

Leona's round, pock-scared face took on an ugly scowl. "I can't do anything for you," she said, dismissing me with a flip of her wrist.

Twenty minutes later I was pulled roughly, partially dragged, from the dorm where I had gone after the fruitless talk with Leona. The guards took me to the warden's office. The procedure lasted less than five minutes. I was not allowed to speak. Afterwards I was taken directly downstairs in Section Three Building, past the scene of the fight, to a dark corridor lined with doors. They opened one, pushed me in, locked the door and left.

It was nearly pitch dark. The tiny room seemed to hold nothing but some bugs, some debris, and me. The warden had said I was to be confined to the discipline cell for a month. It turned out to be two weeks. Later, I found out that Angela had intervened and gotten the time reduced. It was a two-week period of my life that I have no wish to document or recall.

When they let me out, I was unable to walk, I had a tremor in my hands that wouldn't stop, and I might even have been slightly crazy. Fortunately, my memory of it is fuzzy. I do recall being carried to the infirmary, a room with beds lining both walls, full of very sick women. I believe I stayed there for two or three days, passing in and out of consciousness. It might have been longer. They told me I screamed a number of times. I don't remember that.

Teresa came on the last day I spent in the infirmary.

"My poor sponsorera. Eee, you look awful." She gave me milk. "Sometimes it's better not to fight," she said kindly.

I nodded. I had trouble talking. My gums were sore and swollen although the infection was receding.

"They're giving you penicillin," she said. "You will recover. Here, I brought you a book. You're a scholar, no? You probably need a book."

"*Passion on the Nile,*" I read. "Thank you, Teresa."

By the next day, they decided I was well enough to resume my work in the kitchen. Although the clanswomen told me how foolish I was, it seemed there was also some admiration in their responses toward me.

I regained my strength and health quickly. I had become somewhat claustrophobic as a result of my experience in the discipline cell. I also had become angry. I was learning more than I ever wanted to know about interpersonal power, its uses and abuses, and what I was learning made me angry and determined. My anger made the hardness that had begun as a calculated act, take on a more authentic quality. After my confinement in the discipline cell, I became more self-interested, more aware of the price of my own survival. I came to see others as either useful objects or interefering obstacles. I was forceful and ascendent. The deference I got from the weaker people, the respect from the stronger ones increased and so did the gratification I felt from their reactions to me. I was always alert, always prepared to turn away from what did not directly affect me and to defend myself if the need arose.

During the tenth week of my residence at Solera, I told Teresa it was time to nominate me formally into membership in the clan. She agreed and did so. She had no doubt it would go well. The vote was to be held on Wednesday. On Tuesday Leona told me she wanted to see me in her room.

When I entered Leona's lair, she sat enthroned in her easy chair, looking particularly repugnant. I took a straight-backed chair across from her. Vera, her "lady", sat on the bed listening to the radio. Leona had her feet up on a box.

"Take my shoes off, Rogan. My feet are sore. I want a foot massage."

Many women in the clan performed little services for Leona. Others did not.

"We sure could use a masseuse around here," I said.

"Take my shoes off!" Leona repeated, pointing to her feet.

I knew what she was doing. I knew she saw me as a threat to her and needed to solidify her position of superiority over me before I became a clanswoman. I also knew I would not be her lackey. "I don't do such things," I replied, keeping my voice calm and pleasant.

She leaned forward menacingly. "You better start!" she growled.

I paused as if I were considering it. "The truth is, Leona," I said, my tone still light, "it just doesn't suit my character."

"You must like it down there with the filthy debajeras," she hissed.

I lit a cigarette. "I like being treated with respect," I replied.

"I don't believe I like you, Rogan. You are too damn smooth for your own good."

Vera looked toward us from the bed. She turned the radio down as if the conversation were suddenly worth listening to.

"I see," I replied. "Well, we can't really like everybody, Leona, but I believe you and I can get along. I'm basically agreeable, even pleasantly cooperative if I'm not hassled."

"It would be better for you if I liked you."

"I believe it."

"I'd like you better if you took my shoes off now and massaged my feet for me. This is your last chance."

63

"I'd be glad to do a favor for you from time to time, Leona, but not that one."

"Get out!"

I left.

I knew I had taken a chance by defying her. That night and the next day, I went over it in my mind. I did what I had to, I concluded. I could not let her demean me. I'd lose myself if I did. I hoped Leona would turn out to be big enough to deal with it, but she did not.

With much pain and faltering, Teresa informed me that, although the vote had gone well, nearly 100 percent in favor, Leona had vetoed it. I would not be in a clan. I was a debajera.

"Oh, Kat," Teresa's eyes were tear-filled. "I can't stand it." She took a deep breath. "What can we do?" She was crying. "Leona has the final word. I'm...I'm going to quit the clan. I'll be a debajera with you."

"Don't be foolish," I said. I put my arm around her thin shoulder.

At Solera Women's Prison, clanswomen work in the Print Shop, in the garden, or at other relatively appealing jobs. Debajeras never do. Debajeras work in the fields, the laundry, the kitchen, at the most aversive jobs. Clanswomen are all trustees, debajeras never are. Only debajeras are sent to the discipline cells. Guards never beat or rape clanswomen. Debajeras feel blow and abuse at the whim of both the guards and clanswomen.

I was now a debajera, they said, but I was determined that I would not remain one.

I thought about escape. I thought about rebellion. I thought about Leona—the vicious Lion, and about revenge.

I also thought about justice, about fighting the system at Solera, about prison reform, and about Triste and Petrillo and about hiring a private detective. My head spun with thoughts.

I suppose I slept that night, but it didn't seem like it. I rose early, picking my way around the beds filled with sleeping, hopeless, downtrodden debajeras. I hadn't used the debajera john for weeks. Now I had to. It's dilapidation and inadequacy appalled me. I left quickly, needing to be outside. The sun had barely risen. The doors of Section Three Building were still locked and I waited until a guard came and opened them. I had decided what my first step would be.

In the whole time I had been in Solera, I had seen Angela only twice. Once, I saw her walking across the yard escorted by her entourage. Another time I caught a glimpse of her exiting from the Print Shop. I had never seen her in the dining hall. I was told she ate in her room. She was a tall, muscular woman. She wore clean, pressed pants and expensive-looking shirts and boots. They said she was as smart as a professor, as quick as a lynx, as strong as a buffalo, as cruel as she had to be to be what she was. She was the main woman at Solera. To the prison staff, she was the supervisor of the trustees. To the prisoners, she was the top honcho of all the clans. She had conferences with the warden. He relied on her to keep the order. The guards gave her wide berth and some were obsequious with her, currying her favor. She exuded power, had absolute authority over all the prisoners, and an understanding with the prison staff. The clanswomen talked of her frequently, often in hushed tones. The debajeras also talked of her. Angela was feared and admired. "I'll do whatever she wants," Teresa had said about her one time. "So far, only for her," she added flirtatiously. "Even what is not natural for me. What the Angel wants from me, I give to her as if she were the man I love. Sometimes she sends for me and I am happy to go, always, right away. I am lucky. She says I remind her of her first lover. I laugh when she says that. I don't altogether understand these things, but she gets pleasure from me and so I am there to please her whenever she wants. She is kind to me, like you, Kat. But, I know she can be very hard. You too. Some say Angela can be cruel."

Rosa spoke of her, too. And Carlotta. And all the others. There were many stories. How much of it was true, I did not know. I knew she ran the Print Shop. The Solera Print Shop with its old presses turned out reams of material for the government. Angela was the expert. She oversaw every process with the expertise of a seasoned business executive, the efficiency of a first-rate engineer. This is what I had heard and more, much more, about Angela.

I went into Section Five building. I knew that Angela lived upstairs. Although it was quite early in the morning, I could hear people talking. I climbed the stairs and as soon as I arrived on the second floor was intercepted by Lucia, one of Angela's lieutenants.

"Sightseeing?" she asked.

"I'd like to see Angela."

"Oh? What about?"

"Business. Connected with Section Three Clan."

"You're Kat Rogan, aren't you?"

"Yes."

"Wait here, I'll check."

She went to the door at the very end of the corridor and knocked. She disappeared inside for several minutes then returned and told me to come with her.

I couldn't believe what I saw when I entered Angela's room. It felt like years since I'd seen luxurious surroundings, although by most standards, I knew the word "luxurious" could not be applied to this place. There was a double bed, two easy chairs, a small table, carpeting (thin, but in good shape), a wooden wardrobe, curtains on the windows, pictures on the walls and even a battered-looking stereo. The room was nearly twice the size of the one Teresa shared with three others.

I had never been this close to Angela. She was striking-looking although not really attractive in any usual sense. Deep lines were etched along the sides of her mouth. Her sizable nose gave her face a bold, forceful look. She appeared to be in her mid-forties.

"Have a seat, Kat," she said. Lucia left the room. "Can I get you something to drink? A Bloody Mary, perhaps?"

How refreshingly civilized, I thought, relaxing some. "Yes," I said. "You wouldn't have Pepsi by any chance."

Angela snickered. "Pepsi? Ha! You're a strange one." A slight grin crossed her face. "I'm afraid I have no Pepsi, Kat Rogan." She stood with a hand resting loosely on her hip. "But I believe I could dig up a Coca-Cola. Would that do?"

I nodded. "That would be fine."

Angela took a bottle of coke from the bottom drawer of her wardrobe, opened it, then sat on the chair across from me. Her movements were swift and sure. She handed me the coke.

"I've been watching you," she said.

I made sure my eyes remained in contact with hers. "Oh?" I replied. It was easy to feel intimidated by Angela.

"Yes, more closely than most. I like what I've learned about you."

I definitely liked hearing that. I tipped the bottle to my lips. The coke was warm, but it tasted good anyway. "You heard about the veto?" I asked.

"Of course."

66

"That's why I'm here."

"Yes."

"I believe I should be in a clan."

"I agree."

This is going very well, I thought. "I think Leona sees me as a threat," I said, "but I'm sure we can work things out. I propose that the three of us—you, me and Leona, have a conference. I think her veto was rash and not well-grounded."

"A conference won't be necessary," Angela said. She placed her foot up on the table. She was wearing thick leather slippers. "I thought you would come here today. I like how you operate." She leaned back in her chair. "You're not debajera material, Kat. I'll talk to her today. You don't need to be present."

I felt tremendous relief.

"Incidentally." Angela continued. "I understand your friend Durango was quite pleased about the outcome last night. She seems to have taken a great dislike to you. As soon as she learned you were to be a debajera, she got you assigned to field work. Apparently, she had other plans for you as well. I've straightened her out. You can continue on kitchen detail until you hear from me. Take the coke with you," Angela said, standing up. "Enjoy yourself."

I worked all day in the kitchen. Nothing unusual happened. I had no doubt that Angela would take care of things with Leona, but I couldn't shake the disquieting feeling I had. It nagged at me throughout the day. As I was walking back to the dorm, Teresa ran up to me, her face radiant.

"You're in!" she yelled, grabbing me and hugging me, nearly causing us both to lose our balance. "Angela did it! She overrode Leona!"

I smiled and nodded.

"You're a clanswoman now. Halleluja! You'll be living upstairs with us. In Dolores' room." She hugged me again. "Come on, I bet you want a shower. I have some nice clothes for you. Real clothes. No more greens. I just got some grass. Let's smoke it. Oh, Kat, I'm so happy!"

Teresa and I entered the Section Three building, arm in arm. There was a noisy commotion inside. The nurse from the infirmary was moving people aside to make room for the stretcher. Two guards were carrying it up from the basement. As they passed us in the hallway, I could see the pale face of the person under the bloodied sheet. It was Leona.

"What happened?"

"Her hands."

"What about her hands?"

"They..." The speaker was a debajera from B dorm. She looked sick. "Torato, the guard, was taking me down to the basement for...I was the first to see...," she said. "They... somebody cut off her hands."

"Oh God!" Teresa moaned.

Teresa's face was ghostly pale and I had to support her to prevent her from collapsing. We made our way upstairs. Clusters of people were talking quietly up and down the halls and in the rooms. Rosa and I took Teresa to her room and laid her on the bed.

"I'm afraid to think it," she said. "It can't be." Her face was twisted in angry pain.

She would say no more. I stayed with her for a while, then left her with Rosa to see if I could learn more from others. I went from room to room. All that I discovered was that Leona had been found in the basement storage room with both of her hands severed from her body, that she was still alive and being driven to the nearest clinic, about thirty miles away.

No one was saying a word about how it could have happened, who could have done it. Some of the women were appalled, some appeared to be blandly accepting of it, most seemed frightened. "Was she in a feud with someone?" I asked. "Would the guards have done it?" I got no answers. I hated to think of other possibilities.

Later, when Teresa calmed, she and I went outside. Only when we were alone did she begin to talk.

"This afternoon," she said, "Angela sent for Leona. They met in Angela's room. Angela's lieutenants were there and one of them, Lucia, is Anita's friend. That is how I heard. Anita said Angela and Leona talked for a long time. They were talking about you, Kat. Angela knew a lot about you. She knows about everything that goes on here. I tell her things, too. Whatever she wants to know. She was asking Leona about the veto. Angela said you seemed an asset. That was her word, 'asset'. And she was questioning Leona about why she had vetoed you from joining us. Leona got pissed. She has such an ugly temper. She said she resented her judgment being questioned and her turf and her rights as a Section Leader. She said stuff like that. And I guess what happened was that Angela listened to all this but when Leona finally stopped, Angela said that you were to be let in. You were to join the clan. She said that it would be wisest for Leona to announce it herself, to say that she had changed her mind and Kat Rogan would be in Section Three Clan. But, Leona refused. I guess she was pretty obnoxious. But, Angela was calm as always. She said 'then it will be this way: Kat Rogan is admitted into the clan because I override your veto. That's how it is. That's all.' Those were her words, Anita said. But, then, instead of leaving, Leona—Oh Jesus, what a fool she is—she jumped her. She jumped Angela! She went for Angela's throat and was strangling her.'' Teresa's lean body was trembling as she spoke. ''Angela and the lieutenants, Lucia and Ria and Margarita, they had to pry Leona's fingers from Angela's throat. After they did, Angela just stood and looked in her cold way at Leona and then Leona left.'' Teresa shivered, as if a chill had gone up her spine. ''They had to pry Leona's hands off Angela's throat and now Leona has no hands.''

8.

THE CLANSWOMAN

To be in a clan at Solera Women's Prison means some very specific things. There are rules, none written, but everyone knows them. A clanswoman has much independence and power within the prison social system. She belongs to the ruling class, but she is subordinate to two people—her Section Leader and Angela. Clanswomen fight for their own, for others in their clan, when the need is there. It is a tight system. Everyone knows how it operates. The guards, too. They are part of it. It is how it is at Solera Women's Prison.

Leona did not return. There was an investigation. The warden was very angry about the undesirable attention the "incident" brought to Solera. His arrangements with Angela were geared toward avoiding disruptions of any sort. He and Angela had several meetings over this incident, prisoners and guards were questioned, but the investigation came to nothing. It was not the first act of violence left unresolved at the prison.

I had no trouble solidifying my place within the Section Three Clan. I worked on the presses at the Print Shop each day. No one ever hassled me. Lucia was serving as temporary Section Leader. She and I became buddies. She reminded me of Elizabeth and that made me feel both sad and pleased. I thought of home less and less. I have to admit that I fully enjoyed my status as a clanswoman. As well as I'd had it earlier, relative to most newbloods and to debajeras, the differences now that I was "in" were dramatic. Guards not only did not bother me or sneer at me, but they treated me cordially, some even with a degree of deference. Durango stayed out of my way. Clanswomen became more friendly and more open. Debajeras were eager to do favors for me. I actually felt taller. I walked differently. It wasn't exactly a strut, but close. Many of the clanswomen had a swagger to their walk, I noticed.

Other clanswomen joined Teresa and me behind the garage for karate lessons; Teresa was skillful enough now to help me with the instruction. Debajeras outnumbered clanswomen five to one at the prison, and at times, there were attempted rebellions, bandings together of debajeras and threats to our authority. We squelched them easily and the Section Three Clan was especially counted on for this now because of our karate ability. There were times when I felt waves of guilt for my participation in this. I pushed the feelings away. Teresa and I grew closer and closer. I was cautious, but less so than I was at home when I felt this way about a woman. I was letting our relationship develop, slowly.

My former life seemed increasingly remote. I continued to correspond with my friends from home, but their world was no longer mine. Nettie wrote me saying some journalist from Marigua had contacted her. He told her he was writing an article on North American prisoners abroad, people who had been unjustly prosecuted, and wanted to include me. She thought it might be helpful and, at least, it could do no harm. I agreed and gave her permission to tell the man all she wanted, and to tell anyone else he might contact to do the same. I didn't have much hope of its coming to anything.

I had hired a private detective to continue the investigation of Petrillo and the Sundances, hoping that this might be the answer. In his last letter, Triste had some interesting news. He informed me that the folder had disappeared. He had been keeping it in his office, in the file with the other material on my case, and now it was gone. Nothing else had been taken, just the folder. I was glad. It meant that someone was out there who knew the letter was valuable. It gave me hope. Maybe Cornelio Fanta, the private investigator I had hired, could find out who stole the folder. Maybe the burglar was the missing link. Along with xeroxed copies of other documents, Triste had given Fanta a copy of my translation of the letter as well as a copy of the map. I, too, had sent Fanta information but apparently he was not satisfied. He sent me a detailed list of questions covering everything that might be remotely related to the case. He said he hoped my replies would be thorough so I would not have the additional expense of his making a trip to Solera to talk with me. I wasn't particularly bothered by the possibility of incurring such an expense. In fact, I liked the idea of a visit from him. But, nonetheless, I responded to his list of questions immediately with as much detail and thoroughness as I could. It felt good to be doing something that might help me attain my release. I felt more encouraged and hopeful than I had for a long while.

I had now been a prisoner for three months and I had changed significantly. I was hard, tough, authoritative, often unbending and condescending. People either gave me room or tried to ingratiate themselves to me. Weaker women sought my protection. Stronger ones wanted to be my buddy. Some part of me liked all this. I told myself I only behaved this way in order to survive, but on some level I was truly enjoying it. That bothered me and whenever I realized it, I pushed the awareness away and gave an order to some debajera or found an available body to have sex with.

I had not yet had sex with Teresa. It was clear that she was enamoured of me and her feelings seemed to be growing all the time. She flirted with me shamelessly. I had liked her and felt attracted to her from the beginning. That's probably why I stayed away from her sexually for so long, that and her claimed heterosexuality. I knew she would never be the one to initiate sexual contact between us. Nevertheless, she gave clear and frequent cues that she would be receptive to my advances. She was. Our first lovemaking took place on November 12th, Teresa's birthday. It was intense and romantic and soon such sessions became frequent. I began to feel possessive toward her; something I used to fear would happen. I began to expect her to be there for me when I wanted her. She welcomed this. She catered to me. She expressed adoration for me. It was pleasant, making life in prison much more tolerable. It was also somewhat surprising to me that Teresa would want it this way, actually desire to be subserviant to me. How could someone want that, I wondered? I could not have anticipated that in a couple of months, I would want the same thing myself, want it with more intensity than I've ever wanted anything.

On November 13th, I received a progress report from Cornelio Fanta. He was turning out to be a very diligent and, possibly, ingenious sleuth. That's what I wanted to believe, at least. In his report he outlined the steps he was taking both in his thoughts and in his actions. He began with a statement of the overall objective of his search, namely, as per my request, to determine whether or not Peter Petrillo was connected with the Sundances, and, if so, how. He said that a side-effect of his investigation of this might be the solution to the Martin Sundance murder, although that, in itself, was not his objective. His objective was to find enough new evidence to justify a new trial for me. Señor Fanta's thinking, as he related it to me in this first, very lengthy, report began with the question: "How did a letter addressed to Maria Sundance in Postero, Arcedia, Marigua, which bore a stamp cancellation from the Postero Post Office dated June 26th turn up in Martin Sundance's hands, in Chicago, Illinois, on June 28th?"

He then proceeded to speculate on the answer: Either Martin Sundance brought it with him to Chicago, or somebody else did. As there is no feasible explanation for Martin Sundance bringing it, Fanta conjectured, it must have been someone else. Who? Maria Sundance? No. There is firm confirmation that she did not leave Marigua during that time. Peter Petrillo? No, he was definitely in Postero on June 28th. Martin Sundance's partner referred to in the letter? Possibly. But how did he find out Martin sent Maria the letter disclosing the secret? Martin certainly would not have told him. Who could have found out Martin sent the letter, Fanta pondered? It's unlikely that Martin would have told anyone. Who could have had the opportunity to know of and to take the letter? Maria's maid? Yes, but she's a very unlikely suspect and she seemed quite sincere in her denial when questioned, Fanta reported. A Post Office employee? Petrillo? If the partner killed Sundance, which was quite probable, then Petrillo was not the partner, Fanta reasoned, since Petrillo was in Marigua on the 28th of June and, hence, could not be the murderer. (He could have sent someone, I thought.). It could be that Petrillo was not, himself, the partner, Fanta wrote but that he intercepted the letter at the Post Office and gave it to the partner who went to Chicago and killed

Sundance. Or that Petrillo *was* the partner, I thought insistently, and hired a killer to take care of Martin. The number of letters in Peter Petrillo's name fit the code. I couldn't understand why Fanta didn't give that the import it deserved. Fanta said he would continue to investigate the possibility that Petrillo was working with the partner, but he believed there were some very interesting alternatives.

Perhaps, he wrote, this is what happened: Perhaps Maria Sundance received the letter, translated it, told someone about it, and that person then took the letter with him (or her) when he (or she) went to Chicago to kill Martin. Who would Maria tell? This is a question I'm investigating at the moment, Fanta wrote. Why would that someone kill Martin? For the long-lost treasure, of course. People have certainly killed for much less than this treasure seems to be worth.

Fanta went on to tell me of other facts he had uncovered: that Petrillo did deep sea diving as a hobby; that Petrillo took courses at Joaquin University; that Petrillo attempted to rape a Colombian woman two years ago, although charges were never pressed; that Petrillo had large gambling debts; that Martin Sundance, his sister, Maria, and their father (deceased three years) were all archeologists who excavated artifacts of the local Indian tribes for study and display; that seven years ago, Martin deviated from the family tradition and began obtaining certain such items, those of precious stones or metals, for sale abroad; that, as a result of these activities, Martin had become alienated from Maria; that Martin had gone to Chicago on June 27th in connection with the sale of four golden icons.

Fanta also mentioned what he had learned about the earthquake of 1760, how it had disrupted much of the terrain in the Tordad area of Marigua. He said he supposed that could have buried many treasures.

Although Fanta hadn't yet succeeded in connecting Petrillo with the Sundances, I was sure he would. I was very impressed with the report and the obvious attention he was giving the investigation. The information about Petrillo's other rape attempt did not surprise me. I wondered how many others there had been. What did surprise me was Fanta's speculation about Maria, that she may have received the letter Martin sent, that maybe it had not been intercepted. That thought had not occurred to me before. I reviewed the phone conversations I had with her from Chicago, trying to recall if there was any indication that she was lying to me, that she already knew the full contents of that letter. I couldn't tell. I was eager for my next communication from Cornelio Fanta.

9.

THE SECTION CHIEF

One day in late November, Angela sent for me. We sat across from each other on her two easy chairs. I wondered how she got the clothes she wore. They were expensively cut and always clean and pressed.

"I have plans for you, Kat Rogan," she began without preliminaries. "I like how you handle yourself." She smiled, a rarity for her, and it gave her face a slight hint of softness. "You're my kind of woman."

Oh shit, I thought, she's not coming on to me, is she? I found the idea aversive, and wasn't at all sure how I could handle it.

"You are here for life," Angela continued. "In my country, that means life, unlike in yours." She was not smiling now. "Your attempts to fight your conviction are failing. They almost always do, although anyone with any money tries."

She lit a thin, brown cigarette and offered me one. I declined.

"I sincerely hope your attempts succeed, but I don't believe they will."

I listened without comment.

"There are two roles I've been considering for you, Kat. I could use another loyal, competent, lieutenant."

76

I felt relieved. It was not my body she was after.

"I was considering that, but I decided against it."

I waited, anticipating what she would say next.

"Your skills would be better used as a Section Chief." She paused momentarily, watching me for a reaction, perhaps, and then she went on. "That role will involve great responsibilities. As you know, we need a Chief in Section Three. I want to appoint you. Would you like to think it over?"

"No," I said calmly. "No need. I accept."

Angela almost smiled again. "Then this doesn't come as a surprise to you."

"No, the possibility crossed my mind."

Angela nodded. "Yes," she said. "Yes, you *are* my kind of woman."

It wasn't until weeks later that I gave much thought to what kind of woman that was. In the meantime, I lived without analyzing. I used and enjoyed my power and status with little consciousness of what it meant.

My time was filled and passed quickly. I worked side by side with Angela, managing the Print Shop. I played cards, poker mostly, and usually won. I read. I socialized. I ate relatively well. My room had evolved into a comfortable den; Teresa fixed it up for me. I found solitude there when I craved it or tender loving care from Teresa when I craved that. I also began to oversee the drug traffic at Solera, a role Leona used to have. We were growing marijuana in the fields beyond the prison. I made sure the field workers kept quiet about it and the guards content with their share. We traded it outside, through the guards. I acquired a radio, oil paints and canvasses, and numerous books and other possessions.

On Christmas Eve, a month after my promotion to Section Chief, I sat in my room, on the soft, cushioned chair, while a Beethoven symphony played on the radio. I was thinking about Solera and about what I had become since entering this place four and a half months ago. This was the first time I let myself seriously analyze the situation here and my part in it.

I had become autocratic, that was clear, even domineering. I often behaved condescendingly, usually with a humorous edge. I was cold and stern in some of my interacitons and probably not very sensitive much of the time. I did not need to use persuasion with people to get what I wanted; I simply told them what to do, and they did it. I called the shots. It was so easy. Since I did not have to bother with their preferences or their feelings, often I did not. Angela was king with countless vassals and underlings. The guards were no more than an occasional nuisance. I was an excellent Section Chief, I was told.

I knew all along that the whole system was ugly and obscene, and that my role in it was inconscionable, but I think I had lost touch with my conscience, with my consciousness, my values.

I thought about my father. He had ruled our home like a tyrant, my mother and my sister cowed to him. I fought him, fought vehemently as soon as I was old enough to put up resistance, and he never really succeeded in controlling or subduing me. But maybe something worse had happened. Here I was, acting like him, dominating other people, often with little respect for their needs or rights.

Why, I wondered? I had never behaved like this before. What about me and what about this place, this situation, allowed it to happen? Was it, indeed, related to my father? Had his influence, his kind of mentality, festered in me until an opportunity arose where I could act it out? Was it something about the women here? Did I believe it was all right to treat them this way because they were only prisoners? Because there were Latinas? Was I taking my own frustrations out on the people here? Did that inevitably happen in a prison situation? Was I, indeed, a tyrant? Had I become that which I'd always abhorred? I didn't know the answers. I did know that I had definitely been taking advantage of the power I had and enjoying it.

Few people challenged me at Solera and I never had to use force to get what I wanted. A word, rightly placed, or a stern look was enough. And I had my coterie of admirers, followers, clanswomen who looked up to me and emulated me. Especially Teresa. She seemed particularly intrigued by the way I was. She complimented me repeatedly on my strength, my humor, my self-assurance, my sense of fairness when disputes arose, and even on how sensitive, and kind I was with some people. She often said she adored me. She doted on me constantly, and I allowed her to. More than that, I fostered it. I liked it. Of course, I was drawn to Teresa, too. I enjoyed her a great deal and I certainly found her attractive. People had begun referring to Teresa as my "lady".

Although I never lost sight of my wish to be free, there is no doubt that I experienced a certain amount of contentment at Solera. After all, I was adored, admired, appreciated, catered to, sought after, respected, feared, obeyed. For a prisoner at Solera, I was doing rather well.

But something was wrong. I had been aware of it for the past several days. I was growing increasingly dissatisfied and uncomfortable. Maybe I had gotten my fill of being a "top", I thought, as the strains of Beethoven filled the room. I was certainly finding it less and less enjoyable recently. I was no longer getting pleasure from the fact that a path cleared when I entered a crowd and a respectful hush took place. There was no more kick when people fawned over me. Teresa's adoration no longer felt so good or desirable. Maybe I had just grown satiated with it. Or could the change mean that my conscience was returning, my previously-professed values reasserting themselves?

Perhaps it was that debajera, Luella, who set off the change in me. The memory of Luella had been haunting me since I sent her to the kitchen for an orange a few days ago.

"Be quick about it," I said.

She looked very frightened. I watched her run to do my bidding. She came back quickly and held the orange out for me with tremulous fingers. I looked at her face. Her lip was actually quivering. She looked terrified.

"Anything else you want Señorita Kat?" she asked, her eyes downcast.

I was sure that what *she* wanted more than anything else was to be away from me, the Section Chief, away from the grip of the power I wielded. It bothered me. Later, I thought about my sister, how frightened she had been of father. I didn't remember my own early childhood very clearly. Had I trembled like that before him? Had he enjoyed it?

The night after that interaction with Luella, I was in bed with Teresa, resting my hand on the soft hair of her devoted head. She was crouched between my naked legs, gently, passionately arousing and pleasing me with her sweet mouth and tongue. When we finished and her eyes found mine, the worshipful adoration I saw did not feel as it had before.

"What are you thinking?" I asked. I had never asked before.

"I'm not," she said. "Just feeling. Feeling safe. Lucky. Feeling lucky to be yours."

79

I took hold of her chin. "I own you," I said.

"Yes." She smiled and snuggled up against my chest.

"You're not so feisty as you used to be," I said, "with me at least." I knew that Teresa always held her own quite well with others at the prison.

"I never was with you," she said.

"That's true. Just the first day."

"Not even then, really. I fought with you along with the clanswomen, but I knew you were a winner. You had to win. You were so brave. I'd never known another like you."

"Hm-m."

"Are you ready for more?" she asked. She stroked my nipple tenderly.

I sat up, moving her hand away. "Teresa, tell me, don't you resent my...doesn't our relationship bother you sometimes?"

"I love our relationship."

"I dominate you."

"I know."

"It never bothers you?"

"No...well..." Teresa sat upright on the bed, cross-legged. Her naked shoulders and breasts looked very soft and vulnerable. "Sometimes I get this strange feeling...like a sinking feeling in my stomach. Hey, Teresa, I say to myself. Why do you let this woman push you around, huh?" She shook her head. "I never get an answer."

Maybe it was Zita Foralla who contributed to the change that was taking place in me, I thought. She too was a debajera.

"They say you're an educated woman, very bright," she had said to me last week outside the dining hall.

I couldn't believe that a debajera was initiating a conversation with me. A week or two earlier, I would have cut her down, put her quickly in her place. Or, if I found her audacity amusing, I might have let her continue for that reason. But, I guess I was beginning to let go of the need to lord my power over others, so I waited for Zita Foralla to go on.

"I've even heard that at one time you considered yourself to be a feminist and a humanist," she continued.

At one time, I thought? Well, wasn't it true? Could I dare apply those labels from the past to myself now?

"I was with the movement in Marigua," she said. "I fought for women's rights until they stopped me by locking me in here.''

I knew of Zita's background. Although she was a political activist, the crime for which she'd been sent to Solera was robbery. She had lifted a diamond brooch from some contessa. Political prisoners, I knew, were not sent to Solera.

Again, I waited for Zita to go on speaking. I think I needed to hear what she would say.

"When I am released, I will continue the fight. In here, at Solera, a place of all women, in here I find even more oppression and patriarchal-type injustice than I saw out in the world. You were a feminist. I don't understand.''

I didn't understand either. How could I explain the fact that I had not only dominated and participating in oppressing others, and women at that, but that I had found it gratifying. How could I explain accepting Teresa's adoration and service? What was there inside of me that allowed me to do it just because I could? I looked at the young, strong, idealistic woman facing me. If the time were early last summer and the place Chicago, it would have been like looking at a younger version of myself. I felt sick.

"There aren't many alternatives,'' was all that I could find to say. "The system is entrenched.''

She shook her head. "I've heard those words before,'' she said. "Many times, many places. Sometimes we are just too scared, or too weak or blind, or too self-indulgent, maybe, to *seek* the alternatives.''

"Get out of here!'' I had said, and she did.

I tried to forget, to put the conversation out of my mind, but I could not. And I could not forget the admiring and, sometimes, frightened look in the eyes of so many women I had power over, or the worshipful look in Teresa's eyes.

Power is evil, I thought.

The music had stopped. A voice came over the radio but I did not listen to the words. I reached over and shut them off. I don't want it. I don't want this kind of power. It's no good, not for anyone.

The next day, Christmas day, I talked with Angela. She listened respectfully to my views but she saw me as misguided.

"It is essential to have a hierarchy and a class of have-nots,'' she said patiently. "The debajeras serve a vital balancing function, Kat. I thought you understood that. If their status were raised, then the position of the clanswomen would be jeopardized. We need them. We have to have scapegoats for the guards and for the clanswomen. If goods and power were divided equally," she argued, "then we would all be living at the level of debajeras—me, you, the other Section Chiefs, all the clanswomen. We'd all be at the mercy of the guards. The way it is works, Kat. It works because the guards benefit by it; as you know, they get a healthy portion of all the contraband brought in, they get a caste to push around. The warden benefits; he gets high productivity from the Print Shop and the fields, and a relatively peaceful, smoothly functioning prison. This is the way it has to be," she insisted, although she showed no impatience toward me or my ideas about changes. She heard them all, and turned them all down, gently, but adamantly. I made one last attempt that day, for there was one thing that had never stopped eating at me, no matter how blind I had become.

"There are women being raped here." I said.

"Yes, that happens."

"Even by clanswomen sometimes."

"Yes."

"Don't you think we could, at least, make that stop?"

Angela looked at me calmly. "Their fear of it keeps the debajeras tractable," she said.

"That's loathsome."

She shrugged her shoulders.

Angela was apparently as unthreatened by my changing attitude as she was unmoved by my appeals. She had said on a number of occasions that the system was as solid as granite. The grumblings of a conscience-striken Section Chief obviously did not worry her.

10.

THE THEORY

I spent a lot of time alone the next few days and did a lot of thinking—about the way it was at Solera and about getting out. I hadn't had contact with Triste for nearly a month, since he told me the attempt at getting my sentence reduced had failed. That news, though disappointing, was not unexpected. My hopes were resting on Cornelio Fanta. On December 28th, I received my first and last visit from him. He said he wanted to give me his report in person and that there would be no charge for his trip to Solera.

I was surprised by his appearance. Maybe I had been picturing Humphrey Bogart. Cornelio Fanta was a short, fat man with a thin moustache, receding hairline and a slight lisp. He was in his mid-fifties.

"No link at all," he said after shaking my hand lightly and seating himself. "Nothing to connect Petrillo with either of the Sundances. Sorry."

I sat down heavily. Slowly, I nodded my understanding. My face may have reflected some disappointment, but I would not let it show the full depth of my letdown, the devastating feeling of defeat. I had been sure Fanta had come all this way to give me *good* news. "So it goes," I said. "Shit!"

"Yes," he replied. "I must admit, I did think that Petrillo's position at the Post Office might turn out to be relevant. Unfortunately for you, it did not. At least, in no way that I could determine. Although there may have been opportunity, I could find neither motivation nor evidence for Petrillo having intercepted the Sundance letter."

I nodded again but I couldn't accept it. Petrillo had to be involved. He had been stalking me. He searched my room. It couldn't just be coincidence. "Well, did you solve Martin Sundance's murder, at least?" I asked casually, leaning back and lighting a cigarette. It seemed I was more like Humphrey Bogart than was Fanta.

"Yes, I believe so."

"You don't say? What's the story?" How easily it came now, my cool, controlled veneer.

"It's a theory, really. Insufficient proof to take it to court, but I will inform the police."

"So what's your theory?" I asked. I will not stay here forever.

"I believe Martin Sundance was killed by one Manuel Paz."

"Manual Paz? Who is that? Not Martin's partner?" I didn't think that could be. For one thing, the number of letters in the name *Manuel Paz* didn't fit the code. There should be a five-letter first name and an eight letter surname, as in *Peter Petrillo*.

"No, I don't believe so. I suspect that the partner, whoever he is, was also killed by Paz or else joined forces with him."

Petrillo, I thought. "Tell me more," I said. I wasn't liking his theory.

"Manuel Paz is a curator at the Natural History Musuem in Postero. He is also—was, that is, a close friend of Maria Sundance. It is said that they were romantically involved. As I see it, on June 27th, Maria Sundance received the letter from Martin Sundance and immediately translated it, using the necessary book, the book that is now missing, to translate the number code."

Fanta removed his wrinkled, suit jacket and tossed it onto the chair next to him.

"There's some important family background that's relevant here," he said, wiping his oily forehead with his handkerchief. "It seems that Maria Sundance had always been the more responsible and mature of the two Sundance children. Father favored Martin, however. Now, Maria dealt all right with this, favoring him herself, until Martin got greedy and, abandoning the family dedication to science, was lured away by his lust for wealth. Father continued to favor Martin. Maria grew angry and resentful. This part is not theory," Fanta said. "I've spoken to a number of people who know the family well and there is consensus on this point."

I nodded for Fanta to go on.

"After Maria translated the letter and map, she took them to Manuel Paz. A quite natural thing to do."

"The letter does mention an Archeological Committee. Is Paz on the Committee?"

"Yes."

"Does Paz acknowledge that that's what happened?"

"Oh, no. Most definitely not. According to Manuel Paz, Maria Sundance talked with him about the letter only after she learned of it in her phone call from you last July." Fanta's mouth curled into an oily grin. "But, he's lying. He claims she never did give him the details of what was in the letter, but said only that it had to do with a treasure Martin discovered. He claims further that Maria told him the letter was written in code."

"Yes."

"And that she needed to get hold of a book to complete the code translation."

"But, you don't believe him."

Fanta looked at me cooly. "What I believe," he said emphatically, "is that Maria Sundance told Señor Paz the full contents of the letter on June 27th, the day she received it in the mail."

"The full contents? You mean that she'd translated all the code, the book code too?"

"Exactly."

"So, they knew the name of the partner and where the treasure was located."

"That's right. Between the two of them, and whose idea it was originally I do not know, but between them, they plotted to take the treasure for themselves."

"Hm-m," I said. "Go on."

"This would mean eliminating Martin Sundance from the picture. And it would mean lifting the insurance letter from Martin's lawyer's file."

"I see."

85

"And doing something about the partner."

"Eliminating him?" Could I have been an unwitting accomplice? Killing Petrillo for them? No, they could not have expected that Petrillo would end up dead from his encounter with me.

"Possibly," Fanta said. "Or joining forces with him."

"Hmm."

"So, Manuel Paz stole the envelope from Martin's lawyer on June 27th and flew to Chicago on June 28th. I was unable to find a record of Manuel Paz taking a flight on or around that date, but that proves nothing. He could have used another name or flown out of somewhere other than Postero. He may not have gone directly to Chicago."

"But you're convinced that he went there."

"Yes. He was definitely out of town on the 28th. He admits that."

"He admits it?"

"Yes, although he claims he was with Elena Sorra in Puerto Chiaiz. She verifies his alibi, but there are no other witnesses to substantiate that story."

"So she's lying for him."

"I believe so."

"Why would she?"

"Why do people?" Fanta wiped his forehead again. "Many reasons. In her case I believe she believes it's love."

"He was two-timing Maria?"

"Quite possibly."

"You begin to undermine my faith in people, Señor Fanta."

He ignored that and went on. "Manuel Paz flew to Chicago and went to Martin Sundance's hotel room. He had the letter and map with him in a folder. Why, I'm not sure. He may have told Martin he intercepted it, that Maria never got it. Possibly Maria requested this. Possibly she didn't want Martin to die knowing his loving sister was capable of such betrayal and of fratricide. Martin always thought so highly of her." A touch of contempt showed through in Fanta's expression.

"So Martin grabbed the folder and ran."

"Yes."

"And Paz shot him as he was fleeing."

"It fits the report I got from the Chicago Police and what you say happened next.''

"Yes, it fits. And then?"

"And then Manuel returned to Postero to await, with Maria, the arrival of the body and of Martin's possessions, including the folder."

"But the folder never arrived."

"The same object cannot be in two place at one and the same time."

"It was in my dresser drawer."

"An excellent hiding place," Fanta said sardonically.

Out the window of the Administration Building where we were meeting, I caught a glimpse of Teresa. She was laughing and talking with wild hand gestures to Carlotta. These are my people, I thought sadly. This is home.

"When Maria and Manuel realized the folder was not with Martin's other things, they probably got worried," Fanta continued. "Manuel probably concluded that Martin had slipped the folder to that attractive young woman who found him dying on the street. They may have tried to find out who you were," Fanta said. "Or they may just have waited to hear from you assuming you would try to get the letter to Maria. At any rate, I'm sure Maria was not at all surprised when you telephoned. She was ready. She played her part well and got you to agree to bring the letter to her as she and Manuel had planned."

I shook my head. "I liked her."

"Yes, well...hm..."

"Why didn't she just have me mail the stuff to her?"

"She tried that, didn't she?"

"I guess she did. She didn't try real hard."

"Possibly she and Paz wanted to meet you, to reassure themselves that you presented no danger, that you didn't plan on telling anyone else about the strange contents of that folder. So, they lured you to Marigua. But, before they could get to you Señor Petrillo entered the picture. An attractive American woman traveling alone. Why not? Another pleasant evening. Another conquest." Fanta slowly rubbed his puffy hands together. "But you turned out to be less agreeable or less passive than he had anticipated." Fanta looked me in the eye, "Señorita Rogan," he said with great sincerity, "I believe you did get a dirty deal. I think you made a strong case for self-defense. In a more civilized time, in a more civilized place, you would have been acquitted. From those photographs of your neck, I would say it was his life or yours."

"You know," I said, "when I escape from here and live incognito on the Riviera, I'm going to keep my knife right on me, maybe strapped to my leg, but certainly not in my suitcase."

Fanta did not seem to like that remark. He appeared uncertain whether to let it pass or not. "Why did you have a knife with you, Señorita Rogan?" he said at last.

"Self-defense," I said sadly, "as I said at the trial."

"Yes, you are from Chicago where..."

"I was attacked here, in your country."

"It's better for a woman not to carry a weapon. It can be taken from her, as you found out, and used..."

"Tell me more about your theory," I interrupted. "I'm interested in what your thoughts are about Maria's death."

"Cetainly," Fanta replied pompously. He seemed to be deriving significant enjoyment from this conversation. "On the same morning that you received the phone call from Maria Sundance, Sunday morning, Maria invited Señor Paz to her place for breakfast. Señor Paz acknowledges that, as does the maid, Juanita. When Manuel Paz left the villa, I suspect that he took the translation of the letter and the map with him. Very likely the missing book as well."

"And Maria didn't know he took them."

"No, no. He lifted them. She suspected the maid, Juanita. Upset the poor girl quite a bit with her accusations."

"Why would he take them?"

"Part of his plan—his plan to get all the more for himself."

"So you think he killed Maria."

"He had both motive and opportunity. On the day of her 'accident', he was at her house. He could have tampered with her car."

"You know he was there."

"Oh yes. He admits it. And, of course, there's the maid. Maria received a phone call while Paz was there at her home, the call from Triste. While she was on the phone, I suspect that Paz sneaked into the garage. Maria then left to meet Señor Triste and Paz went away to await the news of the poor dear's tragic accident."

I sat quietly for a while, trying to digest everything Fanta was saying. "Why did Paz need the book," I asked, "if he already had the translation of the letter and the map?''

"I'm not sure, Señorita," Fanta replied, unruffled. "Some things remain unexplained. Perhaps some day, Señor Paz will enlighten us on that point."

I was finding Fanta increasingly distasteful.

"After your conviction," Fanta continued, "the only remaining danger to Manuel Paz was the original letter and map which he rightly assumed would be in your file in Triste's office. Of course, he did not know a copy existed. When he took the letter and map he most likely assumed that all he had to do then was wait until whatever occurred—all those untranslated words—and grab the treasure. Too bad no one can translate the code."

"Maybe Juanita could be hypnotized."

"I beg your pardon."

"The maid. Hypnotized to recall the name of the book."

"Interesting," he said, without interest. "I am going to report all this to the Postero Police, Señorita Rogan. I hope they will be wise enough to put a tail on Señor Paz so they can be there when he goes to retrieve that valuable object, or whatever it is, that set off this whole sequence of events."

I felt very tired. I guess it was the anger, the frustration. Suddenly, it all seemed to have so little to do with me. I didn't want to believe the theory. I didn't want it to be correct. Petrillo was involved, I was sure of it. He had to be. And his name had the right number of letters. He must be the partner. "I still think Petrillo was the partner," I said. "Much of your theory would still fit. Paz killed Martin then approached Petrillo and they formed a new partnership. Petrillo went after me to get the letter and ended up dead."

"But why would they use such means to get the letter when you had come all those miles in order to turn it over to Maria Sundance voluntarily?"

I gave that some thought. "Maybe Maria was backing out," I suggested. "Maybe she was haunted with guilt and was going to turn the letter over to the police and confess. Or maybe Paz was forcing her to cooperate and she wanted no part of it."

"Or maybe *you* were one of the partners," Fanta said.

"What?"

"Maybe Maria told you what the letter meant and you insisted on joining the partnership."

I rolled my eyes in disgust.

"And you killed Petrillo so there'd be one less slice taken out of the pie."

"You're making me sick."

"You expected acquittal."

"Do you believe what you're saying?"

Fanta shrugged. "Who knows," he said. "No one is ever above suspicion."

"It doesn't appear that you've been of much help to me, Señor Fanta."

"No, it doesn't."

"I see no need for further contact between us."

"I understand."

11.

THE CONTRACT

The day after Fanta's visit I approached Angela with several ideas about escaping from Solera. She told me stories of previous attempts—of dogs, of gunned down escapees, of rotting bodies found in the jungles south of the prison, of fleeing prisoners relentlessly pursued living in hiding and fear until they were found, of extradition for the few who had made it out of the country. There had not been many attempts in recent years, she said, and those that had occurred had failed. She strongly advised me not to begin plotting and not to talk with others about it.

"If you attempt it, you will fail," she said. "It would upset the equilibrium of the prison, and *that* would upset me."

I took her advice. I talked with no one about escape, although I did not stop thinking about it. I could not. It seemed my last hope for release was gone.

I had gotten Zita Foralla into a clan. She had resisted joining, at first, but her friends convinced her that she'd be in a better position to try to change things if she were in a clan. For a while, I avoided her. I knew full well I had been living out of touch with the self I wanted to be, rationalizing my oppressive behavior as a necessary adjustment. I didn't feel like talking with her or anyone else about it. I had indulged some despicable needs to lord over others the power I had acquired, flaunting it, even somehow managing to think of it as my due. I was glad it no longer gave me pleasure. It was a relief. That part, at least, felt good. It had pleased me to tap and live out that ugly dark side of myself and now it didn't. I felt done with it. I no longer felt the need to be a tyrant. But I was laden with guilt. I did not know what to do.

Zita Foralla seemed to sense what I was going through. She gently sought me out. Gradually, I began to let her be with me, and we had talks together.

"The need you had is not what's bad," Zita said.

"How can you say that?" I asked. "There was something in me that pushed me to take advantage of the situation. That sounds pretty bad to me."

"Some of the things you did were."

"At times I felt heartless."

"Power is seductive," she said. "It takes a very aware person to resist. If one knows of the payoffs of power, and most of us do, and if she thinks she's capable of wielding it, and you are, it's very hard not to go with it if she has the chance."

I shook my head. "I don't think so," I said. "It shouldn't be hard to resist at all, not if your values are decent, if you really respect human beings."

"That's too simple," Zita said.

"Maybe," I replied. I felt like crying. "This guilt..."

"Let go."

"I tuned people out, Zita, tuned them out as people. I used them like objects. No empathy. Very little compassion."

"How about some for yourself right now."

Zita was kind, but I wasn't ready. I couldn't let go. I was obsessed with self-examination. I avoided people as much as I could. I pulled back from Teresa somewhat, too. She was clearly pained by my detachment. Several times, I tried to talk with her about it, but I could not. I couldn't explain. I didn't yet understand myself. When I did have contact with others, I was as sensitive and kind as my position would reasonably allow me to be.

I considered resigning as Section Chief. I considered rash escape plans. I thought about ways to coerce or manipulate Angela into changing things. I contemplated becoming a debajera and fomenting revolution. I had tasted power and smacked my lips on it. I had abused it, feeling stronger by making others act weaker. Something in me had made me revel in my ability to control and dominate others. I had wallowed in it and now it made me sick.

"You've certainly changed how you treat people," Zita said.

"I only changed because it no longer pleases me."

"It no longer pleases you because you changed. You went to the depths of something that most people never do. You went there and you came back."

"How dare I go there! How dare I indulge myself at the expense of other people."

"It would have been better had you not, " Zita concurred.

"To say the least."

"But, you did. That's too bad. But you've stopped now." Zita wrapped her strong fingers around my hand. "You learned, you realized, and you stopped."

"That doesn't erase what I did."

"No, it doesn't. Of course not, the past can't be erased."

"And I'm still part of it. I'm still part of the ruling class."

"So am I. Maybe we can use our power..."

"How? The system's made of cement."

Zita suddenly looked tired. Her shoulders dropped. She shook her head slowly. "Cement," she repeated, looking off into the distance.

I put my hand on her shoulder. "Failure is impossible," I said, squeezing her and smiling.

She looked at me and returned my smile.

"Look at you," she said cheerfully, "a case in point. You're definitely changing."

I nodded. "You know, my sweet little Teresa is not crazy about the changes."

"Teresa's on her own trip."

"I really care about her."

"I know. Are you in love with her?"

I paused. "I care about her," I said at last. "She's a pretty special woman."

"You're a pretty courageous woman, Kat."

I shook my head. "I can't believe you think that."

"It's brave to open your eyes and look at yourself."

"I don't feel brave."

"I know."

93

Despite my talks with Zita, the turmoil continued. I could not decide what course to take, or figure out why I had taken the course I did. It was in the middle of all this that I got the news.

It was on the first day of the new year. I was called into the warden's office. He asked me to be seated. "You have been contracted out to the Neva Prison Farm," he informed me.

I felt an immediate sinking, sickening sensation in the pit of my stomach, then throughout my body. I knew exactly what this meant. Every prisoner here did and every one of us feared such a fate with absolute dread, even the most hardened women, even Angela. I had been bought, purchased, to labor on a prison contract farm. I was to be a slave, to live under the vilest conditions imaginable, to be as powerless as a person can be. I felt dizzy. The warden called for some water to be brought. He said I would be leaving in three days and he said some other things but I didn't hear them.

Somehow, I found my way out of his office and the Administration Building. I felt like a robot, as if I had no volitional control over my movements. My legs took me to my room. My body sat itself in my chair. I was vaguely aware of knocks on the door several times and of the room gradually growing darker, but mostly I was in a numbed state that precluded thought or feeling. I may have slept in the chair, or maybe I just sat in a dazed state all night. What I next remember was the room beginning to grow light again and pressure in my bladder. My body's needs made me move and the cold shower helped connect me once more with my capacity for thought.

I started with questions: Why? Why this now? Why me? Why all of it? My life in Chicago had been a meaningful enough life. I was satisfied. I was productive. I hurt no one. I contributed. Why did I have to be ripped from it and thrown into this unwarranted hell? Why? Why did Sundance breathe his last breath at *my* feet? Why? Why did Petrillo cross my path? Why did I let myself end up living in defiance of my own values? What did it mean about me? And why...this is where I broke down...why did I now have to endure even more. Was this to be my punishment for what I had become?

I didn't really think there were answers to most of these questions. I had no belief in supernatural, overriding plans for such events. I didn't really believe on any level of my being that there was some far-reaching philosophical or spiritual purpose to the course of my life. But I asked the questions, nonetheless, and cried. I cried in the shower. The cold water washed away the tears, but not the anguish and desparation.

Yes, I had heard about the prison farms. Farms, ha! That word usually has a pleasant and comfortable association of rural peacefulness, fresh air, gently rolling hills full of living, growing things. The prison farms in Marigua, I was told, are absolute hell holes. Prisoners who complete their sentences emerge drastically changed, much worse than what I'd experienced at Solera. They become totally hardened and cruel and closed; or they emerge dull, apathetic, beaten, empty, and closed. Some of the prisoners don't survive, they say. Especially the men. They are used as labor and worked mercilessly and some don't make it. But often the fate of the women is no better. They are used as labor, too, or used as sexual slaves. The rumors say there are no limits, no controls at the prison farms, that the "owners" are free to use their "purchases" as they wish, and that there is no such thing as the system we have at Solera where some prisoners come to survive fairly well on the backs of others.

In Chicago I had managed to live at a distance from the blatant cruelties and degradation of humankind. Most of what I knew of it, I knew second-hand. It had never touched me, face-to-face, never, until dying Martin Sundance made that simple request of me. Why did it have to happen? Why was I pulled into it? Why had I become a part of such horrible things, a cooperative part, and why was I now to suffer the worst fate imaginable. Why? I kept asking, knowing there were no answers. I was scared. I was shaking with the terror I felt.

I dressed and then sat again on my chair in the room that had become home. Angela can intervene, I thought, although from what I'd come to understand, she could not. She can get me out of this. Let them buy someone else, I thought, then felt a momentary pang of guilt. How strong our self-preservation is. Let someone else go in my place, Angela.

But Angela said that could not be. Her power was limited, she told me. Her agreement with the warden gave her no control of who was to be "contracted out", for the choices were made by the prison farms. They could choose whom they wanted; they had such say over their "merchandise". Angela had more to tell me than that. She said it was also agreed that if a "contracted out" prisoner were returned, if the prison farm was dissatisfied with her, then she forfeited her chance ever to be a trustee. She could never be in a clan. Angela was neither unsympathetic nor sympathetic as she spoke of this to me. She seemed simply to accept it all as how things were.

All day and the next my torment continued. Teresa was stunned. She moaned and clung to me. I would miss her. Oh, how I did not want to go. How ironic, I thought, to regret the leaving of Solera prison. How odd to feel it as a loss worth mourning—this place of harsh divisions and self-serving alliances, of raw, unpolished power, where the rightness of might or station prevails. How like the world in caricature. Tomorrow I would leave. Today I was taken for the piercing of my ear.

Through my left ear, up high, through the cartilege, a hole was made and a ring inserted and locked in place and welded tight. The ring was inscribed, "Marigua Prison System." It was widely known in this country that convicts who left the prison walls for farms or work-release or hospitals were marked this way. To give refuge to a person so marked was a serious, punishable crime.

On the final evening, I said goodbye to those I considered to be my friends. It could not be called a party for, although a group was gathered and beer was drunk and reefer smoked, there was little laughter and no rejoicing. Angela's goodbye had been a terse handshake at the Print Shop. Zita was strong for me and I felt her deep caring. Teresa was miserable. She rarely left my side. She cried softly most of the time, and when it was time to say goodbye, she clung to me and wept deeply.

12.

THE ESTATE

For my departure, I was made to dress once more in prison greens. Two men arrived from the prison farm. They wore street clothes. I waited in the office of the Administration Building as the men exchanged papers with the clerk. This completed, they took out handcuffs and beckoned for me to come. Teresa was at the gate. We had agreed that she would not come there, but she did. I walked past her, tearfully, heavily, led by the farm guards, past Teresa who had cared about me from the first day, and out through the gates. They clanged shut with an iron finality.

"God, what a wretched place," one of my escorts said as we entered a car. I was directed into the back seat. One of them sat next to me. "I'll bet you're glad to be getting out of there," he said.

I looked at him with disbelief, "Yeah," I replied, "frying pan to fire. I'd be glad if you'd drop me at the airport."

He laughed. "I know what you mean. You'll be very surprised, though, at what it's like where you're going. You're from the U.S., huh?"

"Yes," I said, suspicious of his friendliness.

"We got a couple other Yanks at the Estate. Some kid who got caught with a shitload of grass. And I forget why the other one's there." He thought a moment. "Oh, well. You'll meet him. So, uh, what's the scene like in that place, Kat? You feel like talking about it?"

"Not especially."

"Yeah, I bet it was a bitch. I was at Marigua Fed myself, before *I* got lucky. I smashed a cop in the face at a protest march. They don't go for that, you know. Say, I forgot to introduce myself. My name's Luis, Luis Gomez."

We were traveling along the dusty, unpaved road, headed toward the coast. It's the direction I would have run had I ever actualized my escape fantasies. I used to stare that way through the barred window in my room.

"And that's Paulo Mendez." Paulo nodded to me from the front seat.

"I've been a resident at the Neva Estate for four years, now," Luis continued. "I got three more to go on my sentence."

"You're a prisoner!" I said in disbelief.

"Yeah, well, we don't call it that. We're called residents at the Estate, most of us, that is."

"And Paulo?" I asked. "He's a...a resident, too?"

"Sure. Strictly white collar crime though, eh, Paulo?"

"I'm surprised they send prisoners to pick up..."

"Yeah, well, you're in for a lot of surprises at the Estate."

For the first time in three days I felt some lightening inside myself, the development of a strand of hope. I had decided that rather than submit to humiliation, domination and other dehumanizing treatment, I would fight it with everything I had, fight it to the death, and I expected that that would not take long. Could it be that this would not be necessary? "Tell me more," I said, twisting my wrists in the handcuffs. They were unsual shackles—thin metal lined with some sort of cushion, and a long chain between the wrist cuffs.

"Sorry about those," Luis responded. "We gotta use 'em for the novicios, the newcomers. You won't see much stuff like that at Neva's though. Just for the trouble-makers and for the novicios, until they get the hang of it."

"Get the hang of it?"

"You know, adjust to the change—going from a prison to the Estate. You get a lot of freedom there and it takes a little time for that to sink in, to not go wild with it, you know. And you have to

98

learn about how life is at the Estate and know not to run even though you could. Stuff like that."

"I'm overwhelmed," I said.

"I was, too. I heard prison farms were the pits."

"That's what I heard."

"Most of 'em are, I guess. Neva's is different."

I felt as if I had just ascended from a collapsing coal mine to a tropical paradise. I let myself revel in it for a while as we drove, getting nearer and nearer to the mountains. It crossed my mind that Luis was lying, playing with me in a cruel teasing way. Here I was, sitting in shackles, my ear smarting from the pull of the ring hanging from it, and I was actually believing that I was being taken to a pleasant place? I shook my head. "Where's your earring?" I asked Luis suddenly.

"Sh-h," he said, placing his finger over his lips. "We saw them off." He laughed. "Look." He bent his head close to mine and pulled back his hair. I could see the small hole. "After we've been residents for one year, we get them removed. When the inspectors come, we put them back on. We have a lot of fun when the inspectors come."

I laughed. I really laughed, a hearty deep laugh, for the first time in days. "Wonderful," I said. "But, why? Why are things so good at Neva's Estate. It doesn't make sense."

"Natalia Neva. Contessa Natalia. She is wonderful! Wait until you meet her. Some say she's eccentric. Who knows? I say she's marvelous. She has a little speech for all the novicios. She'll tell you. Wait to hear it from her."

"How about a preview," I said, smiling. "I'm very curious."

It seemed Luis expected this and was, in fact, eager to tell me more. "Contessa Natalia Neva is very, very rich and very, very beautiful. When her husband died ten years ago, she decided to use her fortune and her influence in some unusual ways. It is said that she once had a lover, years ago, who was sent to prison and who suffered miserably and died there. Maybe that's true, maybe not. But, at any rate, she has a private crusade, a rescue crusade I call it, for those imprisoned in this country. Not the "lost ones", as she refers to them, the ones who are the habitual criminals, the psychopaths. These she calls the lost ones and ignores. Among the others, she chooses some who she buys, and brings to the Estate."

"How does she choose?" I asked.

"You tell her that, Paulo."

Paulo had said nothing so far on our trip. "It is part of my job," he now said. "To make the choices. There are criteria we use to decide who, among the prisoners, we will take. We have to limit it. There is not room for everyone who could qualify. I think of myself as an executive searcher—job recruiter." He laughed. "Actually, that's what I did before...that was my job in Juanara where I used to live. I began to make mistakes though, in Juanara. Bad ones. I let some of the candidates make themselves look more attractive to me because of little gifts they offered. Well, sometimes they weren't so little. And once I started that, I got addicted to the luxuries of wealth and even the challenge of getting more in various ways. They call it embezzlement. Ah, well. You did not ask for my story. I go through the files of prisoners, prison records. I study their cases, and I interview people. Your friend, Nettie Dawson, was very informative, and Elizabeth Blakely."

They had both written me, I recalled, about some journalist in Marigua who had contacted them. It must have been Paulo. I had given them permission to talk with the "author" all they wanted, and to tell anyone else the "journalist" might contact to do the same. I hadn't given it much thought after that.

"We must rule out the 'lost ones'," Paulo said. "Some of the people we choose have had very bad luck in their lives. Some have been idealists whose struggles for their beliefs led them to disobey the laws. They all have stories."

Luis offered me a cigarette. I considered asking why I was chosen, but Paulo continued speaking.

"I give Contessa Natalia the information I compile, and she chooses. She and Tallo, her niece. Hey! Look at that! A tapir. Have you ever seen one, Kat?"

The animal was strange-looking. We watched it lumber away from the road and dash into the foothills of the mountains. The scenery was becoming more beautiful each mile that we went. We were leaving barren Solera far behind. Paulo was talking some more about the Estate, but I barely listened. I was wondering if other prisoners from Solera had gone to Neva's Estate and, if so, why we hadn't heard about Neva's, why we only knew of prison farms as places of slavery and misery. I wondered why I was chosen. I thought of how I had treated people at Solera and felt guilty for being given this deliverance.

100

About two hours after our departure, we stopped for something to drink at a small town on a lovely lake. I was feeling euphoric. "The people here are annoyed," Luis was saying, "because of the new dam that is being constructed. When it's done, the river that flows into the lake will be diverted and the level of the lake will be much lower," he said.

"Why are they building the dam?" I asked, only half listening. I was sipping my coke and basking in the beauty of the surroundings.

"To irrigate the Tordad Plain," Luis replied. "It needs water badly."

We continued our trip and soon we reached the sea. The blue beauty of it moved me so, my eyes teared over. We were high in the mountains and all around us was beautiful countryside. We came to a coastal road and drove for many miles, the mountains on one side, the sea on the other. It was early afternoon when we turned off the main road, went a few more miles, then made a turn onto a blacktop road which led to an iron gate. The gate was open. The ornamental sign at its side said: "Neva Estates, Private Property". We entered and drove through winding, hilly, green terrain.

The sea was frequently visible, with sandy beaches here and there along its rocky shore. Soon we came to a town with small houses and larger stone buildings nestled among the hills and greenery. It looked very peaceful and inviting. I was excited. What a lovely place! We continued past the town for another mile or so. Oil rigs became visible at one point. They were in a valley along with oil storage tanks and pipelines. It jarred me to see these signs of technology here, even though Luis had told me Natalia had vast quantities of oil on her land. We continued until we arrived at a complex of about a half-dozen buildings, generously spaced, in Spanish Colonial architectural style. Whiteness was everywhere and orange-red roofs. It looked to me very much like an expensive resort hotel. I laughed to myself. So this is where I am to be a slave. I could not believe my good fortune.

Paulo dropped Luis and me in front of a beautiful three-story structure. It had a balcony hugging it nearly all the way around its perimeter. "I'll let the Contessa know we've arrived," Paulo said.

I stood in the warm sun beneath the clear blue sky taking in deep breaths of fresh air. Flowers grew in profusion. To the left was a pond surrounded by benches and beyond that a garden. Off to the right stood a huge mansion. As I looked that way, my gaze was interruped by the sight of a woman mounted on a shiny black horse. Her hair was nearly as black as the horse, and the sun sparkled on it and silhouetted her form against the mansion in the background. She wore a white shirt with full flowing sleeves and black pants and boots. She looked majestic.

"Let's get something to eat," Luis said, ushering me toward the building with the balcony.

Luis introduced me to several people including the cook. They were all friendly and welcomed me. The contrast between this and my arrival at Solera was striking. I could feel myself relaxing. I felt uncomfortable being in handcuffs, but no one seemed to pay any attention to them. I remember every detail of the meal we had. Browned, spicy chicken. Soft, warm white rolls with butter. Potatoes, spiced deliciously. Guacamole. Artichokes. Cold Coca-Cola. I savoured each bite, making myself eat slowly. It had been a very long time. Two others ate with us and Paulo joined us too. Paulo said that something had come up and the Contessa had left for a business trip of some sort. Tallo, her niece, went too. Paulo also informed us that a storm was brewing. I hadn't noticed until then that the room had grown darker. He said that my interview with the Contessa would have to be postponed.

"Too bad the Contessa had to leave," someone said. "She likes to greet all novicios when they first arrive."

"Yes, she likes to tell the new arrivals, personally, about the scene here."

"Nearly all novicios go through the same routine," Mona said. Mona was a sweet, bubbly woman in her late twenties with striking teeth. They were unusually large, although very white and straight, except for one of the top front ones which was slanted slightly, giving her smile a childlike quality. "You live in the novicio quarters and have a job assignment and go to classes and group."

"Indoctrination," Luis said, laughing.

"Education," Mona said. I found out later that she helped with the novicio program. "And then there will be an evaluation," she said.

"To see if you are ready to become a resident," Paulo said, pouring some wine into my Coca-Cola glass.

I was about to protest that I didn't drink wine when we heard yelling outside. People rose from the table. Mona and Luis ran to the porch.

102

"It's a fire! Everyone, come! The Fortura House is burning!"

I ran outside with the others and could see flames jutting up from one of the lovely white buildings, 500 or so yards away. It cast an orange glow in the darkened sky. People were running toward the burning structure from several directions.

"The hose. We must get the hose from the main garage!" someone shouted.

Several people ran off with him. I went toward the fire.

"Juanita is up there with the children!" a woman screamed.

The front porch of the two-story structure was engulfed in flames.

"Around the back! Maybe we can get to them up the back stairs."

The men arrived dragging the huge hose. They attached it to a spout about a hundred feet from the burning building. I kept looking up to the second story, thinking about the people trapped in there. I ran around the back. The door was open and I could see flames lapping around the stairway that led to the second floor. A man had drenched a blanket in water, wrapped it around himself, and was preparing to run up the stairs.

"Stop!" a strong voice commanded, a woman's voice. "You won't make it," she said. "Jaime, take three or four others and get the scaffolding from behind the main garage. Quickly! Run!" The speaker then walked several yards around the edge of the house. "Aim it at the center window there," she said to the men holding the hose.

I watched her with fascination. She was the woman I had seen on the horse when I first arrived. I couldn't take my eyes off her. She seemed larger than life, the light from the fire casting a vibrant rosey glow on her skin and her shiny black hair. She continued giving orders. Everyone did as she said, immediately, and soon the chaotic situation took on a sense of orderly goal-directedness. The flames in the front of the house were being smothered. The men arrived with the huge aluminum scaffolding the woman had sent for.

"Place it there," she said, pointing. As soon as it was in place, she directed the man with the water-soaked blanket to climb up and another person as well, a tall woman in blue jeans and a plaid cowboy shirt. "Keep the hose on that window," my black-haired hero shouted from the ground.

103

The two rescuers were at the top of the scaffolding. They broke out the window with an axe and the woman climbed in. The man followed her. The crowd below stared at the window they had entered.

Next to me a woman began to cry. "Oh, Juanita, oh, please God."

I put my hand on her arm. She turned to me with her tear-streaked eyes. "Juanita is up there and the three children," she moaned, clutching my hand with hers. "The others got out, but Juanita did not..."

"Look," I said.

The man who had climbed into the window was emerging, carrying someone, an adult, in his arms.

"Is she burned?" the woman implored, clutching with painful tightness onto me.

"Probably not, probably just the smoke," I said.

"Come," she insisted, pulling me with her. "Come with me. We'll see."

Juanita was close to unconsciousness and was given oxygen from a tank to breathe and soon she revived. Her friend had let go of me and run to Juanita's side. The other rescuer was climbing down now, handing one, then two small children to the waiting arms below.

"Where is the baby?"

"I couldn't find her," the cowboy-shirted woman said. Her face was smudged with soot. "The smoke was too thick."

"Bring the hose up the scaffolding," the black-haired leader ordered.

When this was done, she climbed up herself. I could not hear what she said then, but I saw the two men with the hose point it inside the window and then watched as the black-haired woman's powerful form disappeared within. She had put a mask of some sort over her face.

"She won't make it," cowboy shirt said. "It's an inferno in there. The smoke is too much."

I suddenly became aware of my own inactivity and how foolish it seemed to be standing there, motionless, in handcuffs as people around me were risking their lives. I ran to the scaffolding and started to climb.

"No, no. Don't do that," someone said, grabbing hold of me.

"She needs help!" I yelled.

"Stay down. Marinda will make it."

No sooner were these words spoken than the hero emerged from the window she had entered, carrying a two foot long bundle.

"The baby."

They gave it oxygen. It was breathing. It was alive. Juanita and the children were taken away, taken to the building where I had just finished eating. Marinda continued directing the firefighting. It took another hour until the flames were no longer visible. The rain had stopped. I watched the whole time with the rest of the crowd. I heard many comments about Marinda and how fortunate it was that she was near and came and took charge and saved the lives.

"She is wonderful," someone said.

I was inclined to agree.

Afterwards, people gathered in a large living room in the building with the balcony, the building where I had eaten. They sat and talked about the fire and how the lightning had struck and how bad the damage was and how lucky that no one was seriously hurt and on and on.

When Marinda walked into the room, the people applauded her. She laughed a deep throaty laugh, leaning back her head, and I thought her neck the most graceful arching beautiful neck I had ever seen.

The child Marinda had saved, a little girl maybe one or two years old was sitting on the floor placing stones into a plastic carton. She ran to Marinda and Marinda pulled her up and swung her in the air, then sat with the child on her knee and talked and joked with the people gathered there. I sat across the room, staring at Marinda. She had washed herself and changed her clothes. She wore tan pants and a tight black top. Her hair was wet and glistening and I felt a sudden urge to be near her, feel her strong arms encircling me. Someone brought out a guitar and singing began. I watched Marinda sing. I watched her talk and laugh. I watched her until she left. Then nearly everyone else left, too, and Mona told me she would show me my room. I still wore the wrist shackles and Solera Prison greens.

It was a lovely, comfortable room with its own bath. Mona brought me some clothes.

"You'll be staying here until the Contessa returns," Mona said.

I smiled. "I'm quite impressed. You know, this isn't exactly what I expected when I was told I'd been 'bought' by a prison farm.''

"I know," Mona said. "We're very lucky."

"You're a prisoner, too?" I asked. "I mean, a resident."

"Yes."

"Is everyone at the Estate?"

"No, there are many freecomers who live on the property. Many residents have families here and others also sometimes come and stay."

I shook my head in disbelief. "And Marinda? Who is she?"

"Oh, wasn't she wonderful at the fire! She is a draftsperson at the oil fields. A friend of Tallo Neva, the Contessa's niece. Marinda came for a visit one time and then she came back to stay. Do you like these clothes?"

"They're fine," I said with some irritation, barely glancing at them. I wasn't interested in the clothes. I wanted to hear more about Marinda. I caught myself thinking of Mona as a manipulable pushover, someone I could easily control. Clearly, the habits I had developed at Solera were not yet gone. I looked more closely at the clothes. "Yes, in fact, they're very nice," I said. "Thanks." There were several pairs of slacks, cotton or denim, and blouses and a jacket. "When will the Contessa return?" I asked.

"In one week. In the meantime you will stay here instead of at the Novicio Quarters. It is always up to the Contessa whether our new arrivals will go the usual route or not. So you'll just have to wait until she returns."

"And what's the *un*usual route?" I asked, chuckling, but a little uneasy. I was still having trouble believing that this "prison farm" could be so idyllic.

Mona laughed. She was sitting on the dressing table fingering the comb and hairbrush. Again I noticed her crooked front tooth and liked it. "That depends," she said. "A couple of years ago an artist came, Cora Voreamas, a very talented, wonderful artist. Before Natalia allowed her to go through the novicio program, she kept her at the mansion to do her portrait and then several other works. Cora stayed there a long time, nearly a year, before she was allowed to go through the classes and groups and become a resident. She lives in the settlement now."

"Hm," I said.

"And then there is Federico. He is still at the mansion. A very

106

handsome man, very nice. He stays there at the mansion with the Contessa. I don't know why, but there are many rumors. And there is the horse trainer. He was kept at the compound to tend the horses. He never did become a resident and he's been here three years now." Mona paused. "Let me see, I know there are more. Oh yes, Tora. She can do any kind of repair work. Fix anything, I guess. The Contessa was so impressed that she didn't want to let Tora get away and become a resident. She sent her to her friend, Maria del Gasta, who has a place on the estate, near the sea. It's a big place and Señora Gasta is old. Tora keeps the place up and helps others on the Estate too."

"Did they have a choice?" I asked, "Tora and the others."

"I don't believe so," Mona said. "And there is Miguel. He was a brute, a rough and course man. Natalia made him learn to be a nursemaid, to work with the children. He's a resident now. He got a job at the pre-school. That's what he wanted. But these are all exceptions, Kat. Most everybody just goes through the novicio program and then becomes a resident. That's what will happen with you, you can bet on it. You are from the United States, eh? Do you have a husband there?"

I looked at Mona for several seconds, then resisted my temptation to respond arrogantly. "No," I said.

"Oh, well, I'm not married either." She giggled. "You speak Spanish so well. I speak English a little," she said in English.

We chatted a while longer. When she was ready to leave, Mona removed the shackles from my wrists. "Here, in this room, there's no need to wear these," she said. "But, I will have to lock the door," she added apologetically. "If you get hungry, or if you need anything, you can call on that buzzer. I must go now, Kat. I will see you in the morning."

Alone now for the first time since I left Solera, I just sat in the soft, tapestry-covered easy chair, my feet on the leather footstool, and let it sink in. Amazing! This was all so unbelievable. I felt happier than I had since. . . since I could remember. I believe I was smiling. I jumped up and ran to the mirror by the dressing table. Yes, I definitely *was* smiling. I looked at myself. My hair was beginning to grow again. I had been keeping it short at Solera and had been planning to drop in soon on Flora. She was the best hair stylist at Solera. She charged the clanswomen for her work, but not me. She said she was honored to do my hair. I think I'll let it grow,

I thought now, as I looked at my reflection. Maybe very long. My mother had always tried to get me to grow it long. "More feminine, Kat," she'd say. I looked older, I thought. Yes, I've aged. At Solera, many women told me how young and attractive I looked. Of course, it was probably just flattery, I thought. People were always trying to please me there, and I played it to the hilt, didn't I? I wasn't smiling now. I didn't like those memories. How could I have let it happen? I drifted back.

"Hey, Maria, did I say you could sit here?"

"Oh, I'm sorry, Kat. I didn't know you didn't want me..."

"No, no, go ahead, sit. It's all right. You're looking kinda cute tonight."

"Thank you.'"

"I was just thinking maybe you wanted to sit a little closer to me."

"You want me to?"

"Sure, I could use a little warming up...Ah, that's nice...yes, that's very nice."

Pig, I thought. I had become a pig.

"Sandra, I've been thinking about you."

"You have?" She squirmed uncomfortably. Sandra was one of the few other North Americans at the prison. She was quite shy.

"Yeah, I have. I hear you're into leather."

She blushed, her whole face and neck becoming bright red.

"I've been thinking of letting you make me a pair of sandals."

"Oh, yes...yes, I'd be glad to, Kat," she stammered.

"Yes, I thought you would."

I took advantage of them, used them for my own gratification. More memories came.

"You, debajera, carry that box up to my room. Now!"

"Yes, Kat."

I was suddenly crying.

"You, take that bag of groceries into the house. Now!"

"Yes, daddy."

"No, you can't go to Jennifer's house." "I don't like that expression, Katie. Wipe it off your face." "You're late. Go to your room. No dinner." "Because I said so, that's all you need to know." "Don't sit like that, it's not ladylike," "Bring me another cup of coffee."

"Your father's a good man, Kat." "No, you don't, you don't

hate your own father." "Because I love him, Kat. Oh, I know he gets grumpy, but that's how men are." "I've learned how to get what I want from him. Little tricks I have. They almost always work." "Because I love him, Kat." "He's very strong." "I look up to him." "I like to please him. He never hits me." "I feel safe, protected with him. I need him, Kat, I love him."

I don't know how long I sat there before the mirror, remembering. I suddenly became aware of where I was and that it was raining again. I looked out the window, across the compound. I could see the lights from other buildings. I was very sad when mom died. I'm glad, though, I thought, watching the lightning flash, glad that she didn't have to deal with my being convicted as a murderer. That would have destroyed her.

I slept well in the cozy bed in my lovely, carpeted bedroom. I dreamed of a woman with black shiny hair on a black shiny horse, riding in the night up a hill, lightning flashing around her, highlighting her regal form with a white glow. I was at the foot of the hill looking up at her as she rode. I was filled with admiration.

I breakfasted with Mona and Luis and an older man called Huberto. We talked of the fire and of Juanita and her husband, Juan, and I learned some more about Marinda. Everyone seemed to admire her. Luis said she was an excellent draftsman, that the architects relied on her. She had never married, I learned. She came to Neva's six years ago to visit her friend, Tallo, and had decided to stay. She was very kind, they said, but very assertive, too. A strong, strong woman. There were some oblique allusions to her possible attraction to women, but no one took that very far. They seemed to share a great respect for her. I had no trouble understanding why. She haunted my thoughts.

Mona showed me around the compound. Contessa Natalia lived in the mansion. Others stayed there, too. Some came and went, friends of Natalia's and relatives. Federico stayed there. He was a writer and could often be seen on the balcony with his typewriter. The large building where I stayed and where we ate was called the Big House, La Hacienda Grande. Parties were held there, Mona told me, and meetings, and visitors often stayed there. Behind the Hacienda Grande, past the garden were the Novicio Quarters. There were usually not more than ten at a time staying there. In that building were sleeping rooms and meeting rooms and the kitchen and dining hall. Mona said she would be leading a discussion group there later in the afternoon. The novicios were to talk today about the fourth right on the Statement of Rights and Obligations. It had to do with freedom from force and coercion, and behaviors that result in a partial forfeiture of that right.

"We go into all the ramifications," Mona said, "of what each right means and how they must be respected. No rules or laws can be made by any group that violates the rights. No individual can violate them. We talk about why this is so and people give their reactions."

There were other building as well at the compound, including a jail. "For outlaws," Mona said, "residents who have refused to respect the basic rights of others. They go through re-education. Usually, it succeeds, but there are some failures."

We were sitting near the pond, now, on one of the benches. "The Estate is very large," Mona said. "Do you remember leaving the main road and then passing through a gate when you came here?" she asked.

"Yes."

"That's one boundary, where the gate is. The other is miles that way, about fifteen miles. I'll show you a map, later, if you'd like. Natalia's property is like a half-moon along the sea. The sea is one border, the mountains curve around to form the other. The Estate is about fifteen miles long and almost ten miles wide. Where we are now, the compound, is right in the center. You can see that the mountains are there, to the left, and the sea to the right. Behind us, there, is the oil field and beyond that, the settlement. Ahead of us is the only other exit by road. That leads to Amerotos and other towns. There's another gate at that exit."

"So those are the only ways to leave, two exits," I said.

"Yes, by road. The mountains are very rugged but they have been crossed by a few. On the other side of the mountains is the main road, the federal road. And then, of course, there's always the sea. But, that requires a boat."

"Hm."

"I hope you're not thinking of trying to leave, Kat."

"No, not really," I said, "but who knows. Don't you ever get frustrated with having to stay here?"

Mona looked at me with a very serious, strained expression. Her lips were tightly pressed together. "A few people have tried," she said. "Most were novicios. With their shackles and earrings, they did not get far. One who managed to get those signs of his status removed was gone for three weeks. He was found in Mexico and returned to prison—not here. He will never come back to the Estate. No one who escapes can return here. When you go through the novicio program, you will learn that you jeopardize everyone by running. The Contessa gets very upset. She has said many times that she will continue bringing people from prisons to the Estate only if escape attempts are few. If too many occur, she will stop bringing prisoners here."

"So that's the incentive to stay."

"That's only one of them, Kat, obviously." Mona seemed a little annoyed with me. "Life is pretty good here, in case you haven't noticed. That's the main incentive. For most of us, we live better than we ever did before. And, as strange as it seems, we have more freedom. As long as we abide by the Statement of Rights and Obligations and do not leave the Estate, we have an incredible amount of freedom. I'm talking about residents, of course. For novicios it is different, until they complete the program. And for outlaws, it is not so good. Of course, the freecomers come and go as they please. Many residents stay on when their sentences are over."

"They stay?"

"Yes. Why should they leave? I mean it, it's a very good life. I am looking forward to the end of my sentence, though. That will be in 2½ years. I will stay here, but I'll be able to travel. I'll be a freecomer. I have relatives in Postero. It will feel good to go back. Most of them have come here to visit with me. This Christmas, they all came—my mother, my four brothers, my baby sister, cousins and aunts and uncles. We had a wonderful fiesta. Too bad you were not here yet to meet them."

I worked in the garden for a while in the late morning. Mona told me I didn't have to do any work, that I could just lounge around if I wanted, but I chose to do some weeding and transplanting. It felt good. The plants were vibrant from the watering they had received the night before. I also ran some errands for Mona and for Luis, and helped out with the cleanup of the burned-out house. In the late afternoon, Luis asked if I would mind delivering a package to one of the cabins, about three-quarters of a mile in the hills. I asked him what it was worth to him. He laughed. He thought I had a good sense of humor. The package was addressed to Marinda Sartoria.

As I walked along the road, my thoughts were full of her. I pictured her vividly, her strong, angular face with the full lips and slightly flaring nostrils. Intelligent, pensive eyes. I saw her on the horse. I saw her carrying the child from the burning house. I saw her playing the guitar and singing. And then my fantasies went beyond what had actually been. I pictured myself arriving at her house. Marinda would be on her horse in front of the cabin. She would smile at me as I approached. Then she would reach down her hand to me and pull me up behind her on the horse and take off. We would soar through the hills, my arms wrapped tightly around her. We would ride and ride until we came to a clearing, a meadow with soft grass and tiny wildflowers. She would ask me to spread a blanket on the grass. I would do so and she would stand next to me then and look into my eyes and slowly reach her hand toward me. She would take my chin in her soft strong hand and hold it. I would feel a chill of excitement through my body. She would continue looking into my eyes, then pull me to her insistently but tenderly. She would press her lips on mine, hard, deep, and I would. . .

I stumbled on a rock in the path and nearly fell. What is this, I asked myself? Why am I thinking such thoughts? I hastened my pace to clear my head. In my pocket I had the pass Luis had given me. He said that because I was in shackles and wore the earring, I would be questioned if I met someone, so I had to have the pass. It indicated the date and time and my destination and that I was to return to the compound within an hour. I was nearing the cabin Luis had described. Marinda's home. My pulse speeded up. Weird. Her place was quite large, I thought, to be called a cabin. It was constructed of wood, varnished and natural. It had a long slanted roof, a balcony and an enclosed patio draped in flowering vines.

I knocked on the door and waited, feeling foolish for feeling so excited about seeing her. I knocked again, slightly harder. Still no response. I knocked and waited for what must have been a full five minutes and then I tried the door. It was unlocked. The interior was simple, warm and bright and very inviting. There were thick rugs, Indian design, and plants and soft chairs and pillows.

"Hello!" I yelled.

No answer. I was in *her* house. These were *her* things. How silly, I thought, to feel this way. I placed the package on a table knowing

I should leave now. But I didn't. I walked around the living room fingering objects. I went into the kitchen, neat and spartan and full of natural wood, then into the bedroom. I stared at her bed. It seemed huge. I looked out the bedroom window at the hills and the mountains beyond and the road. There were no people. Softly, slowly I sat on the bed. I felt my whole body tingle. This is absurd. I removed my shoes and lay my body across this soft warm place where Marinda slept. My eyes were closed. I lay on my back feeling her there above me, moving slowly down to me, to join her body to mine. I was lost in in when I heard a noise. Frantically, I jumped up, put on my shoes and bolted from the room. I looked all around the house, inside and out. No one was there. I went back to the bedroom and straightened the soft, thick, navy blue bedspread. On the dresser was a carved wooden box. I opened it, tentatively, quietly. There were silver chains, bracelets, necklaces, and turquoise and a thin leather strand with several blue and brown beads. I held the leather bracelet in my hand. I put it on my wrist. It gave me delightful pleasure to do so. I was reaching for a silver pendant when I heard hoofbeats. Quickly, I closed the lid and went out to the living room and then to the porch.

Marinda dismounted and tied her horse to a post in front of the cabin. "Hello!" she said. "What brings you here?"

"I...uh. A package." I said, "I brought a package for you. Luis asked me to. It's inside." I leaned against the porch railing trying to fight this ridiculous nervousness I was feeling.

"I see. And your name is..."

"Kat," I said. "Kat Rogan." At least my voice was steady. I had a flash of myself at Solera. The contrast was mind-boggling.

"Yes. I believe I saw you yesterday, after the fire." Marinda held out her hand. "I'm Marinda Sartoria."

We shook hands. I felt electricity pass from her palm, through my body, to my spine. She seemed oblivious to the shackles I wore.

"Well," she said cordially, "I'd invite you to sit awhile, have a drink with me, but I'm afraid I have to run. We'll be sure to make it another time, all right?"

"Yes," I answered. "Sounds good."

We were standing together in front of the cabin. She started up the stairs.

"Thanks for bringing the package," she said over her shoulder.

I stood there watching as she disappeared inside. I wanted to go to her. I wanted to get lost in her eyes and bury myself in her powerful body and be absorbed by... Suddenly, I felt weak, almost nauseated. I had never reacted this way in my life, to anyone! What the hell was the matter with me? This is nonsense. Ridiculous! I began moving toward the road. On the walk back to the compound, I reviewed, over and over again, each movement she had made, each word she said, every moment of my interaction with her.

"She has a friend she visits in Portez," Mona was saying back at the Hacienda Grande. "Sometimes she stays several days. And she travels from time to time. She used to live in the Columbia, in Bogota. She goes there sometimes. Why do you ask so many questions about Marinda?"

I felt embarassed. "I'm writing a book," I said. "Wait 'til you see my chapter on you."

For the next few days, I hung around the compound, meeting people, talking, working in the garden and in the kitchen at the Hacienda Grande. It seemed like a dream. It was so beautiful and peaceful here, and the people so cordial and respectful of each other and of me. No one seemed to have more status or authority or privileges than anyone else.

One day I took a horseback ride with Paulo. We passed Marinda's cabin. The whole time we were near it my heart was pounding faster than the horse's hoofbeats. I wore her bracelet. I fingered it, stroked it, was constantly aware of it against my skin. You're idolizing this woman, I told myself chastisingly. This is not you. I was reminded of stories my mother had told me about her courtship with my father, about her feelings of adulation towards him. I felt disgusted. Was this the way Teresa had felt toward me, I wondered? I suspected it was.

Days passed and I did not see Marinda again. On the sixth day of my stay at the Neva Estate, I went with Luis to the settlement. We drove along the sea. Between the road and the sea lay rocky stone and stretches of sandy beach. At one point along the beach, at the peak of a group of rocks, I could see something golden glittering in the sunlight. As we got closer, I realized that it was a statue of some kind.

"What is that, Luis, the golden statue atop those rocks?"

"You did not notice it before, Kat, when we came a week ago? That is the Winged Dancer. We will stop and take a closer look at it, if you'd like.''

It was one of the most beautiful pieces of sculpture I have ever seen. It had the grace and strength of the Hellenic Greeks, the vibrancy of a Michelangelo, the nobility of form of a tribal Indian work. Mounted on a natural platform of rock, it stood, soaring. It was a bigger than life-size human figure, dancing. Its graceful body was clothed in loose pantaloons which fell to a place just above the ankles, and in a wildly flowing robe of feathers, thousands of feathers. The dancer's feet were bare and agile and alive. The arms were spread wide and seemed to draw the observer forth, towards the dancing figure, welcoming, enticing. The chin was held high, the face, noble, serene but full of life and joy. I could not tell if it was a woman or a man. I was going to ask Luis what he thought, but then I knew it didn't matter which it was. It was life, human life, happy and healthy and free. It was magnificent.

"It's magnificent," I said.

"Yes. Do you not know the story?"

"No, will you tell me?"

Luis smiled widely. "I love to tell it."

We sat among the rocks at the base of the large soaring statue, and I stared at it as Luis spoke. He spoke for a long time, telling me how centuries ago, before the Europeans came to this part of the world, the only people here were tribal, many different tribes. They were nomadic for many many years, Luis said, until they discovered agriculture and then they developed settlements. Soon after that, one tribe, the Omilato, grew very powerful, more powerful than the rest. There were wars and conquests. The Omilato took over the other tribes, one after another, forcing them to take on the ways of the Omilato. Over the years, the Omilato influence and domination included most of the tribal peoples. The Omilato were a fierce and sometimes cruel people. Very hierarchical. The chiefs and their courts lorded their power over the peoples of the tribes. There were divisions, like classes. It was obviously an extremely nonegalitarian culture. Women were at the very bottom, subject to their husbands' rule, worked and bred to exhaustion and early death. The lower class within the tribe, men and women alike, suffered terrible oppression by the ruling class, the chiefs and their court, the nobles and warriors. The Boweso tribe was one of the last to resist engulfment by the Omilato. Finally, when it was clear that they would be overtaken if they did not leave, the Boweso uprooted themselves and migrated to the sea.

"They settled somewhere not too far from here," Luis said, "on the Suga River. No one is sure exactly where their settlement was because there was this terrible earthquake in the middle of the 18th century. It changed the whole terrain of that area."

"Earthquake?" The interesting little story suddenly became *very* interesting.

"Yes."

"Go on."

Most of the Boweso people were killed as a result of the earthquake, Luis went on, and so were the Omilato who lived near that area, he said. Centuries before, the Boweso had discovered a safe enclosure along the Suga River. The river came from high in the mountains and fell downwards.

"A glorious waterfall it must have been," Luis said enthusiastically, "and then there were several miles of rapids. It was along these rapids that the Boweso made their home."

On one side of the settlement, Luis told me, were the unscalable mountains; on the other the rushing river. In between was fertile land and that was where the Boweso settled. They were invulnerable to attack. The mountains could not be climbed. The river could only be approached from downstream and the Boweso's lands entered at only one place. There they built a high thick wall. The Omilato could not get to them, and soon stopped trying. The Boweso apparently lived a peaceful life, based on a system of equality and justice; a system totally foreign to the Omilato (and to most countries today, I thought). Their land was rich and the climate friendly, Luis said. The Boweso grew many crops and hunted and fished. Men and women alike shared in all the roles and all the work.

"There were not families as we know them today," Luis continued, "but groupings or units, all sharing tasks and goods, and love."

Luis' face was glowing as he spoke.

He told me that laws were few among the Boweso, that leadership was shared and rotated, and diversity was valued. They also developed clothing, cooking techniques, customs quite different from those of the other tribes. Once a year, on the anniversary of the day they discovered this place, all of the Boweso people gathered for a ceremony of celebration. From the river, over the years, they had collected gold. Lots of gold apparently.

"In present terms, millions of pesos worth," Luis said. "Finally, on the 25th anniversary of their settlement, they unveiled a statue—the Winged Dancer." Luis paused here, looking at the golden sculpture that rose above us from the rocks. "That is how it looked," he said. "Or very similar. That replica was made from drawings and descriptions that have survived. The statue itself disappeared when the earthquake struck. Every year the Boweso would bring forth the statue and place it in the center of their village for the annual celebration. It would stay there for one month, then be removed and kept in some secret place in the surrounding mountains. The few Boweso survivors of the quake did not know or would not tell where the statue was hidden. It has never been found although it has been sought for the last century by many different people. The statue has come to symbolize life of freedom and equality, and now the Contessa, well, Tallo actually, had this one made and placed here."

I felt flushed with excitement. "What year was the earthquake, Luis, do you know?"

"1760," he said.

I nodded.

"It's a fascinating story, isn't it?" He stared up at the Winged Dancer.

I could remember much of Martin Sundance's letter almost verbatim. *I have ascertained where the* blank-blank *is located.* Winged Dancer? Could it be? I couldn't remember how many numbers were in those blanks. I hoped there were six and six. I needed to get a copy of Sundance's letter. Triste had one which he had gotten from Fanta after the original was stolen. I assumed Fanta still had a copy, too.

"Do you know how the earthquake changed the terrain, Luis?"

"You seem very interested in the earthquake, Kat?"

"I'm interested. Do you know?"

"Yes. Suga Lake was formed then. The river, the Suga, used to flow through a gorge into the sea and somehow the earthquake blocked the path and Suga Lake was formed."

"The statue's been missing since the earthquake struck?" I asked.

"Yes. It's never been found."

"It must be worth a fortune."

117

"I suppose." Luis looked disappointed in me. "It's real value lies in what it stands for, Kat. Like I said, it's a symbol to the people of Marigua. It stands for freedom, and human dignity. For respect."

I knew I had to get the letter from Triste as soon as possible, and that I had to learn more about the Boweso and the missing statue and exactly what changes the earthquake had caused.

"You know the story is true," I said to Luis, "not just a myth?"

"It is documented," Luis said. "Several anthropologists visited the Boweso. I believe even one from your country. I have the books at the compound. I will show you. We should get going, now, Kat. I am already late for the meeting." Luis did not seem too alarmed about that.

We continued our trip until we reached the settlement. Although I was preoccupied with what Luis had told me, I was greatly impressed by what I saw there. It was a very attractive and cheerful town. I walked around the shops and sightsaw while Luis went for his appointment. I kept thinking of the letter. The dying old man. Was he a Boweso? Several people in the town, very cordially, asked to see my pass, and then some of them chatted with me about the settlement and their lives there and asked about me.

"I am a freecomer now," the bartender said. "This is home for me until I die. Here, I am wealthy and important, as is every other member of the community. Outside I was poor. I lived in a barrio. I could tend bar in Postero or some other city in Marigua, but I would be a fool to leave. Besides, I would have to go alone. My wife loves it here. They sent her for training and now she is a nurse in our clinic. Have you seen the clinic?"

"No," I said. "I was just given a tour of the school, though. It seems very...different. Very free."

"My children love it. They never pretend to be sick so they can stay away. They are learning so fast. I didn't know I had such smart children, even Jose, who was so bad and never studied in Postero where we lived before. No, you will see. You will want to stay...unless you get too homesick for your own country when your sentence is up."

"It won't be up," I said.

"Oh," he replied kindly. "Well, then how lucky you are, lucky to be here and not in some disgusting prison."

How lucky, indeed, I thought.

Tomorrow, the Contessa Natalia Neva would return, and at last I would have my interview and start my program as a novicio and become a resident and find a job, and, in a year, my earring would be removed and I would have few reminders that I was anything but a free woman living a very pleasant life.

When we returned to the Estate, Luis got me the books. During his investigation, Fanta had done some research on the earthquake and I, too, had read some articles he sent. But now everything I read had more meaning. Suga Lake was formerly the Suga Valley through which the Suga River flowed. Popular name. The river still flowed to the sea as it always had, but now it flowed into Lake Suga at one end and out the other side to the sea. The earthquake had created a natural dam and the waters of the Suga River flooded the valley and formed Suga Lake. I thought of Sundance's letter, trying to remember the exact words. The *something* had been *submerged* by *blank blank* since the earthquake of 1760... what then? I couldn't remember. The statue has been submerged by *Suga Lake* since the earthquake... It fits, I thought. It could be...

I also read about the tribes, the Omilato with their oppressive ways, the sensitive, strong Bowesos. There was another tribe, called the Zecundexes, who formed another caste in the Omilato Empire. They were described as small, soft, passive people. They welcomed their annexation by the Omilato for they found protection under the Omilatos' wing, and security. They willingly became the personal servants of the Omilato lords and warriors. They provided comforts for them, soothing them in numerous ways after their battles and hunting expeditions. According to what I read, the Zecundexes idolized the stronger, more aggesive Omilato and were honored to serve them. The Omilato treated the Zecundexes as useful, pleasing inferiors. Sometimes as pets; sometimes as functional laborers and as sexual diversions. The author of the article suggested that the natures of the Omilato and the Zecundexes complemented each other.

I stayed awake long into the night reading and thinking. I thought about the different tribes, about the Winged Dancer and Sundance's murder. I thought about what steps I would take. I thought about Marinda and about the impending meeting with Contessa Natalia.

119

13.

THE WIFE

The next day Mona accompanied me to the mansion. It was a huge building with immense white columns, an expansive stone patio near the entranceway, exotic-looking plants and huge flowers and vines. This was the first time I'd been inside the mansion. The foyer was large with tile floors and grained wood and more plants. A skylight was overhead.

"This way," Mona said.

I wore a pair of loose cotton pants, a cotton blouse, and, of course, the handcuffs. I had become accustomed to the shackles but was relieved when Mona removed them before knocking on a large, carved wooden door. At the bid to do so, we went inside.

"May I introduce Señorita Kat Rogan, Contessa," Mona said, respectfully. "This is the Contessa Natalia Neva," she said to me.

It took me a second to place her, and when I did, I'm sure my face flushed. I thought I saw a look of recognition on her face, too. A momentary frown darkened the smooth beauty of her forehead, for the briefest moment. She wore a long dress and sat on a huge throne-like chair.

"Have a seat, please," Natalia said. Her voice was smooth and refined. I took the chair across from her.

"It often has a significant effect," she said, "to see, face-to-face, the prisoners I have bought. It often affects my decision about their fate. Take you, for example, Kat Rogan. I did not expect you to be as you are, and now that I see you, it stimulates me to modify my original plans for you." She smiled a puzzling smile. "Mona, dear, would you fetch Marinda, please. She's in the library."

I reacted as if the name, Marinda, were not a word but a current of electricity being sent down my spine. I seemed to have little control over my response to her. I did try to calm myself as we waited. The Contessa did not speak nor did I. When the door opened again and Marinda entered, she seemed to take over the room.

"Marinda, this is our new arrival, Kat Rogan," the Contessa said. She was obviously very perceptive, for she immediately added, "Or have you two already met?"

"Yes," Marinda said pleasantly. "We have." When she looked at me, it felt like her gaze penetrated my skin. She nodded at me, then turned back to the Contessa. "What is it you have in mind this time, Natalia?" she asked teasingly.

She was smiling. I felt an overpowering wish to have such a smile directed at me. My heart was pounding. She is so magnificent-looking, I thought. The stark white of her blouse contrasted against the olive skin and black hair. The sound of her deep rich voice sent a chill through me.

"Well, Marinda, I've been thinking...," the Contessa said. Marinda took a seat next to the older woman. Her movements were swift and graceful. I couldn't stop staring at her. "...about Tallo. You know how I worry about her."

"I know," Marinda said, "but needlessly sometimes, I think. Tallo does such a good job of taking care of herself."

"Everyone needs a little help with that, I believe," the Contessa said. "Even Tallo. That girl is too hard on herself, always working, always busy. She rarely ever truly relaxes, and I'm convinced she doesn't eat as well as she should."

"She doesn't seem to be wasting away."

"And that little cabin of hers. It has such potential. She insists she'll get around to fixing it up and making a home for herself, but she never does get around to it."

"I guess her room at the settlement satisfies her."

121

"That tiny cubby hole. Ah, that's no way to live. And she refuses to live here."

"Yes."

"She needs someone to look after her."

"Do you think so?"

"Indeed! She needs a homey home where there is someone who will pamper and indulge her."

Marinda's laugh was deep and throaty. I loved the sound. My heart continued to thump against my chest as I watched her and listened to her.

"Since Melina disappeared, Tallo's been with no one," the Contessa continued.

Marinda nodded.

"She will never marry," the Contessa said.

"No, she won't."

"A man, that is."

"Right."

"And she has shown no inclination to seek a lover."

"That's true."

I was growing more and more puzzled by this conversation, but I didn't want it to end for I didn't want Marinda to leave my sight.

"What do you think of *her?*" the Contessa asked, gesturing toward me.

Marinda looked my way. Her large black eyes again seemed to penetrate me. I felt flustered. She turned back to the Contessa. "I think you're plotting again, Natalia."

"Well, just a little maybe. I want you to be involved in this one, Marinda. Now, hear me out. I have decided to give a gift to Tallo."

"A very unusual one, I suspect," Marinda said.

"Yes, rather," the Contessa replied. "I have decided to give my dear niece...this woman, Kat Rogan, to be her faithful, devoted...wife. Yes, wife. To love, honor and obey her, to make a warm and comfortable home for my precious girl. Isn't that a good idea?"

My jaw dropped. I was appalled. She couldn't be serious.

"Grand."

"I'm not sure you mean that, Marinda. Now, just think about it a minute. We have here, in Kat Rogan, an attractive, intelligent woman of the lesbian persuasion."

Marinda smiled as the Contessa continued. I was dumbfounded,

122

probably close to being in a state of shock, for the Contessa's words seemed to be coming from miles away.

"I have liberated her from her sordid existence at Solera Women's Prison. She owes a debt to society, for her crime, and to me, for my act of charity."

"I suppose it could be looked at that way."

"I want Tallo to be indulged, to be cherished and treated like the princess that she is."

"And so you want to present her with Kat Rogan, to do the honors."

"Isn't it a wonderful idea?"

"It strikes me as the sort of idea you would have, Natalia."

"Yes. Well, now about your role in all this."

"I'm listening."

"Kat Rogan was a Section Chief at Solera."

"Is that so?"

"A very tough cookie."

Marinda flashed me a look that left me feeling anything but tough.

"I'm afraid she doesn't know how to be a wife, Marinda."

"I seriously doubt that she does."

"But you can teach her."

Marinda laughed again in her throaty way and, despite the obscenity of this conversation, I felt liquidy and drawn to her.

"Train her how to serve and indulge dear Tallo in the way of traditional wifehood. Train her by taking her first, temporarily, as your own."

I was feeling digusted now, more with myself for experiencing a contradictory sense of delight as this outrageous prospect, than at the Contessa for suggesting it.

"This is idotic!" I said. My voice came out more loudly than I'd intended.

"As you can see, it will be a difficult job," the Contessa said to Marinda.

"An impossible one!" I shouted. I rose to my feet. "You can't play with people's lives this way. I absolutely won't..."

"Silence!" the Contessa commanded. An angry dark expression covered her face. She looked very much as she had when I let go of her hand at the river atop San Trito. "Marinda, do you think it can be done? Do you think you can do it? Tallo has so many ornery people to deal with in her work and I do so wish for her to have a peaceful place to come after one of those hard trying trips."

"You know I enjoy challenges," Marinda said.

"Ah, excellent. You shall have absolute authority over her during the training, Marinda, and all the help you may need. Do whatever you wish to achieve the goal." The Contessa rose and walked toward the door. "Let's try to keep it secret. I would prefer that Tallo be surprised by this gift." She looked at me. "You are not to speak of our arrangement to others, Kat Rogan. They are to know only that you will be Marinda's helper, her assistant, nothing else." She opened the door and called to Mona to join us. "Mona, take Señorita Kat away for now, will you. Lock her up somewhere."

"Yes, Señora."

"I would like to say something," I said to the Contessa.

She looked at me cooly, then smiled. "Ask Marinda," she replied.

I turned to Marinda. Again a chilling rush shot through me. "May I say something?" I asked, angry that my voice cracked slightly as I spoke.

"I have no wish to hear from you at this time," Marinda said sternly. "Go now."

I spoke no more, but did as she said, annoyed and puzzled by my own docility. Mona was surprised when I told her I would not be going through the usual novicio program but would be Marinda's assistant. We talked of it as she accompanied me back to my room. I was again in handcuffs.

"Well, it certainly could be worse," Mona said. "Being Marinda's assistant does not sound bad at all."

"I'd rather be back at prison," I blurted.

"What? Why, Kat? I don't understand. What's so bad about working for Marinda?"

"I do not want anybody goddam bossing me around," I hissed.

Mona nodded. "You were a boss at Solera, I bet," she said.

I didn't respond.

"If you went back, you would not be a boss. You would be a debajera."

In the morning, Mona brought a very large delicious breakfast to my room. She told me that Marinda would be coming for me soon, that I should be ready. I felt a strange mix of excitement and fear. I wanted to feel anger. I pictured her—tall, dark, graceful, stately, majestic, powerful, magnetic. Stop! I told myself. This is nonsense! I tried again, trying to think of her more objectively. I pictured her face. Deep, dark eyes. A very sensuous mouth. Yes, she was attractive, and obviously she was a self-assured, confident, capable woman. But, a human being, goddamit, I reminded myself. And not a very admirable or ethical one at that. To participate in the Contessa's ridiculous plan makes Marinda no better than she, no better than that condescending, spoiled, capricious, pompous, self-indulgent bitch she works for. They're two of a kind, I thought, playing with peoples' lives for their own amusement, using us as if we were pawns in a chess game or dolls in a doll house. It's much more honest at Solera. There, at least, there is no pretense. Here, they coat it with a pretty covering of grace and gentility but the divisions are as severe, the power as abused. Marinda Sartoria, you are no better than Angela, I thought angrily. Worse in fact. You are like a more polished and refined Leona. Train me to be a docile, accomodating wife! Grotesque! Naziesque! And to think that I could have felt some attraction to you. To think that I could have actually desired, even yearned to be in your presence, that I had felt a deep strong wish to please you, that I felt admiration and. . .What nonsense! I don't feel that way about her. I've never felt that way about anyone and never will. No one warrants adoration. No one deserves my devotion and awe. I've never felt it. I never will. Not for God or Jesus Christ or any messiah or budda or deistic image or human being. No! I don't feel that way. Stop, dammit, stop! She's nothing but a goddam weak, ignorant, cruel, flawed, disgusting mortal. I despise her! I'll fight her every goddam inch, every centimeter. I fought it at Solera from the very beginning and I'll fight it here. I'll never succumb. I'll never let her do it to me. I'll never serve her and do for her whatever pleases her and smooth her lovely brow and massage her soft warm feet and caress her beautiful body and give her pleasure in every way that I can and revel in the privilege of being with her. . .No! Stop. I jumped up, trying desparately to pull myself out of the insane hypnotic spell of whatever it was that was happening to me. I felt sick. The desires that kept haunting me were revolting. Kat, snap out of it! She's a nasty, immoral brute, an asshole of a woman, a woman who has agreed to train you. Listen to that! *Train* you to *serve! Be a wife! Repulsive.*

125

Mona accompanied me outside. Marinda was leaning casually against a truck. Immediately, I felt it. The more I felt the weak, melting sensation, the more I had to fight it and generate anger and disdain instead. Despicable, I thought, as I walked toward her. I'm sure my face must have been twisted into an angry, hateful sneer. I hoped it was.

"You look grumpy this morning," Marinda said. Her voice sounded kind and humorful and caring and deep and rich.

I increased my sneer and made my eyes look cold and hateful and I said nothing.

"Get in the truck," she said. She turned to Mona. "Thanks, Mona. Oh, the handcuff key, yes. See you later."

Marinda climbed into the driver's seat. I sat next to her, the chain from the shackles resting on my lap. I kept my head turned away from her. My heart was pounding. She started the engine and we left the compound taking the road into the hills.

"I imagine Natalia's idea is rather shocking and upsetting to you," Marinda said, after we had driven a minute or two.

Yes, but exciting too, I wanted to answer. Exciting to know I will be with *you,* close to you and be allowed to do what will please you and hear your voice and look at your magnificent face and body. "To say the least," I replied, turning toward her angrily. "As a matter of fact, I find it one of the most reprehensible productions of a so-called 'human' mind that I've ever..."

"Wow! All right, all right," Marinda said. She smiled. "Actually, that reaction's very understandable and that's why I wanted to make sure..."

"And I find *your* willingness to go along with it an indication of your total lack of character," I interrupted, glaring at her.

"Hey, wait a minute. Listen will you, before..."

"Your obvious moral decrepitude. You know, your self-respect must be amazingly low, if not non-existent."

"Watch what you're saying, Kat Rogan. You're getting on my nerves."

"No integrity. Your participation obviously reflects a gaping lack of self-esteem."

I saw her jaw tighten and her eyes narrow, but once I started, I couldn't seem to stop. "To choose to take advantage of an opportunity to lord your unearned power over another human being in such a way," I went on, "is weakness *in extremis,* pure,

126

pathetic weakness." I emphasized each word.

Marinda had slowed down the truck, nearly to a stop. She was looking at me and I at her. I almost shook with the anger and hatred I was ventilating.

"You, my dear," I spat at her, "are the classic example of a weak person in a powerful position. You make me sick! You make me wretch!" I took a breath. "Have I answered your question?" I shouted. "*That* is my reaction to what you and your phoney snit of a Contessa are doing."

Marinda stopped the truck and continued looking at me. I couldn't tell from her expression if it was anger or hurt she was feeling. Or something else. She continued to look at me that way.

"I have infinitely more respect for the dumbest asshole of a guard at Solera Prison than I do for you," I said, "or for that bean-brained Contessa cunt you suck up to."

"Rogan!"

I could read the expression now. It was anger. I wanted to take her hand in mine and beg her to forgive me and explain that I didn't mean it, that I adore her, that I think she's the most magnificent woman I've ever met and I'd be honored to do or be whatever she wants. "Hey, terrific," I said. "So, you're gonna get tough now, huh, big woman? You gonna muscle me? If you didn't have that dim-witted Contessa backing you up, you'd probably be pissing in your boots, you weakling pussy. You're the type of woman I squashed to quivering mush at Solera."

Her eyes glared. "Listen, Rogan," she said. "You just dug yourself a hole with your foul mouth. You just changed the whole game." She shook her head, her mouth in a cold grin. "So it's your turn to listen now. I'm going to explain some things to you."

She had stopped the engine of the truck and turned toward me. She had her right arm over the backrest of the seat. The fabric of her blouse was pulled tightly across her breasts. Her eyes were firey.

"Listen well."

"Fuck yourself," I said.

She grabbed the front of my shirt so rapidly I didn't have a moment to anticipate the action. She held onto the cloth tightly forcing my head back. I looked into her angry eyes. I felt very vulnerable. I also felt an exciting, melting, electric sensation shoot through my entire body. Was this what I wanted? I knew I had

127

pushed her to it. I didn't speak. I couldn't have if I wanted to. I remained suspended. Slowly, she loosened her grip.

"You are a convicted murderer," she said, enunciating each word. "That means, under the laws of this country that your civil rights have been forfeited. The contract Contessa Natalia Neva has with the Marigua Prison system gives her absolute control over you. You might have had it very good at the Estate, like most prisoners here, but you have an outstanding knack for irritating people." She shook her head again. "You have irritated me, Kat Rogan. Too bad for you. You are a prisoner. You have no civil rights, no power. I know this isn't really news to you, but you're behaving as if you're ignorant of it, as if you need reminding. Natalia Neva can use you in any way she wants. She could chain you to a wall, lock you in a box, sell your body, exploit your labor. You have no choice. You sacrificed your freedom of choice when you took Peter Petrillo's life. That's how it works. What you think of this fact is irrelevant. What you think of the morality of Natalia Neva's decisions about you is irrelevant. What you think about my character is irrelevant."

She seemed absolutely powerful and wonderful, the way she spoke, the way she was looking at me. Her anger was magnificently controlled. She was calm but excitingly intense. I loved it and only later did I think it odd or wrong that I should love it.

"I am going to go through with this. I'm going to train you. I'm going to do just what Natalia requested."

I did not respond. I was having trouble looking at Marinda.

"To begin with, your attitude is very bad," Marinda continued. I nodded.

"You realize that," she said.

"I realize you don't like it," I responded. My voice was stronger than I'd expected, stronger than how I was feeling inside.

"It must change."

"Not likely," I made myself say.

Marinda laughed. She had lit a cigarette and was now resting her left arm on the steering wheel. The sound of her laugh sent delightful shivers down my neck to the small of my back.

"You will learn," she said. "You've made me decide that. It will probably be the hard way, but you'll learn. I may even enjoy teaching you."

"Honestly, Marinda, don't you feel disgusted with yourself for being involved in this?" I asked.

Marinda laughed again, then she stopped. It seemed the anger had returned. "Moral decrepitude, eh? Pathetic weakness." She looked at me scornfully. "Natalia paid a good price for you," she said. "She told me to teach you to be a devoted wife and so I will."

I stared at Marinda coldly. "We live in different worlds," I said with disgust. "We operate from totally different premises. There is no sense in trying to communicate with you."

"You're rather taken with yourself," Marinda said simply.

"It's called respect," I replied. "For myself and for other people. A foreign concept to you, no doubt."

Marinda shook her head and started the engine. We drove until we were high in the mountains. The sea sparkled several miles beyond. We rode without speaking. I tried not to look at Marinda, but my eyes kept being drawn back.

"Surely, you must realize that what you're expecting me to do is obscene," I said, breaking the silence. "Catering to someone, subjugating myself." I was imagining catering to her and fighting the pleasure it brought. "It defies everything positive and ascendant about humankind," I said.

"Most women do it voluntarily," Marinda replied casually.

I had to laugh. In a sense, what she said was true. "They think they have no other choice," I said.

"In your case, that is accurate," Marinda reminded me.

I got an electric chill again. I let what she said sit awhile. Finally I spoke again. "What you people think of as a 'wife' is rather overdone, I'd say, certainly obsolete. I believe Natalia used such words as 'indulge', 'serve', 'obey', 'pamper'."

"Actually, such expectations of a wife are still quite popular," Marinda replied. "For many people, that's what wifehood is all about."

"You haven't heard about 'equal partnerships'," I said. "You know, mutual sharing, support, respect, stuff like that."

"I'm talking about reality," Marinda replied. "Not myths. The reality is that wives were invented to cater to men. And I'm going to train you to cater to Tallo. Simple as that."

I didn't respond. I had become lost in fantasies again. I was not thinking about what we had said, but rather reveling in her closeness to me and fantasizing about what else she would do, how

129

I would respond. Wanting it.

"Tallo owns a cabin," Marinda said. "It was given to her. It needs some work. Your training will begin there. You will live at the cabin and work there, and begin to learn how to be a proper wife. Now since you seem unclear about exactly what wifehood entails, let me specify." She cleared her throat, then went on.

"First, a proper wife subjugates her own will to that of her spouse. That's the main principal, and one that I suspect you may have some difficulty learning. You strike me as being rather 'willful'. Not a good trait for a wife. But, you will learn. You will learn to do everything I tell you, exactly, with no questioning, no argument, no resistence, either overt or subtle. You are to obey absolutely and immediately."

"And if I don't," I said, beginning to feel angry again, beginning to need to fight her again.

"Disobedience and disrespect will be punished."

"Barf," I said.

"The amount of punishment you incur will be a direct barometer of your intelligence. If you behave stupidly you will suffer more punishments. Simple. You will end up a well-trained, obedient, submissive, traditional wife. You will get there easily or with difficulty depending on your behavior and the degree of your self-control."

"Pathetic weakness," I muttered contemptously.

"That's an example of a punishable behavior," Marinda responded. "Very soon, I will no longer allow them to go by."

"Very soon I will no longer allow them to go by," I mimicked scornfully.

"The punishments will be periods of confinement," Marinda said, looking at me and then back at the road. "Confinement in a place less comfortable than you've been allowed here so far." I felt immediate fear, almost panic. Ugly, pushed-away memories of the discipline cell at Solera crushed in on me. I lapsed into silence.

A short time later, we arrived at the cabin. It was a mess. It was located in a beautiful isolated spot near a mountain stream, but the cabin itself was in disrepair, dirty and rundown.

"As I mentioned," Marinda said, "this place needs some work. The supplies you will need are in the truck." She walked to the dirty sink in the kitchen and turned on a faucet. "Ah, good, the water still works," she said. "Hopefully that means that the

130

plumbing is OK." She looked at me in the way that rose goosebumps across my back. "Well, unload the truck and get started," she said. "Don't slack off now. There's much to do to make a comfortable home for Tallo." She pushed aside a dusty, broken chair. "You are not to leave the area, Kat. If you want to explore, don't go beyond a radius of 500 meters from the cabin. Any questions?"

I did not respond.

"Your behavior will be observed. Disobedience to my orders will be punished by confinement. Any questions?"

"I'd like to contact my attorney," I said.

Marinda laughed. She laughed uproariously. She seemed immensely and genuinely amused. Her laugh was infectious and I couldn't help laughing with her. We must have kept at it for over a minute. Finally I spoke.

"I'm serious," I said. I chuckled again. "Something new has come up about my case."

"Oh, I see," Marinda replied. "Sure." She wiped away a laugh tear. "Your timing is wonderful. You be good and I'll bring some paper. Now, get to work."

"Marinda."

She looked at me with her beautiful dark eyes.

"What you're asking me to do here," I said, smiling, "is men's work. Such heavy labor is not for wives."

Her eyes smiled. "More mythology," she said. "Go on now, unload the truck."

Marinda walked over to the stream and sat on a rock. I went to the truck and began removing things. There were many items including a supply of food and a sleeping bag. The unloading took quite a while. When I finally finished, Marinda returned to the truck and, without a word, drove off. I was angry with myself for feeling a sense of great loss as I watched the truck disappear down the road.

I had piled the equipment and supplies in front of the cabin. I stared at them for a while then sat on the rickety stairs of the porch. I looked out over the hills. The view was beautiful. The sea did not seem very far away. I fingered the tear-shaped earring hanging from my left ear, and wondered if I should risk trying to get away from here. I began to formulate a plan. I could take as much of the tools and other equipment as I could carry, walk through the mountains until I came to the road on the other side, keep going until I reached Portez, sell the tools and things there. No, I thought, first I have to remove this earring and these handcuffs. Now, getting over the mountains does present a problem. Maybe I could slip through along the sea road to the gate, then sell the tools...Once I had some money, I could take a room someplace, call Nettie or Elizabeth at home and see if they could get me a passport. Then, I could wait until they sent it or brought it. How does one get a fake passport, I wondered? What risk would my friends be taking in doing it? Was it fair to ask? Could I stay in a hotel in Marigua without papers? I was occupied with all these silly thoughts when I heard hoofbeats. I watched the rider coming up the path.

"Olá," the woman said, dismounting. "I am Tina." She tied the horse to a tree branch, and extended her hand. "Marinda thought you should have company."

"How considerate," I said, shaking the woman's hand. She was plump and rather pretty. She seemed a little shy. "Are you to help with the work?"

She shook her head, and shrugged, almost regretfully. "I can't do that," she said. "I am just to observe."

"To observe?"

"Yes."

"For what purpose?"

"Well..." Tina squirmed, seeming embarassed. "You know ...to report...to Marinda."

"I see."

"I'll try not to be in your way."

"That's nice," I said. I laughed then. "Strange place," I mumbled.

"I have some news for you," Tina said, apparently trying to win my good will.

"What's that?"

"You had a visitor at the Estate."

"I did?"

"Yes, he came this morning, just after you and Marinda left."

I couldn't imagine who. "Who?" I asked.

"I don't know his name. I overheard. I was working on the books for the Contessa and just heard part of the conversation."

"What did you hear?"

"He asked for you. He said he was an acquaintance and requested the opportunity to visit with you."

"What did he look like?"

"He was very tall and thin. With not too much hair and a very high forehead. He wore light pants and a nice shirt, a white one. He was maybe forty years of age. Very tall."

I had no idea who it was. "You're sure he asked for me?"

"Oh yes. Kat Rogan. He is your friend?"

"What else did he say?"

"That he thought he might be able to help you with your legal case."

"Hm-m. Is he a North American?"

"No, no. He is from here. From Marigua. He said he just recently heard about your unfortunate circumstances. He talked that way, saying things like, 'unfortunate circumstances'. He seemed very educated. Don't you know who he is?"

"Did he say anything else?"

"No. Let's see, no, that's all. Señora Natalia said she was sorry but you were not available for seeing visitors at this time, but that he could write to you. She said he could write about arranging a visit."

"And then?"

"Well, he left."

"Yes."

"What else could he do?"

I was puzzled. It obviously wasn't Triste or Fanta. Who else? I never met a Mariguan before coming here. Except Sundance, I thought. "Thank you for telling me, Tina."

"You're welcome. Well, I don't want to distract you any more," she said. She went to her horse and removed something from the saddle bag. I watched her string a hammock between two trees and climb in. She smiled at me, then opened a magazine and began to read.

I decided I had better begin working although I had no idea how to proceed. My experience in such tasks was minimal. I had built a bookcase once. As a kid I had played with my father's tools when he was not around. Suddenly, my eyes were full of tears. That happened at Solera from time to time, too. I'd have some memory of my past and then I'd find myself crying. My father died five years ago. He had been a tyrannical, iron-fisted, emotionally distant man. As soon as I was old enough to rebel effectively, I fought his control with all my resources. Fortunately, he did not resort to physical violence to assert his will and in response to my recalcitrant stance, he gradually seemed to give up on me, focusing his despotism on my mother and sister. Poor mom. She took it all. She thought of him as a strong man. She never fought it, never seemed to get angry even. I think she was sad without really knowing why. She served her husband faithfully to his dying day and when she was finally free, she just wasted away and died herself. It was as if she had no self separate from her role with him. She had said, more than once, that it gave her pleasure to please him and when he was gone, she felt useless.

I wiped the tears away and began sorting through the supplies. The handcuffs were annoying, but the chain was long enough that they didn't restrict me. There was a pair of blue jeans among the other goods, and some ankle-high work boots. I changed into these; as I had expected, they fit fairly well. I piled the wood neatly along the side of the porch, and then began a thorough scrutinizing of the cabin, inside and out. I realized the first step should be to clean out the rubbish that littered the four rooms, hoping that as I did this, I would get some sense of what aspect of the repairing I should begin with. There was a book on carpentry among the supplies. I was very hungry by the time I had piled the junk outside and swept the floors. I sat on the porch and called to Tina.

"How about some lunch? You hungry?"

"Yes. I brought something for myself. They told me you have food."

There was a jug of apple cider along with the tortilla chips, cold chicken and guacamole. There was other food, as well, in fact enough for several days. Tina and I ate together, sharing the cider. She was very sweet and pleasant.

"I hit my husband," she said at one point.

"Oh?"

"While he slept."

"Mm-m."

"With a hammer."

"A hammer!"

"Yes. On the head. He got a concussion, but that's all. He is a miserable gorilla. He would drink and hit me, beat me, and sometimes even the children."

I listened.

"I was afraid to leave. He threatened me. He said he'd find me and kill me, and the children, too." Tina was crying now. "So, I planned it. It was the only way. I didn't know his head would be so thick. I said it was a burglar, but no one believed me. In jail, in prison, it was terrible. And then the Contessa rescued me. How I adore her. For my exchange work, I work for the Contessa. I have a house in the settlement. My children are with me."

"They live with you?"

"Oh, yes. They were staying with my sister, and she brought them to me. She wanted to stay herself, but her husband would not allow it."

"You're a prisoner here, aren't you?"

"Yes, a resident."

"And you have a house and your children are with you."

"Yes."

Even though I knew that these arrangments were not uncommon at Neva's Estate, it still amazed me. I poured another glass of cider for myself and some more for Tina.

"So you like being here?"

"Of course. It's a dream come true. My children are happy. People respect us. At the Estate there is great respect for everyone. I never imagined there could really be such a place. I am on the Food Council now. I was elected. They listen to my opinions. I help make decisions. Such great respect for people here."

I laughed. "Right," I said sarcastically.

"I know you are not yet being allowed to go through the novicio training and become a resident, but you probably will soon. Most everybody does. Pretty soon, that's probably what will happen with you, Kat, and then you will see."

I shook my head. "I don't think so. The Contessa seems to have other plans for me. I think she holds grudges," I said. I chuckled. "You see, I met her once before. In Postero. She didn't seem to take to me."

Tina nodded. "Too bad," she said. "Always I have known Natalia Neva to be very fair and good. But, sometimes...well, she does get kind of...she does things I don't understand, sometimes."

Tina got up from the porch and went back to her hammock. I watched her settle in, then found the carpentry book to read about repairing stairs. I decided the porch would be my first project. I read and measured and sawed and hammered. It went better than I had anticipated. It wasn't a perfect job, but the stairs were now solid and safe, and so I turned my attention to the railings. I worked for hours, resting now and then and once I took a walk around the area. A hundred yards or so upstream was a small waterfall. It was a beautiful spot. I sat there enjoying it until I caught myself dreamily thinking of Marinda. I was chastising myself for this strange attraction to her, when Tina came sauntering up the path.

"There you are!"

"Yes," I said.

"I was wondering where you'd gone." She said it in her shy way.

"Now you know," I said.

I returned to my work on the porch and didn't stop until all the railings and floor boards were acceptably fixed. I felt a pleasant sense of accomplishment and fatigue. The sun was getting low when Tina began to pack up her horse.

"You're leaving?"

"Yes. I want to get back before dark."

"And me?"

"I believe you're to stay here."

"Stay here. Oh, I see," I said, matter-of-factly.

"That's what Marinda said. Are you frightened?"

I thought about it. "The idea doesn't thrill me."

"There's a lantern."

"Could I talk you into leaving your hammock?"

"Of course. I should have thought of that. It's very comfortable, you know. When I was a child, my bed was often a hammock." Tina removed it from her saddle bag.

"What will you report?" I asked.

"I will tell Marinda just what happened." Tina gracefully pulled her chubby body up into the saddle.

"And tomorrow?"

"I don't know."

I nodded. "I enjoyed your company, Tina. I hope you come again."

"Thank you," she said, and she rode off.

The darker it got, the lonelier I felt. The lantern light was harsh and cast an eerie glow. I heard all kinds of sounds. I didn't want to be inside the cabin; it was so barren in there. I didn't want to be outside. Finally, I built a fire, a big one, and had some supper. It was peaceful, but I felt edgy. I had ruled out any thought of attempting an escape at night. If I used the lantern, I could easily be spotted moving through the hills, and I'd probably get lost, and it was very dark. The stars helped some. There were many, many stars. The air was balmy and I was sleepy, but I couldn't relax.

I wondered again who my unknown visitor could have been. Manuel Paz? I wondered if there was any way whoever it was could have remained on the Estate without anyone knowing. I felt I needed to remain vigilant. I heard a twig snap at the other side of the cabin and my whole body tensed. I threw more wood on the fire and tried to calm myself. I thought of Teresa, back at the prison and wondered if there were any way I could persuade Natalia to "buy" her, too. I thought about the Winged Dancer. I thought about what an amazing place the Estate was, almost utopic—for residents, that is. Mostly I thought about Marinda. Trained to be a wife. How dare they! They want to demean me, and I will not cooperate with that. I will not feel this way toward Marinda. I'll fight it. I'll fight it all. I stared at the flames. Of course, they do have a stacked deck, I thought. I sat for a long time, my anger growing as the fire's flames began to flicker into dimness and red embers.

I heard another noise, the sound of movement in the brush and trees nearby. Some little creature, I thought, in my attempt at self-reassurance. I had set up the hammock at the same place Tina had hung it, but decided now to sleep inside. I found a way, within the cabin, to hang the hammock. I doused the lantern and wiggled into the sleeping bag which I had laid along the hammock. I used my rolled up jeans as a pillow and a hammer as my companion for security. It was more comfortable than I expected and although I felt a need to remain alert, my eyes began to droop.

My dream was vivid and frightening. I was in a haunted woods, lost and pursued. I ran in circles, the pursuers getting closer and closer. I could hear the breathing. I ran faster but got nowhere. My legs were chained together with ankle shackles. They hampered my movements, catching on every fallen branch. I stumbled again and again. I knew if I gave up I would disappear, no longer be, no longer be me. The pursuers were relentless. They were moving in on me, getting closer and closer.

I awakened with a start. I had heard something. Footsteps on the porch. I felt around for the hammer. My heart was hammering. Something bumped against the door. Oh, God! I struggled out of the sleeping bag, clutching the claw hammer with my sweaty hand. More sounds at the door. I stood now, in my barefeet, T-shirt and underpants, staring at the door, the hammer ready. More footsteps. I edged toward the door, placing myself flush against the wall, ready to attack if the door opened. I waited. The sounds continued. I didn't move. The waiting, the suspense was agonizing. I slid back a few feet toward the window. Slowly, I moved my head so I could see out of the window onto the porch.

My sign of relief and laugh startled the goat and I watched it running off the porch and away. The sun was just beginning to show itself. "A goat," I said outloud. "It was a stupid, god-damn goat." I laughed again because it felt so good. I laughed and crawled back into the sleeping bag on the hammock and slept some more, this time without dreams.

14.

THE CELL

I was pulling out broken bricks and scraping pieces of mortar from the fireplace when Marinda arrived.

"Not bad," she said. "The porch is looking good. I brought some paint and roof shingles for you."

The familiar feeling of excitement was there again. "You're too kind," I said.

"Yes, but you must learn to speak without the sarcasm, to show the respect that a good wife should. Say it again," Marinda ordered.

"You are too kind," I said sarcastically.

"Again."

"You're too kind." This time my tone was matter-of-fact.

"Again."

"Oh, come on."

"One."

"What? One what?"

"One step toward being locked up in a cell I'm saving for you."

I turned away in disgust and scraped a chunk of mortar from the mantle.

"Two."

"How many strikes until I'm out...or in, rather?" I asked. I didn't feel as nonchalant as I sounded.

"Ten today; nine the next time; then eight, seven, six...Understand?"

"You can count backwards. Marvelous. Can you do it in English, too?"

"Three."

"I'm using them up fast."

"Very."

"How long in the cell?"

"Twenty-four hours."

"And how can I avoid it?"

"I know you know."

"Marinda," I said pleasantly. "It was very kind of you to bring more materials for my work here." I smiled. "Thank you."

Marinda returned my smile. "Excellent," she said. "I'm looking forward to a campfire breakfast. I brought some eggs."

"Sounds good," I said.

"Well?"

I looked at her. "I'm to do the cooking?"

"Of course."

It didn't take long to rekindle the fire. I made scrambled eggs mixed with hot sauce and brewed some coffee. We ate silently staring off into the mountains. I had to force myself not to keep looking at Marinda, not to marvel at how the sun glistened on her hair and at the smoothness of her skin. I wondered what Marinda's thoughts were. Mine stayed focussed on her. There was definitely something regal and imposing about her, I thought, even when she wasn't on a horse or fighting a fire. *Regal and imposing.* Those were the same words Lorrie Watts had used.

Lorrie was a young lesbian I had seen around the community in Chicago over a period of years. We had never exchanged more than a few words but I often noticed her staring at me, from across the bar, in the lobby at concerts, at the coffeehouse. At first, it made me feel somewhat self-conscious. She always averted her eyes when I looked her way. Was my face smudged with soot? Did I have a piece of spinach hanging from my nose? I realized at last that she probably had some kind of crush-from-a-distance on me. She never tried to initiate any contact until, finally, one very late night at a dance, when she came up to me and began to talk. She was clearly quite drunk. She made her confession. She told me that ever since the first time she had seen me two and one-half years ago, (she gave the exact date and hour), she had had the most intense, erotic reaction. It wasn't like with women she'd become involved with. This was instant, powerful, overwhelming, she said. It was then that she told me I seemed "regal and imposing" to her.

She said more. She went on to tell me of the fantasies she'd been having since first seeing me, fantasies of my overpowering and dominating her and her own game of resistance then orgasmic submission. It was not unknown to me that there were women, including lesbian women, who experienced such cravings. However, Lorrie Watts was the first woman who had ever spoken of them to me in this way and, certainly, the first I knew of who imagined me as a party to them. I wondered now if Teresa had felt something similar towards me. I had responded to Lorrie with compassion and understanding, assuming her words to reflect an unfortunate, probably deeply rooted, piece of her early conditioning as a female in the culture of the patriarch. I told her I would be happy to discuss it further with her at a future time, but that I had no wish to be involved in the realization of her fantasies. She said, yes, yes, she understood, that she was drunk and stupidly bold, but we should talk again when her mind was clear and inhibitions operating properly. She left the dance then, immediately, by herself. She never spoke to me again, and although I saw her around occasionally, she seemed to judiciously avoid me and I no longer caught her staring.

Regal and imposing, I thought. Damn! How vehemently I had always held my own, resisted any form of even the most subtle domination by another, of either sex, of any status or position of authority. And I had gone to the opposite extreme at Solera. Now I was to be "trained" to "serve" and "obey" another, to subjugate my will to hers. They had the means to force me to act out this role. I resented that less than I resented the feelings (were they "erotic"?) that I experienced in Marinda's presence, and every time I thought of her, and now as I sat next to her.

"Is there anything else you need?"

Marinda's voice startled me. "What?" I said. She looked at me and I felt as if my whole body were vibrating.

"Other supplies, for the work?"

"Oh." I tried to calm myself. "Yes, as a matter of fact, yes.

More bricks. The fireplace is in worse shape than it looked. I'll need at least a dozen more."

"Are you all right?" Marinda asked. "You seem rather...I don't know. Is there...?"

"No. I'm fine. Varnish for the floor would help, unless you want them carpeted. I wouldn't advise that, though."

"Varnish," Marinda said. "Bricks and varnish. No problem. Get me my cigarettes, will you. They're in the truck."

I brought her the pack from the dashboard. She waited for me to light one for her and I got a strange pleasurable feeling as I did so.

"Tina told me she got somewhat bored here yesterday," Marinda said.

"What a shame."

"Oh-oh. That sarcasm again."

"Yes," I said. "A deeply ingrained part of me.

"That's what the training's about, Kat. Change. New learning. Getting rid of some of the old patterns."

"Like self-esteem and pride, in this case."

"Learning humility. It's clearly been a stranger to you. I bet you worship no god."

"You win."

"No belief in such things?"

"No worship."

"Natalia was right," Marinda said. "She reads people so well. Tell me, you know a Federico Jimanos?"

I did not, but I decided not to let Marinda know this right now. "Why do you ask?" I inquired.

"He came to the Estate."

"I see. To visit me?"

"You know him then? The Contessa was somewhat suspicious. He did not have the normal identification papers."

I was unsure how to play this, but I was quite curious about who the visitor had been, and I did not want to give Marinda and her cohorts all the control. I said, "I'd like to see him. Will that be possible?"

"That depends on you. Novicios rarely are allowed visitors. Nor are wives who displease their surrogate spouses. We'll see how the training goes."

I rolled my eyes in disgust but made sure Marinda did not see. I began to think about Federico Jimanos. Who could he be, I wondered? Why had he lied about knowing me? He might be connected with Petrillo or maybe the Sundances. He might be Manuel Paz.

Marinda rose and stretched. "Not a bad breakfast," she said, "but you could probably benefit from some cooking instruction. The Contessa wants Tallo to eat well..." She looked into my eyes, still smiling "and to be well eaten," she added, laughing.

I felt a jolt.

Marinda walked to her truck, and I watched the trail of dust as she drove off. She had brought me stationery to write to Triste and I did so immediately. I thought that, with the information from Luis and the books I had looked at, I could probably fill in some of the blanks in the letter.

The rest of the day went much like the day before. Tina arrived on her horse, this time with some knitting as well as a magazine. She had brought a cushion, too, and placed it where a tree could be her backrest. She sat. I worked. I enjoyed the work. It took most of the day to complete the fireplace. It was late in the afternoon when I finished. Tina was napping in the hammock. I sat on the porch smoking a cigarette and watching the horse swish away flies with its tail. I used to ride horses frequently. I had enjoyed the ride last week with Paulo and decided a little ride would be fun right now. I tossed away my cigarette butt. Quietly, I approached the animal. I stroked its warm muzzle speaking softly to it as I did. I slung the saddle up on its back and fastened it. The horse did not balk when I mounted, but responded quickly to my tugs on the reins. I went up the road a hundred yards or so. Tina continued to sleep. I went a little further, then sped up to a canter. I loved the feeling of the air brushing through my hair and the view here was far superior to any trail I'd ever ridden. I continued along the road.

Suddenly, my joy ride took on another dimension. I realized this would be a perfect opportunity to explore the area with the possibility of finding an escape route, a path that would lead me to the road along the sea and the gate and beyond the boundaries of the Estate into freedom. I spurred the animal on with greater purpose and intensity now. I took a path that diverged from the main road, passing several cabins, all of which appeared to be inhabited. I kept going. I must have ridden for close to half an hour when I saw someone ahead, walking along the path. He had seen me and I decided that to change my course at this point might arouse suspicion. I came abreast of him and slowed to a walk. He looked at me with curiosity.

"Hello," I said. "Beautiful day."

"Yes," he replied. "Most are this time of year." He frowned in a puzzled way, staring at my handcuffs. He was a short, stocky man with a thick black moustache.

I began to move along when he spoke. "Excuse me," he said. "May I see your pass?"

I considered my alternatives. I could bolt. I could lie. The latter seemed the best. "It's at Tallo's cabin," I said.

"Will you come with me then, to my place up the road. I'll have to telephone about this."

"Yes," I said. "I'll meet you there."

I tore off, pushing the steed as fast as it seemed able to go. I felt excited, as if I were in the wild west on the run from the bad guys. I kept going and going, turning onto different paths here and there, guided by the sea, when it was visible, and by the sun. I knew I was heading toward the road that Paulo had driven when he and Luis brought me here. I was hoping, for future use, to find a path in that area that would lead out of the Estate. I could see the dirt road at various times from the horse trails I was taking. At one point, I saw the raised dust of a vehicle about a half mile ahead.

I continued my search. There was a maze of paths criss-crossing the area. I had slowed to a walk as I got nearer and nearer to the sea. I didn't want my route to take me out of the camouflage of the hills when I made my escape, but I wanted to be near the road. I could hear an engine now. I concealed myself and the horse in a clump of trees and waited. The sound got louder. I could see a small section of the road from where I hid. Then I saw her. It was Marinda on a motorcycle.

I stayed motionless knowing it might be unpleasant if she were to see me for she had said something about staying close to the cabin. I could no longer see her, but could tell by the engine sounds that she had slowed down and now was coming my way. Could that little nerd I met on the road have phoned her, I wondered. Damn! The sounds were getting closer so I decided to make a run for it. I tore down the trail away from Marinda and her noisy bike. The brush was thick and the land rocky so I didn't dare risk leaving the trail. I drove the horse on, hoping for an intersecting trail to appear, painfully aware of the decreasing gap between the motorcyle and me. I came to a fork in the trail, turned left, then dismounted and walked with the horse off the trail toward a group of rocks.

The cycle had sounded farther away for a while but now I could tell it was approaching again. I hid with the horse amongst the rocks and waited. The sound of the engine got very loud, then stopped. I waited, figuring there'd be scant payoff for running. I hung onto the slim hope that she would not find me in my little hiding place. But she did.

I was smiling at her as she climbed over the rocks and approached me. "Hi," I said.

She shook her head. "Serious disobedience."

She was holding a coil of rope. From her pocket, she withdrew a heavy pair of handcuffs and beckoned for me to come to her.

"Is this really necessary?" I said. For some reason, the drama both frightened and amused me.

She removed the more delicate handcuffs I was wearing and replaced them with the pair she had brought. She tied an end of the rope to the handcuffs, and led me and the horse out from the rocks and back down to the trail. Her bike was there. It was a hefty-looking Kawasaki. She mounted Tina's horse and looped the rope around the saddle horn. Again, even in these circumstances, I was struck by how majestic she looked. She began moving. I ran behind her through the trails, trying to keep enough slack in the rope to avoid being pulled off my feet. We reached the dirt road and she quickened her pace. I had to run to keep up.

We went for what seemed like miles. I was ready to collapse with exhaustion when we finally entered the compound. I saw Mona on the patio of the mansion, looking very upset as she watched us pass.

Marinda spoke to a man standing at the entrance of the red building. I had met him before at the Hacienda Grande. His name was Huberto. "Put her in Number Three," Marinda told him.

I felt weak.

Inside the building, Huberto looked at me compassionately. "You must have made Marinda very angry," he said. "I have never seen her be harsh with even the most stubborn novicios."

The building was plain and neat, rather hospital-like. Down the corridor I could see a row of jail cells with bars for the front walls. Most of them contained one or two people. I felt immense relief.

145

They weren't dark, closed-in rooms. It wouldn't be so bad. Huberto removed my handcuffs then took me down the corridor to the back part of the building. There were no longer barred cells, but a row of steel doors. He opened one of them. The weakness returned. The room was small, probably eight feet square. There was a toilet, a sink and a cot. On the sink was a washcloth and a small bar of soap. The room contained nothing else. There was no window.

I recoiled from it.

"It will be dark," Huberto said, holding onto my arm, "but otherwise it's not so bad. There's nothing to be frightened of. There are no bugs or anything. It's just the darkness."

We both stood outside the door. He seemed almost as reluctant as I to have me enter the room.

"Do you know how long I'll...?"

"As soon as I find out, I'll let you know," he said. "You'll have meals, of course. The food's not bad. Like I said, it's mostly the darkness."

I pointed to the next door. "Is anyone in there?"

"No," he said. "No, you're the only one in the back cells. I'll tell you what," he said. "I'm not supposed to, but I'll try to come by every couple of hours during my shift. I'll knock on the door and we'll talk a couple minutes. How's that sound?"

I felt an indescribable tenderness toward this homely little man, with the crossed eye and the kindly smile. I remembered, more clearly than I ever wanted to, the horror of my confinement in the cell at Solera. The aloneness had been unbearable. It was crushing.

"Thank you," I said to Huberto. "That sounds very good."

"Well, I think you better..." He gestured toward the cell.

I entered and stood facing him.

"It's 6:15," he said. "Dinner is at about 8:00, OK. See you then."

He closed the door slowly, the light dimming, dimming until it was gone. The lock clicked. "That bitch," I said aloud. A panicky feeling was beginning to develop. The darkness was suffocating. The memories unbearable. I sat on the bed and tried to convince myself that this was no big deal, nothing to be frightened about. "It will be all right," I said aloud. "There's nothing to fear. Relax." I took deep slow breaths. I'll sleep, I thought. Yes, I'm tired. I'll sleep and soon that sweet little Huberto will be back and it

146

will be OK. I lay down and almost instantly everything faded.

The knock was soft and I awakened slowly.

"It's Huberto. I have your tray." He opened the door. "How are you doing?" he asked.

"It happened to you, didn't it?" I said. "You were locked up like this."

"Yes," Huberto replied, handing me the tray. "But not here. Here it is not so bad. I am not allowed to stay," he said. "I must close the door."

I nodded. In the darkness, I set the tray on the bed and felt the food. It felt like it might be a sandwich. I took a bite; it tasted fine. I felt around the tray some more. There was rice and a plastic fork and something else—a cylindrical smooth object...and a pack of matches. I lit a match. Wonderful! I lit the candle. Marvelous! Huberto, you are a dear. I knew I would never tell a soul at this place what he had done. I finished my candlelight dinner and realized I was humming to myself. It really would be OK. I extinguished the candle, knowing I must conserve it for when I really needed it. I lay back on the bed, thinking, maybe dozing off from time to time. Huberto came again. He took the tray and we talked. He told me he did not particularly care for his work assignment at the jail. It was his exchange work, he said.

"What is that?" I asked.

Although Mona had talked about this with me, it would take Huberto a long time to explain, I hoped. He leaned against the door, holding it open, letting the delicious light in.

"Every resident at the Estate," he began, "is entitled to certain things—to shelter and food, medical care, use of the beaches, the roads, the public buildings, the schools for the children. Did you know that?"

"Yes, I heard, but I don't know the details, Huberto. Tell me more."

He crossed his arms. One eye looked at me, the other somewhere else. "In exchange for those things," he said, "for the basics, each person, each adult, must contribute in some way. Must do work."

"And your work here, that is your contribution?"

"Yes. I've done other things, too. There are many ways you can do your exchange work. Some people do no more than the minimum. I think they are lazy, but that's OK. It is their right. Those people live simply, at the settlement dormitory. If you want more than that, if you want a room of your own or even a house of your own and if you want to own things and eat more delicious food..." He smacked his lips at this point, "then you do more than the minimum, more than just the exchange work. You see?"

I nodded.

"Most of us do, but not all."

"And if you don't do *any* work?"

"But you must," Huberto said. "If you don't, you will have no credits. For exchange work, we earn credits. We must each earn 400 credits a year to stay here. If we do not, we must leave. For freecomers, that means leave the Estate. For residents, it means jail." He pointed up the corridor. "No fun," he said. "In exchange for credits, we get to live freely on the Estate and have all those things I mentioned. For those who want it, we also get dormitory room and board."

"What if someone is independently wealthy?" I asked.

Huberto laughed. "Oh, you Yankees," he said. "There are some of those, but you don't understand, Kat. To live at the Estate, everyone must do exchange work. Every resident and freecomer. Even if you are a millionaire. If you don't need the credits for food and shelter, if you have your own private doctors, that's OK. You still must earn the credits, whether you use them or not."

"It's like taxes," I said.

Huberto seemed to give great thought to this. "Yes," he replied at last. "I think it is. Instead of money, you give work."

"Everyone the same amount?"

"Everyone 400 credits. But many, many ways to earn them."

"How many hours of work to earn 400 credits?"

"Depends on the work. Even the best jobs require no more than eight hours a week. This job, at the jail, is not such a good one, so less hours are needed. If I worked here 250 hours a year, that would be enough to earn all my credits."

"Hm," I said, calculating. "That would be about a month of full-time work, eight-hour days."

"Yes, I think so," Huberto said.

"Then you could loaf the rest of the year."

Huberto nodded. "If you like to loaf," he said. "And if you are satisfied with very simple living. I like my TV and I like my hobby, model railroad trains. And I like good food. Have you been to any of the restaurants in the settlement?"

"No," I said. "But, I've been eating very well at the Hacienda Grande. Tell me more, Huberto. What else do you do besides your exchange work here?"

Huberto smiled. "I will. Sometime, I will, but Señorita Kat, I must leave you now. I will come again."

I slept well and when I awoke I felt no fear, for I knew the candle was there. I lay on my cot a while, wondering what time it was. It could be the middle of the night, but because I felt quite rested, I decided it was morning. Huberto had told me I was to be confined here for 24 hours. I lit the candle, used the toilet, then put the candle out again and shoved it under the mattress. After doing some exercises, I began to daydream. Marinda was most on my mind. Marinda, her harsh treatment of me, her strength, her beautiful skin and eyes and hair.

The day dragged by. Each time I felt the darkness close in on me, I lit the candle. I tried to use it sparingly. None of the day guards spoke to me. It was a very long 24 hours. I was much relieved when, at six in the evening, Huberto escorted me from the cell to Mona who was waiting for me. She hugged me. The gesture made me cry for some reason. Mona walked with me across the compound to the Hacienda Grande. She told me Marinda was expecting me. I still wore the clothes from yesterday and Huberto had put the slender handcuffs back on me.

15

THE TALE

Marinda was seated at a desk in a small office. She wore a suede vest and a necklace with feathers. She looked wild and powerful to me despite the civilized surroundings. Seeing her necklace made me think of the bracelet I had taken from her cabin. I no longer wore it, of course. I had taken it off for my interview with Natalia, and had kept it hidden ever since. Marinda looked up from her papers.

"So what did you learn?" she asked.

I stood before her in my wrinkled clothes, my hands shackled in front of me. I felt like the debajeras must feel. It was a most disagreeable feeling. I tried to shake it off. Several smart retorts occurred to me, but I knew they probably wouldn't really be so smart. "That it's not wise to go horseback riding," I said, looking as sincere as I could.

Marinda was wearing glasses. She peered at me over their rims. "Anything more general than that?"

I maintained my sincere look. "That you expect me to do as you say, not as I wish."

"Good," she said, nodding. She removed her glasses and stood. "I often go for a swim at this hour. You shall come with me today." She removed the handcuffs and handed me a woven

Indian-design sack. "Mona packed the things you'll need."

We went by motorcycle. I sat behind Marinda holding onto her waist. She was slim and muscular and I was feeling irresistibly aroused holding onto her this way as we rode through the hills to the sea.

The water was calm; the sun, low in the sky at this hour, made sparkles of light on the gently rippling surface. No one else was at the beach. Marinda spread a large towel on the sand as I looked through the bag for a swim suit. There was nothing of the kind, just a towel, a pair of jeans and a beige-colored cotton shirt. Marinda had taken off her clothes and was strolling over the sand toward the water. Her body moved gracefully, the muscles rippling smoothly under her skin as she walked. Her hair hung straight down her back almost to her shoulder blades. I watched her plunge into the water and swim swiftly and expertly out into the sea. It was a very beautiful sight. The feelings of adoration were growing rather than diminishing. I removed my clothing. The water was pleasantly cool and I glided through it, enjoying its clear blueness and salt smell. I could see shells on the sandy bottom and small stones and little fish. We swam for fifteen or twenty minutes. I loved it. Some prison, I thought. I couldn't believe I was doing this. I felt very lucky.

After we dried ourselves, Marinda put on a pair of shorts and I donned the jeans Mona had packed. We sat, bare-chested, on the large towel looking out at the passing ships and sailboats.

"The birth of Tallo Neva occurred thirty-seven years ago at a place very much like this," Marinda said, still looking out to the sea. "Her mother had a bamboo cabaña built for the birthing. The cabana opened to the sea. Tallo's mother and her dear friend, a wise midwife, came to the cabaña when it was time. It was early morning, just before dawn. At the moment of birth, the sun burst forth from the horizon and spread a rosy glow over everything. As soon as the cord was cut, the midwife carried the newborn Tallo to a small, warm pool of sea water she had prepared and floated her there and washed her, then laid her in her mother's arms. It was the only child Señora Neva ever had, the only one she ever wanted. The husband of Tallo's mother, the rich and powerful Count Eduardo Domingo Neva had wished for a son—until he saw his daughter. He took Tallo to his heart instantly, was captivated by her as was everyone else who came to know her. She was not an ordinary

151

child. Even as a baby, there was a deep wisdom in her eyes."

Marinda paused here. I waited for her to go on, relishing the sound of her voice.

"Tallo grew up along the sea. The animals in the hills and along the shore spoke to her. People knew, they sensed her specialness. Her wits were the sharpest; her mind the keenest; her passions the most powerful. Tallo was special. Her understanding was the deepest; her compassion most encompassing; her anger dreaded; her love sought and enveloping. When she was ten years old, yellow fever swept through the area. Many people died. The parents of Tallo Neva died. Tallo mourned deeply, but without bitterness. She was to come and live here with her uncle, Diego Gerrardo Neva, and his recent wife, the beautiful Natalia Mariana, who had just miscarried a son. Tallo came here to live, to this estate. It was a ten-mile trip and Tallo insisted on making it by horseback, alone. With her arrival, the Estate took on a new vitality. Tallo captured the hearts and the minds of her new family and friends quickly and completely. It became a home.

"When Tallo reached womanhood, she went abroad to study and to experience more of life. Little is known of this period. She went to Europe and then to your country, to Stanford University in California. Her destiny is here, she said when she returned. And here, she has remained. Many men have tried to court and woo Tallo. She let them touch her mind, but not her heart. She remained away from them, above them, aloof from men."

Marinda looked at me now. I was more fascinated by hearing her talk this way than by what she was saying, although the story did intrigue me. I had been aware of tingling sensations since she first began to speak. "As you do," Marinda added. She pointed far up the coast. "Do you see that peak, the second one, the one slightly higher than the rest?"

I followed her finger with my eye. "Yes. I see it."

"That's where it happened. Tallo's friend, Melina, was a woman who, in many ways, climbed mountains. That one she climbed literally, climbed it using ropes and spikes. She never came back. She was never found. Tallo still sits sometimes and stares at that mountain peak, although Melina has been gone for a half dozen years now. Tallo mourned her friend as she had mourned her parents over twenty years before. Her joy of life never left her, but there was a sad part then. Some say Melina didn't die, but climbed so high she just disappeared. Others say she climbed to the top and down the other side and went away, that Tallo was too much for her and she could not say goodbye." Marinda took a handful of sand and let it slip slowly through her fingers. "You see, Tallo has a tendency to overwhelm."

I was listening, spellbound now, and when Marinda paused, my mind filled with images of this woman about whom she spoke.

"She's not an ordinary person," Marinda said. "Her aunt is devoted to her. Tallo is really the guiding force behind the operation of this Estate—much more than Natalia. At any rate, Natalia saw in you—I'm not sure why—she saw someone who might please her beloved niece. She's always looking for ways to please Tallo. It seems to be the driving force of her life. She showers gifts on Tallo and Tallo accepts them all graciously. They please each other, those two. It pleases Natalia to think that you will please Tallo and it pleases Tallo to please her aunt. You are in the middle and you must play your part. It is my job to prepare you for it, and so I'm speaking to you as I am."

The beautiful story had suddenly taken an ugly twist.

"And I'm to please her by being her pseudo wife. It doesn't fit."

"It does to Natalia."

"I think there's more to it than that."

"Oh?"

"I met Natalia once before."

"Yes, at San Trito."

"You know."

Marinda nodded.

"I think she wants to humble me."

"Could be. Natalia is always full of plans and multiple reasons for what she does. She's a very fascinating woman herself."

"Tell me more about Melina, about the 'friendship' she and Tallo had."

"No. I've told you all I choose to about that. There are just a few more things I want to say to you today. Listen well." Marinda's expression had changed now. She looked stern, intense. "You will continue your training with me until all your actions, subtle and more overt, reflect a full understanding of the role you are to play in the drama Natalia is orchestrating. I will teach you as much as I can of how to fully please Tallo Neva. You must learn to read her well, to anticipate her wishes, even those of which she herself may not be aware. Your sole purpose in your interactions with her will be to give her joy, pleasure, amusement, comfort. This is what Natalia wishes. This is how it shall be.''

I should have had a thousand questions and objections, but, for some reason, I was speechless. The sky was orange now. The peacefulness of the early evening and the fascination with being here with Marinda and with what I'd heard, filled every part of me, dissipating my outrage, calming me. I had no wish to speak or move. We remained on the beach for a long time, until darkness reminded us to leave.

16.

THE DISCLOSURE

I spent the next week at the cabin. Tina came by each day, once or twice, but never stayed long. I painted and pounded and scraped. Marinda sent furnishings and appliances but rarely came herself. Electricians came and installed wiring. I no longer thought of escape. I worked hard and long each day and took walks and bathed in the stream and slept well, and read. Occasionally visitors came, residents who lived in other cabins in the hills, or messengers who came from the Hacienda Grande. Mona visited one day, bringing me a special meal, and Luis came by.

I learned more about Natalia's estate. Ten years ago, I was told, the first prisoners arrived. They were given a Statement of Rights and Obligations. They were not to leave the Estate, and they were to abide by the Statement of Rights and Obligations. Those were the only rules imposed by Natalia on the residents. Within the boundaries of the Estate and of the written document, they were to develop a society of their choosing. Luis brought me a copy of the Statement of Rights and Obligations.

"Parts of this look familiar," I said as I read it.

"They say Tallo wrote the original draft."

"I think she plagiarized a bit."

"I believe she drew from the constitutions and bills of rights from a number of different countries," Luis said.

"Interesting," I replied. "It looks like she might have been influenced by the Declaration of Human Rights of the U.N. Charter, too."

Luis shrugged. "Probably," he said. "We all had to study this when we were novicios, and all the freecomers must also."

"Have you brought it to me for that purpose, Luis? So I can study it?"

"Well, sure," he answered, "if you want to study it. I just thought you'd like to see it. How is it going for you, with Marinda?"

"Fine," I said.

"It's strange what happened to you."

"What do you mean?"

"Working for Marinda. repairing this cabin. Being restricted. I thought you'd go through the novicio training and then become a resident like everyone else. Natalia is unpredictable sometimes."

I smiled at Luis, fanning myself with the Statement of Rights and Obligations. "Unpredictable? I don't know about that," I said. "Inconsistent, maybe. She's an aristocrat, right? We can't really expect her fully to believe in other's rights and freedom. That's asking too much of an aristocrat."

"No, you're wrong, Kat," Luis insisted. "Look at the settlement. Look at what she's done for all those people, what she's given them a chance to do for themselves."

I nodded. "Her charity work."

"That's not fair," Luis snapped defensively.

"She has the mentality of a tyrant, Luis."

"How can you say that? She sets people free. Once they're residents, she never interferes."

"But she makes sure some of us don't become residents. She holds onto her sphere of power."

Luis looked torn. "I suppose so," he said. He took a sip of the drink I had made him. "But the good she does far outweighs the bad."

I shrugged.

When Marinda was not with me, which was most of the time, I continued to be appalled and disgusted by the role I was being made to play. When Marinda came, I felt pulled into her spell. I

156

found myself actually wishing to please her, to do whatever she wanted of me. This awareness would push me to rebel, to give her trouble. Then my rationality would mediate and tell me to cooperate enough to avoid confinement, but not so much as to lose my pride and sense of self. I was making sincere efforts to be non-sarcastic and appear agreeable and cheerfully responsive to Marinda's wishes. She continued with the numbers game, keeping track of each time I behaved in a way she deemed inappropriate for my "role". It had reached the point, now, where I was to be allowed only three slips on a given day. If I exceeded my allowance, Marinda reminded me several times, or if I behaved in what she interpreted as an intolerably rebellious way for a good wife, then I would be confined again. I certainly did not relish that prospect, even though Huberto had made it bearable for me before.

It was now late January. I had been at Natalia's Estate for 17 days. I had been in this country for six months. Solera was beginning to seem like a strange, unreal, nightmarish dream. I felt very far from the person I had become when I was there. Very very far. Occasionally, though, I still felt the pangs of guilt. In the environment at Solera, I had tapped a part of my character that I didn't understand or like. I had been pulled (or maybe I jumped) right into what Elizabeth would call the "male power mentality."

My goal was to win. I not only accepted the structure I found, but I became an avid participant in it. And I went beyond merely taking care of myself. I got right into the power. What grated on me most was the gratification I got from it, from seeing others in awe of me or intimidated by me. Some of them seemed to enjoy it. Teresa certainly did. But others clearly didn't. Was I actually cruel to anyone? I don't think so. I probably didn't make things any worse at Solera by my presence there, but I certainly hadn't made things better.

How ironic, I thought, dipping the brush into the paint can, how ironic to be in the position I am now. I spread the paint evenly over the living room wall. My just desserts?

Triste sent me a copy of my translation of Martin's letter as I had requested. I began at once to see if words like "statue", "Suga Lake", "Boweso" would fit. My assumption was that each number in the code stood for a letter.

I have ascertained where the 43-37-1-18-9-19/58-11-15-93-2-14 is located. It fits! Great!"Winged Dancer" fits. *It is in*

14-1-1-21-23-15-7. Neither "Suga Valley" nor "Suga Lake" fit. Ah, but "Marigua" did. I moved on. *The 9-6-3-4-25-31 must stand as a monument...* "statue" of course. I was enjoying this immensly. I knew it wouldn't tell me whether Petrillo was involved, but it was another step toward finding out. I went on to the next sentence...*learned of it from an old man of the 06-12-1-06-16-14-22-9.* Too many letters for "Boweso." Damn! *He 2-39-4-30-5 only the 61-1-01-23-4-19-52 tongue.* He spoke only the...damn! *Boweso* should fit. Why doesn't it? I went on. *It has been submerged by 40-7-34-7/24-15-32-2 since the earthquake of 1760 flooded the 17-3-7-62/37-9-24-14-9-10.* This was the most important sentence and each word fit exactly. *It has been submerged by* Lake Suga *since the earthquake of 1760 flooded the* Suga Valley. I wanted to tell someone. I wished Triste were here or Nettie.

I went on to the next important sentence, confident that I could fill in more blanks. *As the 78-17-2* (that's map, I'm sure)...*As the* map *indicates, the 15-4-16-10-47-12 is in a 17-1-42-3, forty feet below the present 4-8-2-40-5-5-4 of the 12-3-24-6. As the map indicates, the* statue *is in a* (something with four letters) *forty feet below the present* surface *of the* lake. All right, I thought! Progress. Wonderful progress. *When the 18-6-12 is finished and the 12-4-31-5/18-6-50-2-6/15-3-29-2-2-8 the 1-1-3-12-18-6 will become accessible.* The last word was "statue" but I couldn't figure out the others. When the what is finished? What could it be? Three letters. I was stuck. I worked on it a while longer, then put the letter aside and just thought about it.

I decided that, although this new information was great, it wasn't enough to warrant hiring another detective. But I was excited. I knew now what the treasure was, the Winged Dancer, and where, forty feet below the suface of Lake Suga. I decided I needed to get to Lake Suga somehow, that seeing the region might help. According to the map it was less than two hours away from the Estate. We had probably passed very close to it on our way here from Solera. I hoped I could manage to take a trip there.

The next afternoon I was in my bedroom at the cabin, building a platform for my bed, when Marinda arrived in the truck.

"Unload my things," she said. "I'll be staying a while."

My heart raced. Staying here, with me. I couldn't seem to prevent myself from feeling delighted.

There were two small bedrooms in the cabin, in addition to the kitchen, living room and john. Yesterday, I had finished painting the other bedroom, the one I had not claimed for myself, and had hung the bamboo blinds Marinda sent. I brought her suitcase into that room. "Shall I unpack for you?"

"Please," she said, crisply. "You needn't ask such things, just do them."

"Some people are touchy about their possessions," I said defensively, hurt by her curtness.

"I don't want you pestering Tallo with innumerable questions."

"Tallo might like questions," I said, opening the suitcase and beginning to place items in drawers.

"One!"

"Marinda," I said, coming to the doorway. "We have to discuss something." I was trying to keep the irritation out of my voice.

"We *have* to?"

"I'd *like* to," I said. "Would that be agreeable to you?"

"All right. Bring me a rum and coke. I'll be on the porch."

The porch was now comfortably furnished with several outdoor chairs, a small table and two hanging plants. I joined Marinda, placing her drink on the table.

"So, what's on your mind, sweetie?" she asked.

I settled into my chair and put my feet on the rails. "In your view of wifedom," I began, "is the wife to acknowledge having a personality and will of her own, or do you see her as simply being *responsive* to her...her husband?"

Marinda leaned back in her chair with her arms behind her head apparently thinking about my question. She seemed so self-assured and strong. I had an urge to put my arms around her and rest my head on her chest.

"In your interactions with me," she responded at last, "and with Tallo when the time comes, you, as a proper wife, are to be *actively* responsive, Kat. You must use your personality, your perceptions, insights, inferences, sensivity, empathy—use them in order to please and serve me. You are to sharpen your ability to read me, to anticipate what will be pleasing to me at a given moment, sharpen that ability to such a fine edge that you become an extension of my will. That's my view of wifedom."

"Disgusting."

"Two."

159

"I adore you," I said. I did not know I would say this. I guess I could not help but say it, for the feeling was so powerful.

"What?"

"I worship you, Marinda," I said intensely. "Don't you know? I truly do."

"Kat."

I was trembling. I had moved to the edge of my chair and was looking deeply into her eyes. "I...adore you."

"You're serious, aren't you?" Marinda said kindly but with a puzzled expression.

"I can't help it...I feel..." I reached my hand slowly towards hers which rested on the arm of her chair. With one finger, softly, just barely touching the surface of her skin, I stroked her warm, soft flesh. I felt lost, found, transcended, mesmerized.

"Are you all right, Kat?"

I looked into her eyes. "Yes," I said. "I'm very...happy." I continued looking at her. "Don't believe it when I fight you, Marinda. I want, more than anything I ever wanted, I want to please you, obey you, worship you."

"You do?" Marinda asked, then answered herself. "You do. You really do."

"You're my god."

"Oh my god."

I smiled. The spell was broken. I smiled then laughed lovingly at her, at her response. "Don't you want to be my god?" I asked teasingly.

Marinda did not reply. She seemed uncertain. This was the first time I had ever seen her uncertain and it thrilled me and made me adore her more. "The training's going well, don't you think?" I said.

Marinda did not smile. She did not speak.

"Shall I leave you alone for a while?" I asked.

"Yes," she said.

I went into the cabin. I was glowing. I was excited. I was happy. I had told her. I had said it, spoken the truth. I did adore her. I don't know how long I sat inside the cabin, but at some point, Marinda came inside and the glowing feeling intensified as I looked at her and I felt trembling excitement. She sat across from me, looking very serious and very beautiful.

"How are you feeling now?" she asked.

160

"The same," I said. "Only more so. Marinda, I want only one thing. I have only one desire, absorbing everything else in me. I wish to please you, to serve you, to adore you. Nothing more. I know it's crazy, but it's taken over. Other than that one wish, to be for you, I have none. It's whatever you want that counts. The only wish I have is to please you."

"Doesn't that frighten you, Kat?"

"No."

"Such selflessness."

"I want to lose myself in you, merge into you."

Marinda was silent again, looking first at me and then away, at the ceiling, pensively. "You actually *want* to be subjected to me. It's not just to fulfill the role we're forcing on you."

"I want it."

She nodded. "I see. Yes, I understand now." She narrowed her eyes and looked directly into mine. "You shall get what you want, Kat."

I felt intense pleasure and gratification. I moved toward Marinda, but her look stopped me. What was it? Her face was different. Harsh, maybe. I felt confused.

"You will jump when I say jump."

I looked at her quizzically.

"I will use you in any way I wish."

I moved back to my chair.

"You are my instrument, my possession."

Marinda put her leg up, resting her foot on my knee. I was feeling very uneasy.

"If, at times, I feel like being amused by you in some way, then you will serve as an object for my amusement."

Something was wrong.

"When I want you as a functional servant, that's what you'll be. You'll fetch. You'll serve."

I was very conscious of her foot on my knee.

"Sometimes I might merely want you as an invisible background object; there, available, waiting in readiness for me should I have an impulse to use you in some way. Yes, I understand now, Kat," she said. She was smiling. "On occasion, it might amuse me to observe your reaction to things, to see how you respond to stimuli I present you with." She continued smiling. "Yes, I may do that for my amusement at times," she said, "as one might play with a bug

161

or drop ink onto a piece of paper to see how it splashes. You're a potentially interesting plaything, Kat, a toy.''

Angry outrage was churning in my stomach. I clamped my teeth together.

"Oh, oh," Marinda said, observing me. "You musn't show it.'' She withdrew her foot from my leg, and she stood. "You are to please me, remember? Feel and think what you must, but don't show it." She stood over me. "Not even subtly. Show only those reactions that will please me.''

I could not respond. I didn't know what was happening. Everything had changed. The absurd feelings of adoration had evaporated.

"Sing a song!" Marinda ordered.

"What?''

She looked down at me sternly.

This isn't what I meant, I thought. She's not...it's not how...

"I'm waiting. It would please me to hear you sing a song. Now, do it, wife!''

It was all wrong. I had to shift the atmosphere. "Marinda, dear," I said, forcing lightness into my voice. "You're not showing your most adorable qualities right now.''

She placed her foot on the edge of my chair and rested her arm on her knee. "I'm getting impatient," she said. Her voice sounded threatening. "You're not pleasing me. I said sing. Now sing.''

Bitch, I thought. I took a deep breath and tried to smile. "Sure, I'll sing a song," I said. "The atmosphere here could use a change.''

Marinda sat and waited. I chose a love song, one that I had learned from Teresa. It was a happy and sad song, and as I sang I began to feel its meaning.

"Not bad," Marinda said when I finished. Then her face took on that harsh look again. "Now, I want you to kneel, Kat, here, at my feet." She pointed. "Kneel!''

I looked at her for several seconds, then I rose slowly from my chair and approached her, still looking into her eyes. I got quite close to her, looking down at her where she sat, and then I spoke, slowly, emphatically, in English. "GO TO HELL, BITCH!''

I turned my back to her and walked out of the cabin. I went down the steps of the porch, slowly, and continued walking. I heard nothing from Marinda. She did not come after me. I kept

162

walking. If I continued on this road, it would eventually take me to the compound where the mansion was and the Hacienda Grande and the beautiful garden, and if I kept going beyond that, the road would take me along the sea, past the settlement, to the border of the Estate and beyond. I was not thinking of where I was going. My pace had become rapid, not in an attempt to get anywhere quickly, but as a reflection of my angry state. I walked for a long time. I saw no one on the road; I barely saw the road or the hills or the beautiful view with the sea in the background.

By the time I got to the outskirts of the compound, I had calmed enough to begin analyzing what had happened. I knew that I had let myself reach the depth of a hidden, repressed part of myself—that wish to feel adoration, to have someone be above me, worthy of my worship. I had contacted it, that fear-evoking, but enticing, desire. I felt it for Marinda. Adoration. Oh, mother, I heard you. Message denied but message received. I had finally acknowledged it fully to myself. I'd been fighting it. I guess I've been fighting it for years. And then I stopped fighting. I accepted it. And I expressed it. To her. It felt wonderful. Oh, yes, until...Marinda, you changed. It got ugly. No! I shook my head vigorously.

What now, I thought, as I continued walking. Because it turns ugly to me does not mean that I can stop it. I have no choice. I had known from the start that there would be scant payoff for refusing to conform to Natalia's script. Prideful balking would not make her change her plan, that was clear to me all along. I had no doubt that they had the power to control my behavior, and for me to make it hard on them would only make it hard on me. What happened then, back there in the cabin, I wondered, as I continued my trek, getting closer and closer to the compound; what made me have to fight it despite that wish inside of me and despite the inevitable aversive consequences of refusing Marinda's demand? I wasn't sure, but I knew I would not be able to play it all her way. I would kneel to no one! Ever! The bitch!

I walked past the Hacienda Grande toward the red building where the cells were. Several people watched me. I sat under a tree and waited for them to lock me in the black cell.

"She called from Jorge's cabin," Huberto said. "They would have found you if you hadn't come yourself."

"I know," I said.

"Are you ready?"

I used the candle sparingly again. The darkness was suffocating. I tried to talk myself into going along with Marinda, into overcoming my resistance to the way she played the game. I tried to rekindle the feeling of adoration and the wish to do whatever she might ask. It was a battle. You cannot win, Kat, I told myself, but something in me would not accept it.

This time the twenty-four hours seemed much much longer and when Huberto finally set me free, I felt more gratitude at being released than anger at having been confined. I was taken directly to Marinda.

"What did you learn?" she demanded. She looked so strong, alive, beautiful.

"I hate the darkness," I said, shaking my head. "I really do." I stood before her in shackles.

"Kneel!" she said.

She had that look and tone again. God, how I hate the darkness. But I could not do what she demanded. "I can't," I said softly. Then raising my chin. "Marinda, I won't! It's not...me."

"Only part of you," she said not unkindly. "If it came easily, it would mean nothing, don't you think?"

"I used to do a lot of horseback riding," I said. "I once watched them breaking a new one. It had been wild. They had it shipped from somewhere in the west. It was very ugly to watch what they did to it, and how it finally calmed and took the saddle and did their bidding. It felt wrong."

Marinda nodded. She was sitting in a large leather chair wearing jeans and riding boots. "There's a similarity," she said, "but it's not an exact analogy. The meaning of it exists in your thoughts, your consciousness; the horse knew none of that. You *will* kneel when I tell you to. You will come to do whatever I tell you to. It will be now or it will be later, but it will be."

I thought of the darkness. I thought of myself kneeling at the feet of another. Such conflicts should not be. It wasn't right. Nor were jails. Or poverty, or violence, or oppression, for that matter, I thought. Do it, Kat. Get it over with.

But I could not move.

This time, the twenty-four hours seemed like weeks. The candle was gone. The matches were gone. Huberto said he could bring no more. Black is so black. Being alone in the blackness does something to the mind.

"Kneel, Kat!"

I tried to argue. "Surely, that's not what Tallo wants," I said. "She's above that. Why not..."

"Kneel, Kat!"

My legs were trembling.

Marinda waited.

I had already told myself, of course, I will. It's no big deal. It's symbolic. Change the meaning of the symbol. You're being forced. It means nothing. My legs would not bend.

Huberto spoke very little to me this time. It was during the last hours in the darkness that I reached the resolution, and when the time came, I walked out smiling, a bounce in my step. I was brought into the room where Marinda sat. Still smiling broadly, I went immediately to my knees. "You were right," I said, laughing. "Might is right!" I knelt cheerfully in front of her.

"Good," she said.

I looked up at her still smiling. "What else would please you, Marinda. You deserve nothing but the best."

"Don't!" Marinda ordered. "Empty flattering words are not needed. No more of that. You have a long way to go, Kat Rogan. You are very slow at catching on, even though you profess to wish for nothing more. Stop grinning. It annoys me."

I stopped. I remained on my knees at her feet, trying to transcend the situation, to remove myself, to remove any meaning from it save the fact that I had no choice and so my acts had no moral meaning. You could choose to die, I rebutted myself. Or live forever alone in darkness. That's no choice, I replied.

"There will be a fiesta tonight," Marinda said. "You will accompany me and attend me. You will focus all your energy on pleasing me. You will do as I say, instantly. And if I have the trumpets play a loud introduction, and if I then announce, as all eyes fix on us, that you will kneel before me and kiss my foot, what will you do?"

"I will do as you say," I said.

17.

THE SEDUCTION

Mona paraded an armload of dresses before me. We were in the sun room of the Hacienda Grande. "Choose," she said, "for the fiesta. This one, I think, would be wonderful for you. You are so tall." She held up a light-weight printed cotton.

"I'll wear pants," I said. I noticed Mona's look of disappointment. "But maybe a more festive blouse," I added. "Are there any?"

"Gringo-girl," she said, teasingly. "Always you have to wear the pants, eh?"

There was a ten-piece band and strings of colored lanterns between trees and tables of food and drink. People kept pouring in, everyone looking bright and seeming in high spirits. I stood next to Marinda, "attending" her. People were already drunk and dancing gaily. Natalia sat in a large cushioned chair in the center of it all, talking vivaciously, laughing. There was a man at her side, a handsome man, her Federico, no doubt. There were children, too, and games being played. Suddenly, I saw a woman, a very striking woman, coming out from the mansion and walking onto the lawn. I had never seen her before. She seemed to stand out from the others, and drew my eye magnetically. She wore a cool blue silk blouse and black pants. People converged on her immediately and I watched her talk pleasantly with them and sometimes touch their hands or shoulders. Marinda must have noticed the admiring fascination in my gaze as I watched the woman's graceful movements.

"You are not to look at her," Marinda said cooly.

I looked away. I wondered who she was. Chuckling to myself, I also wondered whether Marinda could be jealous. The music had stopped momentarily, and now began again. A samba.

"I want to see you dance."

I rose and looked around among the crowd. I was searching for Luis, but then I saw Huberto, holding a slice of mango in each hand, looking very happy.

"Will you dance with me, Huberto?" I asked.

I could see Marinda watching. I felt somewhat clumsy, but we melted with the crowd, moving to the endless beat. Occasionally, I caught glimpses of the mysterious woman. I saw, in the eyes of those who looked at her, a reflection of my own feelings. Was I imagining it?

I did not get nearer than twenty feet to that woman the whole evening, until the end. Most of the time Marinda had me waiting on her, "attending" to her. She listened while I spoke of life in Chicago to some of the guests. She had told me to amuse them with stories. I did my best and they seemed satisfied. I told some anecdotes, embellishing the stories and making some of them up entirely. "And the traffice jam was so bad on the Dan Ryan Expressway that time that for two days the people stayed, camping there. They played cards and helicopters dropped them fried chicken and they did line dances between the cars. After that it was decided that only blue or white cars could use that road on even-numbered days, and the others on odd-numbered days. There have been no traffic jams since."

It was late and the crowd thinning when Marinda had the trumpets blow and walked with me up onto the band stage. So, she really intends to do it, I thought. The pig.

"For you who have not yet met her," Marinda announced, "I want to introduce our latest novicia, Señorita Kat Rogan."

The people applauded. I felt very uncomfortable.

Marinda had the microphone. "Tonight," she continued, "Señorita Rogan wants to make an offering, to present a token of her esteem and admiration to our own Tallo de Carrizosa Neva."

Oh no, I thought. What is she doing to me? I looked into the crowd of hundreds of faces. On hearing Marinda's announcement, many of them had turned to look at the woman leaning against a tree. It was the woman in the midnight blue blouse. She was looking directly at me. So, that was Tallo.

"Sing the same song," Marinda whispered to me. She handed me the microphone, then spoke to the band leader.

The music began. And soon, I did too. I had sung in choruses, but never a solo, although I was told my voice was pleasant. Looking at Tallo the whole time, I sang the soft sweet strains of the little love song Teresa had sung so many times in that other world.

When I finished and the listeners were applauding, Marinda handed me a flower. "Bring this to her, then return to me. I'll be over there."

Everyone watched as I walked from the stage, past the clusters of people, around a row of tables to where Tallo stood. I stood before her, mesmerized by her black, smiling eyes. I could not stop staring and some time must have passed until I remembered my mission and slowly offered her the white rose.

She took it, smiling, and the applause that followed nearly drowned out the sound of my pounding heart. Somehow I pulled myself from Tallo de Carrizosa Neva and returned to Marinda.

That night I dreamed of her, of Tallo. I gave her a rose. We were alone, and she took it and took my hand as well and kissed me sweetly, deeply on the lips. It was one of my better dreams.

I had spent the night at the Hacienda Grande. In the morning, Marinda took me back to the cabin. We went by motorcycle. Again, the contact with her body as I held onto her waist excited me and my head was filled with fantasies as we tore through the hills. She liked to go fast and I found myself clinging tightly to her around curves. At one point I leaned my cheek against her back, and it was then that the feeling came back full force. Since the kneeling episode, I had not experienced that sense of awe and adulation, but as I sat with my body pressed to hers, I could not prevent its return.

Marinda had brought some work to do. She lay the blueprints out on her drafting table and was soon absorbed. For a long time, I just watched her from across the room. Her movements were brisk and sure. As she frowned in concentration over her work, she looked so wise. Brilliant, I thought. Brilliant and beautiful and majestic and imposing and fantastic. I wanted very badly to kiss her neck. Instead, I brought a cup of coffee for her and her cigarettes and an ashtray and set them on the table next to where she was working. I watched her some more, watched her adoringly, until my body was so stimulated that I had to stop.

I went into the bathroom, thinking that I would finish painting the trim on the cabinets. I did that but only after I did myself. The fantasies were all Marinda. When I finished panting and painting, Marinda was still poring over diagrams. She had drunk the coffee. I sat not far from her, reading, and then I made us some lunch. She worked while she ate, barely speaking. At one point, she had me go through her materials to find blueprint number 403. I was pleased to be of help. I felt strangely honored. It went all day like this. I took several brief walks, read some more, visited with some residents who were horseback riding in the area, and fantasized about Marinda.

At last, as it began to grow dark, she put her work aside.

"Will you spend the night?" I asked.

"Yes," she said. I had fixed her a drink and built a small fire in the fireplace. Marinda was sitting on the sofa in front of it.

"I still adore you," I said. I sat on a footstool to her side.

"I know."

"I want to please you."

"Yes."

I kept looking at her, my longing and adulation probably obvious. The fire was crackling and bringing just the right amount of additional warmth to the room. It was quite dark now. We had not turned on any lights. "I want to please you," I repeated.

She looked at me from the corners of her eyes. "What do you have in mind?" she asked.

"Making love to you." I held my breath.

She looked at me in a way she had not done before. Her eyes went from my face, downward, along my neck, and to my breasts. I felt the electric chills. "Take your shirt off," she said.

I'm sure I blushed. I felt heat pouring through my body. I began undoing the buttons, unable to look at Marinda, feeling a shyness I had never experienced before. She watched each move I made, her eyes burning through me. I put the shirt aside. She took hold of my belt and pulled me demandingly to the sofa. We were sitting side by side then. I could feel the warmth of her solid leg muscles against my jeans. I felt vulnerable. I wanted to reach for her but I could not move. She did the reaching. She touched my face, one cheek, softly, then moved her hand downward along my jaw to my neck. I felt delightful, tingling sensations everywhere her fingers went and further. I was aware of wetness between my legs. Suddenly, she shifted positions and in a flash I found myself lying flat on the sofa, on my back, Marinda's powerful body suspended over mine. She wrapped her hand around my breast, gently at first, her skillful fingers playing with my nipple. Then she increased the pressure, squeezing just enough to make me moan in pleasure. In the middle of my sighs, her mouth covered mine, stopping the sounds, starting the hot flying magic of my body on fire. It couldn't have been just a kiss for I reacted as if the earth had stopped. I was floating, flying, tingling everywhere, melting into her, merging, transported some place where I had never been.

We made love in front of the fire in the little cabin in the hills of Marigua, South America. It was very passionate and very mutual. My mission had been to give pleasure to Marinda. She did, indeed, seem very pleased, but I have no words to describe the joy and ecstasy I felt from her tender strokes, and her strong insistent caresses and the total blending of all my body with all of hers. For a long time afterwards she sat on the rug, before the fire, leaning on the sofa, and I lay with my reeling head resting on her smooth, warm, naked lap.

"I've never felt this before," I said at last, stroking her thigh. "It's like you're all that is, all that matters. You overshadow everything else that ever was or ever will be."

She stroked my head. "Yes," she said. "That's good. That's how it should be."

We stayed there for a while longer, talking. I asked Marinda about the work she did and she spoke some about oil, about the production of crude at the Estate, about wildcatters she knew and about some of the production problems she worked on. She spoke of the Estate's international sales and of Tallo's crucial role in that. "You seemed rather impressed with Tallo, last night," she said.

I didn't reply right away. I did not want to speak of Tallo or think of her. She was a very attractive woman but an ugly reminder to me of why I was with Marinda and what the future held. I dreaded the day when the next step of Natalia Neva's plan for me

170

would be taken and I would have to part from Marinda.

"I want to be with you always," I said, at last.

Marinda laughed. "You're feeling devoted to me, aren't you," she said.

"Yes," I replied, and I surely was, but some old voice in me was crying to be heard. *Don't attach,* it said. *Not to anyone. You will consume or be consumed. You will overpower her and make her disappear. Or, you will melt into the irresistible power you give her over you and be gone yourself.* That's what was happening with Marinda, I thought. But, I did not want to think about it. No more than I had wanted to think about Teresa and how I consumed her. I had been Teresa's Marinda, my mother's husband; I was now my mother, Marinda's wife. Suddenly, I felt so uncomfortable I had to move. I jumped up and grabbed my clothes. Marinda watched me as I dressed and I couldn't help but feel the pleasure as her possessive eyes took me in.

18.

THE LETTER

The next day, I went with Marinda to the oil fields. Her office was in one of the modern adobe buildings there. Neither of us spoke of our lovemaking of the night before. The climactic evening had ended pleasantly and quietly. I had prepared a dinner for us and then Marinda read for a while and went off to her bedroom. I was awakened early in the morning by the roar of her motorcycle. She was gone for several hours and when she returned she told me to get ready, that we were going to the oil fields. She said she could use me to help with some correspondence.

I hated to type, and yet, at first, I did not mind at all doing the typing for Marinda. She introduced me to Anna, the administrative assistant, who would tell me what needed to be done, and then she disappeared. I did not see her again that day. Anna drove me to the cabin when the work day ended, and picked me up again the next morning. Marinda had not come at all. I typed and I typed, working in a small office by myself. Occasionally, I chatted with the other office help and once or twice I thought about how determined I had always been never to be a clerical worker. I guess it was a mistake to learn to type. No, it was a mistake to come to Marigua, I thought.

I was missing Marinda terribly, thinking of her constantly. At one point in the afternoon, as I was typing a letter to Gulf Oil, I looked up and saw her standing there. The impact was instantaneous and powerful. I'm sure I flushed. I felt the effect of her presence vibrating through my whole body.

"You got a letter from Federico Jimanos," she said, tossing it onto my desk.

I suppose she expected me to open it, but I couldn't move. I tried to force myself to gain a modicum of composure. "Thanks," I said, trying to sound casual. With thick fingers, I fumbled with the envelope, eventually managing to open it. "He wants to come and discuss my legal case with me," I said after reading the short note.

Marinda was sitting on the corner of a desk across from mine. The cloth of her pants stretched across her hips and thighs in a way that made my head foggy and my heart pound. I'd like to touch you, I thought.

"I'd like to see him," I said. "Maybe he can be of some help."

"Help? What kind of help?"

"Getting me released."

"Aw," Marinda crooned, pursing her sensuous lips into a sardonic smile. "You don't like it here."

I couldn't quite read what she was doing, how she meant what she said. As much as I was under Marinda's spell, I had not and never would lose touch with my wish for freedom. "I'd rather be free," I said.

Marinda laughed. "The time may come," she replied, twirling a pencil in her long, strong fingers, "when, if you had the choice, you would choose to stay."

"After a lobotomy," I retorted sharply.

Marinda's dark eyes glared angrily at me. I could not be unaffected by this. Part of me wanted to go to her arms, hold her and be held by her, assuage her, do or say whatever would please her, for I wanted to please her. Part of me wanted to tell her to go fuck herself. These were the hard moments, when the conflict was highlighted painfully.

"You've been doing so well, Kat. I don't like this backsliding."

I did not reply.

"Hey!" she rebuked. "You'd better be careful." She strode over to where I sat. "You cannot afford to let foolish dreams of autonomy distract you." She stood directly in front of me, looking

173

down at me. "Need I remind you that you are to subjugate your will to mine at all times."

I started to turn my head away.

"Listen to me!"

I looked back into her beautiful fierce eyes.

"Subjugate your will to mine. That means that you do not have the freedom to make such impudent cracks to me. Since you seem to need it, I will explain." She rested one hand on the edge of my desk as she spoke. "In your role, with me, you are not permitted to express yourself freely. You must gauge things better, Kat. Use that perceptiveness of yours. Anticipate that such remarks will annoy me and then censor them."

I hated what I was hearing. I hated these words coming from Marinda. I hated the lecturing tone and I hated the meaning of what she said. It made me want to smack her arrogant face. It smothered the feelings of adoration. Hearing the words was too obvious a reminder of the obscene basis of our relationship. The ecstatic joy of making love with Marinda, the feelings of devotion and awe shifted now.

"All right," I said, matter-of-factly. I wanted her to leave. Her presence was no more than an irritant and an ugly reminder to me now.

"That's not good enough," she said. "The lobotomy remark was 'one', your present attitude is 'two'. One more and you're gone."

Pig! Bitch! Scummy tyrant! I thought. "What would please you now, Marinda?" I asked, trying to smile seductively and keep my tone soft.

Marinda scrutinized me momentarily, then smiled herself. "How's the typing coming?"

"Fine," I said, still smiling. "This is quite an operation Neva Oil Company has."

"Yes." She walked a few paces away, then turned back to me. "I'm concerned about you, Kat," she said. "Sometimes you seem to be so trainable and other times..." She took a few steps toward me and pointed to the floor. "Kneel!" she said.

Oh shit! Not again. I thought that game was over. Do what she says, my rational judgment told me. Accept that she has the power to force you. I tried to make myself move to obey. My muscles would not respond.

"You have ten seconds," she said.

"Marinda," I said softly. "Wasn't it better the other night, at the cabin. Let me adore you in my way."

Marinda threw back her head in laughter. "No, no, no," she said. "Poor child, you have it all wrong. It is to be *my* way, of course. How quickly you forget and lose touch with what wifedom means. You have two more seconds."

I knelt. I hated her. I had to hate her or hate myself.

"Much better," she said. "OK, get up, wench." She laughed. "*Wench.* I like that." She pulled a chair out from behind a desk and sat backwards in it. "Massage my back," she said. "Wench."

I went to her and stroked her strong, soft shoulders, gently kneading the flesh. As much as I fought it, the excitement and pleasure I got from this contact overcame me. The disdain disappeared. "I adore you," I said, caressing her neck. I continued the massage until my feelings rose to such a peak that I wasn't sure I could restrain myself from falling into her arms. If she wanted me to kneel now, I would feel no struggle at all.

At this point, Marinda rose. "You may contact Jimanos, if you wish," she said, walking to the door. "He can come and talk with you."

I sat motionless, numb, after Marinda left. I could not type. I could barely think. Feelings overpowered me. Adulation, disdain. Worship, contempt. Love, hate. Self-abnegation, self-respect. Mother, father. Submission, domination. Giving, taking. Feeling, thought. The confusion made my head whirl. Only when Anna came into the office was I able to pull out of it.

I looked again at the letter from Federico Jimanos. I was pleased that no one opened my mail here. At Solera, all the mail of the debajeras was opened, although not, of course, of the clanswomen. In his note, Jimanos said that he had heard of my case and was willing to offer his skills in helping me to get a new trial. He explained that when he visited a couple of weeks ago, he had said he was an acquaintance of mine, thinking that it would increase his chances of being permitted a visit with me. He said he would not charge for his services unless he was successful, and requested a meeting. What skills, I wondered? I was puzzled and curious and eager to meet with him. I wrote him immediately to arrange the visit.

19.

THE VISITOR

Over the next few days, I saw Marinda infrequently. I continued to type for her during the day, and stay at the cabin at night. Twice I visited people at the compound and one evening Luis and Mona came to the cabin and we had a pleasant talk in front of the fire.

I expected Jimanos the next day. He had called as soon as he'd received my letter. I had been thinking a great deal about Martin Sundance, wishing desparately that I could find a way to translate the rest of the number code and learn the name of the partner. I still thought it was Peter Petrillo, even more than before, now that I had confirmed that each number stood for a letter. If I could translate the remaining coded words, then I would also learn exactly where the statue was located and how it was going to become "accessible". I hoped it wasn't too late. Maybe someone, the person who stole the folder from Triste, perhaps, had already retrieved the statue and was long gone.

I was sitting in the kitchen at the cabin, thinking of all this when I heard an engine outside. I went to the window. Seeing one headlight, I felt excited. Marinda, on the motorcycle, I hoped.

"Put on some other shirt," she said angrily, as she stomped into the cabin.

"Ooh, bad mood," I said, trying to sooth her. "What's wrong, Marinda?"

She dropped herself heavily into a chair. "Change that atrocious shirt," she snarled, "and get me a drink."

I realized then that she obviously had already had quite a bit to drink. I did what she said.

"Did something happen?" I asked, taking a chair across from her.

"Don't ask questions," she hissed.

I sat back quietly, looking at her. She looked very miserable.

"What are you looking at?" she growled.

"Why don't you talk about it, Marinda. Maybe it would help."

"Get on your knees, cunt." Her words were slurred. "Down here, where you belong. At my feet. Move!"

I had never seen her like this before. Her viciousness made her seem weak. A mean drunk, I thought. But, it was more than that. She had gotten quite loaded at the fiesta last week and was nothing like this. She was clearly in pain about something. I decided to try again. "What is it, Marinda? Why the awful mood?"

"Shut up!" She grabbed hold of my arm. "I think I'll fuck you," she said, through clenched teeth.

My urge was to jump up and flatten her with one well-directed karate chop. I knew I could do it quite easily. Instead, I spoke to her. "Marinda, you're drunk and upset. Why don't you let me help you to bed. Sleep would be the best thing for you right now."

She was still holding onto my wrist. She downed her drink and pulled herself to her feet, pulling me along with her. I took hold of her hand and twisted it until her fingers loosened on my wrist. "Come on," I said.

She let me lead her to her bedroom and she collapsed on the bed. I removed her boots. I think she was already asleep when I left the room.

Marinda slept late the next morning and I was careful not to disturb her. I had coffee ready when she finally emerged from her room. She looked a little gray, but very beautiful anyhow.

She accepted the coffee gratefully and related to me in a soft-spoken, pleasant, almost sweet way. Again, I felt quite drawn to her although I could not erase the memory of her nasty behavior last night.

She gave me a ride to the Hacienda Grande where I was to meet

177

with Jimanos.

Federico Jimanos was just as Tina had described him, although even taller and thinner than I'd expected. He reminded me of a crane. We met privately in a bright, warm room. He shook my hand formally.

"My business is insurance," he said, handing me a card, "but that is not connected with my interest in your case."

We both sat.

"I learned of you in a very strange way. Let me explain." He lit a long, thin cigar, then continued. "It was at a restaurant last July. I was not trying to do so, but, inadvertantly, I overheard a conversation between two gentlemen. I don't know who they were, but subsequently, I have inferred that one of them was your attorney. I heard them talking about the Rogan murder case that was coming to trial. One man was showing the other some papers and asking if he thought he could break the code. It's at that point that I began listening intentionally. I'm interested in codes, you see. In the army I was with the Intelligence Division. The second man scrutinized the documents and said he would work on them, but doubted that he'd be able to be of much help. The first man said that if the letter could be translated, Señorita Rogan might get off. That was all they said about it. Then they talked of other things."

Jimanos paused here and drew on his cigar. I was listening with great interest.

"I didn't give it much thought again until I read of the conviction of Kat Rogan for murder. Nothing was mentioned about a letter or about a code and that puzzled me, but I decided that it probably meant no one was able to decipher the code. Am I correct?"

"Yes," I said.

He nodded. "I considered trying to find out who the attorney was and offering my services," Jimanos said. "I'm quite proficient with many types of codes. I regret to say that I did not act on my altruistic impulse, however, and, in fact, soon forgot about the whole thing."

His story seemed plausible so far, but instead of feeling excited about the possibilities, I was feeling suspicious for some reason. I waited for him to go on.

"Then, several weeks ago, I had dinner with an old army friend. He, too, had been with the Intelligence Division. In the course of our conversation, I recalled the incident involving you. I discussed it with him and he encouraged me to pursue it saying it would be interesting for me and possibly very helpful to you. I remembered your name, possibly because it was such an unusual one, because you are North American. I decided that I would pursue it and, on my friend's suggestion, I ascertained where you were imprisoned and drove out here. They would not allow me to see you at that time but said I could write. You know the rest."

"Well, I'm very appreciative that you would go to all that trouble," I said.

"Would you like me to make an attempt to crack the code?" he asked.

"Yes, of course, but there's a problem." I wasn't sure of the source of my skepticism about this man, but I felt the need to be cautious.

"What's that?"

"It's been stolen. The letter is gone."

"You don't say."

I didn't think he really seemed surprised. "I'm afraid so."

"How did that happen?"

"Someone broke into my lawyer's office and took it."

"I see, and there's no copy?"

"Copy?" I was stalling for time, trying to figure his angle. Was his story true? If not, who was he? What did he want? Could he be Manuel Paz trying to make sure that there's no copy of the letter and map, no way to prove...I was trying to remember if Fanta had given me a description of Paz. I looked at Jimanos. Tall, thin, rimless glasses, balding. Suddenly I was transported back to the scene of Martin Sundance's death. Why didn't I think of this before? The woman in the blue and white dress, the witness who had seen someone watching Sundance stagger down the alley—tall, very tall, thin, rimless glasses, she had said. I felt shaky now. Excited. Frightened. Was this Martin Sundance's killer sitting across from me delicately tapping the ash off his sweet-smelling cigar? "I wish my lawyer had thought to make a copy," I said. I watched his face closely. It appeared to me that he looked more relieved than disappointed at my response.

"Such a shame," he said. "Then there is nothing I can do." With dainty little taps he extinguished his cigar, obviously preparing to leave. I couldn't let him get away.

179

"It is very likely that my other attorney has a copy, though," I said brightly.

"Your other attorney?" He looked distressed now.

"Yes, in Chicago, in the States. She worked on the case, too. She had copies of all the documents, probably the letter as well."

"I see," Jimanos said. "Excellent. Then we're in luck." His voice sounded very flat.

"Very likely," I said. "You really think you could decipher the code?"

"It's quite possible," Jimanos answered.

"I'll have her send it to me."

"Yes, and may I make a suggestion." He leaned his angular body forward. "Since the letter was stolen from one attorney, there is the risk that the same thing may happen with the other attorney. Of course, since I have no idea of what is involved in all this, I can't say whether the burglar would reach all the way to Chicago, but it may be a risk. I would advise that you make sure your Chicago attorney does not make another copy of the documents, but simply sends them on."

"That makes sense," I said. "We wouldn't want them getting into the wrongs hands."

"Exactly. If you determine that she does indeed have a copy of them, you could have her send them directly to me," Jimanos suggested. "That would save time."

A modest proposal, I thought. "Yes," I said, "all right. No, wait. She's very cautious. You know how lawyers are. I think she'd feel better sending them to me." I looked at the card Jimanos had given me. It had his name, "San Trito Insurance Company", a phone number and the same address where I had written him earlier. "I'll contact you as soon as I hear."

"Do that," he said. "Yes, do. I'll be waiting to hear from you."

I walked him outside and stood on the porch as he drove off. I memorized the number on his license plate. Mona saw me on the porch and began walking my way, but I didn't want to talk with anyone. I had to think. I went back inside, to the same room where Jimanos and I had been, and closed the door.

That man killed Martin Sundance, I kept thinking. How can I prove it? I wanted to get to the maid, Juanita, to have her hypnotized. I had to contact Fanta, to find out what Manuel Paz looks like. I had to check out Jimanos. Is he Paz? If not, is his name really Federico Jimanos? I doubt it. No, of course not. Is there a San Trito Insurance Company? I wanted to call the number right now. I wanted to go to Postero, to the address on his card, 47 Montenegro Street. I looked at the goddam shackles hanging on my wrists. Would Fanta help? Could I trust the bastard? I mean, my god, he even suspects me. What a jerk! I'll hire another detective. I should contact Nettie and warn her. Maybe Jimanos will go to Chicago to get the letter he thinks she has. He might be heading to the airport right now. No, he wouldn't do that. Why should he? He thinks I'm getting it for him. He'll wait. Marinda. I need to find Marinda, to ask her to help, to get her at least to allow me to make the phone calls. I wonder how her hangover is.

I was supposed to do some more typing that day anyway and I hoped that Marinda would be at the office and that I could talk with her. I had to wait nearly an hour before anyone was free to give me a ride to the oil field offices. I was being eaten with impatience. When I finally arrived, Anna told me Marinda was in a meeting. She gave me a pile of typing that needed to be done. I took it to the office where I worked and threw it on the desk. There was no way that I could type in the state I was in. I knew that even if Jimanos was the murderer and even if I could prove it, there was no guarantee that Petrillo was involved. It may have no effect on my case at all, I thought, and yet I felt driven to pursue it. If I could get Jimanos, I would get my freedom. I knew it. I just knew it.

There were phones all over the place. I was not permitted to use them. Fuck their permission! I left my office and walked down the corridor. There were many offices, some private ones. I kept walking until I came to a deserted one with an open door. The phone sat on the desk beckoning me.

"Yes. Cornelio Fanta. F-a-n-t-a," I said to the operator. "Thank you." I wrote down the number and was about to make the call when the door opened.

Marinda stared coldly at me.

I did not replace the phone, but returned her stare calmly. "Something new has developed on my legal case," I said. "I have to make some calls."

"Put the phone down."

Feelings of contempt were not strangers to me, but impotent rage was. That was what I was feeling now. Marinda, who at times was god to me, was now nothing but an intensely frustrating obstacle.

181

Play it smart, I told myself. "I tried to find you," I said. "To check it out with you. You were busy." I still held the phone. Marinda stared at me until I replaced the receiver in its cradle.

"Come with me," she said.

I followed her back to my office. She closed the door. I sat in the chair next to my desk. She stood near me, leaning on the other desk, her arms folded in front of her.

"You have a priority problem," she said.

I waited, amazed that, under these circumstances, I could still be struck with how beautiful she was and how strong and powerful she seemed.

"Your thoughts are on your elusive freedom instead of on devoting yourself to your task of unquestioning obedience and service to me."

"This has nothing to do with you," I said.

Marinda shook her head. "As my wife, temporary though that may be, there is no business you have that warrants independent action on your part."

Her talk was hard, but I realized that her eyes were full of the same pain I had seen the night before. I was feeling confused and very frustrated.

"As my strong, protective husband, or whatever the hell you're supposed to be," I said, "I would think you'd want to use your immense, superior power to assist your poor bumbling wife."

"That sarcasm again."

I did not respond.

"Stand up!" Marinda ordered.

I stood.

"My, my. Look at that," she said, gesturing toward her foot. "There's dust on my boot." She lifted her foot up onto a chair. "Take care of it."

The behavior was familiar, but her heart did not seem to be in it. Play the game, I told myself. I got a cloth from the closet and went to her. As I bent to wipe her boots, the closeness of her body to mine filled me with the irresistible sensations that I knew should not be there. I looked up at her face and I knew she read my look.

She smiled. "That's better," she said. "You do know your place. What are you feeling now? Tell me. Tell the truth."

"I'm feeling devoted to you," I said.

"Good." She put her foot down. "I want you to type a letter

now. I want you to type a letter explaining how right it is that you are my devoted wife.''

I pulled the chair back behind the desk and placed a sheet of paper in the typewriter. I looked at her, feeling lost in her spell.

"Type," she said. "I'll be back soon."

After she left, the aura gradually faded. I felt my composure and sense of self beginning to come back. Such a game, I thought. I began to type.

Dear Marinda,

Might is right when it comes to wivery. It is right that I am your wife because you have a kind of power that I do not. You have been given the power to make me behave as a lowly, servile, docile wife. Your power comes from the situation as does my powerlessness. In a society where human...

I had gotten only this far when Marinda returned. "Let me see," she demanded, pulling the paper from the typewriter. She read quickly, shaking her head. "No, no, no," she said. "Sometimes you're so slow, so resistant to the training. Start over, now. Do it right and bring it to me at my place tonight. Nine o'clock." She started to leave, then turned back abruptly. Taking my wrist, she pulled me to my feet and kissed me fiercely, hard, deep, and passionately. Then, she turned and walked out of the room.

I gasped for air as I slid back down into my chair. My whole body was quivering. I felt weak. I sat motionless for a long time.

Gradually, I was able to focus my thoughts. Flashes of Marinda's different interactions with me flitted through my head. What was she about? I wasn't sure, but could it be that Marinda was becoming less interested in preparing me for my role with Tallo than she was in the process itself, her own contact with me and domination of me? I sat for a long time thinking about it.

Finally, I made myself shift gears. I began typing the letter. I wanted to get it out of the way so I could plan my strategy regarding Jimanos.

Dear Marinda, I typed. What could I say that would satisfy her? *It is right that I am your devoted wife because it pleases those who should be pleased.* That's a good start. *While it is an unusual role for me to be playing, what is important is not how it feels to me, but how well I can serve you and, ultimately, Tallo. Your wishing it to be makes it right that it should be. Whether I feel honored or degraded and disgusted about being in such a role is absolutely*

183

irrelevant. My job is to perform as you wish, as a finely turned instrument responsive to each whim you have. That is what being a wife means and if you say it is right, it is. Sincerely,

I signed the letter. I didn't accomplish much else the rest of the time I was at the office. I went over and over what I wanted to do, what needed to be done about Jimanos, but my hands were tied. How true, literally and figuratively. I was sick of having those stupid handcuffs on my wrists all the time. They didn't really interfere with my movements, and they weren't uncomfortable, but I was sick of them. Once, I had asked Marinda whether they were really necessary. She had said "yes", and that was that.

I ate that evening at the Hacienda Grande with Mona, Paulo, Luis and some of the other 'compound' personnel. A pleasant comraderie had developed among us. It was so different from Solera. So nostalgic, reminiscent of how life used to be at home. I'd been thinking of home more and more lately. More than I ever did at Solera. I missed Lana. I missed Elizabeth. I missed Judi and Sharon and Dana and Joel. I missed Nettie. I missed hearing women's music and going to movies and bars and plays and having dinner parties and "intellectual" conversations and mediating people's conflicts and watching TV and my stereo and Jean, my sister, who was married and living in Atlanta with her dippy husband and four kids. I missed my apartment and my bicycle and my ability to do what I wanted when I wanted and go where I wanted and be a free human being and not have to be a bossy Section Leader or a devoted wife. I missed America. God, was I saying that? I missed the English language. I missed the crowded streets of Chicago, the lake front, the zoo. Once I started, I couldn't seem to stop. I missed spaghetti and chocolate chip cookies and tuna fish sandwiches. I missed the arguments about what a feminist is and what a lesbian is and can you be one and not the other. You definitely can, I thought. I wanted to be with Jude or Rit and argue this point with them. "There's no such thing as a genital lesbian." "Says who?" "Eh, your mother uses feminine hygiene deodorant spray." I laughed. Where was this coming from, I thought? No one I know ever said such things. Have I forgotten what life was like there and then? It's here. It's now. It's 8:30 and I have to be at Marinda's in a half hour. Marinda, can one be a lesbian and not a feminist? That would be worth a laugh.

I got dressed. As usual, when I knew I would soon see Marinda, I began to feel excited. I recalled our love-making. I recalled the kiss in the office. I wondered what tonight would bring.

20.

THE SHIFT

Marinda read the letter. She laughed. There was something different in her laugh this time. An edge of sadness, I wondered?

"A good job, Kat," she said. The sadness or sorrow or whatever, was still there in her eyes even though she was smiling. "In fact, an excellent job. You communicated your grasp of the situation and you also managed to slip in your range of feelings, didn't you? I quote..." She read from the letter "'Whether I feel honored or degraded and disgusted...' That's how you do feel, isn't it?"

We were in Marinda's living room. Several candles and a small, dim, rose-hued lamp provided the illumination. Marinda sat on a soft, cushioned chair. I was on a similar one across from her. I didn't answer her question and Marinda did not seem to expect me to.

"You were here once before," she said. "In this house."

I nodded.

"Did you go into my bedroom?"

I remembered it well. Lying on her large, soft bed, imagining her lying there with me. "Yes," I said.

"Why?"

186

"Why?"

"Mm-hm. Why did you go into my bedroom?"

I hesitated. "I don't know."

"Are you sure? I think maybe you do."

"I think I had a crush on you," I said.

"Way back then, huh? But you hadn't even met me yet."

"I had seen you. Watched you."

"At the fire?"

"Yes. But even before that. When I first arrived at the Estate, I saw you. You were on your horse. I...I don't know, I..." I wasn't sure I wanted to go on.

"Tell me, Kat."

This conversation was strange, I thought. We'd never talked like this before. It didn't seem at all like she was ordering me to tell her. It felt more like a conversation between friends, yes, an intimate conversation between two close friends. "I was very struck by you...from the first moment. You seemed different, I don't know. Seeing you stirred up feelings that..." I paused.

"Go on." Her tone was gentle, encouraging.

"I don't know, Marinda. I can't explain it. You just fascinated me. It was like an adolescent crush, I guess."

"Is that why you took my bracelet?"

I felt a sinking feeling. Fear? No. Yes, but not of danger. A different kind—fear of being known, of a secret part of me being discovered. "Yes," I said.

Marinda nodded. "So you felt that way even before Natalia...?"

"Yes."

"Are you in love with me?"

Oh my God. What was happening here? The fear continued. Grew. I felt caught, trapped. I was very tempted to shift gears, to switch into my cocky, arrogant, disdaining way, and to reply sarcastically. I don't know why I didn't. "I thought I was," I replied. "I felt things that I thought were love...but, it wasn't love."

Marinda waited for me to go on. On her face I saw interest, kindness, maybe even caring. But the sadness was still there, too.

"You remember those times when I told you I felt...felt devoted to you...when I said I adore you."

"I remember."

"I meant it."

"I thought you did."

"But it's not love."

"What is it?"

"What is it?" The pain was there in her eyes again.

"Something else. Something that I thought was love. I think it's what my mother thought love was. It was intense, I'll tell you that." I looked at her. She was beautiful. Somehow, in a different way tonight. "I still feel it," I said. "But it's not love." I lit a cigarette. I did not look at Marinda when I continued talking. I looked out the window as I spoke. "I think I was very lonely at Solera." I paused. "In fact, I think I was lonely in Chicago." I took a deep drag from my cigarette and watched the smoke whirl around me. "At Solera, people were...many of the women seemed to see me as...seemed to feel a mix of admiration and fear. That's it. Especially one woman. Teresa. I guess if I had had a bracelet, she might have stolen it. I didn't like what happened to me at Solera. I had a kind of power over those women—especially Teresa. They gave it to me and, damn, did I take it. I got off on it." I looked at Marinda now. "I enjoyed it." I said.

She nodded. "I know what you mean."

"I think it was a dreaded dream come true."

"Yes."

"I was just beginning to pull out of it, to be done with it. Like I'd plunged to the depth of that part of me and explored it, explored me, and I was ready to accept it and reject it...accept that I had that in me, own it, and then exorcise it or rather let go of it, realizing I don't need or want that. I was beginning to do that when I was brought here."

"And here you got in touch with another part of yourself."

"Yes." I was feeling exhilarated by this conversation. Understanding and understood. "The other side of the coin," I said.

"The wish to adore rather than be adored."

"Yes."

"Like your mother."

"Exactly. I'd been my father at Solera and then here..."

"The other side."

"Wow!" I said. I felt both excited and drained.

"Have you explored the depth of that side?"

I looked at her. The soft flickering candlelight reflected on her face and she looked soft and warm. "I don't know," I said. "At Solera, it seemed I had no choice but to be that way...to be tough and dominating. I know I went further than I had to. And, as I said, I came to enjoy it, parts of it." I was still looking at her. "Here, my choices are limited, too. And, the truth is, I enjoy part of it."

"Then will you be disappointed to know that the training is over?" Marinda asked.

I felt a crushing confusion. Over? No more contact with her? Part of me instantly felt very freed. I recalled some of our interactions, the kneeling shit, that night she was drunk. I recalled the deep contempt and disgust I felt. And then there were the other times, the other feelings. They were powerful. Yes, I'm disappointed, I thought. Does she mean it? "Do you mean it?"

"Yes," Marinda said. "As of now—actually, as of a few hours ago, the roles we've played with each other are over."

"Hm," I said. "I wonder if such a thing can simply be decided. Roles sink in sometimes. The parts take over the actors."

Marinda did not respond. I thought I detected that look again in her eyes, a kind of sadness that I couldn't really define.

"Natalia has talked with Tallo, told her of the gift," she said at last.

"Then this was Natalia's decision?"

"No. It was mine."

I realized I was feeling rejected, as if spurned by a lover. How silly. "And I'm to move on now. Go to Tallo. Play the wife role with her."

"That's the plan."

"You know what will probably happen?"

"What?"

"The same thing. Only more so. The prospect of not seeing you, of not...of never...well, it's hard. And then there's Tallo. It will be too easy, I'm afraid. She has some of the same qualities I see in you. At least, that's how I responded to her at the fiesta. And what I know of her, what you told me, didn't help. I'll probably fall under her spell in about two seconds. Damn! The crazy stupid part is that I'm looking forward to it. Oh, mother, if you could only see me now. Of course, it was supposed to be a man." I laughed. "I was supposed to adore and devote myself to a man-husband, not a..." I looked again at Marinda. "Not a Marinda or a Tallo," I

189

sighed. I felt very very drained now. "Life is weird," I said.

"Tell me about it!" Marinda replied chuckling. She got up. "I told you that day you delivered a package to me here, I told you then that you should come by some time and have a drink with me." She was walking toward the kitchen as she spoke. "This is the time," she said. "What would you like? Wait! Don't tell me. I know. You'd like Pepsi, right?"

"Right," I said.

"Will a coke do? That's all we have in Marigua."

"A coke will be fine."

Marinda would talk no more about the training or our relationship or Tallo. She gingerly changed the topic each time I tried and so I stopped trying. We talked of other things, of Mariguan culture and the women's movement here and of lesbians and coming out and fear. Marinda told me some about herself, but not a lot. Her parents had been poor farmers, peasants. She had left their village home as a teenager and, by hard work and luck, had gotten some education. Later, she became an apprentice and learned her craft. I stayed with her, talking in her cabin until close to midnight. She walked with me along the starlit road back to the Hacienda Grande and it was there we said goodbye. I felt heavy with the sadness of our parting. It seemed Marinda did, too, although I could not be sure.

21.

THE NIECE

Early the next day, Mona had a horse ready for me to ride to Tallo's cabin. She told me Tallo was already there, that she'd spent the night there. My night at the Hacienda Grande had not been a very restful one. I don't know what was upsetting me more—the loss of Marinda or the anger at myself for feeling the loss. My thoughts drifted. *Marinda. . . worship. . . Tallo. . . god.* I had never been religious. *I feel adoration for you.* I did go through the training, though. *The power.* My mother insisted that I attend catechism classes and get confirmed into the church. *Kneel!* There was a brief period during early adolescence when I wanted to believe. I was drawn to the idea of someone, some Being, bigger and better and wiser and stronger and nobler and more powerful than I or anyone else; someone genuinely worthy of adoration. *I adore you.* But, I rejected all that. I rejected the existence of such a Being as impossible and I rejected the wish for it as weak, juvenile, demeaning. *Majestic and imposing.* Sometimes the hymns spoke to me; they tapped something, some need in me. *Awe.* It was the same feeling I had gotten so many times when I thought of Marinda and a number of times when I was with her. *Awe. Adulation.* Shit. All this garbage about Tallo's specialness—superstitious nonsense. I was not about to fall for it.

As I rode the big brown mare toward the cabin, I decided to try to maintain an open mind, to give Tallo a chance and not assume she was a pampered snit like her aunt or a bitch or a goddess or anything. I just hoped she didn't share Marinda's need to prove she could force me to kneel at her feet. I made the trip at a very leisurely pace. As I neared the cabin, I saw what appeared to be someone lying on the porch.

I gave the mare free rein and tore forward, arriving at a gallop. It was Tallo. She was lying flat on her stomach, her head at the doorstep, her feet stretched out behind. An image of Sundance lying next to the parking meter on Oak Street flashed in my mind. I dismounted and ran toward the porch.

Tallo moved. I went up the stairs, two at a time. Tallo sat up. She was holding a string in her hand. She smiled. The string ran from her hand, over the doorstep, and into the cabin.

"Possum," she said.

I stopped in my tracks, and stood looking at her, puzzled.

"I almost had it."

"Had what?"

"The possum."

"You're after a possum?"

Tallo nodded.

"With a piece of string?"

She nodded again.

"Lying on the floor."

Tallo laughed. She was dressed in faded blue jeans and a thin jacket. She reeled in the string, rolling it up into a ball. At the end was a piece of something that looked like it might be considered edible by some life form. Tallo stood up and brushed herself off.

"Oh well, I'll get it later. Just watch your ankles." She motioned for me to come inside.

"There's really an oppossum in here?" I asked, seriously wondering if Tallo had a screw or two loose.

"A baby one."

"Your pet?"

She smiled at me, a half-smile really, that showed just the edges of her teeth. Her medium short hair was wavy, black and thick. "I'm told you're to be my pet," she said. "Or something of the sort." She laughed. "Have a seat, Kat."

192

I sat on the sofa in front of the fireplace. Tallo went into the kitchen and came back with a pitcher of lemonade and two glasses. "We have to talk," she said.

I nodded. I heard a scratching sound in the corner of the room, near the bookcase.

"Our guest," Tallo said. She looked around the room. "You really did a fine job on this place. I hardly recognized it, as they say." She poured the lemonade and handed me a glass. "You hungry?"

"No."

"Natalia wants me to have a cozy home."

"I know."

"Fully equipped." She smiled that half-smile again.

I shrugged.

"You've been here, what, about a month? At the Estate?"

"About."

"Do you know much about Natalia Neva?"

"Some."

"She thinks I still need a mommie."

"I thought she thinks you need a wife."

"That too." Tallo took a sip from her glass. "I humor her."

I didn't respond.

"I've found it's the only way to deal with her."

I was staring at Tallo's arm. I wasn't sure I was seeing what I was seeing. "I believe there's some blood-like substance," I said, "trickling down your arm."

Tallo looked. "Oh shit!"

"I believe it's blood," I said. "Even contessa-ettes bleed blood."

Tallo looked at me with amused disbelief. "Hey," she said. "I thought you were well-trained."

I shrugged.

She took her jacket off. Midway up her arm was a wrapping of gauze. It was blood-soaked.

"You're not suicidal, are you?" I asked.

Tallo ignored me and began unwrapping the gauze as she walked to the bathroom.

"Need any help?" I called after her. She didn't answer so I followed her into the john. "Ooh, that's a nasty wound," I said. "You could probably use some sewing up."

"You think so?" Tallo said, looking at her bloody arm. "You

might be right. Can you drive?''

"Of course.''

I had taken a washcloth from the rack and was wiping around the edges of her wound. Then I took a plastic-coated gauze patch, placed it over the cut and taped in on with adhesive.

"Let's go,'' I said. "Where to? The clinic at the settlement?''

"That's the place,'' Tallo replied. She reached into her jeans pocket and gave me a key.

"How'd that happen to you?'' I asked as I drove the white Volvo through the hills. "The cut.''

"A novicio,'' she said. "It's because of one of those novicios.''

"Oh?''

"You didn't hear about Jaime Sanchez?'' Tallo said. She pursed her lips. They were nice lips. "The day he arrived at the Estate, he had his meeting with Natalia. Apparently, he didn't like her plan for him. He grabbed hold of Tina—you know Tina.''

I nodded.

"He held a knife to her, demanding that we remove his earring and handcuffs and get him a car.''

"You're kidding! Is Tina OK?''

"She's fine.''

"This Jaime's an enterprising guy,'' I said. "Did anyone else get hurt, besides you?''

"He did.''

"What happened?''

"I was at the mansion. They told me what was going on so I tried to talk to the man. He was a real nervous type. I couldn't talk him out of it so I told him OK, he could have what he was asking for, except he had to release Tina.''

"Did he?''

"Would you?''

"Probably not, in his position.''

"You got it. So, we made a trade. He got me for a hostage instead of her.''

"Brave girl.''

"I was shaking.''

"Then what?''

"We had the earring sawed off. He was holding the knife to me the whole time. Right here.'' She pointed to her side. It was a nice side. "We had removed the handcuffs and he and I started out in the Volvo. I was driving.''

"You grabbed the knife from him.''

"Hell no.''

"Mm. You crashed into a tree. He was knocked unconscious. The windshield broke and it cut your arm.''

"No.''

"I give.''

"Sometimes it's dangerous hanging around with criminals,'' Tallo said.

"You better believe it.''

"I drove him to the federal road like he wanted. When we got to Portez, he insisted that we change cars. Neither of us knew how to steal a car, to jump one, so we kept looking, trying to find one with keys in the ignition. While he was poking his head into a car, I cracked him on the arm. The knife fell to the street. There were about a dozen people watching us. Estate people. They'd followed us, of course. And all the roads were being watched. As soon as I knocked the knife out of his hand, they jumped him.''

"They got him?''

"Yep. They sure did. He got a black eye though.''

"And you. How'd you get your arm cut?''

"Oh this. I cut it on the lemonade can.''

"What?''

"Yeah, this is because of you, novicia. I couldn't find a damn can opener. I wanted lemonade. So, I used a knife. I didn't do a very good job.''

I shook my head. "How's it doing? Your arm?''

"Your first aid seems to be holding.''

"Was that a made up story, then?''

"Oh, no. That was true. It happened last year. I'm not surprised you didn't hear. People don't like to talk about it. Escape attempts are looked at with great disfavor around here.''

"Are you telling me this for any particular reason?''

"Yes.''

I laughed. "Not this way,'' I said. "If I were going to split, it would be very well-planned. Besides, I'm too curious to leave yet.''

"Curious about me?''

"Yes.''

We were passing the statue of the Winged Dancer. "That's quite a statue,'' I said. "Wouldn't it be great to find the original?''

"That's an understatement. What a day that would be if it were ever discovered. All Marigua would go wild. Do you know where Suga Lake is?"

"I've seen it on a map," I said.

"A lot of people believe the statue's in that area somewhere. That whole region's been thoroughly searched, time and again. You know about the earthquake?"

"1760."

"Yeah. Such a shame. Such a loss. Seems like it's gone forever."

"The Boweso were quite a people, I hear."

"Amazing people. What they accomplished, what that so-called primitive tribe achieved is astounding. Talk about utopia."

"That good?"

"From the information we have, the Boweso people practiced what your basic idealist preaches. They really did it. They seemed a breed apart. I think the child-rearing had a lot to do with it. The kids were genuinely respected. They were listened to. Nurtured. Loved. Encouraged to grow in every way. They counted. I don't know how the Boweso hit on that psychological principal, but I believe that's the key to their success. The adults respected the kids, so the kids respected themselves and that let them respect each other and everyone else. Simple formula, but too complicated, I guess, for any other culture that I know of to actualize."

"Reminds me of the Estate community," I said. "The Statement of Rights and all that."

"They're not unconnected," Tallo replied. "Actually, Neva's Estate is inspired by the Boweso."

"Your doing?"

"Yes," Tallo said.

"You didn't do a complete job," I countered. We were getting close to the settlement now. "There are some people on the Estate who don't get their human rights respected."

Tallo looked at me. "I know," she said. "Nothing's perfect."

I pulled into a parking space behind the clinic. As soon as we entered, people began hovering around Tallo. She was taken into an office or treatment room somewhere. I was pretty much ignored. The car keys were in my pocket. The Volvo was parked outside. The potential for escape was better than it had ever been for me, and yet, I had barely the slightest impulse to attempt it. From what I could pick up so far, Tallo no more wanted a "wife" than she'd want to join a monastery or become a vestal virgin. But then again, who knows? She did say she had to "humor" her aunt. What did that mean?

I went for a walk along the main street of the settlement. I stopped to watch a group of children. They seemed to be building something. There were tools laid out on the grass and boards and wheels.

"These axels are perfect. I'm sure they'll work."

"Lucia got them."

"Hey, great, Lucia. Do you think we can fit them in over on this piece?"

"I hope so," Lucia said. "Jose, can you draw of picture of it for us, of how it should go?"

"Yeah. I think I could. Let me try."

"Here's the pencil," a tiny child said. He couldn't have been more than three years old.

"Thanks, Carlos." The speaker turned to the others. "Carlos is helping with the drawing supplies," he said, affectionately. "Look, he has the ruler stuck in his belt."

One of the boys hugged Carlos.

Jose began to draw. He did a lot of erasing. "I'm not sure just how it should go—the axel has to be attached here somehow." He erased some more. "No, this is no good. Any ideas, anyone?"

"Yes," a very dark-skinned girl in long pigtails responded. "I have an idea."

"Do you want to try?" Jose handed her the pencil.

All the heads bent over the girl as she drew.

"That's good."

One child pulled back from the others. The pigtailed girl kept drawing and the other children made occasional suggestions as they watched.

Jose noticed the child who had withdrawn. "Are you all right, Carlotta?" he asked.

Carlotta looked close to tears.

"What is it?"

The children left the drawing and focussed on Carlotta.

"It's Alfredo. He's working in the dormitory garden. I was supposed to tell him when we were ready to build the cart."

"But, you forgot?"

The girl nodded. She was probably about seven years old. "I

could run for him now, but I don't want to miss anything."

"We'll wait for you, Carlotta."

"Sure we will. We won't touch a thing until you get back."

"I'll go with you," Lucia said. "Come on. Let's go get Alfredo."

Carlotta and Lucia ran off. The other children started tossing a ball around in a circle.

I continued my walk along the street. Unusual kids, I thought. I pictured the statue of the Winged Dancer. Very unusual.

It felt so good to be freely strolling through a town. The handcuffs I wore had become such a part of me that I was oblivious to them. Obviously, however, others were not.

"Excuse me," the man said. "May I see your pass."

"Oh, my pass." I smiled. "I'm here with Tallo Neva. It was an emergency. She cut her arm and I drove her here to the clinic. There was no time to get a pass."

The man nodded. "Very likely what you say is true, but we'll have to check it out. Will you raise your arms please, above your head."

"Hey! Do you have the right to do this?"

"Yes," he replied. "You're a novicia. You have no pass. I must."

I raised my arms into the air and the man gently searched me. He smiled. "Let's go to the clinic," he said.

When we walked through the entrance, Tallo was there with several medical types. She saw me and disappointment clouded her smooth-skinned face. It was a very nice face. Her dark eyes looked even darker.

"She has no pass," the man said.

"Were you planning to go somewhere?" Tallo asked me.

"I considered Hawaii," I said, "but then I settled on a walk through town."

"You weren't trying to leave?"

"No."

"Did she give you any trouble, Raul?"

"No, Tallo. She was just walking along Boweso Street when I saw her."

"Thanks, Raul. My fault, really. I should have thought to give her a pass."

"Is your arm OK?"

"Fine, now. Four stitches."

"Ay, caramba. The Contessa will be sick about it. It will heal OK?"

"She's like an ox," a woman with a stethoscope said.

"You have a good doctor," Raul said to Tallo. "How was New York? You were gone so long this time."

"New York was madness, as usual," Tallo said. "It feels good to be back."

"Have you heard the news? Carmelita had the baby. A girl. The birth was beautiful."

"Yes, I heard. I'm happy for all of you."

"I've decreased my hours at the oil fields. So has Miguel. We're all good parents, Tallo. There are eight of us, now that the baby came. Come see us some time."

"I will," Tallo said. "Say hello to Carmelita and the others."

On the drive back to the compound, Tallo spoke of Natalia and of Marinda.

"You really pushed Marinda's button," she said.

"I did?" I wondered which button she meant. I thought of our evening of love-making and felt the nagging yearning for Marinda.

"She told me what you said, and what effect it had on her."

"What did I say?"

"The first day. About squashing weak little pussies like her, about her lack of integrity and her moral decrepitude."

"I had a point," I said, laughing.

"No you didn't!" Tallo's voice was harsh, the first time I had heard her sound this way. "What you said was real dumb." She paused. "On second thought," she said, "maybe it was calculated. Maybe you knew exactly what you were doing. Tell me this—when Marinda picked you up to take you to the cabin that first day, did you realize she was going to tell you the whole 'training' business was nonsense?"

"Did I realize that?"

"Did you?"

I was driving the car along the coastal road. I looked out over the sea. "I might have."

"I thought so."

"On some level."

"She was going to tell you that to assuage Natalia, you and she would go through some mock exercises and then..."

199

"Well, she certainly changed her mind quickly."

"Yes. Like I said, you pushed her button. She decided to teach you a lesson, I guess."

"She got right into it."

"More than she intended, I suspect."

I smiled. I pictured Marinda. She was something! Then I thought of some of the events of the last few weeks. The kneeling, especially that. And the cell. "She plays rough."

Tallo didn't respond right away. "You do realize that I'm not into this 'wife' garbage?" she said at last.

"I realize it. I'm glad. You were spared your auntie's genes. No blood connects you two."

"No blood, but we are very connected. I disagree with some of the things Natalia does, but I do not defy her if at all possible."

"She's the money source, huh?" From the corner of my eye, I could see Tallo's expression. At first, it was anger and then something else. Disappointment maybe? "Sorry," I said. "That was presumptuous. I don't really know the situation."

Tallo was quiet for a while. "The cabin you made so liveable..."

"Yes?"

"It's very nice. I probably will spend some time there. We'll see how it goes. As soon as possible, I want you to get into the novicio program and get yourself integrated into the community. I've been thinking of how to deal with Natalia. For now, we'll let her think that her plan is moving along as she'd hoped."

"Which means?"

"Which means that you and I will be spending some time together. But, so help me, if you try to 'serve' me and be my 'wife', I'll..." she was laughing. "I'll file for divorce."

We laughed together. Our laughter echoed through the hills. What a beautiful day. What a beautiful day in my life. The sun was high, the sky clear, the sea calm, the hills green, the future bright and full of promise. "I'm not a murderer," I said.

"I know about your case," Tallo responded. "It was self-defense, wasn't it?"

"I think the guy was after a folder I had. It contained a letter and a map."

"Yes, I heard there was a letter."

"You know what I need?"

"What?"

"I need to make some phone calls. I think there's a chance, a good chance, of proving that it was self-defense."

We pulled into the compound. Tallo said she was going to lunch with her aunt and that we'd continue our conversation later in the afternoon. "In the meantime," she said, "make all the phone calls you want. I'll let Mona know it's OK. You do understand the importance of not talking about the Estate?"

I said that I did and she seemed satisfied.

In the Hacienda Grande, things were lively. Juanita's children and some other kids were putting on a play with dancing and drum and tambourine music. I watched them for a while and shouted "Olé" with the others and then I went into a study and called Fanta. He was in the middle of another case, totally immersed, and I had to interrupt him several times, stop him from elaborating on his theories and speculations about how a blond woman could disappear without a trace and weeks later her brunette sister turn up from nowhere. He named no names but talked on in endless detail about the interconnections between the clues and the vital import of the strands of blond hair he'd found somewhere or another. He showed little interest in my case. The Postero police had done nothing with the information he had given them, he said, and there had been no investigation of Manuel Paz. He described Paz.

"Medium height and build. Black, wavy hair, in his late 30's or early 40's."

I was disappointed after the call although not particularly surprised. I hadn't really expected my visitor, the so-called Federico Jimanos, to be Paz. Fanta said he did have a copy of the letter and map and would be happy to forward them to Triste for safe-keeping, though, he reminded me, such things had not been kept very safely with Triste in the past. Did he suspect Triste, I wondered, chuckling.

I called Nettie Dawson next. It took a while for that one to get through, and while I waited, I ate lunch with the crowd at the Hacienda and listened to Juanita sing the praises of Marinda Sartoria.

"How lucky you are to be working for such a woman," Juanita said. "You do that sort of work, too? Make those drawings?"

"No," I said. "I was her girl Friday."

"What?"

"No matter," I said. "I've been transferred. I'm no longer with her."

I wasn't sure if what I felt was sadness. It was seeming right for that chapter to be ended. Marinda and I had played something out, something which, I'm sure, neither of us fully understood. Some day we would talk about it, I suspected. The call from Nettie came. It was wonderful to hear her voice.

"So, what's it like there for you?" Nettie asked. "Your letters say so little."

My outgoing correspondence from the Estate was censored. Several times, I had to redo letters because they conveyed a bit too clearly the conditions at Neva's. "The less others know about what goes on here, the better," Paulo told me. So, the letters to my friends at home and to Teresa were vague in regard to life at the Estate. I got little pleasure from writing them, so I rarely did.

"It's tolerable, Nettie. I'm doing fine. Healthy and getting by." I knew this would not satisfy her. "I don't like talking about it. I hope you understand. Someday, maybe I will tell you stories of this place, but let me tell you why I called..."

We talked for nearly a half-hour. Nettie was excited by the Boweso story and wondered if she could help in any way. I told her I would let her know. She seemed only mildly concerned about the possibility of a break-in at her office. "From what you say, I would think your friend, Jimanos, will wait to hear from you. Apparently, he does not suspect you're on to him."

"Maybe he's telling the truth."

"It's remotely possible. Let me know what you find out about him. Don't trust him until you're sure."

We discussed my plans for trying to continue the investigation and then I listened to stories of life in Chicago; the activities of the new women's crisis line and how they could sure use my mediation services, the gossip about who was with whom now, and the controversy over the purchase of land for the annual Women's Music Festival in Michigan. I loved hearing all this and when we hung up I felt the sad nostalgic homesickness very deeply.

I called information for a listing on the San Trito Insurance Company. They said there was no such listing. They did have a listing for a Federico Jimanos in Postero; in fact, they had three of them. I took down the numbers, then I called the Department of Insurance in Postero. They said they knew of no insurance agency by the name of San Trito and no agent by the name of Federico Jimanos. I called the Department of Vehicle Registration to find out who Jimanos' car was registered to. They said it was a rental car and gave me the name of the company, Los Tigres. Los Tigres informed me that they did not give out the names of people renting their cars. I called the first Federico Jimanos. No answer. The second was clearly not the man who had visited me. His daughter told me he was 87 years old and was sleeping at the moment. The third and final Jimanos on my list turned out to be a young newlywed who was irritated by my call, afraid that his new wife would get the wrong idea. He sounded like he had something to hide. I dialed the first number again, but there was still no answer.

I was able to reach Maria Sundance's maid, Juanita Lupa, but she was reluctant to talk with me. She said she was trying to forget about the whole thing. She insisted she could not remember the name of the book Maria had asked her about. That conversation lasted less than three minutes. I tried the first Jimanos number again. Still no answer.

I decided to try something. I called the number on the business card Jimanos had given me.

"San Trito Insurance." It was a male voice. It could have been his. I hung up.

Tallo and I drove to the cabin. I fed the mare and then we walked down along the stream. "Were you really born in a bamboo cabaña by the sea?" I asked.

"Yes." Tallo laughed. "What else have you heard?"

"That you travel a lot."

"That's true, too, but I wouldn't be surprised if you've heard some things that weren't"

"You do seem to have a mystique around here. Where do you travel?"

"Wherever the buyers are. I sell oil."

"A good capitalist."

"A lousy capitalist. I sell very low."

"Oh?"

"Marigua is a good place for a capitalist, though. It's one of the few countries where property owners also own the subsoil mineral rights. And, Natalia Neva is one of the few property owners who also has her own oil company. We produce a lot of crude over there in those fields. Good, high-quality, low-sulphur oil. We do OK despite the relatively low price we get.''

"Why do you sell low?''

"You're interested in this?''

"Sure.''

Tallo settled back against a rock. She seemed pleased to be talking on this topic. "I trade,'' she said. "Low-priced oil in exchange for high-quality employee relations. You're a feminist, I hear.''

I smiled. "I've been accused of losing touch with it,'' I said, "but, yes. Why? Does feminism have something to do with your oil business?''

"Mm-hmm. It's no secret, at least among people in the business. Oil companies, refineries, importers of crude all know it—if you want to buy from Neva Oil, you must conform to our 'Standards for Employees'. They hate it but they're doing it. Our price is too good to pass up.''

"Tell me more. This is fascinating,'' I said. "You mean you'll only sell to companies with certain standards for employees.''

"Right.''

"What are the standards?''

"Feminist. Equal pay, promotion and benefits for women. Active recruitment on all levels. No overt or subtle discrimination. No 'Old Boys Club'. No secret meetings excluding women executives. None of the usual games. Child care. Flexible hours. Job sharing. It's working. They're doing it. That's the main part of my job, to make sure those companies that agree to our stipulations actually follow through. Some of them try to cheat. It's hard to get away with cheating though, because our agreements include a good watch-dog set up. I go around to the companies, all over the world, but mostly in the States, and interview people, employees, study their reports.''

"I never heard of such a thing.''

"Neither did they before Neva Oil. They fought it at first. But, gradually, more and more firms joined in. The attraction is powerful. Money. The cost hurts them a bit at first. Fairness. Threat to male ego and power. I won't pretend it always goes smoothly, but it's going. There's a hell of a lot of oil on Natalia's land and, as you know, nowadays oil speaks. We're in a very good bargaining postion.''

"And Natalia doesn't mind the loss of profits?''

"Natalia doesn't need her oil. It's just gravy for her. She's an extremely wealthy woman."

"It was your idea—the 'Standards for Employees'?"

"Yes."

"So, the oil company operates at a loss."

"No. We break even. We cover our expenses. We just don't generate any profit for investment. Our money doesn't make money. What would otherwise be profit goes for giving people, women especially, a fair chance."

"That's quite noble."

"I know."

"You do good stuff."

"Yep. It's not changing the world; I don't know how to do that, but it's something."

"And Natalia's all for this? Somehow that doesn't fit."

Tallo smiled. "Natalia tolerates it. She knows it pleases me and she likes me happy. I am. So she is. I try not to give her any trouble. That brings us back to you," Tallo said.

"She wouldn't approve of a divorce."

"Nicely put. I also don't like lying to her, though I do sometimes. As little as possible, though. She wants me to have a home of my own, a cozy nice place close to her, to the mansion. Hence, the cabin. You should have heard her at lunch. Of course, I told her that I found you quite delightful, so accommodating, and that I thought things would work out very well. She was ecstatic. She couldn't praise Marinda enough for the excellent job she did preparing you for this. She also had quite a bit to say about how difficult a person you seemed to be and how she thought that would make you more interesting to me than someone who was more docile and compliant by nature."

I laughed. "Do you know the story of San Trito?"

"Oh, yes," Tallo said. "She enjoys telling that one. 'And as I pulled myself, drenched and humiliated, out of the river, that arrogant girl sat there whistling. The nerve, the nerve!' She told me she had no idea Kat Rogan was the woman who dumped her in that stream when she approved the contract that brought you here."

Tallo and I talked for a long time by the stream and then we went for a walk and talked some more. I found her very pleasant and interesting, and comfortable to be with. My reaction to her was very different from what it had been with Marinda. I was glad. We both talked some about our pasts. Tallo mentioned nothing about Melina, the mysterious friend who disappeared some years ago, and I did not ask. At one point, she tossed me the key to the handcuffs. I smiled at her as I removed them. I was feeling very good. The opposum seemed to have gotten out of the cabin somehow. At least, that's what we assumed as there were no signs of it now. We prepared a light dinner for ourselves and then Tallo played some albums she'd brought back from New York—Holly Near, Cris Williamson, Meg Christian—all the big names.

"This is real comfortable," she said.

"Yes."

"I don't relax much."

"I've heard that about you."

She twisted her head back and forth.

"Would you like a neck rub?"

"Yes."

It was a pleasant evening.

The next morning Tallo left early to go to the oil fields. There was a note next to my handcuffs asking me to please put them on if I decided to leave the cabin. When I was ready to go, I fastened both shackles to my right wrist, wrapping the thin chain around and around. It made a modestly attractive bracelet and it felt much better to wear them this way. I went by horseback to the Hacienda Grande to continue making phone calls. Mona noticed my rearranged shackles.

"That's cute," she said, "but it won't do, Kat. Where's the key?"

"It's OK this way, Mona," I said.

She smiled, showing her endearingly crooked front tooth. "Not OK," she said. "I suppose Tallo has the key."

"Likely," I replied. "Why don't you just let it go, amiga. There's nothing to worry about."

She smiled again. "You have to wear them," she said. "It's a rule we enforce strictly. Until you are a resident or until the Contessa says otherwise."

"I'll go talk with her about it," I said.

Mona argued quite strongly against this, suggesting that I trust her judgment about Natalia. I decided it wasn't important enough to push and allowed Mona to put another pair of cuffs on me. Then I asked her to do me a favor, to make a phone call for me. She was

206

agreeable and we went over her role before calling the number on Jimanos' business card.

"Yes, hello," Mona said. "I am interested in buying some insurance for my car...Oh, someone mentioned your agency. I'm not sure who... It's a new car. I just got it... Yes, I think so. Liability and collision. Oh, I'm not sure... Yes... Yes...

I'll be damned, I thought. He's selling her insurance.

"I would like to think about it," Mona said into the phone. "I maybe will stop in to see you. Are you in El Centro...yes, I got it, yes, 47 Montenegro. Possibly, I will come by to discuss it some more. My name is Luisa LaStrata, and yours Señor...That's J-i-m-a-n-o-s. Yes, thank you."

When Mona hung up, she was beaming. "Did I do well?"

"Great." I said. I was puzzled. Why was there no San Trito Insurance Agency listed with the phone company? I thanked Mona for her help, then called the number of the Jimanos I had gotten from the operator yesterday and hadn't been able to reach yet. A man answered. No, he was not Federico Jimanos. Federico was out of town. Sure, his brother said, he would describe Federico. He was 50 years old, fat and ugly and irresponsible. The brother asked if I was sure I wanted to get ahold of him. I said no.

Jimanos could be legit, I thought. He could be an insurance agent with an unlisted agency. Maybe he's not licensed as an agent for some reason, and gets customers by word of mouth. Maybe he really is an ex-army intelligence officer who wants to help an unfairly convicted stranger by breaking a code for her. Maybe it's just a coincidence that his appearance fits the description the witness gave of the man at the scene of Martin Sundance's death. But why would he not have his agency listed, I wondered?

Who knows, I thought. Maybe they never get over subterfuge once they've worked in intelligence. I wondered how I could go about checking if a Federico Jimanos had actually been in the Intelligence Division of the Marigua Army. If only I could get ahold of that damn book. But, maybe that wasn't necessary. Maybe Federico Jimanos was who said he was and maybe he could break the code. I considered calling him to tell him that I had the letter.

At noon time, Tallo came to the Hacienda Grande. We sat on the balcony together having a drink and talking.

"I think I may have a way to recover the original Winged

Dancer," I said.

Tallo gave me an amused grin. "You don't say," she replied. "You've got a map, right?"

"Right."

"You ran into a long-lost Boweso tribeswoman and she fell in love with you and gave you the map."

"Not exactly."

Tallo looked out over the hills. It seemed she did not intend to pursue the conversation.

"I'm not kidding, Tallo."

"You're not kidding. OK, tell me more."

"You know why I came to Marigua. About the murder in Chicago."

"Yes, I know about it."

"The man who was killed, Martin Sundance, gave me a letter and a map."

"Are you trying to tell me the map shows how to get the Winged Dancer?"

"Yes. Sundance learned where it's hidden from an old Boweso Tribesman."

"So, I was close," Tallo said. "Funny, I'm having trouble believing it."

"That's why he was killed."

"Because someone wanted the map."

"No. Because someone wanted to stop Sundance from giving the statue to the people of Marigua."

Tallo looked much more interested now. When she frowned, the deep lines on her forehead reminded me of an old professor I had in law school. "And you have the map?"

"Yes."

"May I see it?"

"Yes," I said. "It's upstairs. In the room where I sometimes stay."

We went together. I had the documents in a manila envelope I had gotten from Mona. I gave them all to Tallo—the xerox of the original letter and map and my translation of the letter. She looked at them for a long time. She sat on the bed with the papers spread out around her and examined each of them several times, saying nothing.

"Why didn't you fill in this word?" she asked at last.

She was pointing to the first coded word in the sentence; *When the 18-6-12 is finished and the 12-4-31-3/18-6-50-2-6/15-3-29-2-2-8 the 1-1-3-12-18-6 will become accessible.*

"I don't know what the word is," I said. "I haven't been able to figure it out."

"It's *dam.*"

"*Dam?*" I looked at the sentence again. "How do you know?"

"It's obvious from the rest of it," Tallo said. "According to this, the statue is submerged under Lake Suga. Don't you know that they're building a dam there? It's almost finished. In fact March 10th is the projected completion date. I just read it in the paper yesterday. *When the dam is finished and the. . . "* She examined the sentence. *". . . and the lake level lowers,* I'd guess," she said.

"My God," I said, suddenly making the connection. "I've been there! I've been to Lake Suga and I didn't even know it. It's on the route between here and Solera, isn't it?"

"Yes," Tallo said. "Not far from the federal highway."

"We stopped there. Luis said something about a dam and the level of the lake being lowered as a result, but I didn't pay much attention to it. It never occurred to me that that's Lake Suga."

Tallo was examining the map. "You really believe this is authentic?" she asked.

"Three people have been killed because of it," I said. "Yes, I believe it. It makes sense, doesn't it? That's the general region where the Boweso had their settlement."

"Yes."

"So when the dam is done and the lake drops forty feet, then the statue can be retrieved."

"That seems to be the meaning of the letter," Tallo said. "Look here, Kat." She pointed to the map. "This must be the Suga River, and here's the lake. This dotted line probably represents the level that the lake will drop to when the dam is done and the water supply from the river is cut off. I would guess that this 'X' is where the statue is. I wish we knew what this means," Tallo said, pointing to the paragraph of numbers. "It probably describes exactly how to get to the 'X'."

"That's what I figured," I said. "For that, we'll need the book."

"What book?"

"I don't know what book. You see these manacles?" I held up my wrists.

Tallo nodded, looking at me as if I were slipping over the sanity border.

"If I knew what book, and if I had the book, then I wouldn't be wearing these."

"The book has a magic handcuff key hidden in it."

"Yes," I said, laughing. "In a manner of speaking. The book is the key to breaking the code. Once the code is broken, I'll know who killed Sundance. Once I know that, I'm on the road to freedom."

Tallo rubbed her chin. "Right," she murmured.

I laughed. "Let me explain," I said. "Martin Sundance and his sister, Maria, had a code system they used as kids. Each number stands for a letter on some page in a certain book. See here where he says Bookcode 19. I think that means page 19 of the book. Then the first number is probably how many letters you have to count to get to the correct letter. We have to have the book to translate this."

"Hm, that's interesting, clever." Tallo smiled her half-smile, raising her eyebrows. It gave her face a cherubic quality. "Tell me more, Kat. Tell me more about Sundance and all the rest of it."

Tallo sat on the bed and I on the easy chair. I sat on the edge of the chair as I told the story. It took a long time for I gave her every detail I considered relevant. I ended with Mona's phone call to Jimanos. Tallo asked a few questions during my narrative, but mostly she just listened. When I finished, she slowly shook her head back and forth. Her hair glistened.

"I wouldn't trust Jimanos," she said.

"That's my gut reaction, too. He might be the killer. At first I was sure he is, that he's the partner Martin refers to, but now...I don't know."

"For one thing, if you're right about the code, then I don't see how Jimanos or anyone else could possibly translate it unless they had the book."

"Right. But I could be wrong about how the code works. I have a confession."

"What?"

"I don't know much about codes."

"I bet this Jimanos character doesn't either."

"I wish I knew who he is."

"We'll find out," Tallo said.

"*We.* Then you'll help?"

"You're damned right! How could I not? Consider what's involved, Kat, the possible payoffs. First, there's your vindication and freedom. That's a lot, but there's even more than that. There's the Winged Dancer. If Sundance is telling the truth and we could recover the statue... well, I can't describe how terrific that would be. And then there's the possiblity of convicting a murderer. If we accomplish any one of these, it would be worth whatever it takes."

"I think the first step is to check out Jimanos."

"I agree. I want to go to 47 Montenegro."

"Me, too."

"You?"

"Yes," I said emphatically.

"You're a prisoner."

"I hate labels."

Tallo laughed. I laughed with her and somehow we ended up standing, together, our arms around each other, laughing excitedly.

When we calmed down, Tallo spoke again. "How do I know you won't try to escape?"

I looked at her seriously, my eyes filling with tears. "I could end up free," I said. "Legitimately free. That sounds much better to me than running all my life."

Tallo nodded. There were tears in her eyes too. She took my hand. "You know, Kat, if it doesn't work out, your situation still won't be so bad, relatively speaking. You'll become a resident, get a job on the estate, make a life for yourself here. It's not a bad life."

"I know," I said. "I would accept it if I had to. I won't try to escape, Tallo. I want to go to Postero and dig into it." I wanted to go that minute. I couldn't stand still. I was bouncing, my eagerness to get started energizing me.

"With that dumb ring hanging from your ear, there'd be no end of hassles if you were out on the streets."

"I could wear a hat."

"We could remove the earring."

"I hoped you'd say that."

We were both beaming.

211

22.

THE SEARCH

The next day we set out in the Volvo for the four-hour trip to Postero.

"Natalia is very impressed that you're docile enough to be taken on the excursion," Tallo said.

She was driving. The cut on her arm was healing nicely and the amount of bandaging had been lessened. Her hair rippled in the breeze as we roared down the federal highway. We were both very excited.

"What did you tell her?"

"That I had some business in Postero and I decided my 'wife' would accompany me."

I laughed. "I'm glad you're the way you are," I said.

"What do you mean?" Tallo asked.

I was watching her hands on the steering wheel, wanting to look at her but not able to look at her face.

"That you didn't get into it like Marinda did. I think if you had, I might have..." I stared at a passing car.

"Might have what?"

Two identical VW's whizzed by, one after the other, both light blue. "Strange stuff happened with me and Marinda."

"So I heard."

I felt some uneasiness, embarassment maybe. How much had Marinda told her?

"I'm still trying to figure it out," I said. "I think it had something to do with my conditioning." I laughed. "Surprise! Conditioning strikes again!"

"Sex-role, you mean?"

"Yeah. Mom, primarily, but I guess the rest of the culture reinforced it."

"It can be hard to fight."

"I fought it all my life. I think that's why I never fell in love." Tallo was silent. I looked at her face now as she looked at the road. Was she thinking of Melina? "Every time I got close," I continued, "I got scared. I think I was afraid I'd either dominate my lover or let her dominate me. I think I believed it had to be one way or the other."

Tallo nodded slowly.

"How about you?" I asked. "Have you been in love?"

Tallo smiled, but did not answer. I did not ask again. We rode in silence for a while then talked of our plans for when we arrived in Postero. Tallo had suggested we stay at the Tintano Hotel. I vetoed it, explaining why, but later I changed my mind. Somehow, I wanted to go back. Somehow, it seemed right for the Tintano Hotel to be our base of operations. Later, I wished I had never again set foot in that place.

"Do you think they'll recognize me there?" I asked.

"It's possible. If you'd rather stay somewhere else, it really is fine with me," Tallo said.

"No," I replied. "I want to stay there."

An uneasy feeling gnawed at my stomach as we stood at the hotel desk to register. The images came back as I knew they would. It's a hard thing to live with, knowing you've killed a person. It's hard no matter what the circumstances.

Our room was on the first floor. The other time, I had been on three. Since we had stopped on the road for a snack neither of us felt hungry now, and we were both eager to get started with our investigating. We dropped our bags off in the room and went to the gift shop to buy a street map. The clerk stared at me. She didn't say anything, just stared. She probably wasn't sure I was who she thought I was. Tallo had heard of Montenegro Street, although she had no idea where it was. Postero had a population of almost a quarter million people and El Centro was fairly large. The streets were arranged in complicated patterns with many curves and diagonals.

Montenegro turned out to be a short street at the south edge of the city. The neighborhoods it transversed were run-down and seedy-looking. Scores of vendors dotted the street selling various items from small makeshift booths. Many of them had little fires going and cooked greasy food on the street to sell to passersby. I was not tempted. We passed dingy-looking shops and cafes. In the cafes, it seemed all the customers were men. Children ran amongst the cars, most dressed in their blue school uniforms. We reached the block we were seeking. Forty-seven Montenegro was a small, dirty, two-story brick building with a storefront shop. We parked the car and walked to the shop.

"What's upstairs?" Tallo asked the shopkeeper. "Any offices?"

The man was wrinkled and haggard-looking, with several days' growth of beard poking out from his gray cheeks. His pants were dirty and stained, but his wrinkled shirt, I noticed, was perfectly white, absolutely spotless like new snow.

"Who are you looking for?" the man asked. "You bill collectors, eh?"

"No," Tallo replied. "We're looking for San Trito Insurance Company."

"Oh," the man responded, with a change of expression that might have indicated increased interest.

I looked around the shop. It seemed to be a cross between a hardware store, a living room, and a candy shop. In the corner was a cabinet with scores of tiny locked doors. It reminded me of a post office.

"Do they have an office here?" Tallo asked.

The man shrugged as if to say the answer was obvious.

"Does Federico Jimanos have one of those mail boxes?" I asked.

The man looked at me in a dull but scrutinizing way. "Private mail boxes for private people," he said.

"We have some business with Federico Jimanos of San Trito Insurance Company. This is the address he gave."

The man looked blankly at me.

Tallo removed a bill from her wallet, folded it lengthwise and held it up in obvious view. "A piece of that toffee, please," she said. "And keep the change if you feel like talking."

The man eyed the bill. He got the candy, and held out his stubby-fingered hand. When he had the money safely stowed in his pocket, he spoke. "Federico Jimanos has a mailbox here."

"How long has he had it?"

"Not long. Maybe a month. Maybe less."

"Does he get much mail?"

"Jimanos? No. One letter. In all that time, just one letter. But, he comes by every day to check his box."

"What does he look like?" I asked.

The old man wheezed. It might have been a laugh. "Like a hairless bean pole," he replied.

"Do you know where he lives?"

"No."

"Do you know if he uses another name besides 'Jimanos'?"

"No."

"Do you know anything else about him?"

"No."

"Nothing at all?"

"I'm not a bleeding turnip," the man said, shrugging his boney shoulders.

Tallo took out another bill. It was the same denomination as the first. "I would buy another piece of candy, if I knew you would forget about our visit here," she said.

The man handed her a toffee and took the money, grinning a nearly toothless grin. We left the dirty shop and sat in the car for a while, sucking on the candy and digesting what we had learned.

"So, he set it up just for me," I said.

"Looks that way."

"There is no San Trito Insurance Company. That call Mona made...He must have known it was me."

"So, he knows you're checking on him."

"We better be careful. I think our Señor Jimanos is a very dangerous man."

Simultaneously, we each looked out the window, and up and down the street. Then we both laughed.

"I hope our friend in there keeps his mouth shut," Tallo said, "but I don't think that we can count on it."

I didn't want to think about that. I wanted to get moving. "Let's

215

go," I said.

Tallo started the car. We soon came to a pleasanter section of the city and I felt some relief. "So we know that Federico Jimanos is no insurance broker," I said, "and no altruistic breaker of codes. I can think of two ways to find out who he really is."

"One?"

"Hang around 47 Montenegro until he shows up and then follow him."

Tallo wrinkled her nose. "Two?"

"The book. Find the book and translate the missing words, especially the partner's name. Once we have the name of Sundance's partner, we can find out if that person is a 'bald bean pole'."

"How to find the book?" Tallo's eyes sparkled. "I know..."

"Juanita," we said at the same time.

Juanita Lupa was not hard to locate. Her mother told us where her new employer's premises were located and we drove straight there. I hoped a face-to-face meeting would make Juanita more talkative than she had been on the phone the other day. The villa where she worked was on the northernmost outskirts of Postero.

At first, Juanita was not cooperative, but she did listen to us at least, and, bit by bit, I could see her softening. She was a sweet, timid, young woman, probably not more than 18 years of age. She was rather ugly in appearance, though there was a kind of beauty to her, too. We convinced her that she might help me to obtain my freedom. We did not focus on the possibility that Maria Sundance had been murdered. It was clear that it disturbed Juanita to think of such things. I think what really brought her to our side was the fact, which she haltingly shared with us, that she had once been raped. Her tiny little eyes teared up as she recalled that awful event in her life. She wanted to do what she could to help me.

"Do you know what hypnosis is, Juanita?" I asked.

"Oh, yes. I know about that," she said, looking somewhat frightened. "Someone controls your mind. I don't like that thing."

"It can be used to help people," I said gently. "Help them get more control of their *own* minds. It can be used in good ways. Did you know that hypnosis is used to help people do things they really want to do for themselves, like stop smoking, for example?" I realized I had a cigarette burning in the ashtray in the kitchen where we sat. I went on quickly, "Or eat less, or feel less fearful of things or less sensitive to pain for people with lingering illnesses. It can be used for many good things, Juanita. It can be used to help people remember things they have forgotten."

"Maybe so," she said. "That's not what I heard."

"And the person who is hypnotized really does it herself, only what she wants. The hypnotist only helps free her to do what she wants. She is in control, not the hypnotist."

"Why do you talk of this with me?" Juanita asked.

I considered that a reasonable question. "That book that Maria asked you about."

"Yes, that again. I have never stolen. I never will."

"Yes," I said softly. "I believe that. I don't think you know anything about that book, except maybe one thing."

She looked at me, waiting.

"The title of it."

She shook her head. "I can't remember," she said. "The others asked, too. I tried. I told you that on the phone. Señor Triste, and that other one, the detective man. I told them I couldn't remember. I still can't."

"Hypnosis might help you remember. It's locked in your mind."

"Hmm." Juanita seemed to be giving this serious thought. "You want me to..."

"Yes," I said. "It could free me."

"How would it be? What would they make me do?"

"The hypnotist would simply help you get very relaxed and then help you remember that day when Maria asked you about the book. Nothing else. Just relax and then let yourself unlock that memory from your mind."

"Will you be there, too?"

"Yes," I said, "if you want me to. I'll make sure it is OK for you."

Juanita moved her head in a brief nod. "I will do it." Her fat cheeks lifted with her determined smile.

I smiled, too. "We must find someone who can do the hypnosis," I said. "Someone good. We will find someone and arrange a meeting."

I felt very hopeful as we walked out of that ornately furnished monstrosity of a villa and climbed back into the Volvo.

"Let's go find us a hypnotist," Tallo said gingerly.

"Let's go find some food first," I said.

217

The food was no problem, but finding a hypnotist turned out to be more difficult than either of us had anticipated. I suggested starting with the police and seeing if there were any hypnotists they used to help witnesses remember things. Tallo scoffed at this. I insisted. She turned out to be right. She went by herself to the Postero Police Station. I did not want to go anywhere near it. I waited at the cafe down the street.

"They thought I was loco," she said. "They never heard of such a thing. It was funny, Kat. You should have been there. No, you shouldn't have been there. Let's try the Arcedia Hospital."

The woman at the information desk referred us to Dr. Villas who referred us to Dr. Mendez who referred us to Dr. Doreos who gave us the names of two people he thought might be able to help. By the end of that runaround, we both felt tired. It was early evening now.

"How about a movie?" Tallo suggested.

My eyes lit up. It could be *Ma & Pa Kettle Go to Marigua* for all I cared. The prospect of sitting before a silver screen was so dazzling that the specifics didn't matter at all.

I felt differently after we emerged from the film. It was set in the early American West, made in Italy with English dubbing and Spanish subtitles. It was awful. Tallo and I had a great time making fun of it. Afterwards, she suggested going for a drink at the Tintano Hotel bar. I told her to go ahead, I'd rather go see the movie again. She laughed and we compromised by going to an absurd disco near the movie house. Some boys of probably very recent maturity, if that, insisted that we wanted to dance and drink and be with them and so we went back to our room and Tallo told me of how hard it was for women in her country, especially lesbians. The stories made me sad. Angry, too, of course, but mostly sad for the rampant ignorance, judgmental and righteous closemindedness of so many people.

I lay on my double bed across the room from Tallo, who lay on her double bed asleep. I lay there listening to her soft rhythmic breathing. I like that woman, I thought. I like her a lot.

23.

THE NAME

The first doctor was a joke. We went to his "clinic" which was a suite of offices in a building in the center of El Centro. He wore a white coat and a black beard.

"Yes, yes. Age regression, we will use."

I guess he was a psychiatrist. I didn't recognize the names of the institutions on the diplomas and certificates which cluttered the wall.

"And we can take her to other lives. We all have had them, you know. We will have your fair maiden travel beyond her present consciousness and contact previous incarnations. There may be many. We will go way back and gradually work our way closer and closer to her present life. Repressions are all motivated, you know. To find the lost memory we must find the reasons for its loss. We will have to resolve the pressing conflicts of her past lives as we move along, century by century, generation by generation, year by year."

"That sounds like a long trip," I said.

"It can take months, even years, to resolve it."

"I don't believe we can spare that much time," I said.

"Impatient." He tsk-tsked.

219

"Yes, I'm afraid so."

"Well, I could do an abbreviated version."

"That's all right." I stood. Tallo was already standing, quite ready to leave.

We giggled over that one and hoped the other doctor was more to our liking. Our apointment with him wasn't until late afternoon and it was only 10:30 now.

"How about some shopping," Tallo said. "I think your wardrobe and worldly possessions need some filling in. My treat."

"You're sweet."

"Yes."

Did we shop. I think Tallo enjoyed it as much as I. We bought clothing—pants and jeans and shirts and jackets and blouses and shoes and boots. We bought scarves and a leather purse and books and a camera and a watch and a silver bracelet (my plan was to give that to Marinda, although I did not tell Tallo) and two suitcases and toiletries and a mirror and brush and comb. I got my hair cut medium short, the way I always wore it at home, and we stopped for ice cream and watched the street jugglers and laughed at how I bargained in the shops. We ate a huge lunch and took a nap and then set out to see doctor number two.

He was a clinical psychologist, a graduate of Joaquin University, who had also trained in Europe. Dr. Alerna was a calm, bright and inquisitive man, well-practiced in the use of hypnosis. Tallo and I both knew immediately that we had a hit. Dr. Alerna agreed to meet with Juanita the next day. We called her from his office to make the arrangements.

That evening, Tallo took me around the town. She knew Postero well and enjoyed her tour guide role. There was one bar on a quiet dark street, a bar that had no sign announcing its existence, but had a buzzer at the entrance. It was there that I felt the happiest and the saddest. Happy that my sisters had a place. Sad that it was so dark and hidden. Tallo met someone she knew, Marta, and Marta joined us. We did much laughing, but some serious talk, too.

"There are no lesbians in Marigua," Marta said. "That is what people believe. That is what they want to believe. Deny our existence and we will not exist."

"Do you know a woman named Zita?" I asked.

"Zita Forallo? You know her?"

"Yes."

Marta's eyes looked sad and clouded. "She is in prison," Marta said. "She is a strong woman. A wonderful woman. How do you know her?"

I did not answer right away, but finally, when I did I told the important truth. "She came into my life at a very important time," I said. "I sometimes suffer from a tendency toward blindness and Zita was there when I needed her to help me open my eyes."

"She does things like that," Marta answered, not probing for more.

Later I asked Tallo about bringing people from Solera to the Estate. I asked her about bringing Teresa and about bringing Zita. I told her about them, as much as I knew. I did not lie as I told the stories. I did not deny how I had treated Teresa and fostered her idolization of me. Tallo listened without judgment.

"I think I no longer am afraid," I said, "afraid that if I get close to someone, I will do that to her. The worst has happened. I did it to Teresa but I'm done with it now. It's out of my system. I don't want it." We were sitting at the little round table in our room having coffee. A cool breeze came through the window. "The pendulum swung all the way at Solera," I said. "I lived it out, that part that I always feared was in me. It was ugly and I'm done with it. I only wish I could have gotten over it some other way. It wasn't good how I treated Teresa. Or how I was with the other women there. No good at all."

"The male mystique," Tallo said, gently. "Dormant in some of the most committed feminists." She reached across the table and stroked my hand. "We're so complex, so many layers. I guess it's hard to know ourselves completely, to know how we'll act under adverse conditions. We can get sucked in by situations, Kat, do things against our values. We're all vulnerable."

She seemed to understand. I felt very appreciative.

"I will have Paulo check into bringing Teresa and Zita," Tallo said. "From what you say about your two friends, I think there should be no problem. We have a quota, you know, so it may take a while."

That night, I lay again on my bed across from Tallo's, thinking tender thoughts about her, feeling very drawn to her. The heavy warning feeling was not there. I waited for it but it did not come. It seemed OK to let myself feel how I was feeling for her. It seemed OK this time. With that thought I slipped into peaceful dreams.

The next day, we picked Juanita Lupa up from her employer's ostentatious, noveau riche villa and drove her to Dr. Alerna's. Her nervousness disappeared after about two minutes with the gentle man. Tallo and I sat off to the side on a sofa while the psychologist talked to Juanita and she grew relaxed and gradually was induced to recall, as if it were happening right at that moment, the events in early July when Maria Sundance asked her about the missing book. Juanita reported with amazing vividness the words they each spoke.

"Juanita, I'm sure you must have seen it. I kept it in the library, on the shelf to the right of the mantle... No, Señora, I do not know where it could be... Did you take it for some purpose, to lend to someone or to read or use for something, to press a flower, perhaps?... No, Señora, I told you. I do not know... It's all right if you borrowed it without asking, Juanita. I will not be angry. But, please tell me if you did. It's very important... I did not. I did not."

"The name of the book, Juanita," the psychologist said. "Señora Sundance said the book she wanted is called..."

"It has a flowered border, Juanita," Juanita said, her eyes still closed, "and a picture of a delicate plant in the center. It is called the... *The Emerald Hat of Old , Dark Tarzan.*" Juanita said the last part in English, "Yes, I need that book, Juanita. Perhaps you took it home with you without realizing it...No, Señora, I would not do that..."

Tallo and I looked at each other. I grabbed a pen from my purse and wrote down the title.

"Very good, Juanita. You can stop remembering now," Dr. Alerna said. "Just breathe deeply and imagine you are walking through that meadow again...just relax..."

We were all very pleased. "A child's story," Tallo said.

We thanked and paid the psychologist. The charge seemed minimal compared to what it probably would have been in the States. We thanked Juanita heartily and drove her back to her job.

"The Emerald Hat of Old, Dark Tarzan," I said as we drove to the public library. "Sounds racist and agist."

"You're right. Let's forget about it."

"We can't support such literature."

"How politically incorrect that would be."

There was no such book listed, nor was the librarian of any help.

Shit. Back to base one.

"How about a bookstore," I said.

"How about a bookstore," Tallo repeated.

"Let's try."

"Or, how about Manuel Paz."

"Manuel Paz?"

"You said he inherited Maria's books and papers. Maybe he'd let us go through them."

"Yes, but...Manuel Paz?"

"What is it, Kat? I thought you didn't buy your detective friend's theory."

"I don't." I didn't say it with great certainty.

"You're not certain. You think Paz might be involved?"

We were standing on the sidewalk in front of the old gray building that housed the Postero Library. I began walking toward the car.

"No," I said. "I don't think Paz is involved. Fanta's an asshole, right?"

"Certainly prone to false accusations. He did accuse *you*."

I nodded. "OK, let's call Paz."

We weren't far from our hotel so we went there to make the call.

Manuel Paz was at the museum but said he was more than willing to take the time to show us the books and other items he had gotten from Maria Sundance's estate. He said he could meet us at his house whenever we chose. We chose now.

When we arrived at the address he gave us, no one answered the doorbell. Paz had said to go around the back and wait on the patio if we arrived before him. We went around the back. The villa was in an isolated, heavily wooded area. Sitting on the patio, we looked out onto a garden and to jungle-like plant growth beyond.

"This place gives me the creeps," I said.

Tallo looked at me. "I don't think it's just the place," she answered. She looked around. "It is real quiet here."

"Eerie."

"You don't trust Paz."

"You got any weapons in that bag?"

Tallo shook her head. "Do you want to leave, Kat? We could arrange to meet him somewhere else if you're feeling uneasy."

I shook my head. "Nah, it's OK. It's that damn Fanta. He planted those suspicions in my head."

Just then, we heard a car pulling into the driveway.

"Shit," I groaned. I jumped from my chair, and looked toward the jungle growth, tempted to run there.

Tallo watched me. "It's now or never," she said. "Do you want to leave?"

But the back door of the house opened then. A dark-haired man in a light business suit walked out to the patio, his hand extended. "Kat Rogan," he said, looking at me.

We shook hands and I introduced Tallo.

"I know the name," Paz said. "Neva Oil, among other things."

He seemed pleasant enough, but Tallo and I were both wary.

"Sorry to have kept you waiting. Please come in."

We hesitated.

"Is something wrong?"

I imagined his house to be a trap, that as soon as we walked inside, the jaws of the trap would close on me and Tallo, crushing and devouring us. At that moment, a little girl ran out the back door.

"Uncle Manuel, can I play with the xylophone?" she asked.

"Of course, Ramona. Do you remember where you put it?" His voice was tender and full of love for the child.

She ran back inside.

"My niece," Paz said. "What an angel. She was visiting me at the Museum. She loves to do that. I take her in the back and she feels very special," Paz said in his soft-spoken way. "My brother and his wife will come here tonight for dinner. I'm quite a cook. Perhaps you will stay."

Relaxed, we went inside. Manuel Paz turned out to be a sensitive man, gentle, very pleasant and kind. It was clear as we pored over Maria's things that he was still grieving for her. Fanta is definitely an asshole, I thought. He would suspect Mother Theresa. There were no children's books among the items and certainly no book about a dark, old Tarzan. As we were looking the books over one by one, Tallo noticed a paper stuck in the pages of one of them. She shook it out.

"Ah-ha. Look at this. Maria's translation of the letter."

I came to where she sat and read over Tallo's shoulder. All the anagrams had been unscrambled. The number-coded words were blanks. "Do you know where this book was?" I asked Manuel. "Where Maria kept it?"

"I assume in the library with the others. Is this the book you're looking for?"

"I doubt it," I said. It was in Spanish, the novel, *One Hundred Years of Solitude*. I looked on page 19, started counting letters and came up with nothing meaningful. "No," I said, "I'm sure this isn't it. Would you mind if we took it with us, though, Señor Paz, just in case."

"Fine. Of course. I hope it helps you, Señorita Rogan. I can't express how badly I feel for you. And Maria was very sure this letter was of immense importance." He looked at the letter Tallo had found, reading it. "Yes, it does imply that Martin found something valuable as Maria told me." He handed the letter back to Tallo. "It seems important. Maria said that soon she would know exactly how important. Maybe you two can carry on that quest for her."

We had a coffee with Manuel Paz, in his garden. His niece joined us for a minute or two, then ran off again.

Manuel talked lovingly of Maria. "I hoped someday we would marry," he said. His pain was painful to observe.

When we left, Tallo commented on Paz. "I think he's as innocent as his little niece."

"I concur," I said. "I can't imagine him killing a light."

"Say, Kat."

"Say, Tallo."

I was driving this time. We were headed back toward El Centro.

"About that bookstore idea," she said.

"Yeah."

"Picture this... you're Maria Sundance. You got this important message about a super-valuable treasure and maybe about your brother's killer. You need this particular book to translate the message."

"I'm picturing," I said. "It's clear. It's very clear. It's as if I'm living it right now." I spoke very dramatically.

"Shut up!" Tallo said sweetly. "So, you can't find your copy of the book. It's gone. Disappeared. What would you do next?"

"Hire a detective!"

"No. That's not what you'd do."

"What would I do?"

"Get another copy of the book."

"It doesn't seem to exist."

225

"That Tarzan Hat business may not be the correct title."

I gave this possibility some thought. "You're right," I said. "Of course. People often fabricate under hypnosis. It's not lying, they just fill in the blanks in their memory with fantasy."

"So, what would you do?"

"I'd get another copy of the book."

"How?"

"Library."

"Or."

"Bookstore."

"Right. Let's hit the bookstores."

I pulled over to a restaurant. "Let's go in here and see if there's a phone book."

"There won't be," Tallo said. "We'll go to a phone station. There's one about a quarter mile up the street."

We found four bookstores listed in the Postero directory. They were all in El Centro.

"Let's split up," I suggested, looking at the street map. "They're all within walking distance. I'll take the two east of here. You take these."

"Check."

"Roger."

"Roger?"

"Isn't that your real name?"

"Wilco."

"Over."

"Easy."

"How about we meet at that cafe across the street."

"Check."

"Not again."

Tallo got up to leave.

"Do you trust me?" I said. Tallo looked at me. I dangled the car keys. "I may run off with another woman."

Tallo smiled. "I think I'll put the handcuffs on you." She reached into the tapestry bag she wore slung over her shoulder and pulled out a pair of shiney metal shackles.

I was surprised to see that she actually had them. I laughed. "You'll have to catch me first," I said, backing away from her.

"I'm too lazy," Tallo replied. "And much to grown up to play that game. See you at the cafe. Good luck."

The first bookstore was neat and modern and seemed very well-stocked with new and used books. It had volumes in various languages including a large section in English.

"Yes, last July. Probably July 17th or 18th," I said. "Is there any way you can check your orders for those days?"

"Yes, I could. May I ask why?"

"If you received a book order from a Maria Sundance around those dates, then I want to buy that book."

"What's the name of the book."

"I don't know."

"Hm-m-m."

"Is it a lot of bother?" I asked.

The man smiled. He was young with sandy hair and his smile was sweet and boyish. "I'll check. It may take a little while. Browse around."

I did, but I couldn't focus on the books. I found myself wandering through the children's section looking for something about Tarzan and his emerald hat.

The young man emerged in less than ten minutes with a yellow sheet of paper. "Maria Sundance," he said.

"Yes." My heart was crashing against my ribs. "You found it?"

"She ordered the *Rubaiyat of Omar Khayyam,* 1952 edition, published by Garden City Books."

My voice was shakey. "Wonderful," I said. "Do you have the book by any chance?"

"I remember now," the man said. "She was very eager to get it. It was a rush order. She never picked it up. That happens sometimes. I sent a note but never heard from her."

"She died," I said.

"Oh." His face fell. "Sorry to hear."

"Do you have the book?"

He smiled again. He looked to be eighteen years old, but he was probably close to thirty. "I thought of sending it back." Was he teasing me? "But, I didn't. It's on the shelf, over there in the English section. Never sold, but I knew some day it would."

I scanned the shelves. My intensity made my vision fuzzy, but finally I put my hand on the book. My very trembling hand. It was a thin volume. Obviously used. The pages were slightly yellowed. The jacket, which was tattered on the edges, had a floral border and floral center design.

"How much?" I asked.

"Thirty pesos," he said.

"Will you take twenty-five?" I asked, my voice cracking with a silly giggle. "Just kidding," I added.

I gave him the money and ran outside. The cafe where I was to meet Tallo was three blocks away. I didn't want to take the time to walk it. I doubted she'd be there yet anyway. There was another cafe with outdoor tables next to the bookstore. I sat, took out the letter from my purse and opened the book to page 19. I was trembling with excitement and anticipation.

The first sentence with a number-coded word read: *I have ascertained where the 43-37-1-18-9-19/58-11-15-93-2-14 is located.* If our theory was right, those numbers should translate into *Winged Dancer,* I thought. Eagerly, I counted 43 letters beginning with the first word on page 19 of the *Rubaiyat.* "W!" I said aloud. I may have yelled. The waiter who had ignored me up until then came to my table. I ordered a coke. I couldn't remember ever being this excited. I then counted 37 letters from where the "W" was. It was an "I"! I continued, my heart pounding joyfully. Each letter fit. I continued until *Winged Dancer* was entirely filled in. I sat back smiling. I felt like singing. I lit a cigarette.

I had to get through eight more words to arrive at the most important two words on the page, the most important two words in the world—the name of Sundance's partner. I still hoped it would be Peter Petrillo, but I wouldn't be disappointed if it was not. Obviously, there was someone else besides Petrillo involved. If the name was not Petrillo, I was convinced it would be Jimanos' real name. I got through the next word, *statue,* all right, but had trouble with *Boweso* until I figured out the 06 meant skip six lines. I noticed that the waiter was staring at me from the doorway. I disregarded him and continued working. I had a little trouble with the next three words but decided either Martin Sundance or I was not always counting accurately. I finally ended up with *Moran Hills Hospital. He* spoke *only the* Boweso *tongue* was easy.

I was now at the crucial words, the name of the man who, I was sure, was Sundance's killer and who, I was sure, again, if he weren't Petrillo himself, could prove Petrillo was connected with Sundance. I got the first letter done, a "D". A "D". Not Peter Petrillo, then. I was counting my way to the second letter when, suddenly, someone was sitting at my table. I had been so absorbed that I was unaware of anyone approaching. I jumped, dropping my pencil and upsetting my coke glass.

Tallo helped me pick things up.

"What's all this?" she asked. "Did you find something?" She patted at the table with a paper napkin. "I was worried," she said.

"Worried," I repeated, distractedly, staring at the table. What she said hadn't really registered.

"You didn't show up at the cafe."

"Tallo!" I grabbed her by the shoulders. "I got the book!" I shouted. "Look, look! This is it!" I pounded my finger on the slim volume. "*The Rubaiyat of Omar Khayyam.* I'm at the name. I'm translating it. It's working. I almost have the name of the partner."

Tallo's expression said everything I was feeling. The page of the book had turned in the confusion. I found the right page and resumed my task. Tallo hovered over my shoulder.

"i", I said. "D-i" so far. His first name is "D-i" something." I kept working.

Tallo didn't interrupt. I was fully aware of her intense presence at my side. "Diego Orrimano," I said at last. "His name is Diego Orrimano."

Tallo was about to respond but I was back to counting. Finally I finished. "Sundance's partner is Diego Orrimano of Joaquin University." I threw my pencil up into the air. The waiter watched me with what appeared to be condescending pity.

I sat back now, beaming, really looking at Tallo for the first time since she'd arrived. We looked at each other. Two glowing faces. We shook hands across the table. That wasn't enough. We stood up and embraced. That wasn't enough. We kissed. That was a lot. I was very shaken. The waiter, by this time, must have thought we were insane. Tallo called him to us and ordered a coffee for herself and another coke for me.

I told Tallo how I had gotten the book and we laughed about the title. "*The Emerald Hat of Old, Dark Tarzan* isn't bad," Tallo said.

"Sure," I replied. "A ruby, an emerald. Very similar. Omar Khayyam, Old dark Tarzan. Juanita made a good try."

"Do you think this Diego Orrimano is our friend Jimanos?" Tallo asked.

"Yes."

"Let's make sure."

"What do you have in mind, Tallo?"

"We could go to Joaquin University."

"We could. Or, call."

"You don't want to run into him."

"Do you?"

"No." Tallo laughed. "This might be getting dangerous."

"I know. Do you want to back off, Tallo? It's all right if you do. I'll pursue it on my own. It's certainly more my battle than yours."

Tallo smiled at me. She leaned forward as she did, looking directly into my eyes. "Don't be silly," she said. "We'll do it together. You and I, partner."

I took her hand. "I'm glad I met you," I said. The waiter approached our table just then, as we were looking into each other's eyes, her hand in mine. I transformed the handholding into a handshake. "You're a good partner," I said. We moved our arms away, making room for the drinks on our table.

"There's something I'm still curious about," Tallo said when the waiter withdrew after having stared at us again in that strange way. "There's a sentence in the letter...after he says that they did some things that weren't honest and fair..." She took the second page of the letter. "Here it is," she said. *"We had to have* blank *as the* blank *of* blank *and* blank. Can you continue counting until you fill in those words?"

I did. It took a while because there was a whole paragraph I had to get through first and from time to time I made counting errors and had to backtrack. Tallo sipped her coffee as I worked. I was aware of her watching me. That may have contributed to some of the errors. I imagined her eyes caressing me, going along my neck and across my cheek. When I was done, I read the sentence aloud. *"We had to have Bartezo as the Commissioner of Dams and Waterways."*

"I'll be damned," Tallo said.

"No, the Suga River will be dammed," I replied, laughing.

Tallo did not laugh. "What is it?" I asked.

"Arturo Compaña was the previous Commissioner of Dams and Waterways," she said angrily. "When the press started publishing stories about his proclivity for male sexual partners, Compaña was forced to resign from his job and go into seclusion."

"Your basic homophobia," I said.

"Yes," Tallo replied, "but from what Sundance says here, it

appears that Compaña may not really be queer."

"Too bad."

Now, Tallo laughed. "How do you mean that?" she said.

"Both ways," I replied. "So, Sundance and Orrimano framed Compaña to get their boy in as Commissioner."

"Pretty slimey."

"Are you ready to get that creep?"

"I'm ready," Tallo said.

We went to a phone station. I called Joaquin University's personnel office and finally got in touch with the academic dean's office. The clerk there told me Diego Orrimano was a professor of Linguistics and that his specialty was South American tribal languages. Keeping my voice calm, I told her I thought I may have met him once before and asked for a description. Tall, thin, rimless glasses, balding, smoked cigars. There was no doubt now. Orrimano was Jimanos!

I was thinking.

"What are you doing?" Tallo asked.

"Thinking," I said.

She waited.

"Petrillo attended Joaquin University," I said at last.

Tallo's eyes lit up.

"Yes," I said. "That could be important." I was feeling scared for some reason. "Now all we have to do is show they knew each other," I added, trying to stifle the feeling of anxiety and dread. "Well, that's not *all* we have to do," I amended, lightly. "But that's the next step. Agreed?"

"Agreed."

"You call this time," I suggested.

I watched Tallo nodding as she talked on the phone. She had told the clerk in the registrar's office of Joaquin University that Petrillo was a job applicant and that she was calling to verify his academic record.

"He took four evening courses," Tallo said after she'd hung up. "Advanced English I," she said slowly, teasingly.

"Yes." I felt like biting my nails.

"Advanced English II." She waited.

"Go on." I felt like biting Tallo.

"The Statistics of Probabilities."

"And?" I was holding my breath.

"And...tah-dah...Linguistics."

"Hah!"

"Who do you think his teacher was?"

"I think it was Diego Orrimano."

"Good think."

"I'm convinced, Tallo. Orrimano got his student, Peter Petrillo, to find me when I arrived in Marigua and to get the folder from me."

"I'm convinced of that, too. Do you think a judge would be?"

"Probably not."

"We have to prove that Orrimano's and Petrillo's relationship went beyond teacher-student."

"I got it! Señora Petrillo. She might know. We'll ask her."

"What will we say?" Tallo asked. "That we're trying to prove that your dead rapist husband was involved in a murder or two?"

"We could be more subtle."

We were, but Señora Petrillo was still not cooperative when Tallo called her to ask if she could come and talk with her about a professor of her husband's at Joaquin University. Señora Petrillo demanded to know who Tallo was and why she wanted the information. Tallo said she was a student of journalism writing a feature article on Professor Diego Orrimano. Señora Petrillo refused to grant the interview. Tallo left her number in case Señora Petrillo changed her mind.

We considered taking all the information we now had to the police and turning it over to them. Tallo felt rather strongly that that would be a mistake. "They'll bumble it, if they investigate it at all," she said. She didn't have much confidence in the Postero Police Department.

We didn't know what to do so we went to the park. Postero had a very lovely park with rows and rows of flowers and flowering plants and vines and little gazebo-like things stuck here and there in the gardens. We sat in one of them. The sunshine through the trellised roof of the structure cast lovely dancing patterns on Tallo's face and arms. We began reviewing all the facts that we had. I kept getting distracted by how attractive Tallo looked. We decided we could go to the Moran Hills Hospital and maybe get some additional information there and we could go to the Post Office where Petrillo had worked and see what we could learn there. Neither of us felt like doing those things just then. It turned out that we felt like going to the beach. It was 7:00 p.m.

It took us a half-hour to drive to the shore. We found a deserted spot and spread out the Tintano Hotel towels on the ground.

"I went to the beach with Marinda once," I said. "That's when she told me the story of your life."

We sat side by side in our newly purchased swim suits. Although I had acquired a tan in Marigua, Tallo's skin was several shades darker than mine.

"Woven with lies, I suspect," Tallo said.

"Why would she lie?"

"To help you play your role with me."

"Didn't she know you wouldn't want that?"

"She knew, but, as you know, she got carried away with her assignment."

"She told me you had a friend named Melina."

"That part was true," Tallo said. She hesitated for just a moment, then went on. "Melina Castillo. She and I were lovers."

I nodded. I looked out at the sea gulls gliding around in the sky, wondering if Tallo would say more.

"Did she tell you about Melina's disappearance?" Tallo asked.

"Yes," I said. "She told me Melina climbed into the mountains and never came back."

"That was a long time ago."

"It was hard on you."

"Very."

"Still is?"

"Yes. Melina and I were very, very close."

"Mm-hmm."

"Too close for Melina. She was afraid."

"I know the feeling."

"She couldn't stay and she couldn't leave."

"Yes. And no one knows what happened...?"

"I know."

I waited.

"I received a letter from her a year ago."

"She's alive!"

"She's living in Venezuela. She's happy there, she says. I never told anyone. I never felt the wish to or the need to."

"Do you understand it?" I asked.

"I think so," Tallo said.

We looked at each other. What I felt was not the wild, powerful, electrically-charged chills I'd known with Marinda. It was quieter, deeper. What I felt was not the pleasant, secure, ego-boosting gratification I'd known with Teresa. It was more complex and strong than that. From Tallo's expression, it appeared that she was feeling something too.

Our eyes touched a while longer and then we looked away, out at the sea. We didn't speak again for a long time. We watched the birds. We gathered shells. We walked along the beach and went for a swim. We hadn't eaten since breakfast and neither of us seemed to be feeling hungry for food. We lay on the towels and looked at the waves and somehow began talking about our mothers.

Tallo's memories were of walks together on the beach, of evenings in their villa, of talks in the garden, of trips they took, of her mother's strength and love. My memories were less positive.

"My mother was more loyal than strong," I said. "Strength of commitment, maybe. Endurance. There was a lot of love, but. . ." I grew silent.

"It's hard for women." Tallo said softly.

"I know. Have you ever been with a man, Tallo, or men? Sexually? Emotionally?"

"Yes."

"Me, too."

We were lying on our backs and, at that moment, turned simultaneously to face each other."

"I prefer women," we said in unison.

We laughed. Tallo's hand was resting on the towel inches from mine. I moved my fingers toward hers. She moved hers toward mine. It was a soft, tentative touch, a gentle connecting of our hands and eyes. Tallo's smile faded. Her face grew serious.

"Something's happening to me," she said.

"I think I know what," I answered.

"I'm. . .I'm really liking you, Kat."

"Yes." I began laughing.

Tallo looked a little hurt.

"I'm just remembering," I said quickly, "the first time I saw you—at the fiesta, remember?"

"Marinda made you sing a song to me."

"The bitch."

"It was very lovely."

"I was shaking with stage fright."

"You looked at me the whole time."

"I know. I thought you were very.... I thought if I looked at you while I sang I could forget about all the other people watching and listening."

"Did it work?"

"Yes. Marinda had told me you were this special super-human creature. That was my first reaction to you."

"And now?"

I laughed again. "That's what struck me as so funny a moment ago, Tallo," I said. "The next time I saw you, you were lying on your stomach on the porch with your head half-way in the door, pulling on a string." I laughed some more. "You didn't look so super-human then. I love the contrast."

"And, am I super-human?" Tallo asked.

I was feeling very serious now. "You're super," I said.

"Thank you," Tallo replied quietly. She sat up, drew her knees to her chin and wrapped her arms around her legs. "I didn't expect to like you," she said. "I was irritated with Natalia and expected you to be a nuisance who I'd try to get rid of as soon as possible. I was trying not to hold it against *you,* though. It wasn't your fault that my aunt got her hair-brained idea. And now it's turning out that I like you. A lot. You're not a nuisance at all, Kat."

"Thank you."

We were looking into each other's eyes.

"Wow!"

"Yeah."

We went for a celebration dinner. We felt like we had so much to celebrate. We went to a French restaurant, the only one in Postero, and lingered over our meal for nearly three hours.

It was so easy to talk with Tallo. She told me it was the same for her. Our conversation was serious, and then silly and then flippant and then serious again.

235

24.

THE LECTURE

It was late when we returned to the hotel. At the desk, the clerk gave Tallo a message. Her aunt had called to see how she was enjoying her little vacation.

"I guess she didn't believe it was a business trip," Tallo said, chuckling. "That woman. She says she'll call tomorrow."

"And there was a visitor," the clerk said. "He did not leave his name."

"A visitor?" Tallo's tone changed radically. "What did he look like?"

"Well," the clerk said, pursing his lips. "Let me see. He had black hair, very neat. Small eyes. A moustache. A very tall man. Skinny."

"Did he wear glasses?" Tallo asked.

"I don't recall," the clerk replied brusquely, as if annoyed that Tallo was not satisfied with his rather detailed description.

We both looked around the lobby. "I don't think we should go to our room," Tallo said.

"Shit!"

"Right."

"Let's call the cops."

Tallo thought about this. "I don't know," she said. She thought some more. "OK."

We waited in the lobby for nearly an hour before two uniformed officers arrived. It was close to two in the morning. Tallo showed a paper identifying herself as an agent of the Mariguan Penal System and explained our suspicion that a potentially dangerous criminal was in our hotel room. The room was around the corner and down the corridor from the lobby. One officer went around the rear to check the window. The other took the pass key and went down the hall. Tallo and I waited in the lobby. After about ten minutes, both officers returned saying they had found no one. Tallo thanked them and they left looking more bored than annoyed at the false alarm.

We requested a different room and asked the clerk to tell no one of its location. The bellboy helped us move our things to the fourth floor. Because of our shopping trip, we had accumulated what seemed to be a ton of luggage. I had just finished tipping the bellboy and was going back into the room when I saw a man turn the corner and come toward me. He was very tall and thin. Although he had dark hair and a moustache, I knew instantly who it was. Jimanos! He pulled out a gun and pointed it at my head.

Jimanos gestured me into the room then slipped inside behind me. Tallo jumped when she saw him, dropping several clothes hangers. Jimanos' attention was focussed on Tallo long enough for me to give his arm a sharp crack. The gun clattered to the floor. I darted for it but I tripped or Jimanos pushed me, I'm not sure. He grabbed for the gun. Tallo and I tore for the door.

We made it out of the room and through the exit door across the hall. We flew down the stairs, two and three at a time. His footsteps clattered on the stairs above us. We kept running. I was terrified that at any moment there would be the cracking sound of gunfire. I opened what I thought was the door to the main floor, but instead of the lobby there was a deserted corridor. Damn! We had gone too far. Jimanos' footsteps continued racing down the stairs behind us. We ran through the carpeted corridor of the basement to another door. I was about two feet ahead of Tallo. We ran into the room and closed the door. I noticed with strange amusement that Tallo had her tapestry bag draped over her shoulder.

The room was dark. I could see the dim outlines of furniture, rows of folding chairs in the front, a large table, and a section of sofas and easy chairs in the rear. We ran to the rear and ducked down behind some easy chairs. We waited. The room was absolutely silent. We were both breathing heavily, and trying not to. We waited. I was hoping desparately that he would not come in here, and, hoping, if he did, he would not see us.

Slowly the door opened. It let in a stream of light from the corridor. He was silhouetted there in the doorway, the tall, thin figure, his arm extended, the gun in his hand. Tallo and I pushed ourselves down lower behind the chairs. We were pressed against each other. I thought I could feel her heart banging too. I raised my head just enough to see. Jimanos slinked inside the room moving his head, jerkily, back and forth, the silhouetted gun following his head movements. I wanted to move back further into the far corner of the room and merge with the wall. But I remained absolutely motionless, watching the eerie figure creep along slowly, his left hand brushing against the wall as he moved. Suddenly, the room was flooded with light.

I put my head down as far as I could, pushing against the rough fabric of the chair I prayed would conceal us. We had been far enough ahead of Jimanos that I knew he could not have seen us enter the room. He would see the room was empty and he'd leave, I hoped. I could hear his muffled footsteps slowly moving toward us. And then from the corner of my eye, to the right of where Tallo and I crouched, I saw an amazing sight. I almost cried out. On the couch about twenty feet from us, lay two partially nude people, clinging to each other, looking terrified. When they saw I saw them, it looked as if they were about to rise or say something. I put my finger to my lips to silence them. They remained as they were, a young man and a young woman, their eyes jumping with fright. I could hear Jimanos continuing to move past the rows of chairs to the back of the room where four fearful people hid.

"There you are," he said calmly.

I raised my head. He was looking right at me. Tallo mumbled a curse. The couple on the couch did not move.

"Come out from there now, girls, or I will have to shoot you. Hands in the air."

We rose, slowly, our arms stretched above our heads. Keeping the gun pointed at us, Jimanos glided back to the door and closed it. With his left hand, he turned a knob, locking it. He was smiling.

The black wig and moustache he wore gave him a sinister although somehow laughable appearance. I watched every move he made, and from the corner of my eye I watched the young couple. They did not move. Jimanos could not see them. He peered around the room. Near the front where he stood was an elevated platform containing a lectern and behind that a blackboard. Facing the platform were rows of chairs. Over to the side was a large conference table.

"A classroom," Jimanos said, still smiling. Then he laughed a hollow laugh which echoed in the room. "All right students, take your seats." He gestured to us with the gun.

Tallo and I moved out from behind the chairs.

"Sit near the front," Jimanos said.

We walked toward him. My knees were shaking. The barrel of the gun seemed to be pointed right at my pounding heart. I thought of Martin Sundance and felt closer to him at this moment than I ever had.

"Throw the purse over there," Jimanos said.

Tallo tossed her tapestry bag toward the front of the room and Jimanos went to it, dumping its contents on the floor, watching us all the while. He looked through Tallo's things, then pushed them aside. Except for the handcuffs. Those he put in his back pocket. His eyes looked menacing despite his calm demeanor. I was wishing we'd had the foresight to arm ourselves. You should never go hunting a killer unarmed, I said to myself, as if for future reference. I was wishing we had not run into this room or, at least, had waited at its door to grab him when he entered.

I was wishing I were in Chicago. I was wishing I were strolling through Lincoln Park Zoo with Elizabeth, staring safely at the caged wild animals. I was wishing that life were softer. I was wishing that Tallo had not gotten involved with this. There was no doubt in my mind that he was going to kill us. We moved slowly toward him. Will he shoot us here? Will the lovers on the couch be able to do anything? Will he shoot them, too?

Tallo and I sat down in straight-backed chairs.

"All right, let us begin," Jimanos said, sounding very professorial, as if this were a classroom at Joaquin University and he was about to begin a routine lecture on phonemes. He had walked onto the platform and stood now behind the lectern. He laid the gun on the surface of the lectern, removed his wig and moustache and tossed them on the floor. Tallo and I were sitting about twenty-five or thirty feet in front of him, several rows of chairs between us and him.

"The topic of tonight's lecture," Jimanos said, rubbing at his upper lip, "is..." He paused briefly. "The subject," he continued, "is *The Role of Dichotomies in the Recent History of the Winged Dancer.*" He smiled with self-satisfaction, then backed up a step or two, toward the blackboard. He took a piece of chalk and wrote the word DICHOTOMY on the board, printed it in capital letters.

It crossed my mind that he was nuts, psychotic, and then the word "evil" occurred to me. He had us in his power. He was playing with us.

"Dichotomy," Jimanos said, "the division into two, contradictory categories. A most intriguing and relevant theme in the Winged Dancer's history. I expect active participation from you as we explore this topic, class."

He looked at the two of us, each in turn. I felt a shiver of repulsion and fear.

"I want you to pay close attention to what I say and I expect you to participate. Ask questions and be prepared to answer questions that I ask you."

Tallo shifted her position in her seat, pushing her leg against mine. I wondered what she was thinking. I was sure her thoughts were not much different from my own.

Jimanos moved again to the blackboard. *Life and death,* he wrote. "Life and death," he said. "The primal dichotomy. By the time I am done speaking to you tonight, class, I will have decided that question in regard to you."

Evil, I thought. He's not crazy, he's cruel, sadistic. I could see Tallo looking at him with anger and fear. I moved my hand a few inches so my fingers touched hers. Jimanos continued speaking.

"The most recent chapter in the history of the famous lost statue begins at Joaquin University in the offices of the esteemed Professor Diego Orrimano." He began pacing casually across the platform. "It begins nearly one year ago when the professor received a communication from a Señor Martin Sundance inquiring as to the professor's competency in comprehending orally-communicated Bowesan.

Oh, Jesus. So, that's it, I thought. The ghoul is going to make his

240

confession. He's going to stand there with a gun on us and tell his story, and then he's going to kill us. I prayed there was watchman, or some hotel employee, anyone, who would come. Maybe someone was on the way now.

"It was Sẽnor Sundance's wish to hire the professor's services as a translator. Professor Orrimano accompanied Señor Sundance to a local hospital where a very old and withered man lay dying in a darkened room. The man, though fluent in Spanish, refused to speak it. He would speak only Bowesan. It was Señor Sundance's hope to learn from him the secret location of the long-lost golden statue of the Winged Dancer. He presented Professor Orrimano with a list of questions to ask the tribesman."

Orrimano had been looking at the ceiling through most of this recital with occasional glances at us. Now, he looked directly at us.

"Class," he said. "I expect that you are sufficiently familiar with the Bowesos to have some speculation about the stance the tribesman would likely take. You, Señorita, on the aisle seat, your name, please."

"Neva," Tallo said crisply. "Tallo de Carrizosa Neva."

Orrimano nodded his head slowly toward her. "Yes. I'm honored," he said flamboyantly. "Your presence in my humble classroom adds an aura of aristocracy. The Neva's are a most esteemed family. Tell me, Señorita Neva, what stance would you predict the tribesman to have taken?"

Tallo made a sound which I interpreted as exasperation, but then she smiled.

"Orrimano," she said pleasantly, "I'm very interested in what you have to say about the Boweso man and about the Winged Dancer, but this is a rather strange way of doing it. Why don't we just sit together and talk. Maybe in our room upstairs."

A bold move, I thought. I hope it works.

"No," Orrimano said vehemently, looking flustered. "We will do it my way!" He pounded his fist on the lectern, then seemed to calm again. "I want to enlighten you, class," he said, resuming the professorial tone. "You were seeking knowledge and you shall receive it."

"I see no purpose in this farce!" Tallo rebutted angrily. "If you want to tell us, then tell us but this..."

Orrimano grabbed his pistol. "I do not tolerate unruliness in the classroom," he said angrily. "You will respond to my questions."

241

He was waving the gun as he spoke. He leaned then on the lectern, aiming the gun directly at Tallo.

"From what I know of the Bowesos," Tallo said, "I would predict the tribesperson would very politely tell you that he had no knowledge of the location of the statue." She spoke matter-of-factly. Her voice was calm, but I could feel the tension in her leg, still pressed tightly against my own. I squeezed her hand.

"Good prediction," Orrimano said. "But wrong." He placed the pistol back on the lectern. "The old man's name was Dulato. He told me his story." Orrimano leaned both hands on the lectern. "Dulato's life had been a hard one, a life on the margin of an increasingly dehumanized technological culture. Another dichotomy, I believe: the Boweso past, the lost culture, versus the reality of modern life. The Bowesos who survived into this century were few. They tried to remain together. They tried to retain their heritage. When I met Dulato, all the other Bowesos were gone. I listened with compassion as the poor creature spoke to me of his people and of his life. When the last of his fellow tribesmen died, Dulato was alone. A man alone among alien beings."

Orrimano paused dramatically at this point. Was it just for effect, I wondered, or was he really feeling Dulato's pain? I could not tell.

"He had withdrawn from life. He barely spoke to anyone. And yet he spoke freely with me. Why?" Orrimano leaned over the lectern, looking down at us.

I was torn between my desire to know more of Orrimano's story and my awareness that the more Tallo and I knew, the more danger we were in. He waited for a response, staring intensely at us. I returned his pointed stare wishing that looks *could* kill, or at least maim.

"Because you spoke Bowesan," I said.

"Yes, that is why he began. He told me many things and he spoke of the Winged Dancer. That glorious, coveted, piece of gold."

Orrimano's eyes seemed to glitter.

"He said it was gone forever, that he knew exactly where it was as did every Bowesan who survived the earthquake and all their progeny. They all knew. As you may be aware, the statue was immeasurably meaningful to them. It was the symbol of what they had been and what they lost and, to a person, they kept the knowledge of its whereabouts to themselves.''

''But he told you,'' I said. I knew I was being drawn into the story, intrigued by it. I was feeling less fearful now, or at least, less in tune with my fear.

''He was the last,'' Orrimano said. ''They wanted the earth to have the Dancer, he told me, not the madness that was humankind. And yet, yes, he told me where it was. The only Boweso who had ever spoken of its exact location to a non-Boweso.''

Orrimano walked in front of the podium now.

''Why, students,'' he asked, ''why did he tell? There are three reasons.'' He slowly held up three fingers. ''Can you infer any of them?''

''Because he assumed it could never be retrieved anyhow,'' Tallo said flatly.

''Very good. That is one.'' Orrimano looked to us waiting for more, holding up two fingers now.

''Because you offered him something?'' I asked. I was actually getting hooked, getting caught up in the student role, taken back to my law school days. Contracts, considerations, exchange. What Orrimano could have offered that dying man, I did not know.

''Yes,'' Orrimano said, ''I offered him his final chance to speak in his native tongue to a fellow being with interest in and sensitivity to and knowledge of the world he'd lost, the world he'd never had. It made him very happy. It made him want to give me something in return.''

''How nice,'' Tallo said.

Orrimano ignored her remark. ''And the third reason?''

Neither of us responded. I was thinking again of the young man and woman on the couch. They were never completely out of my mind. The back of the couch faced us, totally concealing them and I was sure they could remain undetected if they stayed there. I wondered what they were thinking. I wondered if there was another exit back there and if they could get out, maybe already had, and if the police were on their way to free us from this demented man.

''The third reason...'' Orrimano said. He withdrew a slender cigar from his breast pocket and lit it. ''...was based on this fact: Dulato knew that with his death would die the knowledge of the statue's location. He did not want the knowledge to die with him. He wanted to die with the hope that someday another Bowesan culture would come to life and the Winged Dancer would be there.

This is theory, you understand, simply speculation on my part, but quite probable, I believe."

"So, he told you," Tallo said, impatiently. "And then what?"

"We musn't rush history, Señorita Neva," Orrimano reprimanded. "We must unfold it, slowly, as life unfolds." He smiled condescendingly at her. "A statue deep within a cave, submerged under tons of water, surely would not be recoverable, our old tribesman thought. But he wanted someone to know before he died. Together, we drew a map. He and I."

Orrimano drew on his cigar and let go a huge puff that lingered over his head like a cloud over a mountain peak.

"The Boweso knowledge of the location of their settlement survived intact. The map was accurate. How do I know this, students? How do I know it wasn't myth?"

He paused, waiting for a response from his "class".

"I don't know," Tallo said, folding her arms.

I shook my head.

"I knew because I went there—into Lake Suga, forty feet below its clear, smooth surface. There I found the cave. Dulato's description was excellent. An immense round boulder blocked its entrance, just as he had said. On the boulder was carved a Bowesan poem. We had found the spot, my divers and I, but there was a problem. A major problem."

Orrimano paused dramatically.

"The boulder could not be moved," he said at last. "The pressure of the water held it firmly against the mouth of the cave. Ah, but I'm jumping ahead in my story. Let me continue chronologically."

I was thinking about Orrimano's first dichotomy—life or death for Tallo and me. The gun sitting on the lectern made it hard, at times, to concentrate on the "lecture", and yet I was fascinated by his story, at the filling in of so many gaps.

"Dulato told Professor Orrimano exactly where the treasure was. Sundance, present during the entire interaction, knew what was happening and believed he had a claim to the treasure. Being a reasonable person, Orrimano could understand Senor Sundance's position and so a partnership was formed."

Orrimano was leaning against the blackboard now, puffing on his cigar between sentences.

"The expectation was that, with the map and some well-equipped divers, the statue could be retrieved. The cave's location in the lake was ideal for the project since it was within an isolated cove. We could excavate the treasure, put it on our truck and leave with no one the wiser.''

We knew enough! I looked at Tallo from the corner of my eye. She looked strong but vulnerable. We knew too much! We would never leave this room.

"Professor," I interrupted. "Would you escort Señorita Neva and me to the Postero Airport. We were planning to leave the country—to leave for good."

I felt Tallo tighten momentarily, and then immediately switch. She nodded her head, confirming what I was saying.

"Our plan was for me to make my escape. Tallo and I. We plan to change our identities and live away from here, always.''

Orrimano looked at me with patient tolerance. He placed his index finger before his pursed lips, shushing me. Then, giving no further acknowledgment to my interruption, he went on.

"As I mentioned earlier, the boulder, unfortunately, could not be moved. We ruled out dynamite or any other means except drawing some of the water from the lake."

Stop, I was thinking. Please don't say any more.

"The only way to accomplish this would be to build a dam."

Orrimano went to the blackboard again and began sketching.

"Here is the Suga River," he said, "flowing in here..." He drew a circle. "Into Lake Suga, and out here..." He indicated an area of lower elevation on the other side of the lake. "And into the sea. As you may have heard, the proposal for a dam to divert the course of the Suga River had been under consideration for many years. The Tordad Plain, here," he indicated it on his diagram, "needed the irrigation badly."

Orrimano put the chalk down and took a few steps away from the blackboard. He brushed chalk dust from his trousers. I was staring at the gun, searching for some pretext to get to it.

"Professor Orrimano," I said. "I'm not quite clear about the geography you're describing." I rose from my chair and began moving toward the platform.

"Stop!" he ordered. "Return to your seat."

I remained where I was. Orrimano picked up the pistol. Should I call his bluff, I thought? I'm going to die anyway. I should try.

"Sit, Señorita Rogan. I advise you to sit. Otherwise, Señorita

Neva will have to hear the rest of the lecture by herself. I mean what I say."

I went back to my seat next to Tallo. Orrimano went over the diagram again, as if I really had been unclear. He explained how a dam would lower the lake level. He went over it very thoroughly.

"Is it clear now, Señorita Rogan?"

"It's clear," I said.

Orrimano smiled. "The building of a dam is a major project," he continued. "Quite expensive. Carlos Campaña, the Commissioner of Dams and Waterways opposed it. But Orrimano and Sundance needed that dam built." Orrimano spoke with vehemence. "What could they do? Señorita Neva, you are a Mariguan. What do you know of this?"

"You orchestrated Compaña's downfall," Tallo said.

Orrimano smiled down at us. "'Very good," he oozed. "And here we have another dichotomy—him or us. The scandal, as you know, grew ugly. Compaña resigned and our man, Arturo Bartezo, moved into the spot, as we knew he would."

Tallo and I looked disgusted. Orrimano apparently picked it up.

"The practical vs. the idealistic," he said, almost defensively. "So many dichotomies. Señorita Rogan, you are attending to that recurrent theme, I trust."

"I'm attending," I said. "Ethical vs. unethical."

Orrimano shrugged. "So many dichotomies," he repeated. "Like winners and losers." He looked at us significantly, raising his eyebrows. "So," he continued, beginning to pace again, "with Bartezo in charge of the Office of Dams and Waterways, it was not long before plans for the project were underway. The actual building began in June of last year. The newspapers gave it thorough coverage, as you may recall, Señorita Neva. Everything was going smoothly. It could have been so simple." He shook his head, his arms now folded in front of him. "So simple," he repeated. "But, unfortunately..." He began the pacing again, "one of the co-conspiritors in the Orrimano-Sundance adventure, the loser, as it turned out, began to be pricked with foolish pangs of guilt. The ethical-unethical dilemma you mentioned, Señorita Rogan. Foolish man. 'That statue belongs to the people', he said. Nonsensical rhetoric, but it made me nervous."

At that moment, I heard a muffled scraping sound in the back of the room. It was very faint, but I had no doubt I'd heard it. I did not turn toward it. I hoped Tallo would not either. Orrimano stopped speaking and looked back there. His hand went to the pistol, reflexively it seemed. He waited, staring toward the back, not moving a muscle. My mind was racing. If he went back there, he might discover the others. On the other hand, I realized, it could be the diversion we need, the opportunity to somehow overpower him. He still stood motionless. Would he investigate? I feared for the young couple. If he found them, surely he'd...

Orrimano began to move cautiously away from the platform, looking from us to the rear section of the large room. Not a sound could be heard. Not even the sound of Orrimano's feet as he moved slowly across the carpet and down the aisle. He was almost abreast of us. I was ready. Two more steps and I would spring. My muscles were tensed. I rehearsed mentally the exact movements I would make, going for his hand with mine and then his solar plexus with my foot. He took one more step, then stopped. I remained like a coiled spring, waiting. Two more seconds and it would be over, one way or the other.

Suddenly, Orrimano retreated. He walked backwards several steps, then returned to the lectern. He stood behind it, crouched down, pointing the gun to the rear of the room, his form mostly concealed by the wooden podium.

"You back there, stand up!" he yelled.

The resounding shock of his voice shook the air, seeming to vibrate the objects in the room. Silence. I had turned in my chair and was looking back toward the couch and easy chairs. I saw that a window was open a foot or so, a window near the chairs where Tallo and I had hidden. I turned back to Orrimano. "You're pretty jumpy," I said. "What's the matter?"

He ignored me and continued looking beyond where Tallo and I sat.

"How are you holding up?" I whispered to Tallo, placing my hand on her knee.

"It's not looking good," she replied. "His jitteriness may work to our advantage," she whispered.

"Sh-h," Orrimano said.

There was another sound from the rear, just like the earlier one. This time, Tallo and I both turned. We could see the drapery being moved by the breeze. It happened again, the same noise. This time, we could see the fabric of the drapery pushing against a tin ashtray causing the scraping sound as it receded. I looked back at Orrimano. He was still concealed behind the podium, with his gun hand poking out from the side of the lectern, but now he stood up to his full six plus feet.

"The ghost," I said.

Orrimano asked me to go and close the window. As I did I flashed the quivering couple-of-the-couch what I hoped was a reassuring smile. I was immensely relieved that they had not been discovered. I looked upon their presence in the room as a potential help to us. I wasn't sure how. Maybe only as witnesses after the fact. Maybe they'd help convict Orrimano of my murder and of Tallo's. My legs felt weak as I walked back to my chair.

Orrimano resumed his "lecture". "As I was saying," he said, "Sundance began to express doubts about our enterprise."

The professor seemed barely to have lost a beat from the interruption.

"Now, trust between the two of us had never been high. In fact, we each had 'insurance' against the betrayal of the other."

Orrimano elaborated on this, telling us how each partner had placed a letter in the hands of a trusted person of his choosing, a letter (one might call it an 'expose,' he said), to be disclosed upon the death of he who wrote it. When Orrimano decided that Sundance must go, he knew the insurance letter must go, as well.

"How easy that was," Orrimano said cockily. "Poor man, he had given it to his lawyer. So obvious. That was the first place I looked, but I took the 'insurance' letter only after I was convinced that Martin Sundance had to be eliminated. Do you know how I became convinced?"

I was nodding. It was all falling into place. The bastard.

"Señorita Rogan."

"Martin Sundance's letter to his sister," I said, "But how did you know about the letter?"

"The fates," he replied, smiling. "Fate." Now he laughed. It was a hollow, ugly laugh. "It was through a chance meeting that I found out about the letter."

Orrimano went on to tell us that on the evening of June 26th of last year, he was having a drink at his favorite tavern. An acquaintance of his, a very attractive woman, he said, who also frequented that establishment, was present. Her name was Dolores Diamonto.

"She was romantically involved with someone to whom I, myself, had introduced her," Orrimano said, "Martin Sundance by name. A very handsome couple they made. On the evening in question Señorita Diamonto was not happy. We sat together, she and I, and she confided to me of her concerns. They were about Martin. Poor girl. It seems that Martin had cancelled an engagement the two of them had that evening, claiming work he had to do. Señorita Diamonto was suspicious." Orrimano chuckled. "She thought, perhaps, another woman was involved. To satisfy herself, she stopped in at Martin Sundance's apartment, hoping she would find him there alone, fearing she would not. He was there. He was writing a letter which Señorita Diamonto could see on the table. She could see the salutation, *Dear Maria*. He told her he was writing to his sister. Martin was to fly to the United States the next day and he chose to spend the night before his departure writing a letter to his sister. Dolores Diamonto was hurt and distraught, that was clear, but she was not as distraught as I about this news. I knew I had to stop him. I left the tavern and took a taxi to Martin's home. He was not there. I assumed my betrayer had gone to mail the letter. What did the professor do next?" Orrimano asked. "Anyone?"

"Do go on," Tallo said.

"What the professor did," Orrimano went on, "was to contact his student and his sometime friend, Peter Petrillo."

I felt the sweat suddenly break out over my body. This was it! The connection confirmed! I had to get Orrimano's gun away from him. He seemed oblivious to my reaction to the name he had just named.

"Peter needed money," he continued. "I needed a letter intercepted at the Post Office. The deal was quickly made. He assured me his inspection of the mail to Arcedia would arouse no notice. The next day, I had the letter in my hand."

Orrimano held up his hand, grasping an imaginary letter.

"What a foolish letter it was. Written in some silly coded way. And the map was there, too. Our map. Our secret map. That man deserved to die."

Orrimano's gaunt face twisted into a malevolent sneer.

"I placed the letter and map in a leather folder and drove to Salsente where I caught a flight to Caracas and from there to Miami, then to Chicago, Illinois, U.S.A. This pistol," he held it

249

up for us, "went with me on my trip. Dolores had told me Sundance would be staying at the Endicott Hotel and that is where I found him."

Obviously he plans to kill us, I thought again. No way would he confess like this and then just let us go. Somehow, we must outsmart him. We must get that gun. He's disgustingly egotistical. How can I use that against him?

"Señor Sundance was surprised to see me, as you might suspect," Orrimano continued. "We talked in his hotel room. He did not like what he heard. He looked very frightened."

Orrimano smiled malevolently.

"The folder began to tremble in the poor man's hand, and then he bolted from the room."

Orrimano continued to smile.

"He did not get far, as you know. And at this point, another important figure enters the story. A North American."

Orrimano was still smiling. The man is really enjoying this, I thought. Sick. Sickening.

"With his dying breath, Sundance makes a request of this person. Señorita Rogan, exactly what was said?"

"He asked me to get the folder to his sister," I said.

"And what else?"

"That's all. Not to use the mails."

"I see," Orrimano said. "Yes. I wondered why you didn't send it. I'm so glad you didn't. You see, I assumed initially that the police had the folder and would forward it with the body. Had you sent it, we would not be here right now." He smiled wickedly, then continued. "There's a Sargent Marcus of the Chicago Police with a soft spot in his hard little heart. Hearing of my bereavement he told me many things."

Orrimano was chuckling as he said this. He was looking very smug. I thought again of the two people in the back. I still wasn't sure if Tallo knew they were there. I wished I could think of a plan.

"But the folder was not with Sundance's other worldly goods," Orrimano said. "So, who did I call? Tallo Neva? Who?"

Instead of answering, Tallo asked a question of her own. "How did you know the folder wasn't there?"

"A tedious detail, Tallo dear, but I appreciate your inquisitiveness. Professor Orrimano, being a scholar, as you know, and not a criminal, enlisted the appropriate assistance for some of the undertakings necessary to pursue his mission. He hired a helper familiar with such things.''

Orrimano's tone continued to reflect pedantic condescension.

"As far as determining that the folder had not arrived with the corpse, my helper tells me that a few pesos to a baggage worker at the Postero Airport sufficed. Now, back to my original question, Señorita Neva. Who did the professor call when he discovered the folder was missing?''

"I don't imagine you'd have called Maria Sundance?'' Tallo said.

"If Maria Sundance had the folder, if Martin had slipped it to Señorita Rogan who then mailed it to Maria Sundance, then either a) I would have been arrested immediately, or b) they would wait at the site, at Lake Suga, to catch me in the act of retrieving the statue. Since a) had not occurred, I assumed either they were waiting for the dam to be completed or Maria Sundance had not received the letter. If Maria Sundance had not received the letter, then that woman in Chicago must have it. Who did I call?''

"You didn't call me,'' I said.

"I didn't know your name.''

"You called the Chicago Police,'' Tallo said, "to find out her name.''

"Yes, I called Sargeant Marcus again. He assured me that everything that had been on Sundance's body and everything of his from the hotel room had been sent. He would not reveal the name of the woman, your name, Kat Rogan.''

"So, how did you find out?'' I asked.

"You told me.''

Orrimano paused, apparently awaiting my amazed reaction. I did not respond.

"On July 16th, you had a phone conversation with Maria Sundance. The next morning, you had another. You gave me all the information I needed.''

"You tapped her phone.''

"Of course. Although *I* didn't actually do it. What would I know of such mundane things. That is where my underworld friend came in. Of course, he also came in before that. It is he who breaks into people's files and takes the things I need, not me. He took Sundance's 'insurance letter'. Later, he visited the offices of Señor Jorge Triste.''

251

I had to admit, I continued to find this very fascinating. I was imagining all of it being said in a court of law. "So, you knew I was coming and sent Petrillo to meet me at the airport."

Orrimano nodded.

"But how did you know Maria would not be there, too...Yes, of course. You messed with her jeep. You caused her delay."

"I'd never been to the site of an archeological excavation before. I found it quite interesting. Maria Sundance was most gracious in discussing her work with me. Pulling out the wire and removing that little screw from her jeep presented no problem."

"So, you and Maria Sundance met each other," I mumbled, regretting now, more than ever, that I had never met her.

"Yes. Charming woman. Believe me I took no pleasure in, as you say, 'messing with' her *other* car, the one that went out of control on the highway."

"How did you manage that?" I asked, "To tamper with her car?"

"Now, now. Let us not jump ahead. You arrived in Postero, Kat Rogan. Petrillo, a very charming man, I agree, flirted with you and wooed you. He picked you up at the bar of this very hotel."

"No," I said.

"No?"

"He did *not* pick me up."

"Whatever you say," Orrimano said. "Call it what you will. Now here's the point where the student knows more than the teacher. I read the transcript of the trial. Was your story true?"

"Yes."

"I'm inclined to believe you. Petrillo behaved like an imbecile. His assignment was merely to relieve you of the folder. I suppose he got what he deserved. With you in jail and Maria Sundance determined to get the folder, the next step was obvious."

"Obvious," I said sarcastically. "Kill her."

I was thinking of what Orrimano would consider the next obvious steps. From the look on Tallo's face, so was she.

"Life and death," Orrimano said. "Maria Sundance presented the most imminent danger, for she, I assumed, could translate the coded material. She needed a book to do so, a very well-known book, the *Rubaiyat of Omar Khayyam*."

"How did you know that?" I asked sharply.

"Think, student, think. Did I not know of all her phone

conversations? She made a call to Julia Pontora, a former maid of hers. Señorita Pontora acknowledged that she may have borrowed the book and packed it with her things when she left three years before. She promised to search for it and let her former employer know the minute she found it. I have no idea whether she found it or not, but that no longer matters. Maria Sundance was a danger to me and she had to go. Her garage was unlocked. I'm sure death was quick. The newspapers said she had a broken neck.''

Orrimano took several steps to the side as if to walk away from Maria's death. He continued. "With Maria Sundance gone, the only danger lay in someone else translating the letter and map.''

"So you stole them from Triste's office," I said. "But you waited so long. Why was that? Why didn't you take them right away?'' Again my curiosity was overtaking my fear.

"I should have taken them right away. You would have made a good consultant, Señorita Rogan. I believed, however, that there was no real danger. I believed that only Señorita Sundance could translate them and with her gone and you convicted to life in prison, I felt very much at ease.''

"So, what changed your mind? Why did you steal the folder later?''

"I told you, *I* did not steal it. My hireling, remember? I sent him to Señor Triste's files only after discovering that you had hired a private investigator. There was a remote chance that he would find some way to break the code.

"And how did you know I hired a detective?''

Orrimano left the platform, taking the pistol with him, and seated himself on a chair, facing us, several rows away. "Señora Petrillo,'' he said. "She's been most helpful to me. Inadvertently, of course.''

I felt sickened. This man was a snake.

"She works in a tobacconist shop not far from here, on Grande Street. I go there from time to time. We are acquainted. I taught her husband, as you know. I have been to dinner in their home. Señora Petrillo has great respect for me and at times would tell me things.''

Orrimano stretched his endless legs into the aisle.

"For example,'' he continued, "she told me you telephoned her, Tallo Neva. She told me that you called and said you were a journalist writing an article about me. She told me that and she told me how to reach you, here, at the Tintano Hotel. But last summer, what she said was that a detective was asking her questions about the stabbing of her husband. It upset her, poor child, and she needed to talk about it. People do confide in me. So nice of them. When I heard, Señorita Rogan, that you had hired a detective, I decided it would be safer if I had the folder in my possession. So, I got it. No problem. And then I relaxed, waiting for the dam to be completed."

Orrimano lit another cigar.

"You're probably wondering why I came to you at the prison farm," he said. "Why would Professor Orrimano feel a need to do that? Any ideas?"

Neither Tallo nor I responded.

"Señora Petrillo again," Orrimano said. "She's my leak. She told me she'd received a call from some young man claiming to be writing an article about American prisoners in Marigua. He asked questions about you, Señorita Rogan."

"Paulo," Tallo whispered to me.

"That concerned me," Orrimano said. "I didn't know what it meant but it concerned me and stimulated me to visit you in prison to determine if another copy of the letter and map existed. I went to Solera. Hideous place. You had been transferred, I learned. I went to the Neva Estate. You were incommunicado temporarily, but then, as you know, we arranged a visit. You seemed to trust me." He paused, shaking his head. "Too bad you didn't," he said. "Too bad. I believed that you did, however, until I received that phone call at my newly acquired phone number, the call about car insurance. And then when I received the news from Señor Torenno at 47 Montenegro, I knew for sure that you knew I was deceiving you. I assumed you would contact Señora Petrillo. How right I was. The rest you know. Have I left anything out of the history?"

"Yes," I said, "but only because you are unaware of some of the facts."

"Do enlighten me."

"There are two other people who know everything."

"Is that so? Who, may I ask?"

"They're very impressed with you and want to meet you."

Orrimano smiled. "Martin Sundance tried the same thing," he said. "I didn't believe him either. When I told him that day in the Chicago hotel that I had 'cancelled his insurance', had removed the letter he'd left with his attorney, and when I showed him the folder containing the letter to his sister, Señor Sundance laughed. He was trying so hard to be convincing. He laughed and said he had an additional insurance policy. He wanted to make a deal with me. I did not believe him, and it turned out that I was correct. Do you now wish to make a deal with me?''

"Possibly," I said. I was sweating. "The people I referred to are at Neva's Estate. They're expecting to hear from us in the morning. We could invite them here and..."

"Come now."

"They would love to hear how you were able to get Dulato to..."

"Señorita Rogan. Enough!"

"If they don't hear from us, they'll..."

"Enough, I say!"

He walked back to the platform, and, with the piece of chalk, underlined the words *life and death*. Then he stared at us for what seemed an interminable length of time.

"There have been enough killings," he said at last.

I wished I could have felt relieved.

"We will go to my cabin at Lake Suga. You will both remain there until I have the statue. At that point, I will disappear. As soon as I am safe, I will contact the police, telling them where you are and you will be freed from my cabin. These are my plans," he said. "How do you like them?"

I did not believe him, of course. I was more sure than ever that his intent was to kill us. "Interesting," I said.

"Then, class is dismissed," Orrimano replied. "But, don't leave hastily." He took the handcuffs from his pocket. "The keys, please," he said to Tallo.

Tallo caught my eye. I don't think she believed him any more than I. She went to the pile of things Orrimano had dumped from her bag. From a small coin purse, she removed a key. She approached Orrimano with it. I was hoping she wouldn't do anything foolish, but I was hoping she would be able to do something.

"Stop!" he said. "Throw it, please."

Tallo tossed the key. It landed on the rug. Cautiously, Orrimano picked it up, then, pointing the gun at us, he walked over to the window and removed two ties from the draperies. "That handkerchief," he said, pointing toward the pile of things from Tallo's purse. "Pick it up, please. I'm going to have to gag you. I must insure your silence while I do a little exploring. Nothing to worry about." He pulled a handkerchief from his pocket. "One for each of you," he said. "Who first?"

We both stared at him, neither speaking. "No volunteers? Señorita Rogan, then. Roll the handkerchief into a ball and put it in your mouth."

I looked at him with disgust. He raised the pistol. I did what he said, after which he tossed a drapery tie to Tallo. "Tie it around her mouth. I'll check the tightness, so do a good job."

Tallo did what he said, making sure that I could breathe all right. Orrimano then had us do the same procedure with Tallo, after which he told us to sit on the floor near the table. He had Tallo place one shackle on her wrist, weave it between the table leg and a cross board and fasten the other end on my wrist. He tied our free wrists together with another drapery tie.

"I'll be back in a minute or two," Orrimano said, leaving the room.

Tallo's eyes caught mine and then our eyes held each other. I sent her my concern, my caring and fear, and she sent me hers through her eyes. Our wrists were linked together, our eyes, and our lives were now linked together and maybe our deaths. I could not wipe the tears that came. I could feel them, two tears, one for each of us. I felt Tallo's visual caress. It can't end this way, I thought. It's just beginning.

I turned toward the rear of the room, hoping the two people would go now, run for help, get the police. There was no movement back there. Why don't they do something, I thought angrily. Tallo seemed unaware of why I was looking there.

25.

THE ALLEY

Within a few minutes, Orrimano returned. He tossed us the key instructing us to unlock the shackles. As usual, he held the gun and kept his distance from us. How to stop him? We were now standing and, as per Orrimano's commands, had shackled ourselves together, wrist to wrist. Was his plan to kill us now, I wondered? We were still gagged.

"I'm going to take you to a storage room I found," Orrimano said. "It seems to be unused. I am going to leave one of you there while I take the other to my cabin. Then I shall return for the one I left behind. You are in no danger, believe me."

I did not believe him for a second. Was that room to be our execution chamber?

"Come now. Walk slowly ahead of me. If you try anything, I will not hesitate to shoot."

We walked out the door, Orrimano following behind. The corridor was empty. It must have been near four in the morning. He told us to keep walking until he said otherwise. We went through a door that led to an unfinished section of the basement. It was dimly lit, musty and cluttered.

"Stop. Open that door," Orrimano said.

I opened the old wooden door to a small, dark room. I thought of Solera. I thought of the cell at the Estate, and of Marinda.

"Who will stay?" Orrimano asked. "You, Señorita Neva." He placed the key on a box then backed away. "Unlock the handcuffs."

Tallo complied.

I have to do it now, I thought frantically, when my hand was freed. I worried about endangering Tallo. I worried about dying. God, how much I wanted to live! I have to do it now. Get the gun and smash this evil bastard. Orrimano told me to handcuff Tallo to a pipe within the little room. I moved as if to do so. Orrimano was a near as he'd been to us. It had to be now. He was going to take me somewhere to kill me, then come back to take Tallo and do the same to her. I had to do it now. I took in a deep breath, clenched my teeth, then swung the pair of shackles and let go.

They caught him somewhere on the face. There was a thud and a clang. He staggered. The light wasn't good. I couldn't see the gun. Where was the gun? Had he dropped it? Did he still have it? I lurched toward him. So did Tallo. I feared that the next sound I would hear would be the explosion from a pistol.

I was right. The sound was deafening in the small room. I saw the flash of light, too, and I waited for the pain and blackness.

"Don't move a muscle," Orrimano said to me.

He was pointing the gun at my face. His own face was full of blood. Apparently I was not hit. Tallo! He must have gotten Tallo! She lay motionless on the floor. Oh, no. I rushed to her. The light was so dim. Oh, God, he's killed her!

"Get back," Orrimano ordered.

I was bending over her. Her leg moved slightly. I tried to see, to tell where she was hurt. Her eyes seemed closed but I couldn't tell for sure. I reached to touch her.

"Get back," Orrimano repeated.

There was wetness near her neck. Oh, God! She lifted her arm, reaching toward me. Orrimano jerked me to my feet. He handed me the cuffs.

"Put these on her or I'll shoot the bitch again." His voice was full of rage. "Fasten it to the pipe. Her wrist to the pipe. Do it!"

Slowly I wrapped the circle of metal around Tallo's limp wrist and locked it into place. She lay helplessly, stretched out on her back on the dirty floor.

I started to untie my gag, but Orrimano yelled for me to stop. I felt Tallo's forehead. Her skin was warm. I couldn't tell exactly where the wound was. Her neck and shoulder and chest were wet with blood. I gestured toward Tallo's injury, hoping he'd at least let me bandage it.

"Come on," he hissed. "Out."

I was unable to make myself move. He pulled me roughly to my feet and closed the door with Tallo inside.

If we left her, she would die. She would bleed to death. Orrimano was too far away for me to try to strike him. He held the omnipresent pistol on me.

"Come now," he said.

He was wiping at his face with a dirty rag. There was blood all over his forehead from where I'd hit him with the handcuffs, and spots of it were on his shirt. He took me to a door down the hall.

"Remove your gag, now," he said. "Remember, if you yell, you die."

I undid the tie and pulled the handkerchief from my mouth. "Orrimano..." I began.

"Not one sound," he hissed viciously. "Out the door."

I opened the door. I felt sick. I walked outside into the dark alley, Orrimano behind me.

"Walk," he said through clenched teeth. "That way, to the VW beyond that second passageway."

There were a number of cars parked in the alley and garbage cans and piles of junk. Narrow, dark passageways cut between the buildings. I moved toward the car he had indicated. I was weak. Numb. Nauseated. It seemed my life was to end now, just when... It wasn't fair. Not fair. I love you, Tallo. I forced my sluggish feet to keep moving.

I was only a yard away from the VW when the crashing came, the banging racket. It assaulted my head, my ears. He must have fired the pistol. I must be hearing the sound of death inside my head. Bullet penetrating my brain. Setting off a million synapses. Crushed neurons.

There was shuffling and yells. I wheeled around. Orrimano lay flat on his back in the dirty alley with one policeman straddling him and another pinning down his arms. He no longer had his pistol. It was over. He no longer had the power.

259

26.

THE WINGED DANCER

The crowd was huge. There were journalists and photographers from all over Marigua and some from other countries. There were police and soldiers. Thousands of sightseers lined the rim of the cove at Lake Suga, waiting for the moment when the Winged Dancer would finally be within sight. It would be soon now. Natalia was there. Marinda was there. And Mona and Paulo and Luis and most of the other residents from the Estate. It seemed the entire town of nearby Portez had turned out. Ripples of tension moved through the crowd, for the large round boulder had been rolled aside and the crew had entered the cave. People waited tensely, straining to see. Tallo and I stood side by side. Every so often, one of us would take the other's hand and squeeze it.

The trial had gone quickly. Orrimano pleaded guilty and the courtroom procedure was mostly a ritual. The heroic couple-of-the-couch turned out to be Maria Guadope, a hotel maid, and Juan Forrera, a worker in the hotel kitchen. People smiled about the reason for their presence in the lower level conference room that night three weeks ago. There was some teasing, but mostly the young couple was treated as the heroes they were. As soon as Orrimano had taken Tallo and me from the "lecture" room, the couple had run to the lobby and reported what was taking place. The police were called, but Maria and Juan were not satisfied with that. They ran outside to an all night cafe they knew was frequented by police officers. They were taking no chances. Three officers were there, and another contingent of police arrived just minutes before Orrimano and I emerged into the alley.

The bullet had not touched the bone in Tallo's shoulder. I went with her in the ambulance crying tears of relief and concern. It was in the ambulance that I told her. I told her that I loved her. That was the first time I'd ever said it. I've said it many times since and so has she. In the ambulance, I whispered it in her ear as she lay there on the cot, her shoulder wrapped in white bandages. Her eyes were filled with happy tears and she nodded when she heard the words.

Orrimano told everything. I felt sad for Señora Petrillo. She had wanted to believe her husband had been a better man than he was. I was freed. Fully acquitted. I expected a rush of joy when the judge made the declaration. The rush came, but not then. It came later, at the Estate, when Tallo and I, two free and loving women, embraced and held each other.

We went down to the stream near the cabin. We walked along the water's edge for a long way, far more than 500 meters, until we came to a small clearing of grass and tiny wildflowers. Tallo sat on the soft grass looking at the water and I sat next to her, looking at her. When she turned to me, her smile said everything I felt. We made love under the blue sky. Her body was soft and warm and strong. I felt no fear. I was free and in love and free to love and I held her, touched her, kissed her, stroked her everywhere and she let me in, welcomed me, and I let her in.

Day followed fabulous day at the cabin. We lived each moment and we talked of the future.

"What now for you, Kat?" Tallo asked. "Now that you're free and can do what you want, what will you do?"

"You will like Chicago," was my response.

She smiled. "Of course, I will go there with you, Kat. But this is my home, you know."

"Mine too," I said.

We talked then of our plans. Two homes in two countries. Integrating our lives. The cabin with the wonderfully repaired porch and fireplace in Marigua. An apartment in Chicago. Two

261

lives. Not a dichotomy at all.

"I'll resume my mediation work in Chicago. I'm looking forward to that. I can travel back and forth with no problem. Of course, I'll have to work here, too." I pushed back a strand of hair from Tallo's forehead. "I've been thinking...," I said.

"Yes?" Tallo tilted her head and gave me the half smile I liked so much.

"I've been thinking of spending some time with Natalia, having some good talks with her."

"Oh?" Tallo had been stroking the bare flesh of my shoulder as we lay on our bed in the cabin. At the mention of Natalia, she stopped.

"I think the settlement is beautiful," I said, "the concept and actuality. It's evolving into something as close to a utopic community as I've ever heard of."

Tallo nodded.

"But there's a major flaw."

"A flaw?"

"Mm-hm. Natalia. She has too much power."

"What do you mean? Not at the settlement. She has no power at all there. She can't interfere in any way with the residents and freecomers."

"I know. That's not the problem. It's the novicios. Natalia should not have the power to decide who can go through the training and become a resident and who can't."

Tallo nodded. "You want it all, don't you?"

I laughed. "Of course. There's something incongruous, don't you think that side by side with the Statement of Rights and Obligations, we have a princess who, on a whim, can keep certain people oppressed, under her thumb."

Tallo nodded again.

"So, I think I'll do some talking with Natalia Neva."

"That's up to you," Tallo said, looking away.

This clearly was an area where Tallo and I would *not* be partners. I felt I could accept that. "And I've also been thinking of something else," I said lightly.

"What?"

"Of applying for a job at Neva Oil. I think they could use a mediator's services. I'll prepare a resume and apply."

Tallo laughed. "A wonderful idea. I'll write a letter of recommendation for you if you'd like."

"What will you say?" I asked, turning her over on her back and massaging her gently and deeply. "I want to know exactly. Especially the part about my magic fingers."

One day, near dusk, about a week after Orrimano's capture, Tallo went to the clinic to have her shoulder wound checked and I went to the beach with Marinda. We went by motorcycle. I held onto Marinda's waist as I'd done before and it still felt good, but in a very different way now. There was not that thrilling feeling of delight and awe and adulation. Instead there was a sense of greater understanding, of respect, though neither was complete. I still felt disturbed about how Marinda had been with me. I had a hunch the invitation today was to talk about this.

We had seen each other only a few times since the 'training' ended, and only once alone. That was for the brief moment when I gave her the silver bracelet I had gotten in Postero.

"That's nice," she said, taking the gift. "Very nice. I will treasure it, Kat."

I raised up my hand revealing the leather and bead bracelet I had taken so long ago from her bedroom. "May I keep this?" I asked.

She smiled. "You don't need to ask. It's been yours since you first expropriated it. I want it to be yours. And will you treasure it?"

"I always have."

We were interrupted then and it wasn't until our trip to the beach that we really spoke again. I laid out the towel. It was the same spot we had sat before. This time, we did not swim.

"You brought out something in me that I didn't know was there," Marinda said.

"What was that?" I asked, fairly certain that I knew.

"I'm not sure how to label it," she said, "but I know it has to do with power. A weird kind of power. Power over another, over you. It started as a game, mostly to teach you a lesson, but it turned into something else for me."

She seemed uncomfortable. I was too.

"You began to enjoy it," I said, "to enjoy it too much...too much for your own comfort, I suspect."

"Exactly." She looked intensely at me. "It's what happened to you at Solera, isn't it?''

"I think so," I said. I looked away.

"Do you understand it?''

I continued looking outward, at the sea. "Partly," I answered. "For me, I think it was an old dichotomy. At Solera, I got into one side of it." As I spoke, I saw two ships moving slowly toward each other. "I think we learn in all kinds of ways that to be something in this world, to feel really worthwhile and adequate, we must have power over others. You and I each had the opportunity. I think we each used it to meet some need we'd been taught to have.''

"I don't like it.''

"Me neither.''

"But I liked it, too.''

"Me, too." I looked at her. "I think I'm finished with it, though, that part of it.''

"Do you feel finished with the other side as well?" Marinda asked.

I chuckled. "Yes. It was exciting for a while, to believe another person was god-like. Exciting, but... No, I am not god, Marinda, nor are you.''

"Are you angry with me for what I did?''

"Yes," I said.

"I don't blame you," Marinda replied.

She was wearing the white blouse that contrasted so beautifully with her smooth tawny skin. The breeze rippled it.

"I knew better," she said, "but I did it anyway.''

"Do you feel guilty?''

Marinda thought about this. "I feel responsible for what I did," she said. "And I believe that what I did was in error; it wasn't fair. I don't feel good about it. If that is guilt, then I feel guilty.''

"Is it eating at you?''

"No.''

"Good.''

"I learned from it. And you...you seem OK. You are, aren't you?''

"I am. I definitely am. I learned some things, too, you know. A lot, actually. To tell the truth, Marinda, I don't think I'd be able to love Tallo the way I do if you hadn't helped me go to the depth of that part of me, that 'other side' of my dichotomy.''

I thought I saw Marinda's face grow pale; her mouth slacken.

264

She turned away, then turned right back, smiling. The smile seemed forced.

"You're really intrigued by that 'dichotomy' business," she said casually.

I was puzzled, unsure how to respond to her now.

"Dichotomies everywhere," she said lightly.

"Yeah, I guess Orrimano's lecture made an impression on me. But, do you know what I mean, Marinda, about your role in freeing me to love."

"Yes, I understand." She looked away again.

"What is it?" I asked.

She did not answer. I searched my mind for possibilities. She looked pained. Her eyes were so sad. Oh, no, I thought. Could she be in love with Tallo, too? Oh, no! I never suspected. What am I doing?

"Marinda, tell me," I said softly. "Is it Tallo? Do you...?"

"No. Not Tallo."

Not Tallo. Then...

"You," Marinda said. "But I'll get over it."

This time, *my* face must have paled. I sat there silently.

"I had no idea," I said at last.

Marinda said nothing. Nor did I for a long time.

"I'll be OK," she said.

I nodded. There was more silence.

"You and I shared something pretty big."

"Powerful," I said.

Marinda laughed. She put a cigarette in her mouth. "Light it," she commanded.

I hurried for my matches. "My pleasure," I said, bringing the flame to her. "You know, I do adore you." I blew out the flame.

She laughed again. "And I adore you."

We held each other. The sun was beginning to set. We held each other and then we moved apart.

"I'm glad for you and Tallo."

I nodded. I was feeling very deeply moved. Very very happy and very sad.

"You're two people I'm real attached to. Will you stay on at the Estate, Kat?"

"Part of the time."

"Good. I expect to see a lot of both of you."

265

"Definitely," I said, giving her hand a squeeze.

"And I understand Teresa's coming too."

"Yes, we'll all be here."

Marinda laughed and shook her head. She looked regal and imposing. I laughed with her. She'll be fine, I thought. Just fine.

I felt very good. I even felt good when Natalia gave Tallo and me that smug look and flaunted her success.

"I knew you'd make a good wife," Natalia said.

"How about partner?" I corrected.

"There you go again, Kat Rogan, telling me what words I should use. 'It would make more sense for you to say please'," she mimicked.

All four of us laughed. Tallo and I were dinner guests at the mansion. It was the first dinner I had there. It wouldn't be the last. Federico sat at Natalia's side, being charming and attentive. I guess he was her 'wife'.

Those pleasant days on the Estate passed very quickly and soon the time arrived when they were ready to bring out the Winged Dancer. Our bags were packed, Tallo's and mine. They were in the Volvo. As soon as the Winged Dancer was freed from its cave, Luis would drive us to Postero for our flight to Chicago.

The first two members of the crew emerged from the cave. The crane was in place, ready to lift the statue the forty feet up to where we all stood, onto the edge of the now much shallower Lake Suga. The statue was wrapped in something, canvas perhaps. The cloth was dry. Apparently no water had gotten into the cave. It looked huge as they rolled it out on the wheeled wagon. The crowd applauded. The workers tied the statue securely and hoisted it slowly up the edge. We watched silently. I felt tense anticipation. They set it carefully on the platform that had been prepared for it. I waited breathlessly with the others for the moment of the unwrapping.

Someone approached us.

"Here comes the Mayor of Portez," Tallo said.

He came up to me. "Señorita Rogan, we would be very pleased if you would do the honors."

Tallo gave my arm a squeeze.

The Mayor of Portez escorted me to the base of the still-covered statue. A ladder had been placed at its side. I began untying the cords, feeling very excited. One by one I unloosened the ropes, climbing the ladder to reach the higher ones. I could feel the thousands of eyes watching each move I made. I got to the last tie, and undid it. The cloth now hung loosely over the huge figure. I climbed down the ladder, looking from the hushed crowd to the immense statue. I took hold of one corner of the canvas and began to pull, slowly, walking backwards as I did. The tip of the winged cloak appeared first, the brilliant gold gleaming in the sun. A unison croon arose from the crowd. I continued pulling on the canvas until the entire statue was visible. The cheers were deafening.

It was magnificant! It was awe-inspiring! Imposing and regal!

The expression on the dancer's face was one of serene vitality, deep peace and joy. Its dancing feet were full of the spirit of life and its hands were beckoning us, all of us, to come, to come out together and dance and dance.

A few of the publications of
THE NAIAD PRESS, INC.
P.O. Box 10543 • Tallahassee, Florida 32302
Mail orders welcome. Please include 15% postage.

WINGED DANCER by Camarin Grae. 228 pp. Erotic Lesbian
adventure story.   ISBN 0-930044-88-6 $8.95

PAZ by Camarin Grae. 336 pp. Romantic Lesbian adventurer
with the power to change the world.   ISBN 0-930044-89-4   8.95

SOUL SNATCHER by Camarin Grae. 224 pp. A puzzle, an
adventure, a mystery—exciting Lesbian romance.
                                          ISBN 0-930044-90-8   8.95

THE LOVE OF GOOD WOMEN by Isabel Miller. 224 pp.
Long-awaited new novel by the author of the beloved *Patience
and Sarah.*   ISBN 0-930044-81-9   8.95

THE HOUSE AT PELHAM FALLS by Brenda Weathers. 240
pp. Suspenseful Lesbian ghost story.   ISBN 0-930044-79-7   7.95

HOME IN YOUR HANDS by Lee Lynch. 240 pp. More stories
from the author of *Old Dyke Tales.*   ISBN 0-930044-80-0   7.95

EACH HAND A MAP by Anita Skeen. 112 pp. Real-life poems
that touch us all.   ISBN 0-930044-82-7   6.95

SURPLUS by Sylvia Stevenson. 342 pp. A classic early
Lesbian novel.   ISBN 0-930044-78-9   7.95

PEMBROKE PARK by Michelle Martin. 256 pp. Derring-do
and daring romance in Regency England.
                                          ISBN 0-930044-77-0   7.95

THE LONG TRAIL by Penny Hayes. 248 pp. Vivid adventures
of two women in love in the old west.   ISBN 0-930044-76-2   8.95

HORIZON OF THE HEART by Shelley Smith. 192 pp.
Sizzling romance in summertime New England.
                                          ISBN 0-930044-75-4   7.95

AN EMERGENCE OF GREEN by Katherine V. Forrest. 288
pp. Powerful novel of sexual discovery.   ISBN 0-930044-69-X   8.95

THE LESBIAN PERIODICALS INDEX edited by Claire
Potter. 432 pp. Author and subject index.
                                          ISBN 0-930044-74-6   29.95

DESERT OF THE HEART by Jane Rule. 224 pp. A classic;
basis for the movie *Desert Hearts.*   ISBN 0-930044-73-8   7.95

SPRING FORWARD/FALL BACK by Sheila Ortiz Taylor.
288 pp. Literary novel of timeless love. ISBN 0-930044-70-3   7.95

FOR KEEPS by Elisabeth Nonas. 144 pp. Contemporary novel
about losing and finding love.   ISBN 0-930044-71-1   7.95

TORCHLIGHT TO VALHALLA by Gale Wilhelm. 128 pp.
Classic novel by a great Lesbian writer. ISBN 0-930044-68-1   7.95

LESBIAN NUNS: BREAKING SILENCE edited by Rosemary
Curb and Nancy Manahan. 432 pp. Unprecedented auto-
biographies of religious life.   ISBN 0-930044-62-2   9.95

THE SWASHBUCKLER by Lee Lynch. 288 pp. Colorful novel
set in Greenwich Village in the sixties.   ISBN 0-930044-66-5   7.95

MISFORTUNE'S FRIEND by Sarah Aldridge. 320 pp. Historical Lesbian novel set on two continents.
                                        ISBN 0-930044-67-3   7.95

A STUDIO OF ONE'S OWN by Ann Stokes. Edited by
Dolores Klaich. 128 pp. Autobiography. ISBN 0-930044-64-9   7.95

SEX VARIANT WOMEN IN LITERATURE by Jeannette
Howard Foster. 448 pp. Literary history. ISBN 0-930044-65-7   8.95

A HOT-EYED MODERATE by Jane Rule. 252 pp. Hard-hitting
essays on gay life; writing; art.   ISBN 0-930044-57-6   7.95

INLAND PASSAGE AND OTHER STORIES by Jane Rule.
288 pp. Wide-ranging new collection.   ISBN 0-930044-56-8   7.95

WE TOO ARE DRIFTING by Gale Wilhelm. 128 pp. Timeless
Lesbian novel, a masterpiece.   ISBN 0-930044-61-4   6.95

AMATEUR CITY by Katherine V. Forrest. 224 pp. A Kate
Delafield mystery. First in a series.   ISBN 0-930044-55-X   7.95

THE SOPHIE HOROWITZ STORY by Sarah Schulman. 176
pp. Engaging novel of madcap intrigue.   ISBN 0-930044-54-1   7.95

THE BURNTON WIDOWS by Vicki P. McConnell. 272 pp. A
Nyla Wade mystery, second in the series. ISBN 0-930044-52-5   7.95

OLD DYKE TALES by Lee Lynch. 224 pp. Extraordinary
stories of our diverse Lesbian lives.   ISBN 0-930044-51-7   7.95

DAUGHTERS OF A CORAL DAWN by Katherine V. Forrest.
240 pp. Novel set in a Lesbian new world.ISBN 0-930044-50-9   7.95

THE PRICE OF SALT by Claire Morgan. 288 pp. A milestone
novel, a beloved classic.   ISBN 0-930044-49-5   8.95

AGAINST THE SEASON by Jane Rule. 224 pp. Luminous,
complex novel of interrelationships.   ISBN 0-930044-48-7   7.95

LOVERS IN THE PRESENT AFTERNOON by Kathleen
Fleming. 288 pp. A novel about recovery and growth.
                                        ISBN 0-930044-46-0   8.50

TOOTHPICK HOUSE by Lee Lynch. 264 pp. Love between
two Lesbians of different classes.   ISBN 0-930044-45-2   7.95

MADAME AURORA by Sarah Aldridge. 256 pp. Historical
novel featuring a charismatic "seer."   ISBN 0-930044-44-4   7.95

CURIOUS WINE by Katherine V. Forrest. 176 pp. Passionate
Lesbian love story, a best-seller.   ISBN 0-930044-43-6   7.95

BLACK LESBIAN IN WHITE AMERICA by Anita Cornwell.
141 pp. Stories, essays, autobiography.   ISBN 0-930044-41-X   7.50

CONTRACT WITH THE WORLD by Jane Rule. 340 pp.
Powerful, panoramic novel of gay life.   ISBN 0-930044-28-2   7.95

YANTRAS OF WOMANLOVE by Tee A. Corinne. 64 pp.
Photographs by the noted Lesbian photographer.
                                        ISBN 0-930044-30-4   6.95

MRS. PORTER'S LETTER by Vicki P. McConnell. 224 pp.
The first Nyla Wade mystery.   ISBN 0-930044-29-0   7.95

TO THE CLEVELAND STATION by Carol Anne Douglas.
192 pp. Interracial Lesbian love story.   ISBN 0-930044-27-4   6.95

THE NESTING PLACE by Sarah Aldridge. 224 pp. Historical
novel, a three-woman triangle.   ISBN 0-930044-26-6   7.95

THIS IS NOT FOR YOU by Jane Rule. 284 pp. A letter to a
beloved is also an intricate novel.   ISBN 0-930044-25-8   7.95

FAULTLINE by Sheila Ortiz Taylor. 140 pp. Warm, funny,
literate story of a startling family.   ISBN 0-930044-24-X   6.95

THE LESBIAN IN LITERATURE by Barbara Grier. 3d ed.
Foreword by Maida Tilchen. 240 pp. A comprehensive
bibliography. Literary ratings; rare photographs.
                                                    ISBN 0-930044-23-1   7.95

ANNA'S COUNTRY by Elizabeth Lang. 208 pp. A woman
finds her Lesbian identity.   ISBN 0-930044-19-3   6.95

PRISM by Valerie Taylor. 158 pp. A love affair between two
women in their sixties.   ISBN 0-930044-18-5   6.95

BLACK LESBIANS: AN ANNOTATED BIBLIOGRAPHY
compiled by J.R. Roberts. Foreword by Barbara Smith. 112
pp. Award winning bibliography.   ISBN 0-930044-21-5   5.95

THE MARQUISE AND THE NOVICE by Victoria Ramstetter.
108 pp. A Lesbian Gothic novel.   ISBN 0-930044-16-9   4.95

LABIAFLOWERS by Tee A. Corinne. 40 pp. Drawings by the
noted artist/photographer.   ISBN 0-930044-20-7   3.95

OUTLANDER by Jane Rule. 207 pp. Short stories and essays
by one of our finest writers.   ISBN 0-930044-17-7   6.95

SAPPHISTRY: THE BOOK OF LESBIAN SEXUALITY by
Pat Califia. 2d edition, revised. 195 pp.   ISBN 0-930044-47-9   7.95

ALL TRUE LOVERS by Sarah Aldridge. 292 pp. Romantic
novel set in the 1930s and 1940s.   ISBN 0-930044-10-X   7.95

A WOMAN APPEARED TO ME by Renee Vivien. 65 pp. A
classic; translation by Jeannette H. Foster.
                                                    ISBN 0-930044-06-1   5.00

CYTHEREA'S BREATH by Sarah Aldridge. 240 pp. Women
first entering medicine and the law: a novel.
                                                    ISBN 0-930044-02-9   6.95

TOTTIE by Sarah Aldridge. 181 pp. Lesbian romance in the
turmoil of the sixties.   ISBN 0-930044-01-0   6.95

THE LATECOMER by Sarah Aldridge. 107 pp. A delicate love
story set in days gone by.   ISBN 0-930044-00-2   5.00

ODD GIRL OUT by Ann Bannon   ISBN 0-930044-83-5   5.95
I AM A WOMAN by Ann Bannon.   ISBN 0-930044-84-3   5.95
WOMEN IN THE SHADOWS by Ann Bannon.
                                                    ISBN 0-930044-85-1   5.95
JOURNEY TO A WOMAN by Ann Bannon.
                                                    ISBN 0-930044-86-X   5.95
BEEBO BRINKER by Ann Bannon   ISBN 0-930044-87-8   5.95

Legendary novels written in the fifties and sixties,
set in the gay mecca of Greenwich Village.

VOLUTE BOOKS

JOURNEY TO FULFILLMENT	Early classics by Valerie	3.95
A WORLD WITHOUT MEN	Taylor: The Erika Frohmann	3.95
RETURN TO LESBOS	series.	3.95

These are just a few of the many Naiad Press titles—we are the oldest and largest lesbian/feminist publishing company in the world. Please request a complete catalog. We offer personal service; we encourage and welcome direct mail orders from individuals who have limited access to bookstores carrying our publications.